T. J. FROST

FIGHT
FOR
LIFE

This book is a work of fiction.

All characters, locations, situations and events are the product of the author's imagination or are used fictitiously. Any resemblance to actual persons, living or dead, or to real places or events is purely coincidental.

Copyright © T. J. Frost 2017.

The right of T. J. Frost to be identified as the author of this work has been asserted by him in accordance with the Copyright, Designs and Patents Act 1988. All rights reserved.

No part of this publication may be reproduced or transmitted in any form or by any means (electronic, mechanical, or otherwise) without the prior written permission of the author.

ISBN 978-1977925848

Author's website:
www.timothyfrost.com

For giving so generously of their time and expertise, my thanks to Dudley Bennett (medicine), Dr. Brian Cox (genomics), and Rev. Canon Jonathan Charles (liturgy). Any errors that remain are my responsibility.

For Lizzie

1

The specimen resembled a head of coral: symmetrical, brain-like, otherworldly.

The geneticist operated a joystick to centre the image on the monitor.

The financier watched. "So your technique works?"

"Yes."

"Our client will be pleased. What more do you need to deliver on the contract?"

"Third-generation sequencers. Five of them. Thirty million US dollars total."

"You got it. What else?"

The geneticist looked up from his instrument. His piercing blue eyes betrayed no emotion. "More of what we are looking at here. Much more. Only alive."

2

RACHEL PHELPS ARRIVED at the Willows Care Home and parked next to her husband Paul's pickup.

She hurried inside and found Paul in earnest conversation with the manager, Guy Lane. An attractive young woman sat on a sofa nearby. Rachel recognised her as the home's visiting PC tutor.

Guy Lane shook her hand. "Good evening, Mrs. Phelps. Thank you for coming so quickly. Eve is distraught, I'm afraid. She's refused all her medication and keeps calling for you. It seems to be something to do with her bank account, so I asked Leelo to come in too, as she was helping your mother yesterday with online banking on her iPad. Shall we go up?"

On Eve's floor, Primrose, they met Alma, Eve's favourite carer, petite and blue-aproned. "She asking just for you, Mrs. Phelps."

Guy Lane said, "Paul and I will be in the lounge at the end of the corridor if you need us."

Rachel knocked and entered.

Her mother sat in her wing chair, a shrunken figure, a rug over her bony knees. To one side stood an overbed table with a tray of supper, untouched.

Eve Miller stretched out her arms and called in a wheezy voice, "Rachel darling, I've been such a stupid old woman. I don't want to live another day. I want to go to sleep and wake up in heaven . . . or the other place, more likely."

Rachel sat on a footstool and took her mother's hands in hers. "Mum, whatever is the matter? It can't be that bad."

"Yes it is, darling. I've been fooled . . . tricked. Whatever was the word dear Leelo used? Spammed—no, scammed. And I thought I was being clever . . . helpful."

Rachel felt the colour rise in her cheeks, as happened so often these days when she got stressed. The redness would spread down her neck and chest like a rash. "Mum, slow down. Take a deep breath. Just tell me the problem."

Eve buried her head in her hands, and for a moment the only sound in the room was of her quiet sobs, which transitioned into a chesty cough. She looked up with tear-filled eyes and spoke so quietly that Rachel had to lean close to make out her words.

"I have been robbed, Rachel dear. Robbed of all my money. The lot. All the proceeds from the house. The whole two hundred thousand pounds. The money I needed to pay for my care here and to secure Robbie's future when I'm gone. And it was all my own stupid fault. Pass me some water, would you, darling? I'll try to explain so you can get the police straight on to their wicked tails. Do take my lavender bottle and spray around. And turn the thermostat down. I'm always asking dear Alma to lower the temperature, but it seems to creep up again until I can hardly breathe."

Rachel did as she was asked. She sat, picked up a copy of *Saga* magazine, and fanned her burning face.

Eventually, Eve spoke again. "I received a call yesterday morning on my private telephone line, from the bank."

"Nice Mr. Plumb?"

"No, not lovely Howard. This man said his name was Fletcher, and he was an investigator from head office in London, the City. He spoke so nicely . . . such an educated voice. He warned me in confidence that Howard Plumb was suspected of fiddling the books and stealing money from clients through the online banking. They thought he had me in his sights. They'd been watching him, you see, through the computers. This Fletcher told me the safest thing to do was draw my money out straight away and put it into an account at head office. Told me I'd receive a better rate of interest too.

"Well, you could have knocked me over with a feather! Howard Plumb a crook! Yet I'd been worried about this online banking. Dear Leelo told me lots of things—about not opening attachments, whatever those are, or giving out my secret passcode. Which I never did!"

Rachel's pulse pounded. This couldn't be happening. She forced herself to listen to her mother's story.

"Fletcher telephoned again yesterday, just after dear Leelo had left. He gave me the details of the new savings account he had opened for me in the City. Then he told me to get down to my branch and arrange the wire transfer, but without alerting Howard Plumb. Oh, the devil! This was the clever bit. He said, 'Pretend you are taking the money out for the purchase of a property for one of your children!'"

"Mum, I don't believe what I'm hearing. You went through with it?"

"Yes, darling. I phoned Terry the Taxi this morning, and he pushed me right into the branch. There, I tricked poor Howard! I said the money was for a new house for Robbie. Shame on me!"

"Maybe the transfer hasn't gone through yet. We must call telephone banking and halt it."

"No, darling! Too late! When I arrived back here, feeling pleased I'd secured my savings and helped the bank catch a crook, I signed into online banking on my iPad. Sure enough, the Bonus Saver account showed zero. I sat here looking at the number for a moment. Then the penny dropped. I spent a fruitless hour trying to call head office and speak to this Fletcher, but of course there was no such person. Then I had a sort of breakdown and have been crying ever since. My world has shattered, changed in an instant. Oh, that smooth-talking devil! On top of everything, my cold is no better. Let's hope it turns to flu and kills me off!"

Rachel shifted into coping mode. "Here's what we do, Mum. Whatever mistake you made, and even if your savings are gone, it's not the end of the world. We'll get by. Robbie will be fine. I'll call Simon when I get home."

"No! Don't bother dear Simon. He has such a stressful job, and he can't do anything, being so far away. I implore you, don't worry him."

Rachel sighed. "I fail to see why Simon shouldn't be informed."

Eve seized Rachel's hand in a fierce grasp. "Not yet. Promise. Simon has so much on his plate."

And I don't? Rachel thought, but she said, "Fine. Tomorrow morning, I'll start making calls. I'm sure the money isn't lost. The bank will compensate you. They should never have transferred out such a large sum. Now I will ask Alma to bring you a cup of warm milk and put you to bed."

Her mother smiled weakly and released her grip on Rachel. "All right, darling. Thank you for coming. I hope you can sort me out, but I fear the worst. Off you go home with dear Paul before you catch my cold."

3

RACHEL FOLLOWED Paul's pickup, her hands clenched on the steering wheel and her mind in turmoil.

Despite her reassurances to her mother, she knew it would be a crippling blow to the family if they'd lost so much money.

She'd watched a documentary about such a scam, perpetrated on a Newcastle couple in their eighties. The bank had denied all liability, stating they had simply complied with their clients' request to empty their account.

The traffic lights ahead changed from green to amber, and the brake lights of the pickup flashed as Paul slowed for the junction with the bypass. The family firm owned two trucks: this one was a Ford Ranger 4x4 with personalised plates and Phelps & Son, Builders on wraparound colour graphics. The other was a rusty, drop-side tipper in plain white.

The liveried pickup seemed to reproach her every time she saw it.

Paul was the son in question, and he would have loved a son of his own to carry on the family business.

The lights changed, and the pickup turned onto the bypass. It took Rachel half a minute to close the gap between the two vehicles, her Fiat 500 bouncing along like a tiny puppy struggling to catch up with its mother.

She loved her car. Despite its diminutive size, there was plenty of headroom for her six-foot-one-inch frame.

They passed the Shell filling station in convoy, turned off the bypass, and wound down the dark country lanes. Soon, the two vehicles crunched on the gravel drive leading between the beech trees to their bungalow.

Paul parked next to the rusty white tipper and Rachel drew up in front of the Phelps & Son office—converted long ago from a double garage by Paul's father.

Their beloved rough collie, Raffles, leapt from the cab—which served as his mobile kennel during the working day—and rushed to greet her, tail wagging. She stooped to scratch his downy ear.

"You've got the right idea, boy," she told him in confidence. "No worries about money or ailing mothers, just live for the moment." The dog seemed to grin back at her in agreement.

In the kitchen, Rachel dried Raffles's paws, tossed him a dental stick, found a lasagne ready meal in the fridge, set it in the microwave, and finally poured a generous glass of red wine for Paul and a smaller measure for herself.

They sat facing each other over the pine table.

"How bad?" Paul asked.

"She seems to have been tricked out of everything in the saver account. Just over two hundred thousand."

Paul puffed out his cheeks. "Two hundred grand. Bloody hell." His blue eyes, the feature she had first noticed about him all those years ago, seemed duller tonight. "You'll get on to the bank and the police tomorrow? Anything I can help with?"

"I'll handle it. You don't need any distractions."

"Too right. I must make those four cottages weatherproof before winter sets in. It's slow going in all the mud and rain. I wonder if that computer-training woman, Lilo or whatever her name is, had something to do with the scam? She could have gained access to your mum's accounts, seen the savings, and passed the details on to her boyfriend. A lot of these care home workers are Romanian. They're behind all kinds of criminal activity."

Rachel considered this. It was a plausible scenario. "Assuming the police get involved, I'll alert them. I'd better warn Guy Lane of our suspicions."

"How are we going to pay your mum's fees if she's lost the money? Even in the short term?"

"Seven hundred and fifty a week? We'd exhaust our own savings in three months. And we need to keep a reserve in case anything else goes wrong with your cottages. Mum was so happy at the Willows in the summer. Now this. She looked a hundred years old tonight, Paulie, and said she wanted to die. That's not the mum I know." Rachel's eyes pricked with tears. "In the longer term, there's Robbie to consider. Speaking of which, I must text him something to reassure him. He guessed something was up when I rushed out of the class."

She took her phone from her bag and keyed, *Mum fine, just a problem with her bank, R xxx*

Paul sighed. "Babe, we can't pay her care home fees, even for a month. You know that."

As if to emphasise his words, the ancient microwave pinged like an old-fashioned cash register.

4

AFTER A RESTLESS, hot, and sweaty night with less than five hours' sleep, Rachel set about her to-do list at the stroke of nine o'clock.

Howard Plumb at the bank confirmed the facts of Eve's visit and the transfer, and expressed horror as he listened to Rachel's account of the scam. He promised to report the incident and investigate the beneficiary, though pointed out that this would be unofficial, as Eve had given no power of attorney to her children.

Next, Rachel spoke to the local police. She explained what had happened, emphasising that her mother was eighty-six, frail, and vulnerable. The duty officer transferred her to a detective sergeant named Jim Ryan who arranged to visit Rachel and Eve at the Willows that same morning.

Rachel called her mother, who picked up at once.

"Any luck with the police?" Her voice was weak.

"Yes, a detective will meet us in your room at ten thirty."

"Well done, darling. I couldn't eat any breakfast, but soon dear Alma will help me get washed and dressed and put on my makeup."

Rachel took her umbrella from the stand and hurried across the tarmac to the Phelps & Son office. Fallen leaves swirled around her ankles.

She entered and quickly closed the door against the driving rain.

Kizzy, their Jamaican secretary/bookkeeper, turned from her computer. Her wide smile seemed to light up the gloomy morning. "Hiya, Rache. Ready for a coffee?"

"Thanks, Kiz. I could do with something a lot stronger, but coffee will have to suffice."

"What's up, sister?"

"Mum's been scammed." Rachel launched into a breathless account of the fraud perpetrated against her mother.

Kizzy's mouth fell open as the words tumbled from Rachel's lips. "Oh my God," she said when Rachel drew breath. "Your poor old mum. Poor Robbie. Not to mention poor you."

"Poor is the word, all right. At least the police are showing concern. Now please give me some good news about the cottages. Are we back on track?"

Kizzy heaved herself to her feet and waddled to the kitchenette. She chose a coffee capsule, slid it into the machine, and turned to Rachel. "Didn't Paul say? We need to underpin not just the end cottage but all four. He's there now with the surveyor."

"No, he never mentioned it. Didn't want to add to my woes last night, I imagine. How much?"

"Another ten grand, maybe fifteen."

"That's all the profit from the development gone, then. I knew that four derelict cottages would overstretch us."

"Yeah. Guess that's why they went so cheap at the auction." Kizzy handed the cappuccino to Rachel and slotted a second capsule into the coffeemaker.

Rachel's spirits sagged again. She was riding an emotional seesaw at the best of times these days. Jaggy, excitable highs alternated with soul-sapping lows when life seemed bleak and every move was an effort, every step like wading through treacle. Her hormones ebbed and surged, unruly as a two-year-old's.

All the time, Rachel needed to appear confident, happy, and in control—for her brother Robbie, for her mum, for her dancing pupils. And, more and more, for Paul, if she was honest with herself.

The news about the cottages was another hammer blow.

Rachel caught sight of herself in the wall mirror. She put down her cup and dipped her head. "I look sixty. Young men will be offering me their seat on the train any day."

Kizzy stepped across to her. "Come here, you. Hug time." She reached out and enveloped Rachel in her plump arms. "You look as gorgeous as ever. What's not to like?"

"All those blotches on my neck and face."

Kizzy laughed. "I don't see no blotches. I see a very tall, slim, beautiful blonde who could pass for thirty-five, with a figure I could only dream of having. You concentrate on looking after your mum, Rache. Leave me and Paul to sort out business. We've got two diamond lads in Trevor and Billy — hard workers, reliable, and honest. Paul's got you, you've got him. Money is just numbers on a spreadsheet. Numbers change all the time. You don't have to fuss. Now sit in the comfy chair, finish your coffee, and let me get on with the bills."

Rachel complied, happy to be bossed and looked after for a few minutes by young Kizzy. She took her phone from her jeans pocket and scrolled to her calendar. The evening's class was Latin Technique, for her eight adults studying for the bronze medal exams just before Christmas.

She texted Paul about the police meeting.

He replied, *Good luck Babe, Love you xxxxxx*

She smiled. Kizzy was right: she and Paul had each other. Their strong marriage had survived the disappointment of not having children.

"Thanks for the coffee, Kiz, and the moral support. Just what I needed." She grabbed her umbrella and headed out into the rainy morning.

5

AT THE WILLOWS, an ambulance stood in the loading bay by the front doors, its blue lights pulsating.

The ambulance crew, one male and one female, hung around in the reception area. They seemed relaxed, chatting about last night's TV. Rachel puffed out her cheeks in relief. Just a routine pickup—two bored health workers waiting to take a resident to chiropody or the fracture clinic.

She signed in. The receptionist, an Eastern European girl like so many of the staff, buzzed her through.

On Primrose, the door to Eve's room stood ajar. Voices came from inside.

Standing around her mother's bed were Guy Lane, Dr. Jonathan Thorpe, Eve's GP—and also Rachel's—and Alma.

Guy Lane turned his head. "Mrs. Phelps! They didn't tell me you were here. We've been trying to reach you. Let's go to the lounge." Before Rachel could reply, the manager was in the corridor, ushering her to the visitors' room where Rachel often played Scrabble with Eve.

"Why are we going in here? I want to speak to Mum."

"Please take a seat."

"But—" Then Rachel saw the expression on Lane's face.

"I'm afraid I have sad news. Your mother passed away a very short time ago."

"Passed away? I spoke to her earlier this morning."

"I'm so sorry, also that you were allowed to come up to the room."

The door opened, and Dr. Thorpe entered. He was a tall man with a long nose, who always wore a three-piece suit and tie and had a pompous attitude too, in Rachel's opinion.

"Mrs. Phelps, my sincere condolences."

He didn't sound in the least sorry or sincere. Not for the first time, Rachel pined for Thorpe's predecessor, kindly Dr. Harwood. Everyone had loved him. He'd retired in the summer.

"Mrs. Phelps, I appreciate this is a difficult moment, but as I am here and I do need to know: is your mother to be cremated or buried?"

"What does it matter, Doctor?"

"If cremation, I will require another doctor to confirm the cause of death."

"How can you know the cause? She's only just died and was well and cheerful enough when I called her earlier."

"Mrs. Phelps, I do know the cause. I regret that sudden death is very typical of bronchial pneumonia in this age group. They often rally shortly before the end and appear quite lively, but that's merely the fever making them more talkative."

Rachel said, "Pneumonia? I had no idea—"

Guy Lane said, "Dr. Thorpe, Mrs. Phelps has received a tremendous shock. This really isn't the time. I'll catch you later, or leave a message at the surgery."

"Very well. Please excuse me then, if there's nothing else." Thorpe strode out.

"Not the best bedside manner," Guy Lane murmured. "Would you like to sit here quietly for a few minutes?"

"No, I want to see Mum now."

"Of course." He held the door for Rachel and accompanied her back to Eve's room.

Her mother lay curled up in the foetus position, eyes closed. At a glance, you could think her asleep, yet the sheets covering her remained still and her face was like a waxwork's.

In death, Eve seemed to have shrunk even more.

"Shall I leave you alone, Mrs. Phelps?"

"Thank you, Mr. Lane. Do get on with your day. Please ask Alma to come back in."

"Once again, my condolences. I'm sorry I didn't reach you before you arrived. Take your time. We'll all miss her."

He left.

Alma entered and joined Rachel at the bedside. "Very sad, very sad. I love her so much. My favourite."

"What happened, Alma?"

"I wake Eve at eight, same as every day, and bring her a cup of tea. She say she not hungry for any breakfast. I put her in her chair, in her dressing gown. Later I look in and Eve say, 'Rachel and a man are coming to meet me at half past ten, Alma. Help me with my makeup, won't you, dear?' I say, 'Yes, when I finish clearing breakfast, I come straight back and dress you.'"

"And when you returned you found her?"

"No, Miss Leelo find her."

Rachel, bending over her mother's frail body, jerked her head around. "Leelo? The computer woman? What was she doing in here?"

"I see Leelo knock on the door as I come from the kitchen. Leelo goes in. Then she runs out shouting, 'Alma, quick!' I go into the room, then to the nurses' station. Duty nurse call the ambulance. They come, but can do nothing. Then Doctor Thorpe arrive for his rounds and take over."

Rachel said, "Let me get this straight. You left Mum alive and well. How long before Leelo arrived?"

"A short while, Mrs. Phelps. It hard for me to tell time when everything busy busy. Maybe five minutes."

"And Leelo immediately came back out and raised the alarm?"

"Yes, at once, or almost. I reach the lounge door, I believe." The tiny carer looked troubled. "I do something wrong?"

"No, Alma. I'm just trying to understand the sequence of events. This is such a shock. And that wretched doctor! He was so rude!"

"Dr. Thorpe hurry hurry, in, out, in, out."

They stood in silence for a while. A thought occurred to Rachel. "Who put Mum back in bed?"

"Me and duty nurse. But no time to make her pretty or comb her hair."

A knock sounded on the door. Guy Lane entered. "Mrs. Phelps, sorry to disturb you, but a police detective is waiting downstairs. Says he has an appointment with you and Eve. I gave him the sad news. Shall I tell him to contact you later—or tomorrow?"

"No, I'm coming. Give me five minutes."

"I'll sit him down with a coffee." Guy Lane closed the door behind him again.

"Police?" Alma said, her eyes big and round. "Eve was in trouble? Or danger?"

Despite herself, Rachel smiled. "No, silly. Of course not."

"Eve very upset after she visiting the bank with Terry the Taxi. She tell me she had been a stupid woman and she loved you all."

"Alma, whatever Mum told you, please don't talk about it to the other girls, love. Or to anyone else. It's private family business."

"I understand, Mrs. Phelps. No more talking." The little carer exited the room, leaving Rachel alone with her mother and her thoughts.

She pulled a chair over to the bedside and sat. She reached out and touched Eve's cheek. Still warm. Her mother's mouth was open a fraction, as if she were about to speak.

What would you like to say, Mum?

It was the shock of the fraud that had killed her, after the stress of the visit to the bank. Of that, Rachel was certain. It was also obvious Thorpe had failed to diagnose Eve's pneumonia until too late. Rachel should have telephoned him days ago, insisting on antibiotics. That man was casual at best, incompetent at worst.

Not that it made any difference now.

She wondered if Robbie would want to see his mother lying dead. And Paul? He'd been fond of Eve and the two of them had rubbed along well together. While Eve lived alone in the family home, Paul had popped in all the time—to replace a light bulb or fuse, to glue down a curling piece of vinyl floor. He'd been a model son-in-law.

And what of elder brother Simon, in Australia? Despite being Eve's favourite, he had not been back to the United Kingdom for three years. He managed a copper mine near Perth and, according to Eve, entertained a steady stream of gorgeous girlfriends. Rachel thought he was gay. Whatever. He'd left all the duties of caring for Robbie and Mum to Rachel.

Time up. She glanced around the room. Her mother's valuables lived in a safe in the wardrobe. They could stay there for the moment. Just her handbag, really. She bent over and kissed her mother on the forehead. "Goodbye, Mum. Sleep tight. I'll take care of everything for you."

In reception, a young man in leather jacket and jeans rose to his feet. "Mrs. Phelps? Detective Sergeant Jim Ryan. I'm sorry about your sudden loss. I'm sure you have a hundred things to do, but if you can spare me a few minutes, I'll set the investigation in motion. Time is crucial in cases like this, before the trail of the money goes cold. Let's sit in the bay window."

Rachel eyed the policeman up and down. He was fresh faced; still in his twenties, she guessed. She took a seat on a leather sofa and resisted the urge to lean back and close her eyes. The morning's events, following the previous evening's drama and a restless night, were taking their toll.

None of this seemed real yet.

Ryan perched on the edge of an armchair at right angles to her. "May I record our conversation?" He set his smartphone on the coffee table. "Please start at the beginning."

"My husband Paul received a telephone call yesterday evening from my mother's carer here at the Willows. Alma. I don't know her surname. Alma said my mother was in distress and asking for me. I left my class—I'm a self-employed dance instructor—and arrived here around seven thirty p.m. My mother, Eve Miller, who is—was—eighty-six told me she had been to her bank with the tame driver—they use him because he has a wheelchair taxi and is kind and patient. Terry the Taxi. She'd taken calls on her private landline the previous day from a man calling himself Fletcher who claimed to be from the bank's fraud-prevention team."

"I'll need that number. And your mother's mobile, assuming she had one."

"Yes, she had a mobile, but only for backup. The signal isn't great here, so she mostly used the landline with her cordless phone. Hold on, the mobile may be right here." Rachel opened her mother's bag. "No, it's not."

"Just the numbers will do for now."

Rachel passed her own phone to the detective, who read out the two numbers for his recording. "Do carry on, Mrs. Phelps."

"This Fletcher stated that Mum's account was in danger of being robbed by the branch manager, Howard Plumb. It was ludicrous, but he gained Mum's confidence and persuaded her to go straight to the bank and transfer all her savings into an account Fletcher had given her. Mum pretended the money was to buy a house for my younger brother, Robbie. He's forty-one and has Down's syndrome. When she arrived back here, Mum realised she had been tricked."

"The amount taken was . . . ?"

"Just over two hundred thousand pounds. We put Mum's house up for sale when she moved into care. She didn't qualify for any help with the fees, owning her own place. The house sold a month ago, and the cash was in a savings account while we decided what to do with it."

"Did anyone else have knowledge of your mother's affairs and assets?"

"Yes, I suspect that the volunteer who helps the residents with their phones and tablets, she's called Leelo, may have known about the large amount in the saver account. Mum trusted this woman, who could have peeked over her shoulder while showing her how to use online banking, or sneaked in when Mum was in the dining room. I'm even more suspicious since I learned that Leelo was in Mum's room this morning. In fact, she was the one who discovered her dead. What reason could she have had for being in there?"

"Good question. I'll get this Leelo's details from the manager and interview her. Do you know if either Leelo or Alma are married, or have boyfriends? They can be the problem. They use their women as spies to case out prospects, sometimes without the women even realising."

Paul had made the same point. Rachel thought before answering, "I'm pretty sure Alma doesn't have a man. Mum was always talking about 'poor little Alma, an only child, an orphan, no one to care for her and yet she cares for me.' No idea about Leelo."

"Anyone else with access to your mother's accounts?"

"No. She didn't even give me power of attorney. Too independent. Also, she said it would have to be shared with my brother Simon, who lives in Australia, which would be impractical."

"Mrs. Phelps, I have enough to begin enquiries. I'll report back to my superior and phone you with developments. I'll type your statement up, but you'll need to come in and sign it."

Rachel took a deep breath. "Sergeant Ryan, my mum was old and frail, and not in good health. Even so, it seems extraordinary she could call me, lucid and positive, earlier this morning, but be dead by the time I arrived less than two hours later. I think my mother's death should be treated as suspicious."

6

BACK HOME, Rachel resisted the urge to rush into the office, tell Kizzy the news, flop into the comfy chair, and burst into tears while Kizzy fixed her another cappuccino.

Instead, she made herself a mint infusion, took the magnetic pad from the fridge, and wrote: Paul, Robbie, Simon, Kizzy.

That was the proper order of things.

Paul answered straight away.

She said, "I just got home from the Willows, love. Mum died earlier this morning. Pneumonia."

"Babe, I am so sorry. I expect the business with the bank brought it on."

"Yes. Poor Mum. To spend her last day on earth being scammed of her life savings and to die a pauper." Rachel's hand shook as she sipped her mint tea. She choked back a sob. "Oh Paulie, I never said goodbye to her! What's worse, that Leelo woman was the one who found her!"

Paul didn't reply. Had the connection dropped? No—she could still hear the mini-digger in the background. "Paulie, did you hear me?"

"Yes. That's bad news, because we agreed last night that Leelo might be connected with the scam. I don't suppose you saw the police after all this?"

"Yes, the detective arrived while I was there."

"Does Robbie know yet?"

"I'm on my way to him next."

"I'll be there to help when you get back from the kennels."

"No, love. Stay and press on with the cottages. Don't waste time and diesel coming home now. I'm fine, and I've got lots to do."

"That's my girl. Will you cancel classes tonight?"

"No. Life carries on. Cha-cha-cha."

"I'll bring a takeaway, so at least you'll get your tea before you go out for once. You must keep your strength up."

Rachel unlocked the drawer in the sideboard and took out the folder of her mother's paperwork. She found a copy of the will, dated four years ago. Its provisions were simple. Apart from the jewellery, promised to Rachel, Mum had left everything to Robbie, with Rachel and Simon as trustees. In the event that Robbie predeceased his mother, the assets were to be divided equally between the two surviving children.

Rachel phoned the Willows and spoke to the receptionist, making her repeat the instructions to be sure she had understood. "Please tell Mr. Lane I have now checked the will, and my mother wished to be cremated."

She couldn't give Robbie her news over the phone. He had a mental age of around ten. Provided he kept to his routine, he coped well and enjoyed life. But he could descend into a black depression—or erupt in sudden anger—when things went awry. He might even behave unpredictably and be a potential danger to himself or others.

Her kid brother needed kid-glove treatment at times of crisis.

As she drove to the Korner Kennels, Rachel kept coming back to the computer trainer, Leelo. Why had she really been at the Willows the previous night? Why had she returned the next morning, before normal visiting hours, and let herself into Mum's room?

Rachel didn't like it at all, but was she overreacting? Were her suspicions rational?

She drummed her fingers on the steering wheel and hoped that Detective Ryan proved as efficient as he seemed.

At the kennels, she found Julia, the owner, and explained the situation. Julia showed Rachel into the staff rest room, which was furnished with metal chairs and tables and decorated with posters of prize pedigree dogs and cats. She returned moments later with Robbie.

Her brother's broad, flat face wore a troubled frown. "Hi Sis. What's up?"

Rachel reached across the table and took his chubby hands in hers. "Sorry, Robbie. Mum died this morning. Pneumonia."

"I had a bad feeling after Paul called you away from the hall last night." Besides working at the kennels, Robbie acted as DJ for Rachel's dance classes, cueing up the waltzes, foxtrots, and quicksteps.

They sat for a moment in silence. Rachel said, "I'll take you to see her, if you like. To say goodbye."

"A bit late for that, Sis. I guess she had to die eventually." His face brightened. "Does that mean I get all the money now?"

This was no time to talk about money—or the lack of it—so Rachel said, "Yes love. As we know, Mum left everything to you in a family trust. You won't have to worry about it. Life will carry on as normal."

"Can I buy a car?"

"No love, you can't buy a car."

Robbie pouted. "How about a new stereo!" he exclaimed.

"That sounds possible ... but hey, love, we need to remember Mum and be sad together first."

"Yes. Let's do that."

They sat for maybe a minute, until a small dog started barking somewhere outside.

Rachel said, "Would you like to go home now? Or would it be nicer for you to stay until normal finishing time?"

Robbie valued his routine, so Rachel was a little surprised when after a moment's thought he replied, "Go home and think about Mum and be sad. There's only six dogs and four cats in today, and I cleaned all the kennels already. Julia will make up their dinners. Shall I come to Latin class this evening?"

"Up to you, Robbie. I can cope with Barry and Monica."

"I think I'll stay in then, watch *Milo and Otis*."

"Good plan. Off and change, get your bag, and let's go. I'll call ahead so they know you're coming home early and why."

"Thanks, Sis." Robbie's lower lip wobbled. "I've never not had a mum before."

Rachel squeezed his hands in hers and smiled. "Me neither, Robbie. Me neither."

7

PAUL ARRIVED with a takeaway curry at six o'clock. This was the last thing Rachel felt like eating, but she didn't say so. She forced down some of the greasy chicken Madras and a poppadum as she briefed her husband on her day.

Paul cracked open a second can of Belgian lager. "Sure you don't want a drink? Calm you down?"

"No thanks, Paulie. I've got to drive and work, remember. Latin bronze medal class."

He took a long draught. "Did you get through to Simon?"

"Yes. I woke him at two in the morning, I'm afraid. He said flights are no problem."

"He'll turn up at the crematorium hotfoot from the airport with a minute to spare, knowing him." Paul drank from his can. "So everyone has the news now? Auntie Audrey—and Eve's old neighbours?"

"Yep, I think I got them all. I left a message for Howard Plumb at the bank."

Paul finished his can, let out a slight belch, and set down the empty among the litter of tinfoil and cardboard containers. Rachel said, "You didn't tell me about the structural problems with the other cottages. You must keep me in the loop, love. Money will be tight."

"It's all under control. While you were running around this afternoon I sorted it. You never needed to know, with everything that's on your mind and you not feeling yourself anyway. I'm not keeping anything from you, babe. Please don't micromanage my business as well as yours."

Rachel raised her eyebrows. "Under control? Kizzy told me we were in for another ten to fifteen thousand."

"I did a deal with Mervyn from the groundworks company. He owed me a favour after I put work his way on the Satchell Estate. He'll underpin all four cottages for five grand, and he doesn't want paying until we sell the lot, however long that takes. So you can stop keeping tabs on me and Kizzy, right?"

Rachel sensed the colour rising in her neck. The spicy curry was to blame. She'd feel bloated for the rest of the evening and suffer another bad night. She resisted the urge to complain about Paul's choice of supper. At least he'd taken the initiative.

To change the subject, she said, "Thorpe was a pig today. I have an appointment with him tomorrow, which I've waited two weeks for. I'm thinking of changing surgery. He never told me anything useful about Mum's condition, anyway."

"He's not supposed to. Patient confidentiality. Even with members of family."

"That's ridiculous. He should have informed me he was treating Mum for pneumonia. If he was."

Raffles, asleep in his basket after an early supper and a scamper around the wet field beyond the back garden gate, snuffled and snorted as if agreeing with her.

Paul attacked a naan. He spoke through a mouthful of the doughy bread. "Thorpe now has a second certificate confirming the cause of death?"

"I don't know. The police have taken over."

"I agree that Leelo's involvement is unfortunate, and she might be part of the scam, but are you seriously suggesting she helped do away with Eve? That Mum's death was suspicious? Aren't you being . . . paranoid?"

"Why was Leelo in Mother's room so early this morning?"

"Maybe to reassure her that she was *not* a party to the fraud. Leelo must have heard the details from Lane. He did call her in last night on standby."

"Yes. I thought that was odd in itself."

"Babe, this is all the subject of a police investigation, so let matters run their course. It's sad that Mum has passed away, but at least she won't suffer the aftermath of what she did. The urgency's gone. It's not as if we would have seen any of the money."

Rachel grimaced. Her stomach was already protesting. "Paulie, we've known that all along. Everything goes to Robbie during his lifetime. We need the money for him. Robbie is fit and healthy now, at least as much as he could be. But his Down's will catch up with him. Accelerated ageing is the reality. We might require private carers, even need to build him his own home. Hare House is great, but they don't have specialist equipment, or wheelchair access, or medics living in. So while Robbie is alive, and pray it will be for many years, he's the top priority."

"And that's how it should be." Paul eyed the remaining four cans in his six-pack. "You haven't eaten much."

"Quite enough, thanks. I'll fix myself a bowl of cornflakes when I come in." Rachel glanced at the kitchen clock. "I must go."

In the hall, she put on her raincoat and ankle boots, grabbed her handbag and her carry bag of dancing shoes, and opened the front door. The porch light illuminated a dense, drenching rain that fell vertically now the wind had dropped. She turned back and called towards the kitchen. "Paulie, have you seen my umbrella?"

"Sorry, no, babe."

She'd had it that morning at the Willows. She realised she must have left it in the care home, perhaps in her mother's room.

Bother.

The Fiat knew the route from the bungalow to the school hall and could almost steer itself there like one of Google's driverless cars, giving Rachel ten blessed minutes alone with her thoughts. The heater blared on full power and the interior of the little car soon warmed up. She turned the fan off before the rising temperature brought on another hot flush.

Tomorrow, she'd see Thorpe for her appointment—with any luck the last with the wretched man. She would make it clear she was unhappy with his treatment, both of her and her mother.

The other practice serving their postcode was in Hilworthy, some ten miles north. A village surgery, it offered fewer facilities, but she'd heard that they compensated with old-fashioned family doctoring. She'd try and sign on with a lady GP, and an older one at that, who understood women's problems and showed a little sympathy.

Like mother, like daughter.

Eve had started the change of life in her early forties, even younger than Rachel. She and her dad had got careless and next thing they knew, Eve was pregnant with Robbie. Back in the 1970s, there had been no routine screening for Down's syndrome.

Robbie. How will he cope with the reality of Mum's death, and the funeral?

She imagined him in his cosy room at the hostel, watching his cat-and-dog movie for the hundredth time.

Like one of Robbie's scratched old vinyl LPs, Rachel's mind kept skipping back to the question of the bank scam and the woman Leelo's involvement.

Paul is probably right: the urgency is off the investigation now Mum is dead. Will the detective follow through at all?

As the Fiat purred down the bypass, Rachel had an idea. And a good one. She knew she mustn't interfere with the police, but she could help them with some undercover enquiries of her own.

I owe it to Mum.

8

THE LATIN STUDENTS proved to be on good form, warned of Rachel's bereavement by her trusty assistants Barry and Monica, and confident with their reverse turns, cucarachas, closed-hip twists, and chassés.

After the class, Rachel found her umbrella on the back seat of her car.

How did it get there? I keep losing things these days!

Arriving home, she waved through the office window at Paul, working late at his PC—unlike him. Raffles lay at his feet, head between his paws, thoroughly bored.

A good opportunity to start her own detective work, and staying busy would maybe keep the reality of her mum's death at bay for a while. It certainly hadn't sunk in yet. She'd been racing around all day like a demented chicken, in total denial.

She took her mother's handbag from the kitchen dresser and set it on the pine table. She made herself a hot, milky drink and poured the bowl of cereal, noting that no beer cans remained in the fridge from Paul's six-pack. While she ate, she extracted the contents of the bag one by one and examined them forensically. She set aside two lipsticks, a comb and hairbrush—both clean and free from hair—half a packet of tissues, a powder compact, an unopened tube of Love Hearts sweets, and a nail file.

She took out Eve's address book and diary. The detective wanted these; Rachel had arranged to drop them in to the station the next day and sign her statement. She'd needed the books in the meantime, for the telephone numbers of friends and distant relatives. Now Rachel leafed again through the two books. She was looking for anything relating to Eve's iPad, online banking, or email.

Nothing stood out: just names, numbers, and addresses—the older entries neat and tidy, the newer ones more scrawled.

She examined the diary.

"Hair," "Chiropodist," "R&R," for Rachel and Robbie, featured regularly.

And lots of "Leelo." She counted them up: one a week in August, two a week in September, and four this month.

There were six "Paul" entries in the two weeks before her death. Paul tried to pop into the Willows when he was passing, and Eve had continued to save up little jobs for him: hanging a picture, or changing a light bulb for a stronger one. All tasks for the care home maintenance man, but Mum had invented lots of excuses to see Paul and make him feel wanted.

All the same, six visits seemed unusually high, particularly when Paul was supposed to be focused on the cottages.

She turned to the endpapers looking for codes, numbers, anything of that sort.

Zilch.

She searched around in the now-empty bag. Here was one more little zippered compartment. Inside, she found the safe key.

Maybe the banking codes and passwords are in the safe—along with the elusive missing mobile phone. And Mum's iPad, come to that.

Annoyed with herself for failing to realise that the safe might contain more than jewellery, Rachel threw the used cosmetics and other personal items into the kitchen bin. She looked at the forlorn, empty handbag. Tatty, stained: no good even for the charity shop. Fighting back the tears, she lobbed it into the waste as well.

A wave of tiredness swept over her.

Whatever Paul was doing in the office was taking forever. She trudged along the corridor to the master bedroom, washed, undressed, slipped under the duvet, and fell asleep in seconds.

9

SHE AWOKE next morning to find herself alone in bed, sun shining through the curtains, and her pillow not even drenched in perspiration.

With a yawn, she reached for her alarm clock. It was 8:30 a.m. Her best night for weeks! Despite the curry!

Rachel felt guilty at having slept so well; it seemed disrespectful to Mum. She should have lain awake all night in grief.

She opened the curtains. No liveried pickup: Paul and Raffles were already at work.

She showered in tepid water, dressed in a skirt, cashmere jumper, and jacket to boost her confidence, and arrived in good time for her appointment at the town surgery.

Twenty-five tedious minutes later, the bleeper sounded and her name scrolled on the sign above reception.

Thorpe sat behind his desk, buttoned up as usual, writing busily on a pad. He kept Rachel waiting for a full half minute. When his hooded eyes flicked up to meet hers, they were wary.

"Mrs. Phelps, once again my condolences. What can I do for you today?"

"Doctor, the hot flushes are really bothering me now, and I'm not sleeping, and sweating at night, and recently my memory is letting me down too."

"Have you tried one of those little handheld battery fans? A lot of my patients swear by them. Menopause is not an illness, it's a natural process of ageing as your body readjusts to declining fertility. As for the sleep hyperhidrosis, to give it its proper name, you could place a freezer block under your pillow. When you're too hot, turn the pillow over and the other side will always be nice and cool. Just two commonsense solutions that avoid medication. You can Google them all. The *Saga* site is very helpful."

"I think I'm beyond that stage. This is affecting my work. I have to look good, fit, and healthy for my dance pupils, and I can't demonstrate the foxtrot holding a fan in my hand."

The doctor sighed and turned his expensive-looking pen around in his fingers. "Everyone in your position thinks that hormone replacement is the magic bullet. The problem is, HRT doubles your chance of breast cancer. I have to tell you that. I'd like you to persevere with the DIY remedies first, see how you cope, and if you really can't get by after another month or two, we'll consider the HRT route. Agreed? Anything else on your mind?" He twisted his lips into an attempt at a sympathetic smile.

"Yes ... my mother's death. It was so sudden. Please tell me, had you diagnosed her with pneumonia in the days before?"

Thorpe stiffened, and the patronising smile disappeared from his thin face. "I attended your mother within the requisite fourteen days prior to her death, and as I explained to you at the Willows yesterday, it was certainly bronchopneumonia. I spoke to Brundall at Hilworthy, who saw the body and confirmed the cause."

"That's not answering my question, Doctor. If you knew Mum had pneumonia, why didn't you let me know? Or start her on a course of antibiotics?"

Thorpe stopped twirling his pen. He glanced at his watch. "Antibiotics, antibiotics, you all want antibiotics! Mrs. Phelps, have you not been keeping up with the news? Overprescription of antibiotics is resulting in dangerous resistance that threatens us all. Every practice in the United Kingdom is under strict instructions to decrease routine use of them as a 'just in case' solution."

Rachel's face started to colour. "If someone's dying of pneumonia, what's to be lost?"

"Firstly, there are several types of pneumonia, only one of which responds to antibiotics. Secondly, your mother was not dying of pneumonia when I last saw her alive. She had a wheezy cough, but no *rales* or *rhonchi*. Mrs. Phelps, pneumonia can kill a young, fit, and previously healthy adult male in twenty-four hours. Imagine how much more rapidly it can overcome an elderly person, in bed a lot and therefore more prone to lung congestion. What would you have had me do, mount a bedside vigil?"

"Dr. Thorpe, I resent your tone of voice. Did you in fact diagnose her with pneumonia at all?"

Thorpe's face was turning puce. He raised his hands. "Mrs. Phelps, I understand yesterday's events were distressing for you, but I will not be harangued in this way. Yes, I had diagnosed pneumonia. However, as you have now involved the police, I do not wish to discuss the matter further. You were entitled to refer the death, but I fear you will regret it. An inquest, if ordered, will pile distress on you and your family, and I hope you realise the process could take six months or longer."

"Regardless of what the coroner decides, I'd like to see my mother's records for the last two months, please."

"Assuming you are her executor, that is also your right. Ask at reception for the forms. On your way out. Simpler still, ask the coroner, who has them right now." He turned his cheesy smile back on. "I'm sorry about your mother. I am. It's never easy losing a parent, even at that advanced age. Be assured, your mother received appropriate care both from me and from the nurses on the floor at the Willows. And her death, though sudden, was not unusual. I've seen dozens slip away like her.

"Coming back to your change-of-life woes, I'm not heartless. It's just that HRT is a major decision. I won't roll over and print out a script at the second time of asking. Did I give you my leaflets?"

"Yes, Dr. Thorpe. Let's leave it there. Goodbye."

Rachel's face burned red. She stood to go. Thorpe picked up his pen and bent to his notes without further word or acknowledgement.

Outside, she took the forms from the receptionist, her hands shaking so much that the woman asked Rachel if she was all right.

Back in the sanctuary of her Fiat, she cried a little. She scrabbled in her bag for a tissue, blew her nose, and consoled herself that she'd never need to speak to that bastard again. She'd register at Hilworthy immediately.

Rachel steadied her breathing and checked her list.

The police station, to sign her statement and check on progress.

Then the solicitor, to get his advice on the bank scam and go through the will.

Shopping, at the Tesco's on the bypass.

She added at the bottom, *Sign on at Hilworthy.*

Feeling a touch paranoid, she hadn't written down her final appointment—at the Willows, with Leelo.

10

DETECTIVE RYAN greeted her with a sympathetic smile and waved her into his office. "Everyone else is out, so we can talk here. I wouldn't want to inflict our sweaty interview room on you."

He produced the typed version of Rachel's witness statement, which she initialled and signed where indicated. She handed him the address book and diary.

He said, "I'm interviewing the care staff, and DC Timmins will work on the phone records. I've met briefly with the coroner. Here's the interim death certificate you'll need for probate."

"Thank you, Detective. That was quick."

"We do our best. I'll be in touch once I have something concrete to report."

She walked up the high street for her next appointment, with her mother's solicitor.

Gerald Smithers had been a golfing buddy of her father's and was a familiar figure in Rachel's life. The old boy still practised, in the same office above the chemist, though he only worked two days a week now, having handed most of the duties to his junior partner—himself well into late middle age, but always referred to as "Young Mr. James."

Smithers welcomed Rachel into his antique-furnished inner sanctum with avuncular charm. The receptionist brought in a silver tray with a black coffee for the solicitor and a glass of water for Rachel—she'd cut down on caffeine, rationing herself to a small mug of tea at breakfast and one of Kizzy's cappuccinos midmorning.

"I was so sorry to hear about Eve. I sense she knew her time was limited, which was why she had me update her will only"—he peered over the top of his spectacles at the document in front of him—"one week ago."

"She never told me that."

"Don't look so worried! Do you have the death certificate, please?"

"This is an interim one. There may be an inquest."

"I understand. Just one bequest added to the will. A worker at the home, who your mum said had helped her beyond the call of duty and become something of a friend. I questioned her closely, because such gifts can be inappropriate. Eve was adamant, her mind was sharp as ever, and the amount was not so great in the scheme of things, so—"

"May I see?"

Smithers handed over the will.

The first clause revoked all previous wills and named Rachel and Simon as executors.

The second clause dealt with the funeral arrangements and cremation.

The third clause left Eve's jewellery to Rachel.

All as before.

The fourth clause read, "I leave the sum of £10,000 to Leelo Vesik, c/o the Willows Care Home."

"Leelo! And nothing for sweet little Alma!"

The fifth clause left the balance of Eve's estate in trust to "my dear son Robbie, for his care, comfort, and maintenance during his lifetime," with any residue to be shared equally between Rachel and Simon, assuming they survived Robbie.

Rachel said, "That's very disturbing for several reasons. First, it's a large bequest to someone she met only recently. This Leelo character was helping Mum with her iPad and taught her how to use online banking. Then, just before she died—the day before, in fact, that's why I've come to you so soon—Mum was cheated out of her life savings in a wicked wire scam. She went to her bank and transferred over two hundred thousand pounds to an unknown account, thinking she was safeguarding it. The police are investigating, but I'll bet the money is far away by now. The bank is certain to deny responsibility, because of the way the fraudsters tricked Mum into lying when she made the withdrawal."

Gerald Smithers's mouth had fallen open by stages during this recitation. He shook his bald head in disbelief. "My dear girl, that is heartbreaking news. For you, Simon ... above all Robbie. This happened when?"

"The day before Mum died."

"You suspect this Leelo Vesik of worming her way into your mother's trust and affections ... even setting up the scam?"

"Worst of all, Leelo was the one who found Mum dead the next morning."

"Most unfortunate. So as of today, what is the value of Eve's estate? Roughly?"

"Almost nothing. The house proceeds are gone. Her current account has a thousand or so in it, but the care home will have a final bill. Apart from that, she held a handful of shares in utilities that Dad bought in the Thatcher era. British Gas, the National Grid, and so on. They're worth around fifteen thousand."

Smithers took off his reading spectacles. "Rachel, that means, after funeral expenses, there will likely be just enough to pay the bequest to this Leelo, but nobody else will benefit unless the missing funds are found. The bequest takes effect first, you see. You could challenge the will, but the costs would likely exceed the amount in question."

"I won't allow Leelo to cash in."

"Are you in touch with her? I wouldn't tell the woman about the gift until the will is proven and probate granted. I see you have brought your passport and ID with you, so we can get the formalities under way. Isn't it ludicrous that I have to request those documents? I've known you since you were two years old, and a very pretty toddler you were, although you're even more gorgeous now. Sorry if that's politically incorrect—I have no patience with modern manners."

Rachel smiled. "Compliment gratefully accepted, as I'm going through the change of life and feel bloated and befuddled half the time."

"No sign of either, Rachel. Chin up, dear. Call me anytime. You can even text or email me. I've got one of those smartphone thingies now."

From the solicitor's, Rachel drove to Hilworthy Surgery and filled in the forms to transfer to that practice. She learned she could make an appointment then and there, so she did, for the following Thursday, a week ahead.

She was now nearer to the Willows than to the bungalow. She fought with her conscience but resolved to continue with her plan despite Gerald Smithers's warning.

At the care home, she signed in and confirmed her appointment. On Primrose, she paused outside her mother's old room. For a moment she imagined Mum inside, watching an antiques show on TV. A sharp pang of loss ran through her, making her shiver.

She opened the door and entered.

Paul had collected Eve's few pieces of furniture, her pictures, books, clothes, and disabled aids the previous day.

The bed was made and covered with an old-fashioned candlewick bedspread. All ready for the next occupant.

The safe was bolted to a low shelf inside the wardrobe, above the shoe rack. Not the most accessible place, even for a fit and able person. Rachel had to kneel on the carpet to see the keyhole. She inserted the key. Really fiddly and stiff. After some jiggling, the heavy door swung open.

She removed the contents: the jewel case and the iPad in its pink cover. She ran her fingers around the dark cavity. Nothing else. No notebooks or scraps of paper. No mobile phone.

A quick look confirmed that all the jewellery was present and correct: Eve's engagement ring, her pearls, the three-stone diamond eternity, Dad's signet ring, and, in a pouch, Granny's collection.

She opened the cover of the iPad and the device lit up. She didn't know the code, so entered Eve's birthday. No luck. She tried her own birthday, then Robbie's.

Not knowing how many attempts Apple allowed, Rachel closed the cover and sat in Eve's armchair. She pulled out her phone and checked it. Three more condolence emails, two from friends and one from a dancing student.

A knock sounded on the door, followed by the entry of Leelo Vesik.

"Mrs. Phelps, we meet properly at last." Leelo's big, wide-set blue eyes met Rachel's. She didn't smile, but neither was she unfriendly.

Self-assured, Rachel thought.

She wore a short cardigan with three-quarter-length sleeves over a plain white blouse, the top two buttons undone. On her shoulder she carried a pink laptop backpack. Bangles on each wrist jingled as she sat on an upright chair.

She made Rachel feel old, fat, and overdressed.

Leelo's face showed solicitous concern. "Sorry for everything that happen—at the bank, and then Eve passing away so suddenly."

Rachel murmured, "I know Mum was very fond of you."

"Oh, and me of her. My best pupil on the iPad, sharp and quick, and her typing improved very much in just a few weeks. We became good friends, and I miss her so! Please, when is the funeral? I must come to pay respects."

Rachel felt her lips pursing. "It's not fixed yet, and may not be for some while. In the meantime, I need to unlock this iPad."

"The passcode is 1946. The year Eve met your father, she told me."

Why had Mum confided in this young woman? Maybe she'd reminded her of a younger me.

Her hair was the same natural blonde, albeit straighter and shorter than Rachel's had ever been. Also, Leelo's calm and serious nature would have appealed to Mum, who scorned "silly little girls," as she termed them.

Leelo opened her laptop bag and produced a designer loose-leaf notepad. She tore out a sheet and handed it to Rachel. "Here is it all—Eve's email password, her banking membership number, her Amazon account details, though I do not feel she ordered anything."

Rachel scanned the sheet, handwritten in neat, rounded blue ballpoint pen. "Is that all I need for the online banking?"

"You also require the passcode. I do not know that. I must be most careful with my clients' data. All personal information I encrypt in a secure file on my laptop. I write nothing down, unless like just this sheet to give you." Leelo stared at Rachel, wide-eyed and serious-faced.

"So how did you set Mum up, without knowing the passcode?"

The girl put her head on one side. "Mrs. Phelps, when we come to that stage of the registration, I look away and tell Eve to think of a number she could remember, not the same as her unlock code, and then never to tell anyone—not you, not me, not someone phoning up, not even a policeman, and not to write it down. It is part of my training for the olders, to alert them to cyber threats and make them very aware of dangers online. So I am horrified to hear of the bank trick. I want to die when I learn of it. I am also very surprised that your mother was fooled. She was so intelligent. My best pupil. She listened with care to everything I said."

"I agree. I am as surprised as you. Unfortunately her generation is very respectful of authority, and these tricksters appeal to their sense of justice. Mum thought she was helping the bank catch a crooked manager."

"I already tell the policeman all I know, Mrs. Phelps. I showed him my credentials and references. He thanked me and told me not to worry."

"I see. May I ask you, Miss Vesik . . . ?"

"Please call me Leelo, like everyone."

"Leelo, I'm fascinated. How do you come to be in this country?"

Leelo tucked a wayward strand of hair behind her ear. "Back home in Tallinn I worked for the government. We have the most advanced systems in Europe, even the world. Estonia was the first country where you can vote, file your income tax, access all public services online. I came to England on a six-month secondment to work in the Treasury in London, advising your chancellor's special project team, to bring your country's systems up to date. At a function I met a lovely Englishman who could make me smile. They say that is an achievement, to get a laugh out of an Estonian girl. We are shy and serious. My secondment ended, but I chose to stay. I had fallen in love with my boyfriend and your country. I signed up with the charity Age-Alert and made a vow to dedicate until the end of this year to helping people like Eve. Because I already had security and police clearance at government level, it was simple to obtain a Disclosure and Barring Service check for the role. I teach here at the Willows and three others in the county. I love coaching the older people. Every evening I go home to my man and cook him lots of proper food such as dill, herrings, cabbage, and potatoes."

Rachel felt mean and small-minded. How could she have mistrusted this young woman? After spending ten minutes with her, Rachel could not conceive that Leelo had played any part in the scam. What of the bequest? It made more sense now; it was exactly the way Mum would have rewarded a selfless person. She'd hated greed and the grasping attitudes of what she called the "me-me-me" generation.

A final question remained. "Leelo, I'm sorry you were the one to find Mum dead. I'm puzzled. Why did you go in to see her that morning, so early?"

The Estonian closed her spiral notebook. Her bangles clinked. "Alma left a message at reception for me to visit Eve as soon as I arrived. I was not surprised. I was sure your mother would want to discuss the bank fraud with me, maybe ask if I could help."

Rachel cast her mind back. *Had Alma mentioned that?* Rachel didn't think so, but she'd been in shock and grief. Anyway, this seemed to clear up the last trace of suspicion against Leelo.

So she said, "Leelo, I do appreciate what you did for Mum. I'll leave word with Mr. Lane about the funeral." She remembered two other things. "Did Mum always keep her iPad in the safe? And what about her mobile phone—it's gone missing. Any idea where it could be?"

Leelo, packing up her notebook and pen, replied, "Eve always had me lock the iPad away after our lessons. I recommended this, even though the device has the passcode set. At some places, not the Willows, I am less happy with the honesty of the staff."

"Could Mum get it out of the safe herself—to use in between lessons?"

"I doubt. That safe is tricksy to open. She would ask Alma if I was not here."

"The phone?"

"That lived in her handbag all times. She used it only a little, when she went on a trip with Terry the Taxi, or an outing in the minibus." Leelo paused. "We had such fun at the village fête! I shall miss Eve dearly."

The Estonian rose, shook Rachel's hand with a respectful bow of the head, turned, and opened the door.

Alma stood outside, her hand raised as if about to knock. The petite care assistant said, "Mrs. Phelps, Mr. Lane ask that you leave the safe key at reception."

"Of course, Alma."

Rachel said her goodbyes to the two staff. She packed the jewellery and iPad into a carrier and paused to look around the room for the last time.

During the short drive home, she asked herself why Alma had been listening at the door.

11

RACHEL UNLOCKED her own front door. The telephone was ringing. She put down her shopping carriers and grabbed the handset from the hall table.

"Detective Sergeant Ryan here, Mrs. Phelps. Thanks for coming in earlier. I now have something to report."

"Go on."

"I took statements from Leelo Vesik and Alma Puusepp, who are both from Tallinn, Estonia, but say they only met each other here in England. Timmins has spoken to everyone else at the Willows who had regular contact with your mother. I also got hold of Terry the Taxi. I've spoken with the serious fraud team at the bank's head office. So far, nothing helpful at all, I regret. The bank is keen for us to step aside and leave investigations to them. As for your mother's death, we believe your fears are unfounded, having spoken to the doctors and nurses."

"I have come to a similar conclusion."

"That's a relief, because the coroner is of the same mind. He will authorise the body to be released so you can go ahead with the funeral and cremation."

"I think I was a little paranoid yesterday. Mum's death was such a shock. I'm only starting to believe it now. How about the phone records—did they give you a lead on the bank scam?"

"No, but here is the surprising thing. On the days in question, no unusual calls were made to your mother's landline, and none to her mobile. The only incoming calls were from Audrey, who is her sister I believe, your husband Paul's mobile, and the bank, which would be confirming the appointment to make the withdrawal. I searched back two days in case she had muddled the dates up, but again I found only calls from people in her address book. As for outgoing calls, during the day of the fraud she telephoned the bank and Terry the Taxi, and there were two calls to your home number that evening and one to your husband's mobile. Did your mum's mobile phone show up yet?"

"No. Still missing."

"It's not switched on, and its last recorded location was at the bank. They don't have the phone at the branch. She may have turned it off for her appointment with the manager, taken it away, and left it somewhere else. The taxi driver says she didn't leave it in his minibus. So we are at a dead end. The absence of any number to link to the purported Fletcher character is most odd. Is it possible he called the switchboard at the Willows, rather than dialling your mother's direct line?"

Rachel thought about this. "Mum said the call came in on her private telephone. The extension from the switchboard goes to a phone on the wall by the door and is for staff and emergency use."

"Still, she could have been mistaken?"

"It's possible."

"I spoke to the duty receptionist on the day in question, who said no calls had been received and transferred to your mother's room. My superior says he can't justify the time and resources to go through the home's phone records in case the receptionist was mistaken. He would like to wait until the bank's fraud team have completed their trace of the money. It's frustrating."

Rachel thanked the detective and rang off. The display on the handset showed a missed call. She didn't recognise the number, which was a mobile, so she pressed Redial.

"Howard Plumb."

The bank manager! "Rachel Phelps here, Howard, returning your call."

"Rachel, my sincere condolences. To think Eve was here in my office only a few days ago! I am sorry."

"Thank you."

"Now, this is unofficial, as I have handed your mother's case over to the fraud team, so I'd be grateful if you kept the information between you and your husband for now. I thought a quick call could save you months of anxiety, and even help you to … um … reconcile yourself to an unwelcome conclusion."

Rachel tensed. She felt her pulse rate increase and the colour rise in her cheeks. "Go on."

"The beneficiary for your mother's transfer was a private bank in the City of London called Grimshaw's. They are being extremely uncooperative and state that the account holder is a reputable customer of many years' standing. They refuse to divulge his or her identity, claiming this person was expecting the transfer, and the amount does not represent unusual activity for the account."

"That's impossible!" Rachel almost shrieked. "Mum was conned! She told us in great detail how she was tricked by someone from your bank calling themselves Fletcher."

"I'm trying to help, Rachel. I shouldn't be telling you this."

"I'm sorry."

"I don't wish to alarm you, but I must warn you we are unlikely to make any swift progress on your claim. The fact that the recipient appears to be *bona fide* has seriously compromised the investigation. Grimshaw's is one of the oldest banks in the country, like Coutts, and it serves only the very wealthy: entrepreneurs, royalty, landed gentry."

"I see. Thank you, Howard, for your candour. Have you told the police about all this?"

"Yes. Do you have a date for the funeral? I plan to attend, having known your family for so many years."

"I'll be sure to let you know. Your information will stay within these walls."

Rachel rang off. Still holding the phone, she bent down and picked up the post from the doormat, dropped in by Kizzy, who received all mail. She entered the sitting room and sat on the sofa to open it.

Two cards from old friends of Eve, their spidery condolences testament to their own advanced ages. She placed them on the mantelpiece alongside others delivered earlier by hand.

She fanned her burning face with an empty envelope. Perhaps a battery-powered fan was not such a bad notion. She could order one on her phone from eBay.

A better idea came to her.

She fetched her mother's iPad.

Much easier on the bigger screen, and quicker than booting up the laptop.

Back on the sofa, she opened the tablet's cover and keyed in "1946."

She logged into the house Wi-Fi—password "Raffles," which after talking with Leelo she realised was dumb.

The home screen apps included BBC iPlayer, Amazon, Google Chrome, and a sketching app. Rachel selected Chrome and navigated to eBay. She signed in with her own ID.

Her phone chimed. She extracted it from her bag. Four new emails.

She pressed the envelope icon and her heart skipped a beat when she saw they were all from her mother.

She breathed out. Of course! They weren't communications from beyond the grave, just unsent messages that had been processed when she fired up the iPad.

She opened the first.

My dalrign Rachel,

A false start, with Send pressed instead of Delete.

The next message ran,

My draling Rachel, I amtyptin this qll by ywerl withouf my spces so I hop ucam undsrotbe.

She smiled. Mum's keyboard skills hadn't improved that much, despite Leelo's praise for her progress. Her occasional emails had always been hilariously mistyped. Rachel imagined Eve, all alone in her room, without her reading specs on, pecking out a message she obviously considered important, pressing Send by mistake, starting again and again. Only, the iPad was not connected to the Willows Wi-Fi, so the emails had remained in her outbox until now.

Third message coming up.

> *My darlling Rach3l, I am typgins this qll byu fmyslef*

You're not making any sense, Mum!

Rachel opened the final message.

> *Alsma is a nauthy little girl, a beastly liar, WICKED, dont beleve a word she says. Lov you alwaysm, Umm xxx.*

Weird, or what?

Eve had always loved Alma and sung the tiny carer's praises. Even on the morning she died, she'd spoken warmly of her.

The detective should know about this development. She took Jim Ryan's card from her purse and dialled his direct line.

"Nobody is available to take your call . . . Please leave your message after the tone."

"Rachel Phelps again, Detective. I've received strange emails from my mother. I won't try and explain, I'll forward them to you now." She hung up and forwarded the four messages from the iPad.

The house phone rang again. Jim Ryan? No, a local number she didn't recognise.

"Brown Brothers Undertakers here, Mrs. Phelps. Is this a good time?"

"Yes."

"We have just heard from the coroner's office that we can go ahead. The crematorium has had a cancellation and we can book next Thursday at eleven."

Wondering why a cremation would be cancelled—deceased come back to life in the mortuary?—Rachel replied, "That's ideal. I'll call in with Mum's hymns for the Order of Service and choose everything."

Next she telephoned her new surgery. "Sorry, I need to change the appointment I just made. I have a funeral that day."

"Are you by any chance free within the next hour? Dr. Clare Tomkins has accepted you on to her register and she has a late cancellation. I know you were only here this morning, but if you don't mind coming back?"

It seemed to be a day for cancellations to work in her favour. Rachel had nothing else planned, so she said, "Great, I'll jump straight in the car and be there in twenty minutes."

As she finished this call, her mobile rang. "Jim Ryan here, Mrs. Phelps. I received the messages. Can you shed any light on them?"

"No, I can't. They arrived from Mother's iPad."

"Will you drop the iPad in, please? Put it in a plastic bag so it gets no more fingerprints on it. I'll fingerprint you when you arrive, so we can eliminate yours."

"No problem. I have to go over to Hilworthy, so I'll stop by afterwards."

In the hall, she took Eve's jewellery case and stowed it in her knicker drawer in the bedroom. She popped the iPad in a plastic freezer bag, which she put into her handbag.

Outside, a visitor's car—a shiny black BMW SUV—was carelessly parked by the Phelps & Son office. Rachel heard raised voices. She crossed the tarmac. Through the Venetian blinds, she saw Kizzy in heated conversation with a man she did not recognise.

She hesitated. She couldn't hear much, but clearly an argument was in progress.

The secretary and the man stood face-to-face. Kizzy was saying "right out of order."

Intervene?

It was probably a dispute over brick quantities or, more likely, given the car, that the visitor was a client unhappy that his project had been delayed by the extra work at the cottages.

The pair were not coming to blows. Kizzy could stand her ground.

"I'm not keeping anything from you, babe. Please don't micromanage my business as well as yours."

Rachel turned away to her Fiat, Paul's words resonating in her head.

She had enough to worry about.

12

"SO YOU APPROVE of your new doctor?" Paul crossed to the fridge. "Chardonnay, babe?"

"No thanks. I'm right off alcohol for some reason. Dr. Tomkins was sweet. *Very* sympathetic. She gave me a full exam and took samples. My blood pressure is a little high, but hardly surprising. She said I was a prime candidate for hormone replacement therapy. I'm fit and active, which is in my favour. I told her what Thorpe had said and she replied, 'He's correct. Your risk of breast cancer is doubled, but only from 0.8 per thousand to 1.6.' So I hope she'll put me on it soon. I can't take the flushes, and the mood swings, and the bloating, and the night sweats, and my boobs sore all the time. I expect you've had enough of it too."

Paul poured wine for himself, took a good swig, and refilled the glass. With his hair tinged with grey streaks, swept back over his high forehead, and his square jaw, he reminded Rachel of George Clooney in his younger days. "I'm so glad I'm not a woman."

"Me too." Rachel grinned.

"Now tell me all about your day, including these emails from the *Twilight Zone*. Your summary while I was showering was, shall I say, breathless. Sit yourself down, count to ten, and start again from the beginning."

Rachel sat as she was told, aware she had gabbled all her news to Paul the moment he arrived home. She remembered reading somewhere that men hated that. They needed to switch off from work and unwind before they could turn their attention to home life. She ticked the points off on her fingers—unstained by ink, since Ryan had used a tiny mobile reader to take her fingerprints.

"One, the funeral is next Thursday. Simon flies in the day before and will stay with us."

"Great."

Rachel looked sidelong at Paul, unsure whether he was being sarcastic. He was no admirer of her elder brother. "Two, the fraud investigation is going nowhere. The beneficiary is some Mayfair toff who was expecting the money."

"I'll bet he was. Won't Grimshaw's Bank have to divulge his identity?"

"Apparently not. The crooks set up the scam to make it look as if Mum intended everything the way it happened. She's not around to contradict that. The only person who knows what she said and did is Howard Plumb, at our branch. He broke with procedure to tell me all this. You mustn't breathe a word to anyone—not Kizzy, not Auntie Audrey. Promise?"

Paul raised both hands in mock protest. "Whoa! Ease up, pardner," he drawled in his best Wild West cowboy accent. "You and me's not talkin' any loose talk."

She grinned again, grateful for his attempt to lighten the mood. "This all happened at once, within a few minutes. Three, I received the weird emails from Mum. Only the last message made sense."

"Tell me again what it said."

"'Alma is a naughty little girl, a beastly wicked'—in capitals—'liar, don't believe a word she says. Love you always, Mum.'"

Paul stroked his dimpled chin. "You say they were from Mum. They were from Mum's iPad. Anyone could have sent them."

"No, it had to be someone who could get the tablet out of the safe and knew her passcode. Only Leelo. Or Alma, but she would hardly compose messages like that about herself. I think it was Mum."

"But it doesn't sound like your Mum's words. When were the emails composed?"

"Can't tell. They went into her outbox because the Wi-Fi didn't connect."

They sat in silence for a moment. Raffles, sensing his opportunity, appeared from the utility room, head cocked on one side in a manner calculated to appeal, his lead in his mouth. Paul half turned. "We'll go out soon, boy. Back to your bed for now."

Raffles gave the doggie equivalent of a shrug and did as instructed.

"I'll take him. I could do with the fresh air. No classes tonight."

Paul tapped his fingernails on his empty wine glass. "Your detective laddie will need to visit the Willows again. You say he can't identify any unknown callers to Mum on the day Fletcher rang?"

"That's right. Her direct line, her mobile, and the home's switchboard all drew a blank. The only people who telephoned her that morning were Aunt Audrey and you."

"We must assume Aunt Audrey is innocent. Anyway, she's not a man. And I remember my call. I picked up a voicemail from Eve and called her back. It was about your birthday present. She wanted to order for you from Amazon and asked me the brand you used."

"I won't be getting that present now." Rachel wiped a tear from the corner of her eye.

"Unless she ordered it before she died, and it shows up. You'd better be prepared for a bottle of Coco Chanel."

"Unlikely. The rest of that day she was preoccupied by the bank scam, and I'm sure she would have been too busy and distracted the day after. Next morning she was dead. Oh Paulie! I'll never get a present from her again, or a birthday card!"

"Or another email, hopefully." Paul reached out and grasped Rachel's hand, much as she had done with Robbie in the kennels that fateful day. "Cheer up, chicken."

But Rachel didn't want to cheer up, she wanted to cry her eyes out. She'd held it together so far, but now, safe at home with the man she loved, her rock and protector and constant admirer, she dissolved into grief and self-pity. "Oh Paulie, she was never a granny! I let her down. She never said anything, but I know she would have loved grandchildren and been the best grandmother in the world." Rachel looked away from Paul as the tears streamed down her cheeks. "I let you down too. I don't know why. Just one bit of my body that wouldn't work."

"We had a lot of fun trying, though, didn't we?" He stroked her hair with the gentlest touch. "Don't beat yourself up, babe. None of this is your fault. I love you. I loved you from the moment I set eyes on you, and I always will."

Rachel snuffled but managed a smile. She took a tissue from her jeans pocket and dabbed her cheeks. "The Red Cross Ball. You were the only man who even knew a waltz was in three time. What would I do without you, Paulie?"

The silence that followed was broken by a rattling sound and a hopeful whimper. Raffles poked his head around the door, lead in mouth once more.

They both laughed. The collie was a joker, with immaculate timing.

Rachel blew her nose. She felt better now. She hadn't cried properly since Mum died.

"Thanks, love. I think I needed that." She got up, took a glass from the wall cupboard, and filled it with mineral water from the fridge. *Have plenty to drink*, her new doctor had advised. She bent down to Raffles and took the lead from his gentle mouth. "Come on, dog. You got me for tonight's walk."

She put on her parka and wellies, grabbed the torch from the shelf above the hall radiator, and exited into the night. Raffles bounded ahead, towards the gate into the field.

They took a left on the public footpath leading to the church and the village. The constant recent rain had made the ground muddy. She threw back her hood and let the cool night air circulate around her head for a moment.

In truth, she'd wanted a few minutes alone, because things Paul said had unsettled her.

To begin with, she didn't use Coco Chanel. She found the warm spiciness of Coco cloying. That was her mother's favourite. Rachel used No. 5. It was odd for Paul to confuse them; his mind was like a calculator. He never needed to write anything down. In fact, he wasn't great at writing. Luckily, he could remember: measurements, tile quantities, telephone numbers, the odds on the favourite at Towcester. Unlike him to get a brand name wrong.

Another thing was that on the previous evening, Paul had asked about the "second signature confirming cause of death?" She was surprised he even knew of such formalities.

More puzzling by far, though, was his comment about Grimshaw's Bank. Unlike Paul, Rachel couldn't trust her memory right now. She'd forgotten the name of the bank, and in her "breathless" summary through the shower curtain earlier, she was certain she had referred to "some posh private bank in Mayfair." At least, she was 99 percent certain that's what she had said.

Had Howard Plumb also telephoned Paul with his news about the bank transfer? No—because Paul would have mentioned it when I finished gabbling at him.

So how did Paul find out the name of the bank? Or is my short-term memory now severely compromised?

She'd also forgotten to ask Paul about the mystery visitor in the BMW who had squared up to Kizzy in the office.

Maybe it isn't the menopause—am I showing the first signs of early onset Alzheimer's?

That was an even less welcome possibility than the alternative: that Paul knew more about the bank scam than he was admitting.

A gust of cold wind blew across the field from the east. She shivered, put her hood back up, and trudged after Raffles.

13

AFTER BREAKFAST the following Monday, the week of the funeral, Rachel sat at the kitchen table in her dressing gown.

She needed to choose flowers for the coffin and had promised Robbie he could come to the florist's with her.

The proof of the Order of Service should be ready to check later that day. All three children were to speak. Simon would read "Death Is Nothing at All," requested by Eve. Robbie would recite "Jellicle Cats" from *Old Possum's Book of Practical Cats* by T. S. Eliot, for no better reason than it was his favourite poem of all those that Mum had read to him in bed as a toddler. Robbie said, "She read it for me enough times. Now it's my turn to read it for her."

To Rachel fell the duty of the eulogy. She'd made six pages of notes and needed to condense these down into four minutes of speaking. The funeral directors had emphasised they mustn't overrun their allotted twenty minutes.

Rachel ticked off the boxes on her to-do list. There had been no further developments in the fraud investigation, and she wouldn't pursue it this week.

She would have to tell Robbie what had happened.

Not before the funeral, she'd decided.

She finished her mug of tea and was about to head down the hall to the bathroom when the landline rang.

"Mrs. Phelps? Dr. Tomkins here. Your test results are in, and your medical records arrived electronically from Practitioner Services. Having reviewed both, I do need to see you urgently. It's nothing to be alarmed about. Sorry, I can't be more specific over the phone. Can you make it in this morning?"

Rachel's pulse raced. This was the last thing she needed, this week of all weeks. "Yes, I can."

"Ten o'clock?"

"I'll be there."

She showered and dressed in double-quick time, jumped into the Fiat, and set off to Hilworthy, her mind in turmoil. Dr. Tomkins had said not to be alarmed, but she would say that, wouldn't she? It must be something serious for the doctor to have summoned her at such short notice.

On arrival, she endured an agonising ten-minute wait until Dr. Tomkins emerged from her room and beckoned Rachel in.

"Mrs. Phelps, sorry to summon you so dramatically. You are healthy, apart from somewhat raised blood pressure, and I suspect I know the reason for that too. I checked your notes. I'm sure it's not the case, but I must confirm: have you recently undergone fertility treatment? Privately, perhaps? I notice you had three courses in your midthirties."

Rachel shook her head in bewilderment. "No. Not since then. We gave up."

"You see, IVF treatment can give a false positive. If we rule that out, then I can advise you—and I hope this is happy news—that you are pregnant."

Rachel's mouth fell open. For a moment she said nothing, and the only sound was the ticking of the clock on the wall. Then she managed to say, "How could that happen?"

"In the normal way, I imagine. You know the procedure."

"I'm menopausal. My periods have been erratic for a year, and I haven't had one at all for three months."

"Can you by any chance put a date on the start of your last known period?"

Rachel considered. "Yes. I'd gone several months with nothing and was experiencing symptoms—the hot flushes. Then I had a light one. I remember because it was a very warm day and we were going to Nando's to celebrate Robbie's blue belt award. I wore a frock instead of trousers for comfort and to keep cool, what with the heat of the restaurant and the spicy chicken." She consulted her phone calendar. "The eleventh of July."

Dr. Tomkins turned to her PC screen and tapped on her keyboard. "Excellent. We'll send you for an ultrasound to date you more accurately, but it seems you are around fourteen weeks on. It's unusual, but possible to conceive during the perimenopause. There may be a psychological element: a woman like you who has tried for years thinks the time has passed, and somehow the pressure lifts."

"I suspect the same thing happened to my own mother, but she was only forty-three. Aren't I much too old to have a baby . . . I mean, I've wanted a family all my life . . . and Paul . . ."

"We'll take the greatest care of you. Forty-eight is not so ancient these days, even for a first child. You're not the oldest patient of mine to conceive for the first time."

"My younger brother has Down's syndrome. That doesn't run in a family, does it?"

"Not usually, and the blood tests I ran last week included a Down's probability. That result is inconclusive, unfortunately. Now I know you're pregnant, we'll do the second part of the test during your dating ultrasound. I'll arrange a priority appointment. The sonographer will look at baby's neck for tell-tale signs. That check isn't one hundred percent reliable either, but it gives a clearer indication of risk. If that turns out to be high, we'll discuss further tests and the choices they involve.

"There are risks associated with later pregnancy. Go home and share the news with your husband. Don't spring it on him—break it gently. Lay off the wine. You might want to wait a few weeks more before you go public." The doctor reached into a drawer and took out a handful of leaflets. The top one showed a smiling, expectant mother aged about twenty, hands resting on her bump.

Dr. Tomkins smiled too. "In shock?"

Rachel picked up the leaflets and leafed through them. "Yes. Can I carry on my business? I'm a dance instructor."

"That sounds fun. Tell me about it."

"I've been dance mad since I was about three. Mum gave me ballet lessons. I preferred music with more of a swing, tried ballroom and Latin, long before they were so popular and fashionable, and found my true calling. I qualified and worked in a Leicester studio for years. When my husband's building business got in a muddle after his father died, I resigned from the studio, stepped in, and took over the admin and bookkeeping. But the dance bug wouldn't go away, so I started my own business, hiring the village hall once a week to begin with. Things mushroomed with the popularity of *Strictly Come Dancing*, and now I have over a hundred regular pupils and hold classes four evenings a week in the primary school. I also do one-to-one teaching, mostly for couples getting married. I love the work, and it's a useful addition to the family income."

"Good for you. Do carry on your business. In fact, you can continue with any activity you wish, including sex. Just listen to your body and rest when it tells you. But I must sound a note of caution. Miscarriage is much, much more common in women of your age. There's up to a thirty percent chance. The most dangerous period is the first four months. That's why I wanted to see you at once, to make sure you stop taking any over-the-counter medications and cut out painkillers, particularly ibuprofen. I already mentioned about alcohol. Reduce caffeine too, if you're an addict. It's all in the leaflets. Also, I recommend a prenatal vitamin." She tapped more keys on her PC. "You're in the system now. Any questions?"

"Why did you suspect I was pregnant when you checked me last week?"

"Menopause and pregnancy share many of the same signs and symptoms. What made me wonder was your blood pressure. You are slim, fit, and active, and you'd never had the problem before. Let me check your numbers now." The doctor wound the cuff around Rachel's upper arm and pumped the bulb. "We'll manage it carefully. There are safe medications if we need them, but I hope we won't." She held her stethoscope to Rachel's skin, and air hissed out of the device. "It's 147 over

95. Nothing to fret over. The important thing is to avoid stress. Spend time with your feet up, listen to music, get early nights when you're not working. I'm sure your husband will step up to make your life as easy as possible."

"Unfortunately we have a funeral this Thursday—my mother's."

"I'm sorry to hear that. I'm sure you'll take it in your stride. Can I confirm that this pregnancy is good news and you'll want to keep the baby?"

"Yes. It's the most wonderful and delightful surprise."

Outside in her car, Rachel resisted the urge to text or phone Paul. In a flash, the symptoms she had been experiencing became insignificant. Presumably the hot flushes would reduce. Fatigue, dizziness, bad nights—all were minor annoyances now.

She must focus on the healthiest lifestyle possible.

She must keep the baby and give birth safely and naturally.

If only I'd changed doctors sooner! That idiot Thorpe! It could have been months before he realised!

If I'd had the news earlier, Mum would have known, and maybe recovered from her illness, and lived to see her grandchild.

No point dwelling on it. Just give thanks for the precious chance to have a family.

She consoled herself with the thought of her mother looking down from above, smiling and approving.

It will be a spring baby—around mid-April. What a perfect time of year! Easter eggs and chocolate bunnies at the little birthday parties!

She'd need maternity clothes. Paul would have to put one of the lads on to decorating the back bedroom as a nursery.

He would be pleased—no, overjoyed. He'd stoically borne the disappointment of all those barren years and the miserable experience of unsuccessful IVF treatment.

He will make a wonderful father. He'll rediscover his confidence, sort out the building business, get to work to earn the money to keep his growing family.

And Robbie will be an uncle!

She glanced at her watch. Time to pick him up en route to the florist's.

14

THEY CHOSE a double-ended wreath for the coffin, in Eve's favourite shades of blue, pink, and lilac, including lilies, lisianthus, and lots of roses. Robbie asked for some golden autumnal leaves among the blooms and greenery, because they would be "sad but nice." The young florist thought this a tremendous idea.

Next, they stopped by at the funeral director and collected a proof of the Order of Service.

"Let's go and have a coffee," Rachel said.

"And a bun!" Robbie sang out, grinning.

They found a window seat at Costa, bathed in autumn sunshine. Rachel ordered a hot chocolate for herself and a coffee and Danish for Robbie. On a whim, she turned back. "Give me another pastry." She was eating for two now!

Robbie studied the leaflet for a full ten minutes before pronouncing himself satisfied with his "Jellicle Cats." Rachel said she would read the rest at home.

Her brother seemed as happy as ever. He chattered about the kennels and how Julia had trodden in a bowl of dogfood and used a "very bad word."

Rachel did her best to respond, nodding and smiling as he wittered on in his usual Robbie manner. So far, he'd coped well with his mother's death. Maybe the funeral would bring the reality home to him.

All the time, Rachel's mind held but one thought: *You're going to be a mum yourself!*

Minute by minute, her excitement grew.

After twenty-four years of marriage! At last!

"Sis, did you hear me? Planet Earth calling Rachel."

"Sorry, Robbie, I was miles away. Yes, it must have been funny when the Scottie met the Doberman."

"They wanted to get it on, but the Scottie was the dog and the Doberman the bitch!"

"Shh, love. Not so loud. If you've finished, I'll drop you home."

With babies on the brain, she delivered Robbie to Hare House and turned the Fiat into her gates minutes later.

The same big BMW was parked, or rather abandoned, in the middle of the drive, preventing her reaching her own front door.

Paul's Ranger stood outside the office, in its usual space.

What the . . . ? Remember, no stress!

She got out of the Fiat and walked up to the office door.

Through the blinds, she saw Paul, Kizzy, and the same man as before. Paul faced up to the visitor, who was as thickset as her husband but expensively dressed in a grey suit and striped shirt with no tie. Paul, in jeans, work boots, and leather jacket, had come straight from a site.

The two men's raised voices left no doubt that the visitor's problem remained unsolved.

Kizzy stood to one side, her head swivelling this way and that like an umpire at Wimbledon.

The visitor stalked to the door, flung it open, and barked at Rachel, "You're blocking me in. Move that car—now!"

Before Rachel could reply, Paul burst out of the door and shouted, "Don't you speak to my wife like that, you piece of shit!"

The man said, "If that stupid little Noddy car isn't clear by the time I turn round, it'll get flattened. Move it now!" He strode towards his BMW.

"Better do as he says. I'll explain later," Paul growled under his breath.

No stress! Think of baby!

Rachel put on her sweetest smile and said, "Moving it now." She got back into the Fiat.

The BMW was already underway. The driver gunned the engine, and the heavy car shot towards her. In a panic, she spun the wheel and reversed onto the grass bordering the drive, ending up in a rose bed.

The BMW thundered past. Gravel sprayed up, and some stones clinked on her bonnet.

Heart racing, Rachel selected first gear with a crunch. Wheels spinning, the little car lurched and jolted onto the driveway. Paul opened the driver's door.

"Come into the office, and I'll explain."

The three of them sat around the meeting table.

"He's right out of order," Kizzy said. "Gone back on his word."

"Who is that specimen?" Rachel asked.

Paul said, "Phil Fletcher, founder and owner of Fletcher Groundworks."

"Fletcher? That's the name of the man who conned Mum."

Paul said, "This guy is a contractor to the Council and the Highways Agency. He's connected. Owns a place near Derby worth three million. Doesn't seem likely he would be involved in scamming Mum. All the same, better ask the detective to question him. It's a strange coincidence at least. These big men think they are above the law. I wouldn't put it past him, if only to get at me."

"So what's this Fletcher's beef with us, a little family building firm?"

"I hired his small-works division to handle the underpinning on the cottages. I told you."

"You said you'd done a deal, he owed you a favour, they would give us a special price and extended credit."

Paul said, "This doesn't go outside the room. Kizzy knows everything. I did the deal with Fletcher's small-works manager, Mervyn. There was a . . . cash incentive."

"Cash? As in bribe?"

Paul looked at the table. "Yeah. If I paid Mervyn five grand in holding-folding, he would undercharge me for the cottages.

He'd bill us five thousand instead of twenty. So we'd end up paying ten grand and getting credit on a half-price job."

"Fletcher found out?"

"Not quite. What happened is bloody Mervyn took the cash but didn't honour his end. He billed the full whack. Money up front! We couldn't pay, the work had started, Fletcher comes round last week and gives Kizzy the third degree, then he's here again today."

"All for a few thousand on a job that must mean nothing to him? It makes no sense." Rachel felt the colour rising in her cheeks. This was precisely what she needed to avoid.

How long has Paul been carrying on this kind of shenanigans?

When Rachel handled the books, everything was above board.

What have Kizzy and Paul been up to?

"If Fletcher's company started the work, that's up to them. If they're not happy, they can just down tools until we pay them something."

Kizzy said, "Would you like me to leave? This is family business."

Paul said, "No, Kiz. I'm the one who's leaving. Rachel, love, Mervyn turned it all on me. Said I'd promised a cheque a week ago."

"Why did this Mervyn character rat on us? He must know you'll be out for his blood."

"I'm going now to meet him, ask him just that—and get my five grand back. Failing which, I shall kill him."

Rachel looked sidelong at her husband. "Take care, love. Keep your temper. We can work this out. It's a setback, sure, but don't turn it into a major drama."

Paul picked up his weighty bunch of keys and headed for the door. "I'll sort young Mervyn out and be home for tea. Sorry you had to witness all this."

Rachel and Kizzy sat in silence. Paul's pickup receded down the drive.

"Coffee?"

"No thanks. Just tell me, Kizzy, did you know about all this?"

The black girl hung her head. "Yeah. Paul said not to worry you, what with you being so easily upset these days."

"I thought we trusted each other."

"Sorry, Rachel. We do. We is friends. Can't you see, I was torn? Paul said he'd done this kind of deal many times. 'Just oiling the wheels of commerce,' was how he put it."

"Not in my time as administrator, or when he worked with his father. They had old Mrs. Saunders on the books and she would never connive in anything dodgy. Tell me, where did Paul get the five thousand? And how did you account for it?"

Kizzy sighed. "He won it at the races when Newsome's invited them all to Southwell."

Rachel said, "That's the day he took Robbie instead of me because I had the gold medal exams that evening. I don't remember him coming home with news of a big win."

"I'm sure Robbie will confirm it. The point is, it was 'free money,' as Paul put it. No need to record it or pay tax on it. Perhaps he had lots of winners in his time and used them for the benefit of the business."

It didn't sound likely to Rachel. She picked up a leaflet about insulation and fanned her cheeks. "So when did you learn of this—and the problem with Mervyn?"

"Last week. Then, when Fletcher showed up here, I realised the secret deal had gone wrong. You was outside. I so wanted you to come in and rescue me from him. They say he's a hard bastard and enforces his terms with a couple of heavies."

"It still makes no sense that someone with hundreds of employees and big contracts would waste time driving around threatening a small outfit like us."

"It's the way he is. Twenty grand is twenty grand. He wouldn't want to write that off."

"This business with Mervyn is weird. Why would he take Paul's money and then not honour the deal?"

"I guess he had second thoughts. I'm sure he'll hand the cash back to Paul."

The telephone rang. Kizzy crossed to her desk and answered it. "Phelps & Son, how may I help you? Oh, Mr. Jackson. Paul says sorry he didn't get round to you today. The rain has held him up. He'll be with you Thursday, no fail. Yes, I understand your frustration. We can't control the weather. Yes, I will tell him that . . ."

No way would Paul be seeing any clients on Thursday—funeral day. However, Rachel said nothing and raised a hand in farewell to Kizzy, who smiled back.

One thing was clear. All was not well with the business. She'd get to the bottom of the problems, but without stressing herself.

It was her fault for not taking a closer interest; after all, she was a director of the company.

As she crossed to the bungalow, Rachel reached another decision. She wouldn't break the news of her pregnancy to Paul just yet. She'd save it until the day after the funeral.

The next evening was Rachel's second beginners' class—she'd had to leave them ten minutes into their first lesson the previous week. They revised the waltz steps and everyone made good progress around the hall while Robbie played "Edelweiss."

Wednesday passed in a blur of funeral arrangements. The telephone rang all morning, with questions and condolences from mourners, or the undertakers checking some detail of the service.

Nothing more was said about Fletcher's visit, or Mervyn, or the financial affairs of Phelps & Son. It was as if they had an unspoken agreement to shelve all such discussions until after the funeral.

She took a call on her mobile while out shopping for tights at lunchtime.

"Jim Ryan here, Mrs. Phelps. I couldn't reach you on your home number."

"I can't talk, I'm in Accessorize. What's happened?"

"Could you drop in at the station as you're in town? There are developments."

Rachel looked at her watch. She was due at the Dog and Duck to discuss the wake, but that could wait.

"I'll come now."

15

RACHEL PHELPS, flanked by her husband Paul and brothers Simon and Robbie, entered the crowded anteroom of the crematorium. A low murmur of greeting hummed around the room to mark the arrival of the principal mourners.

She scanned the sea of faces. There was Howard Plumb from the bank and Gerald Smithers the elderly solicitor, both in dark suits and Rotary ties.

At the end of one row of the cheap plastic chairs sat Guy Lane from the care home, with Leelo Vesik by his side. He too wore a suit and tie, while Leelo had chosen a midlength check skirt and cashmere cardigan.

Aunt Audrey, looking tearful, sat with her daughter Emma, Rachel's first cousin. All seats were taken, but Guy Lane leapt to his feet and ushered Rachel to his place next to Leelo. Leelo smiled in sympathetic acknowledgement.

Rachel's brothers stayed standing among a knot of other mourners.

She counted heads. Twenty-eight. *A pleasing turnout.*

The family had ridden together in a Brown Brothers limousine from the bungalow, following the hearse. No one spoke much on the short journey. On arrival, the driver got out and held a golfing umbrella to shelter Rachel from the worst of the rain, propelled horizontally by gusty, gale-force winds. The others ran for it.

Elder brother Simon had arrived on time from Perth; Rachel had collected him.

Simon had kept his good looks and physique and he was brown as a nut from the Australian outdoor life. Taller than Paul, though not as tall as Rachel, he was more casually dressed than most of the other men, wearing a black leather jacket with no tie; yet he exuded self-confidence. Paul, in contrast, though he smartened up well enough, always looked awkward in a suit, like a schoolboy brushed up to meet a visiting dignitary on Speech Day.

Rachel wore a dress in navy jersey with dark tights and matching shoes with a square heel. Robbie wore corduroy trousers and a V-neck pullover. He didn't own a suit, as far as Rachel knew.

At home the previous evening, after a family supper of spaghetti Bolognese, the three siblings had practised their readings around the kitchen table. Robbie wanted to recite his poem from memory, but the others had instructed him to have the Order of Service open and ready in case he stumbled.

Everyone had approved of Rachel's simple, informative, and heartfelt eulogy, which Robbie timed on his phone at three minutes and fifty-five seconds.

After the rehearsals, Robbie, Paul, and Raffles headed for the sitting room to watch the Manchester soccer derby live. Simon helped Rachel clear up in the kitchen.

"How's life treating you, Rache?" her brother asked.

"Fine," Rachel said. She couldn't tell him about her baby. And she didn't want to tell him about the firm's money problems.

"You're looking great, in the circumstances. Paul's put on a lot of weight."

"A bit, perhaps. You haven't seen him in three years. He does less labouring now. The lads do the heavy lifting."

"Paul used to have a raffish charm. Now he just looks dissolute. I would say you are the one doing the heavy lifting in your relationship. Keep on top of him, Rache."

"Don't start, Simon. I don't need the big-brother treatment. And you haven't exactly been much support. You could have made it back for Paul's dad's funeral."

"You still smarting over that? I had an industrial dispute in full swing. I apologised at the time, and do so again now."

"You could have come since then, to see Mum. She adored you. You were always her favourite."

Families!

Rachel forced herself back to the present moment. At least Simon was here today. She looked around the anteroom and breathed in and out a few times to steady her nerves. The last time she'd been at the crematorium was for Uncle Jack's funeral, three years ago. Mum had kept hold of her arm then, in this very room, and they'd comforted each other.

She took a tissue from her bag and dabbed her cheeks. She put a hand on her tummy. One life had ended, but another had begun. If Dr. Tomkins's calculations were correct, Rachel was a week into her second trimester. This evening, after the wake, she would break her news to Paul. Then Robbie and Simon, and tomorrow to Kizzy and everyone.

Had word got out earlier, it would have complicated today with the danger of Rachel upstaging her mother's commemorations.

The door opened, and the crematorium superintendent leaned in. Organ music became audible. "All is ready. May I remind you, ladies and gentlemen, to silence your phones. Would the family come through?"

They'd chosen not to process in with the coffin, and to take their seats first.

Mum would await them inside.

Rachel opened her bag again and took out her phone. She'd debated whether to bring it, but she had in case there were messages from mourners stuck in traffic or delayed by trees down on the road.

As she reached to silence the smartphone, it pinged.

Paul, by her side, extended his hand to help her to her feet, a gentle smile on his rugged face.

She swiped the screen to view the text.

Her heart missed a beat.

Rachel gasped, and her free hand flew to cover her mouth.

The superintendent held the door. The mourners stopped talking. Rachel remained seated as if glued to her chair.

"Come on, love," Paul murmured. "Time to go."

Pulse racing, Rachel allowed Paul to help her up. She walked zombielike by his side into the chapel, holding her mobile. He put his arm around her shoulder.

On the dais, the vicar awaited the congregation. The organist, a plump woman in an electric-blue suit, played "Chanson de Matin" by Elgar, Eve's favourite composer.

The coffin, with its long, double-ended spray, rested on its catafalque.

Bernard Brown, the funeral director, handed each of them an Order of Service as they passed.

In a daze, Rachel followed Paul into the front row of pews. They sat.

Robbie arrived next and took the pew on the other side of her. Then Simon took his place.

Rachel raised the phone to show the three-word message to Paul. The screen was blank. She swiped to wake it up.

"Time to put that away, love," Paul whispered. "Like he said."

"I just got a text from *Mum*," Rachel whispered back. "I mean, not from her, but—"

With firm fingers, Paul removed the mobile from her grasp, slid the ringer switch to silent, and flipped the leather cover shut.

Robbie spoke up in his sing-song voice. "Something wrong, Sis?" Rachel twisted in her seat. The pews behind were filling up. The organist took more music from the bench beside her and "Nimrod" sounded around the crematorium.

"No, no, Robbie. Nothing."

Paul squeezed her hand. "Try to hold it together, babe. Whatever's eating you, leave it until later. I know you're upset, but we must give Eve a dignified send-off."

Rachel's eyesight blurred. She reached for the phone in Paul's grasp. He transferred it to his other hand and then his jacket pocket. "Rachel, behave yourself," he hissed. "People are looking at you."

Robbie spoke again, his voice quavering a little. "What's the matter, guys? Don't you want me to read after all?"

Rachel reached to her right and patted Robbie's thigh. "It's fine, love. Ignore me. I'm upset."

Robbie fidgeted. "I knew we should have brought Raffles. Mum loved Raffles." The organ swelled as "Nimrod" approached its climax. Being rather deaf, Robbie often spoke too loudly anyway. Now his voice cut over the music. "Why couldn't we bring Raffles, Sis?"

From his other side, Simon murmured in a rumbling undertone, "Calm down, Robbie, my man."

Rachel's cousin Emma, seated behind her, leaned over the back of the pew and said, "Would you like a glass of water, Rache?"

More heads were turning in their direction to observe the disruption.

"Yes please," Rachel said. She needed time to think. Everything was happening too fast.

"Don't tell me to calm down," Robbie said. Simon put a hand on Robbie's shoulder. Robbie pushed it away with an angry pout.

"Sssh, everyone," Paul said. He leaned across Rachel. "Raffles wouldn't have liked your poem about the cats, Robbie. He's happy at home with Kizzy."

"Raffles is a dog. He doesn't understand poems," Robbie grumbled, but he sat back and folded his hands in his lap.

Emma worked her way out of her seat and headed down the aisle towards the waiting room and the water cooler.

The vicar, a short, grey-haired retired cleric from the other side of the county — the only one available at a week's notice — had been observing the goings-on from his position on the dais. He stepped down and approached the family. "We need to start."

The organist was improvising on quiet stops, glancing over at the vicar, awaiting her cue for the service to begin.

Emma's heels clacking on the tiled floor signalled her return. She handed a paper beaker of water to Rachel, who had to hold it in both hands as she was shaking so much. She took a sip. What could she do? She managed a weak smile.

The vicar continued, "Rachel, if you're too upset to speak, let your elder brother take over. It's nothing to be ashamed of. I must begin now. Ready?"

Rachel nodded like an automaton.

The cleric turned, mounted the stage, and moved to the lectern.

The organ fell silent.

"Here, wipe your eyes," Paul said.

Rachel took the proffered tissue. Her handbag slipped off her lap to the floor. She felt her world tilting out of control, events lurching in a direction utterly unanticipated. She itched to look at her phone again, to see if another message had arrived and to read once more those three doom-laden words:

I was murdered.

16

RACHEL HAD SUSPECTED it since the day of Eve's death.

The message was clearly from whoever stole Mum's phone. Rachel had a good idea who that was: Alma, the petite carer, whom Detective Ryan had failed to interview again—or fingerprint—because she had disappeared.

The vicar held out his arms. "'I am the resurrection and the life,' says the Lord. 'Those who believe in me, even though they die, will live, and everyone who lives and believes in me will never die.'"

His words rolled around the chapel, amplified by the sound system.

"Welcome to this celebration of the long life of Eve Miller, much-loved wife to Earl; mother to Simon, Rachel, and Robbie; and sister to Audrey. I'm so pleased you have all made it here on this blustery autumn day. I hope you brought your biggest, strongest brollies."

He paused and smiled at the congregation, then continued.

"As we come to this place, to remember and give thanks for the life of Eve, let us also consider our own life and its meaning, as she has given meaning to our lives. Let us unite our hearts together in a moment of silent prayer and meditation."

Rachel's mind whirled in torment. *How can I stand and deliver a eulogy in these circumstances?*

The silence was broken all too soon for her as the vicar continued, "Eternal Father, before Whose face the generations rise and pass away; and in Whom we live and move and have our being, by Your holy spirit, reassure us, so that in this brief life our eyes may see the light of Your eternal truth, beyond the shades of earth, and find abundant grace in this our time of need. Hear us, O God of our salvation, for the sake of Jesus Christ, our Lord."

Rachel's "Amen" came out as a croak. Paul squeezed her hand.

"Let us stand for our first hymn, 'Lord of All Hopefulness.'"

The organ struck up the introduction. To Rachel, holding the front of the pew for support, the funeral seemed to be racing along.

> "Lord of all kindliness, Lord of all faith,
> Whose strong hands were skilled at the
>   plane and the lathe..."

She sobbed into her tissue, her hands shaking. She swayed when she took her supporting hand away from the pew.

"Sit down, love, if you feel faint."

She needed no second invitation; she sank down to the unforgiving wooden bench.

> "Be there at our sleeping, and give us, we pray,
> Your peace in our hearts, Lord, at the end of the
>   day."

Rachel wanted to shout out, "How can I have peace in my heart? My mother was murdered!" She clenched her teeth to prevent an involuntary cry of anguish escaping.

"Please be seated for Simon's poem."

Her elder brother mounted the dais, looked around, and waited for all rustling and shifting of feet to cease before reading in a clear baritone.

> "Death is nothing at all. It does not count.
> I have only slipped away into the next room.
> Nothing has happened.
> Everything remains exactly as it was.
> I am I, and you are you,

and the old life that we lived so fondly
together is untouched, unchanged.
Whatever we were to each other, that we are still.
Call me by the old familiar name.
Speak of me in the easy way which you
always used . . ."

He finished all too soon. Robbie's turn next. He rose and walked to the lectern.

Come on, Rachel! she scolded herself. *Get a grip! You'll be shown up by your kid brother with Down's at this rate!*

Robbie spoke in a loud, clear, sing-song voice.

"'The Song of the Jellicles' by T. S. Eliot. He was a very famous poet, but I only like his cat poems. This is my favourite, and Mum's too."

Rachel bent to retrieve her handbag. Robbie recited, word perfect. Any moment now and she'd be out there, facing her family, all Mum's friends, the professionals . . . She took out her three pages of printed tribute. Her hands trembled so much that she dropped the sheets, which fell with a crack at her feet. Paul scrabbled for them.

"Would you like me to read your speech?" he murmured as Robbie launched into the final verse of his poem, in which the Jellicles readied themselves for the Jellicle Moon.

"No, I should be fine . . . just nervous . . . and that text . . . can't think straight . . ."

Paul sorted the pages into order and pressed them into her hand. "There's my girl."

The vicar was saying, "Thank you, Robbie, for that wonderful reading. Those moggies were so lifelike, I felt I was going to the Jellicle Ball myself! Now Rachel will share some memories of Eve and her long life."

"Let go of your bag, love."

"Oh. Yes." She'd been clutching it to her like a lucky talisman, her knuckles white.

Simon swung his legs into the aisle to let her out. Robbie stood, waiting for her to exit the row before resuming his own seat.

She smiled at Robbie. "Well read, love."

She felt all eyes boring into her back as she took the few paces forward and up onto the dais.

She turned.

A shock as of electricity ran through her when she saw Detective Sergeant Ryan in the back row of the congregation.

The murder suspects must be here—in the crematorium!

She cleared her throat and glanced from face to face. Some wore sympathetic smiles. Others had dropped their gaze to the floor, or were intent on studying their service sheets, in evident discomfort at her distressed state and concerned for her ability to perform.

Silence descended. Rachel looked down at her three pages through blurry eyes.

"Sorry," she whispered.

A further long pause ensued. Just as the vicar moved to intervene, she spoke.

"Eve Atkins was born on the twelfth of April twenty . . . no, sorry. That's the year she died. Start again. She was born on the twelfth of April, *1930.* Can you hear me?"

No one answered. Rachel had backed off from the microphone on its stand. She stepped up and spoke right into it. "Eve was a London schoolgirl when World War II broke out, and she and her sister Audrey were evacuated from their home in Wapping to Brandon, in Suffolk." Now her voice echoed around the crematorium, too loud and sounding like a little girl's. She pressed on. "The two sisters remained after the war as their parents, our grandparents, were kadly silled . . . sorry, stadly . . . *sadly* killed . . . by a German doodlebug in 1945. When she was sixteen, Eve met a tall, dashing, young Canadian airman called Earl Miller. Dad was . . ."

She broke off, dropped her gaze to the floor, and choked back a sob. With a superhuman effort, she carried on. "Dad was an aircraft fitter. By the time he left the Royal Canadian Air Force, he had fallen in love with England as well as the girl who was now his fiancée, so he stayed, which he could do, being a Commonwealth citizen. He worked as an electrician, then set up as a general building contractor. We three children appeared late and at widely spaced intervals, a bit like our 26B bus service, with dear Robbie the most recent arrival."

No chuckles greeted her little joke. She realised her voice had dropped to a whisper, although her words were still audible thanks to the amplification.

People shifted in their seats.

She tried to enunciate clearly without sounding shrill. "Having three children so different in ages must have been a challenge. But all three of us were treated with equal love."

Now she sounded like Margaret Thatcher! She shook her head to clear it and felt a little dizzy. Still, she was getting through it—stumbling, tearful, but at least on her feet.

"Mum was the glue that held the family together. When Dad died . . ." She tailed off again. She'd lost her place on the page. She turned to the next sheet, noticing, out of the corner of her eye, the vicar glance at his wristwatch.

She decided to skip to her conclusion, to bring the proceedings back on schedule and put an end to her miserable performance and the torture she was inflicting on everyone, not least herself.

Is it pregnancy hormones kicking in, making me so dumb and weepy? Or the shock of that text, arriving when it did? And why did it arrive then?

The answer to her own question popped into her head.

Somebody in the waiting room sent the message! In the certain knowledge that it would unsettle, even derange me!

Who would do that?

Why?

She hadn't spoken for maybe ten seconds now. She cleared her throat again. "In later years, Mum and Robbie lived happily together—until Robbie launched himself into the big world and moved to Hare House. Mum's health began to decline. She stayed on stoically at the family home, keeping all three children's rooms ready with beds made up, in case we should descend on her *en masse* for the weekend.

"She bore her increasing frailty bravely, though it must have broken her heart to move out of her own home and into care. Yet she remained cheerful and active almost until the end, and very much in control of her faculties."

At this point, self-pity, guilt, and fear combined to overwhelm Rachel like a wave breaking over an unsuspecting swimmer. "Until the end . . . if only . . . just one day spoilt it . . . so soon before she died . . . it must have been awful . . . how could we have let it happen? And then to die the very next day . . ." Rachel was talking to herself as much as anything. "We . . . no, *I* . . . let her down. And she never knew, never knew about me. And now it's too late. She's dead. How could it have been so quick? She's gone, done away with, and it's all my fault . . . I'm sorry, Mum. So, so sorry!"

Rachel had turned away from the microphone and now faced the coffin on its stand in front of the curtains. Whether the congregation heard her final words, which she uttered in between sobs, she could not be sure. She noticed Paul's presence on one side of her, and the vicar's on the other. Each man took hold of an arm and guided her back down the step to the aisle. Robbie and Simon shuffled up. Paul helped her to sit.

Feeling faint again, she bent over, her head between her knees.

Through the mist that threatened to engulf her, she heard the vicar's voice over the PA. "Thank you, Rachel, for your tribute. We share your pain and sorrow. Now we will stand to sing the second hymn, 'Love Divine.'"

Paul remained seated, his arm around Rachel. "Don't worry, babe," he murmured.

She replied, "I should have told you, before today. I messed it up."

"Shh, sit quietly. Nearly over."

She looked for her handbag and spotted it out of reach, by Robbie's feet. Paul anticipated her need and passed her a paper handkerchief. "Breathe," he commanded as the organist played the introduction. "In, out. That's it."

Once again, the hymn galloped by.

Before the echoes died away, the vicar intoned, "Please remain standing. We have but a short time to live. Like a flower, we blossom and then wither; like a shadow, we flee and never stay. In the midst of life we are in death . . ."

The organist played the opening bars of Handel's "Largo."

"We have entrusted our sister Eve to God's mercy, and we now commit her body to be cremated: earth to earth, ashes to ashes, dust to dust. In sure and certain hope of the resurrection to eternal life, through our Lord Jesus Christ . . ."

The curtains drew apart, and Eve started her journey into the darkness.

Rachel fixed her gaze on the coffin. A thought popped into her head unbidden. *What happens to the handles and fittings in the incinerator?*

Perhaps they were plastic, in which case they would burn without trace, leaving no evidence.

No evidence . . .

Rachel tore away from Paul's embrace and leapt to her feet.

"Stop the service!" she screamed.

Gasps sounded out from several directions. The vicar halted in midsentence. The organist played a wrong note, and the instrument fell silent.

Rachel turned in her place and yelled, "Detective Ryan! Stop the cremation! Tell them what happened!"

The detective remained standing in his place.

Paul, also on his feet, said, "Babe, have you gone mad?" He took hold of her arm.

"Let go, Paul!" She tore away and pushed past him, her feet tangling with his, stumbling, slipping, almost falling in her desperation to escape from the pew.

Robbie cried out in anguish, "I knew we should have brought Raffles!"

Simon was saying, "Rache, for the love of God . . ."

Rachel paid no attention. Now in the aisle, she raced forward and mounted the dais. She grabbed the vicar by the arms. His surplice flapped around her as he struggled to shake her off. Rachel yelled right in his face, "Stop the service! Cancel the cremation! Mum was murdered, and we must get an autopsy!" Her voice, amplified by the vicar's clip-on microphone, echoed from the walls of the crematorium, followed by a screech of feedback.

Cries of horror and a buzz of loud conversation erupted from the congregation. Paul and Simon headed towards her like a pair of rugby forwards with the evident intention of restraining her.

The coffin continued its slow but relentless progress. Half of it was through the open curtains.

The vicar said, "Rachel, let go. You're hurting me with your nails."

With a wild cry as of a wounded animal, Rachel released the vicar. She turned her head. Simon and Paul advanced, warily now as she flailed her arms around like a mad woman. Rachel saw Ryan at the back of the chapel, on his mobile phone. Calling for reinforcements, she hoped.

Robbie's voice cut through the hubbub. "Mum? Mum! I love you, Mum! Don't leave us this way! Tell her to stop, someone! I wish Raffles was here . . ."

The congregation remained in their places, unsure of their role in the unfolding drama but unable to tear their gaze away from the anguished scenes playing out in front of them.

The vicar, freed, crossed himself. "Will the mourners please return to the waiting room?"

Paul and Simon would prevent her taking any further action. Paul had his hand on her arm.

A few of the older mourners were attempting to leave now, but others remained in their places. An undignified scramble began as those obeying the vicar's injunction found their exit impeded by those who preferred to stay and watch.

Rachel broke away and made a dash for the catafalque.

She climbed up onto it and lunged towards the coffin.

The rollers spun beneath her, and she fell face-first, almost striking her head on the end of the coffin. She pulled herself forward, reached out, and shoved the wreath off the coffin lid.

It dropped away ahead. She clawed her way up and lay full length on the casket like a surfer on a surfboard.

She'd either stop the cremation or die trying—and just then she didn't care which.

The coffin trundled on. Blackness loomed ahead. The shouts and raised voices from the chapel faded as mother and daughter continued their bizarre final journey together.

The curtains closed behind Rachel's feet, and darkness engulfed her.

17

ARE WE still moving forward?

No light penetrated the chamber, and the voices from the crematorium had faded to a distant murmur.

The flames would erupt from all sides at any second.

Rachel's heart pounded. There must be an emergency stop button for the apparatus! Perhaps the visiting vicar didn't know where it was.

The whirring of the conveyor mechanism ceased.

She held her breath. Lights flickered around her. She put her hands over her head and closed her eyes.

"Now I've seen everything!"

She opened her eyes again. Not flames, but fluorescent lighting blinked and then steadied.

Two crematorium workers, in blue boiler suits, leaned over her.

"Down you get, love. Mind your tights on them sharp edges." The taller man helped her climb off the coffin, which rested at the end of the conveyor like an outsize DIY purchase on the checkout at the superstore.

Words tumbled out of Rachel's mouth. "Don't burn her . . . you mustn't . . . the police are coming."

"What happened? How did you get in here?"

"Are we in the oven?" She glanced around, taking in a white-walled room with three metal hatches in the far wall, an illuminated control panel beside each.

"No love, they're behind them steel doors. Everyone thinks the coffin goes straight through the curtains into the flames like in the Bond movie. It doesn't, and we don't run the cremators all day. I think we'd better get you round the front and into the office. Are you hurt? Can you walk?"

"So you'll delay the cremation?"

"We wouldn't fire up until four thirty this afternoon anyway." A thought seemed to strike him. "You wasn't in the box?"

"No. My mother. There's been an error. The cremation can't proceed."

The door swung open, hit the wall, and rebounded with a crack. In burst Ryan, Paul, the vicar, and the crematorium superintendent.

Paul rushed to Rachel and took her in his arms. "Are you all right, babe? I've called the ambulance." He held Rachel's handbag over his arm, incongruous against his well-built, suited frame.

"I'm fine. I'm not ill and I'm not mad. Paulie, give my phone to the detective and he'll see why I acted that way."

The superintendent looked at his watch and swept a hand through his thinning hair. "We can't remain talking here. The mourners for the next cremation are outside in the rain because the waiting room is full of your guests. We must inform them what's happened. Will you carry on with the wake as planned, or should the minister request everyone to return home?"

Paul said, "We can't hold the wake after this. Babe, you are going to hospital for a check-up."

The vicar said, "I'll explain that Rachel is unwell. There's no need to say the cremation has been postponed."

The superintendent said, "That's a matter for the police, surely?" He turned to Ryan. "You're a detective? You attended the service?"

"Yes, but not in my professional capacity. What's this about your phone, Mrs. Phelps? What do you have to show—"

Paul interrupted. "We can't stand here discussing phones. Vicar, please do as you suggested. Tell everyone we will be in touch, that Rachel is in good hands and on her way to hospital."

"I'm not going to hospital. For pity's sake, Paul, hand over the phone to Detective Ryan!"

"Rachel, you—"

"Do it!"

With obvious reluctance, Paul retrieved Rachel's smartphone from his jacket pocket and passed it to Ryan.

"Look at the most recent text," Rachel implored. "Whoever sent it must still be in the waiting room. Detain everyone. The passcode is '1,1,2-2-1.' Like a quickstep."

Ryan entered the code and prodded. He looked up at Rachel. "Nothing received today."

Rachel snatched the handset from him.

No texts at all showed for that day. The most recent incoming message was from Simon the previous afternoon: *Landed on time. Meet you in arrivals.*

"Where has it gone? It was there! Paulie, you saw it."

"I didn't see any text, love. The screen had blanked, and I didn't wake it. Sorry. I didn't understand what your problem was in there, or why you went ape and shouted all that crazy stuff. You wrecked the service, love."

"The text was there! *'I was murdered!'* It was, it was!" Rachel jabbed her phone again and again, but to no avail: the message had vanished.

If I ever received it. Am I losing my sanity?

No—the three words inside the speech-bubble graphic had etched themselves into her brain. She couldn't have imagined it.

"Paul, did you delete it?"

"No. What are you—"

"Detective, take the phone and examine it. See if there's a deleted text." She thrust the handset at Ryan.

An approaching siren penetrated the room. The superintendent addressed the two operatives. "Direct the ambulance to the rear loading bay." The pair, wide-eyed, turned to leave, though by the expressions on their faces they would have much preferred to stay for the conclusion of the drama enlivening their working day.

"Do you have a list of the mourners?" Ryan asked Paul.

"Not with me. The funeral directors left slips of paper on the pews for everyone to fill in."

"In that case, I'll go with the reverend and make sure I get everyone's name and address before they leave. Come on, Vicar. We can do no more here. Mr. and Mrs. Phelps, I'll be in touch. In the meantime, the cremation must not proceed. On my authority." Ryan produced his warrant card and held it up for the manager, who nodded.

Paul and Rachel followed the vicar, the superintendent, and Ryan out.

Rachel twisted her head to snatch a last glance at her mother's coffin on the rollers in the centre of the room. On the floor beside it lay the squashed remains of the wreath, Robbie's sad autumn leaves scattered around.

Stars burst in front of her eyes, followed by a fierce stab of pain in her forehead.

Her knees buckled, and blackness engulfed her.

18

"CAN YOU HEAR me, Rachel?"

She opened her eyes and tried to focus.

"Look at me, Rachel. Any pain in your chest?" She recognised the female paramedic. The same one who had attended her mother.

"No. I'm fine." Her words came out in a hoarse whisper and didn't convince even herself. The ambulance rocked on its suspension as the vehicle took a tight corner, then sped up. The siren wailed.

"She collapsed during the funeral and again just now." Paul's voice.

"Any weakness of arms or legs, or blurred vision, or headache, Rachel?"

"A blinding headache. I've had it for days. I put it down to the stress of the funeral."

"Did you take anything for it?"

"No, nothing."

Paul said, "Why not, babe? I'd no idea you were poorly. Why didn't you tell me?"

"Sir, please let me do my job. Any swelling of the legs, Rachel?"

"Well . . . yes. Nothing much."

"Any other symptoms?"

"I'm a touch . . . dizzy . . . and I feel sick."

The paramedic reached for her stethoscope. She loosened Rachel's clothing and placed the cold instrument against her chest.

She checked her watch and listened, then turned on her penlight. "Look into the beam, please, Rachel. Now the other eye."

She produced a blood pressure cuff and tightened it around Rachel's upper arm. The automatic device whirred, pumped, and hissed.

The paramedic's expression gave nothing away, but she took a clear plastic headset-like tube with two short prongs and tucked it behind Rachel's ears so the prongs entered her nostrils. "A little oxygen. Breathe normally. Try to relax. I know it's not easy with the motion."

"Is she all right?" Paul's voice wavered.

"You relax too, Mr. Phelps. We'll be at the hospital soon . . . please stay in your seat, sir!"

But Paul was on his feet. He leaned over Rachel and took hold of her hand. "That was quite a show you put on back there."

Rachel managed a weak smile. "I hope nobody was filming it on their phone. It was worth it to stop the cremation. I could never forgive myself if I'd done nothing."

"What were you trying to say about a text? From Mum?"

"From her—or from her phone, at least. Three words: *I was murdered.*"

"*Murdered?*"

"Please sit down, Mr. Phelps. Fasten your seat belt. It's not safe for you to be standing while we are on the move. Rachel, this isn't helping. Don't talk any more. Try to keep calm."

Aside to Paul, the paramedic whispered something that Rachel couldn't hear. Rachel saw alarm register on his face before he reluctantly took his seat.

The ambulance careered on, swerving from lane to lane and cycling through its repertoire of siren sounds. Then the vehicle braked hard and stopped.

With a clatter of trolleys and shouted instructions, they lowered Rachel to the ground. Automatic doors hissed and slid apart at their approach.

She turned her head from side to side as much as she was able. Mercifully, Accident and Emergency appeared less busy than usual. The ambulance crew signed her over to the care of the hospital and departed at a trot for their next mission.

A male porter shuffled up. With Paul alongside, he wheeled Rachel to a cubicle, pulled the curtains around them, and left.

A nurse looked in with a clipboard, confirmed Rachel's name and address, and asked permission to access Rachel's Summary Care Record.

"Is that necessary? I'm sure I'll be going straight home."

Paul said, "Of course it's necessary! Why wouldn't you want them to have your records?"

"All right, then," Rachel whispered.

The nurse departed.

They waited.

And waited.

Outside the cubicle, footsteps approached and passed and snatches of conversation floated in.

Paul kept checking his watch. "They shouldn't have left us this long! That's fifteen minutes now. I'm off to find someone."

"Paulie, they're always busy here. I'm not an emergency. Do you think I can take this oxygen thing off? I can't be needing it."

The curtain rattled back and a short, dark-skinned woman looking little older than a student stepped into the cubicle, smiling.

"Rachel Phelps?"

"Yes. I'm much better now. I'm sorry to have caused this silly fuss. May I go home, please?"

"Babe, hush."

The dark woman said, "I'm the duty triage doctor. I just checked your electronic Summary Care Record, which I was pleased to find up to date. You've recently changed your GP, I see." She spoke with a European accent that Rachel couldn't place. Portuguese, perhaps.

Paul said, "What's the matter with her? I wish someone would explain what's going on."

"You are Rachel's partner, sir?"

"Husband. Paul Phelps."

The doctor applied yet another blood pressure cuff to Rachel. "Breathe evenly, Rachel. Relax."

Rachel wished they wouldn't keep saying that to her.

How am I supposed to relax, flat on my back in A&E, after everything that has occurred?

She needed to brief Ryan at length. Also, she was worried about Robbie. Presumably Simon had taken him home. Robbie had been in such a state, poor dear. All thanks to his big sister's histrionics.

The doctor pumped the bulb, applied her stethoscope to Rachel's inner arm, and listened as the air hissed out.

"A bit better than in the ambulance, but still very high: 175 over 115. We need to bring those numbers down. I'm going to admit you. We'll monitor you until we stabilise your BP. It's vital we do that, both for you and the baby."

Rachel, glancing guiltily at her husband, thought she had never seen such a mixture of bewildered astonishment and shock on Paul's rugged countenance.

The young doctor looked from face to face. She put her stethoscope in her jacket pocket and said to Rachel, "Do I understand your husband doesn't know you are pregnant?"

19

PAUL OPENED the rucksack. "I think I got everything. Toothbrush, hairbrush, socks, a nightie I didn't know you possessed, your Kindle, and some other reading material." He hung up the clothing in the bedside wardrobe, put the toiletries in the drawer, and pulled up a chair. "What news? Apart from the obvious."

"Paulie, I'll never forgive myself that you heard it that way. Believe me, love, I thought it was for the best. I wanted to give you the surprise of your life, not the shock to end all shocks in the A&E Department. And I didn't want to upstage Mum."

The monitors attached to Rachel bleeped in a gentle syncopated rhythm.

"You failed there, I'm afraid. You even made the early evening local TV bulletin."

"Whoops." She managed a smile.

"How are you? Have you seen another doctor?"

"Yes, and I've had an ultrasound. The good news is, the baby is fine. The sonographer detected a strong heartbeat. Only, because of the way the baby is lying, she couldn't get a clear view of the neck."

"Why is that important?"

"They look at the folds of skin. It's an indicator of Down's."

"So they don't know the risk?"

"No. I had an earlier blood test, but that was inconclusive too. I have to decide whether to have an amniocentesis."

"What is that?"

"They stick a very long thin needle into my tummy and take a sample of the fluid surrounding the baby . . ."

Paul grimaced.

"Which tells us if the baby has Down's. However, the procedure itself carries a small risk of miscarriage. A few percent."

"Phew. Tricky choice. How long do you have to make up your mind?"

"Not much time. I'm further on than Dr. Tomkins reckoned. Almost four months."

"Nothing to show for it yet."

She smiled. "No, hidden by my flab."

"That's enough about baby. How are you?"

She raised her arm. "This drip is a medication to lower my blood pressure. It's working and I feel one hundred percent better and a complete fraud taking up this bed."

Paul puffed out his cheeks in obvious relief. "How long will they keep you in?"

"A couple of days, until everything is stable. After that they want me to monitor my BP at home and go to the surgery twice a week for tests. They advised me to stop working for a while. So I really, really need a phone."

"Done." Paul handed over a paint-spattered Nokia. "Charged and loaded with twenty quid. I called Barry like you asked, and he'll take the medal class with Monica. They both send their best wishes."

"Thanks."

"Are they happy with mobiles in here?"

"Yes, as long as you keep your voice down."

"I suppose it's too much to ask you not to pursue the police right now?" He raised his eyebrows.

"Paulie, I need to know I'm not going mad. Ryan will be able to retrieve the text from my phone—or failing that, from the mobile network provider."

She thought she saw a trace of scepticism, or worry, flit across her husband's face. "You do what you have to, love. I'm just the backup man. A big old mushroom, me. Kept in the dark with bullshit shovelled over me from time to time." He smiled. "To think we'll be a family after all these years. It's a miracle. How long have you known?"

"Only since Monday." She smiled too, and they held hands. "Any calls at home?"

"Phone ringing off the hook. Mainly the guests wanting to know how you are and what happens next. I've told no one about your pregnancy except Robbie. That was a mistake."

"Did he take it badly?"

"He got hyped up. Well manic, according to Mrs. Fisher. He was holding court in the dining room, telling the others he was going to be an uncle and that his mother was murdered in her bed with a silenced revolver. Mrs. Fisher took him aside and talked him down."

"Simon?"

"Gone. Couldn't change his return flight. Or wouldn't. I didn't want him around at home any more than he wanted to stay with me."

"I meant, did you tell Simon?"

"No. I'll leave that pleasure to you, babe. And I guess I must stop calling you 'babe' now there's a real one on the way."

"Thanks to you, you big stud. Any word from Phil Fletcher?"

"Nope. Kiz says they stopped work on the cottages. He's just mouth and trousers, that arsehole. Forget him."

"Paulie, you did the right thing phoning for the ambulance. I owe you. Correction, *we* owe you."

"What else could I do, seeing my wife launch herself on the conveyor to the ovens?"

Paul stayed another twenty minutes. The moment he left, Rachel switched on her loan phone. She couldn't reach her bag because she was connected to so many tubes and wires, so she pressed her call button. An orderly arrived and helped her. With Ryan's card on the sheet in front of her, she dialled his mobile.

"The person you called is unavailable . . . please leave your message after the tone."

"Detective Ryan, Rachel Phelps here. This is my new number." She read it off the scrap of paper taped on the back.

"*Please* call me with any developments. I'm fine. I'm being well looked after and on the mend."

She called the police station, but they said Ryan was out on duty. Investigating, she trusted. She recited her new number to the duty officer who promised to pass it on.

The orderly reappeared with the drinks trolley. "No caffeine allowed," she told him. "Just a juice, please."

She sipped her drink and replayed the extraordinary events of the day in her head. Her overwhelming emotion was of relief: relief her baby was still alive, relief she had stopped the cremation. Those outcomes mattered more than the humiliation she had heaped on herself, or the distress caused to her family and friends at the crematorium.

She'd have to watch Robbie. With the mental age of a primary-school child, he could overreact to emotional situations. People forgot that because he coped so well with everyday life, provided he kept to his routines. A few of her dance pupils had even failed to realise he had Down's. Short, plump, and broad of face, with folds of extra skin around his neck and dodgy teeth, he resembled many so-called able-bodied men carrying too much weight.

She picked up the copy of *Hello* magazine Paul had brought. It was full of celebrity couples and their perfect babies. Since she'd learned of her pregnancy, she'd seen nothing but babies on all sides: in the street, on TV, in the papers.

She leafed through the pages with listless fingers. The missing text continued to gnaw at her.

Had Paul deleted it? That would be understandable in the heat of the moment, with the whole family present and the service about to begin. She could forgive him, if that's what he did. *But he should own up, not string everyone along. Wouldn't that be wasting police time, to conceal what he'd done?*

Did my husband delete the message for a more sinister reason: to forestall further enquiries?

Could she confront him?

She didn't have a good record of standing up to Paul. He would bat away her questions like shooing a fly, or evade the issue, or turn it into a joke, or give her the silent treatment, or kiss her gently and tell her not to worry.

How easy would it be for Ryan to retrieve a deleted text, in any case? Her phone was reputed to be as secure as an iPhone.

Ryan could, however, get the details of numbers called and received, with dates and times, like he'd done with Mum's phone.

If a text had been sent by a mourner—and Leelo was again the prime suspect—then Ryan would soon find out.

The other possible texter was Alma. The little carer had disappeared. Rachel had learned that much before the funeral, though Ryan had been hazy about the circumstances, and hadn't told her if the petite girl was even still in the country—if he knew.

Alma was also the subject of the mystery emails from the iPad purporting to have come from her mother. Ryan had returned the iPad to Rachel, having learned nothing useful from it, and offering no thoughts on the weird messages.

Rachel's thoughts kept circling back to the three-word text that had so discomposed her in the chapel.

I was murdered.

Written as if by Mum. Why would Alma do that, instead of sending a more helpful clue, such as: *Eve was murdered. Alma.*

Why would anyone murder my mother? It had to be connected with the scam and the theft of Eve's life savings.

With a jolt, she realised that one beneficiary of Eve's death was Paul. Now there would be no more care home fees, no calls on the Phelps's precarious finances.

Could Paul be a party in Mum's death? She felt guilty even thinking about it.

Rachel's heart told her to get out of hospital and back on the pursuit of answers about her mum—and justice.

Her head told her to put the baby first. A precious new life that she had jeopardised by her actions that day. She was very old to have a first baby, despite Dr. Tomkins's assurances.

Miscarriage remained a real threat. The hospital sonographer who had played her baby's heartbeat on the loudspeaker had confirmed that. The other big risk was preeclampsia later in her term—the commonest cause of death in unborn babies.

And their mothers.

A scary thought.

She must keep her blood pressure down.

"Nurse . . . nurse . . ." A feeble cry floated across from the ancient, shrunken woman in the far corner of the ward. Her call button had fallen out of her reach, or she was too weak to press it.

A few minutes later, she called out again, her voice only just audible above the hums and bleeps of the equipment.

There was no response, no hurrying footsteps of a nurse, so Rachel pressed her own button.

The elderly are so vulnerable in hospitals, as in care homes. They have a right to protection.

Rachel would not rest until she uncovered the truth about her mother's death.

20

RACHEL SLEPT FITFULLY, disturbed by the comings and goings of the nurses attending the patients' incessant calls. When she did drop off, she dreamed about herself as a child. She'd been riding her bike, the pink one, up and down the cul-de-sac on a hot summer's evening, one of those evenings that only occurs in childhood and in the summer holidays. She was aged around seven.

Arriving home, she flung her bike down on the front lawn and ran inside, hoping for a cold juice.

Dad was home. His toolkit stood in the hall.

She could sense her parents had something to tell her. They exchanged furtive glances. She couldn't work out from their faces if it was good or bad.

"Rachel, darling. Daddy and I have some news. You're going to have a baby brother or sister. It's a wonderful surprise."

"You said I was the last one!" She felt betrayed. She and her bossy big brother Simon, Mummy and Daddy, plus Flannel the cocker spaniel—the family was complete already.

"Babies come if they want to. You'll love it. You can help me dress him or her, choose clothes and toys, play with the baby."

Despite their brave faces, it was obvious to Rachel even then that the new arrival was unplanned.

Her dream fast-forwarded to six months later.

The first snows of winter carpeted the garden and lane. Her pink bike was safely locked in the shed. Brother Simon was on a school skiing trip in Davos.

"Mummy's coming home this evening, and Auntie Audrey will be leaving," her father announced. "Mummy's bringing Robbie. Your brand-new baby brother. He's very, very special. We'll have to be careful with him, and I want you to be a good girl and help Mummy because Robbie isn't quite the same as the rest of us."

What does Daddy mean?

She hadn't been allowed to see Robbie in the hospital or visit her mother.

Then she was in her nightie, ready for bed. The front door opened, and an icy blast of wind swirled into the cottage.

"Hello Mummy!"

"Hello darling."

The carry cot seemed to fill the entire hall. Rachel bent over the sleeping figure.

"He's quite sweet, but he's tiny and he's got funny ears."

Her mother burst into tears.

21

AFTER TWO NIGHTS on Ramsey Ward, Rachel yearned to go home. They couldn't arrange her discharge at a weekend, so she was obliged to endure Saturday and Sunday in hospital.

The consultant had said it was better to be safe than sorry anyway, although her blood pressure had stabilised within twenty-four hours of admission.

Ryan returned none of her calls.

On the Monday morning, sitting up by her bed, dressed and hair brushed, she called Paul from her loan phone. "I'll be ready to pick up at ten. Just waiting for some paperwork."

Silence greeted her announcement. Then: "Babe, we've got an emergency at the cottages. I'm sending Terry the Taxi for you. I'll see you at home as soon as possible. The heating's on and I've briefed Kizzy to make your lunch."

"I'm not in a wheelchair. I don't need Terry the Taxi. What's the emergency?"

"I'll fill you in later. Don't worry yourself. I'm on top of it. You just get home and settle in."

"Anyone hurt?"

"No, no, nothing like that. Everyone's fine. See you in a bit. Love you."

Of course Paul must deal with a building emergency. Probably a collapse. The Victorian cottages had turned out to be riddled with dry rot, the wooden lintels above the bay windows hollowed out and encircled by sinister tendrils of white fungus. Still, part of her felt neglected.

Could he not leave the site for an hour?

Trevor and Billy, the two lads, could mind the shop. Although they always called them lads, only one—Trevor—

really qualified. He was eighteen, while Billy was sixty-four and an experienced tiler and bricklayer.

Terry the Taxi showed up on time, at ten. Despite her protestations, they put her in a wheelchair. Terry pushed her to the lifts and they emerged into the gloom of a grey autumn day.

At least the rain has stopped.

They crossed the road and entered the massive car park, full even at this hour. Terry folded out the tail lift on his taxi.

"I'll sit up front with you," she said. "I'm not arriving home like an invalid."

He agreed cheerily. "Useful to have the chair for now, just in case."

They set off. "So sorry about Eve," Terry said. "She was a great lady."

"She always spoke warmly of you. You took her on her final outing—to the bank. How did she seem that day?"

Terry stole a sideways glance at her. His face, lined but somehow boyish, gave no clue as to his age. Anything between forty and sixty. "Nervous. She kept looking at her mobile phone, as if expecting a call or message."

"And on the return journey?"

"Quiet, for her. I put it down to tiredness. It was quite an expedition, what with getting into the bank and manhandling her chair in and out."

"Did she have her phone on the way home?"

The minibus drew up at the traffic lights leading on to the bypass. Terry didn't answer at once, considering his reply. "If so, she didn't call on it or keep checking it like on the way there. Sorry, I can't remember for sure. Are you still searching for the phone? It was only a cheapie."

She hesitated. "Someone has it and is using it."

"Not me. I told that detective. I was surprised they got involved in a stolen mobile worth a fiver. It's simple: call the company and get it cancelled."

Terry knew nothing. They were home, anyway. The minibus crunched up the drive and past the rose bed with the tyre tracks leading into it. Kizzy's old Renault stood outside the office.

Groggy after so long on her back wired up to monitors, Rachel allowed Terry to help her indoors.

"Your rucksack is on the hall chair. Paul's paid already. You take care now."

If he knew about Rachel's pregnancy, he didn't let on.

A vase of autumnal flowers stood on the kitchen table: red, orange, and gold gerberas. Plus a note, propped up against the glass, in Paul's round, schoolboy-like hand.

> *Babe and tiny babe, welcome home. I've had to take a business trip for a couple of nights. Don't go up to the cottages. I don't want you fretting, and it's all under control. Kizzy is briefed to look after you till I get back. Sorry for the cloke-and-dagger stuff. All will be revealed. I love you so much, but with money tite I need to sort this out. I hope you understand and forgive me.*
> *Love, Paul xxxxxx.*

She stared at the words in disbelief, then took the paint-spattered site phone from her handbag and dialled his mobile number.

"Hi, this is Paul Phelps of Phelps & Son Builders. I'm not available right now. You can leave a message after the tone or call our office number—"

Not the homecoming she expected or deserved. With her coat still on, she crossed the tarmac and entered the office, holding the note between thumb and forefinger.

Kizzy looked up from her monitor. "Hi, Rache." The chubby West Indian painted a smile on her face. "You got the message. Bit of a surprise for me too. How are you feeling?"

Raffles, lying in the basket that Paul kept in the office for him, uncurled himself, stretched, and padded over to Rachel, tail wagging.

"Hello boy." She scratched his ear. "Kiz, I'm better for now. Or at least I was until I read this note. What's happened at the cottages?"

"Oh, some structural issue. Paul said not to worry."

"Don't mess me around, Kiz. What is the problem? Why has my husband disappeared on a 'business trip' without notice? Tell me everything."

"Rache, I don't know nuffing. That's God's honest truth."

"Are Billy and Trevor up at the site?"

"Nah, they went over to the Ayres. Their extension roof has sprung a leak."

"Take me to the cottages. Please, Kizzy."

"Paul said you must rest . . . not get stressed out."

Rachel spread her hands open in exasperation. "How do you think I feel, arriving home after four nights in hospital to find my husband gone and a note on the table? What am I expected to do—sit and watch daytime TV?"

"It's a bummer, Rache. Sorry, but I'm only an employee. This shit has got me right wound up too. I'm stuck in the middle here."

"Take me to the site now, Kiz, or I'll get in my own car and drive myself."

"Sorry, Rache, no can do. I need to be here for the phones. We have other jobs on, you know. Every day Mr. or Mrs. Jackson comes on, bending me ear, begging us to make a start on their conservatory."

"Right. If you won't do me that small favour, I'm going."

Rachel turned and strode out of the office. She hurried across to the bungalow. Inside, she looked again at Paul's note. No indication of where he had gone, or why. On top of that, he'd switched off his phone. It was too bad.

She opened the hall cupboard.

The keys to her Fiat were missing from the rack.

They weren't in her handbag, because the last time she'd left home was in the Brown Brothers limousine, and she remembered hanging up her car keys. Even so, she fetched her bag from the kitchen table and rooted around in the bottom.

Not there.

She returned to the hall cupboard and looked on the floor, in case they had fallen off the hook into a shoe. Then she searched the pockets of the raincoat she'd worn to the funeral.

No keys anywhere.

She marched back to the office, phone in hand, trying to keep calm for her sake and the baby's. "Kiz, where are the keys to my car?"

"Don't know. Sorry, Rachel." The PA didn't look up from her screen.

"He's hidden them, hasn't he? To stop me driving."

"Don't know. Sorry, Rachel," Kizzy repeated.

"Right. I do not understand what's going on in this business, but I am about to find out. If you won't drive me, I'll call Terry the Taxi back."

Kizzy sighed and rose from her chair. "I'll take you. I'd like to see the situation meself, to be honest. I'm with you, Rache, but you and Paul can't expect me to be a go-between and police a neutral zone between you. It ain't fair. I know you got problems, you bent me ear about your Mum and the scam. Then you halting the funeral saying she was murdered—"

"Who told you that? Paul?"

"Nah, it was on the local radio news. Everyone who's come in here or phoned seems to know too. Let's go. We can talk in the car." She reached over and switched on the elderly answering machine.

Raffles, hoping for an outing, positioned himself by the door, tail wagging. "Sorry, boy, no room in Kiz's car for you. Stay here and mind the shop."

The collie looked up at Rachel with mournful eyes, then turned and padded back to his bed. With a harrumphing sigh he flopped down and curled up, nose resting on the edge of the basket.

Rachel locked up the bungalow. Kizzy wouldn't lock the office: Raffles was an excellent guard dog. Rachel preferred not to shut him in anyway, in case of fire.

The engine of the PA's rust-streaked Renault started on the third attempt and they were off.

"Y'know, Rache, if you want to find out what happened to your mum . . . and I'm not being funny now or winding you up, this is dead serious. Sorry, didn't mean to say that—*totally serious,*—you could try asking her."

Rachel, staring straight ahead through the streaky windscreen, said, "You're talking about your church, aren't you?"

"Yeah. You know me and me mum go regular. It's a proper church, Rache. I told you before—every week ordinary people like me and you get in touch with the spirits of their loved ones. Only yesterday a woman heard from her husband who was killed in Afghanistan. He said he was sorry he'd not mown the lawn the day before he left. He and his missus had a little tiff about it, and the soldier said he didn't want to do it on his last day of leave, and his brother would come round. The poor wife said something like 'your brother knows how to look after his family,' which she'd regretted. Just she was upset he was going back to Helmand for a third tour and she'd had some premonition. Anyways, they got in touch through the medium, and she apologised to her husband and said she loved him and he said the same back, and she cried and cried but it was a real release for her. No way the medium knew about her or the lawn or anyfing before the service. So if your mum did meet a sticky end, she could want to get a message to you." The girl paused in her breathless delivery.

Rachel had heard such stories from Kizzy before. Excitable accounts of contacts from the other side. Rachel wasn't overly religious, but she did believe in a higher power. Nor did she deny the possibility of life after death. She'd listened to the words of the vicar at the funeral, said "Amen," and hoped that Eve's spirit was at peace.

Fat chance, with her body back in the freezer at Brown Brothers.

The Renault struggled up the hill leading to the cottages. Kizzy changed down. Over the noise of the engine labouring in first gear, Rachel said, "Let me think about it. I don't want to upset myself."

"Me and me mum will be there on either side of you. You'll be very welcome. I won't go on about it or mention it again. Promise."

"Thanks." Kizzy's words were kindly meant.

At least she's here, beside me—unlike my husband.

They heard the roaring of a powerful diesel engine before they crested the hill.

Phelps & Son had bought the row of four terraced Victorian farm labourers' cottages for what had appeared to be a bargain price. Once part of the Satchell Estate, the bleak, redbrick homes stood in a lonely, windswept crescent at the top of the hill just off the B-road.

Except they didn't stand there now.

A huge, yellow JCB digger with "Fletcher Groundworks" on its grabber arm was busy demolishing the only cottage still standing.

As they approached, the driver raised his bucket high and swung it into the gable end. The flimsy, single-brick wall swayed like a sheet on a washing line, folded over, and crashed to the ground in a cloud of brick dust. Gunning its engine, the JCB reversed. The caterpillar tracks of the monstrous machine turned as it lurched clear of the falling masonry.

The digger lowered its bucket and advanced on the remaining stub of wall, which stood like a row of broken teeth. With one shove, the final section of building crumpled to the ground.

All that remained of Paul and Rachel's investment was a pile of brick, plaster, tile, and wood, with two rafters pointing upwards at different angles in an ironic V-sign formation.

The digger lowered its arm, rotated so the cab was in line with the tracks, and the mighty engine throttled back to a throaty idle.

"Bleeding 'ell. That's a structural issue an' no mistake," Kizzy said, her voice full of awe. "Guess we should have paid the man."

"Did you have any idea . . . ?" Rachel's pulse pounded in her ears.

"Well, he did say he'd do it that last time before, when you arrived."

"It's criminal damage. I'll call the police." Rachel reached once more for her Nokia phone. Kizzy put her hand on her employer's arm. "Steady on, Rache. Let's just think this through. Maybe Paul ordered the demolition. Them cottages was a load of rubbish. Perhaps he decided to cut his losses and start again."

"Without telling you or me? Unlikely. And he said 'emergency' on the phone. We don't have the money for a new build. If we did, we wouldn't have chosen this site. The idea was to smarten them up, fix the roofs, whack in flatpack kitchens and budget bathrooms, and sell them on as starter homes. Let's ask the operator."

Before Kizzy could protest, Rachel was out of the car and striding across the muddy grass towards the scene of devastation. She approached the digger and waved both arms at the driver to attract his attention.

He cut the engine and climbed down from the cab. "Watch your step, lady. They put basements in these places. You from Planning?" He was a heavyset man of late middle age with a beer belly, but friendly enough.

"No. I'm Rachel Phelps, a director of Phelps & Son. We own this site. Can you tell me what you are doing, please?"

The driver frowned in puzzlement. "Demolishing the terrace, as instructed by my boss. You'll need fencing and signage today. Don't want kids playing in the ruins. Lots of sharp objects and holes to fall into."

"So my husband ordered this?"

"Guess so. Not my business, love. I do what the foreman tells me. Why don't you ask your husband? I'm finished here, waiting for the transport." He dug a packet of cigarettes from the pocket of his low-slung jeans and lit one with a coloured plastic lighter. He leaned back against his vehicle.

Rachel picked her way through the mud to Kizzy's car. Inside, she took charge. Someone had to.

"Kiz, organise temporary anticlimb fencing and get the lads here pronto to erect it. And site safety signs. Also call the electricians to check the power situation and make sure it's safe. Same with the water company. There's no gas supply, thank heavens.

"If Paul had ordered the demolition, he would have discussed all this and arranged it with you. We have to assume this was deliberate vandalism by Fletcher out of petty spite over the unpaid bill. When we get back to the office, after you've done all that, I want you to phone round and track down Paul. Start with Fletcher Groundworks. See if he went there. Then everywhere else he might have gone."

"Sure thing, Rache."

"What else do I need to know about?"

"Nuffing, Rache." Kizzy turned the ignition key and coaxed the engine to life.

Rachel hoped that Paul wouldn't do anything reckless. Laid back by nature, he still had a breaking point—like most people. She'd seen him lose it big time only twice, but on both occasions he'd scared her.

She didn't want him taking any retribution.

He'd placed her in a dreadful quandary. Without knowing the situation for certain, she couldn't involve the police. They would take little interest in a commercial dispute anyway. It wasn't as if the tumbledown cottages were prime real estate.

She leaned back against the headrest as the car bumped onto the tarmac road and coasted down the hill.

On the journey home, neither woman spoke again. Rachel consoled herself with the thought that the cost of the demolition would have likely equalled the outstanding underpinning work.

Even more worrying was Paul's disappearance. She tried his mobile number again and the same voicemail announcement sounded in her ear.

Where has he gone—and why?

To murder Mervyn and dispose of his body?

22

RACHEL UNLOCKED her front door.

With a sigh, she boiled the kettle and made herself a decaf coffee. She grimaced at the bitter taste, emptied it down the sink, and rinsed her mouth with a glass of tap water.

The house phone rang.

"Detective Sergeant Ryan here, Mrs. Phelps. I trust you're feeling better? Is this convenient?"

"Yes, though I'm not sure if I feel better after this morning." Outside the kitchen window, a light drizzle fell.

"Oh dear. Anything relevant to my enquiries?"

"Yes. Paul has disappeared."

"Disappeared? As in gone—vanished?"

"Not exactly. He left a note saying he was going on a business trip for a couple of days."

"That may be inconvenient, but it's not a police matter." Ryan's voice sounded warm and reassuring.

"What news of the investigation? Why didn't you return my calls?" Rachel paced around the kitchen table.

"I went through your phone and examined all the text messages. I couldn't find one on the day of the funeral. It could be there, deleted but potentially retrievable. I don't have the tools here to delve into the database or poke around at chip level. I'm sorry. It's a dead end."

"Can't you send the phone to your specialist police lab where they do have the tools?"

"Yes, if I had the authority. I asked. I'm only a humble sergeant."

"You can get the records from the provider again. That will at least show that a text arrived when I said it did, and from that number."

"Yes, but you said the text came from your mother's phone. The metadata would simply confirm that fact."

"I told you what the message said. Three words. *I was murdered.* We need to know who had the phone and sent it. You must track the location of Mum's mobile, find out if the caller was in the crematorium or somewhere else—if so, where?"

A pause followed, and Rachel could hear Ryan tapping his pen on his desk. When he spoke again, his tone was apologetic. "I could do that. But let me repeat, the phone companies only keep the metadata: who texted who, and the date and time. It wouldn't confirm the words in the message. Without that, I don't have authority to pursue your allegation."

"*Allegation?*" Rachel ran the fingers of her free hand through her hair. Her normally thick and glossy locks felt lank and greasy.

The silence lasted so long that Rachel wondered if the line had dropped.

"Ideally, I would order a complete tower dump from the mast nearest the crematorium, which would flag up all calls and texts made and received and could reveal the location of the caller. But that is time-consuming and therefore expensive. I cannot obtain authority without clear evidence that a crime has been committed. I'm afraid the consensus is that your recollection might be, shall I say, compromised. You *were* in a dreadful state from the moment you entered the chapel."

"Yes, because I had just read the text."

"You were also ill and distraught. I learned from your husband the reason was you were experiencing early complications with your unplanned pregnancy."

"Paul told you all that? He said *unplanned*? *Unexpected* is what he would have said."

"Not according to my notes. He said you were worried about the possibility of Down's syndrome, having a brother with it. And you hadn't told a soul you were expecting, even him, and you were uncertain whether you would continue the pregnancy or not and you had only a few weeks to decide."

"He said all that? Seriously?"

"Yep."

Rachel tried to steady her breathing and her racing pulse. "That's all so personal and not relevant to your enquiries. Of course I'm going to keep the baby."

"I'm afraid it is relevant, and I apologise if I've upset you. I imagined Paul would have discussed all this with you in the hospital."

"No, he didn't even mention you had contacted him."

"It was all urgent, you see," Ryan said. "We had to decide whether to involve the coroner again. Look, this has turned awkward. It would be better if we continued the conversation face-to-face. I can come straight over."

"A bit late for that," Rachel commented, half to herself, through gritted teeth. "Go on with your news."

"I discussed the position with my boss. He decided I'd spent too much time on your investigation. I then met again with Paul. He said there had already been enough upset for the family with the debacle at the cremation. He requested no further action be taken on your murder allegations, but that we continue to pursue the fraud enquiry. Although I have to say, that is also in the pending tray. We will of course keep our files open—"

Rachel almost shrieked down the phone, "My husband authorised you to abandon the investigation into my mother's suspicious death? After I got that text?"

"He said he'd discussed it all with you. I'm in a difficult position here, because he clearly didn't."

"No, he didn't. I'm the next of kin. You had no right to make that decision."

"Paul said you were very poorly and he was concerned for your life and the baby's. He forbade me to come near you or telephone you in the hospital. I suggest you take it up with him, Mrs. Phelps."

"When he returns from his business trip."

Another pause. Then: "Yes."

"In the meantime, what's happening with Mum's body?"

"You need to contact the undertakers about that."

"I'm not happy with any of this." Rachel struggled to keep her voice calm and level. "Seems to me you don't believe my version of what happened that day."

"It's not that I don't believe you. I have to account to others for my time, Mrs. Phelps. And your husband was adamant that the family, including you, had suffered enough. Are you able to get around? Will you call at the station and collect your phone?"

"I could drive if only my husband hadn't confiscated my car keys."

"In that case, I'll come by later today and drop it in. Mrs. Phelps, the bottom line is this: I can't persuade anyone that a crime has been committed, either with the bank business or your mother's unfortunate decease. It's understandable that you are upset by both. Sometimes it is better to move on—"

"Detective, the fraud and my mother's sudden death must be connected. I will not 'move on,' as you and my family and everyone else seem to want. I should never have agreed to go ahead with the funeral. I will not rest until I establish the facts. With or without your help."

Ryan said, "I'll raise your concerns again with my detective chief inspector. That's all I can do."

"One more thing, Detective. Why did you attend the funeral if you didn't have suspicions?"

"To show my respects."

"So you had time in your busy schedule to sit in at a funeral, and would have partaken of our hospitality at the pub, but you can't do any useful investigations?"

Ryan lowered his voice. "I'd been working two weeks without a break, Rachel. It was my day off. I felt for your loss and the distress you have endured. I wanted to show I cared."

Rachel, who had been pacing around and around the kitchen table and had completed about a dozen circuits during the call, froze in her step at this, the first use of her Christian name by the young detective.

"I'm sorry. I have taken my frustration out on you. It was good of you to attend. I look forward to seeing you later, so I can thank you for your efforts. I understand the situation. Goodbye for now, Detective Ryan."

She pressed the red Cancel button on the handset with a shaking forefinger. Her nails, she noticed, were in a dreadful state, chipped and dull.

She hurried out to the office in the drizzle.

Raffles, in his basket, opened one eye, but realised he wouldn't be going walkies and closed it again.

Kizzy, on the phone, smiled up at Rachel. When the PA had finished she said, "All sorted at the site, Rache. The lads are there waiting for Newsome's to arrive with the fencing. The place will be safe, secure, and legal by this afternoon. While I was on to Carrie at Newsome's I asked if she'd seen Paul today, she said no. Just then I was on to Fletcher Groundworks. I know the girl there too, Sharon, and she wouldn't bullshit me. She said no way was Paul around there today. I tried the Dog and Duck—no joy there either. I guess he's on the road and turned off his phone. We have to wait for him to contact us. Bummer for you."

"Kiz, do you know anyone who can do techie stuff with a mobile phone? Like unlock them, retrieve data that's been deleted, scan the databases down at chip level?"

The girl crossed her chubby arms over her ample bosom. "D'you mean hacking? Illegal stuff?"

"No. It's my phone. It's to do with the scam on Mum."

"I thought the cops had your phone for that? Paul said they took it away, which was why he came to me for the old site Nokia and had me top it up an' all."

"The police are winding down their investigation. I'm going freelance."

"You know Mahesh, who runs the stall at the market on Thursdays?"

"I've seen the guy. He replaced a broken touchscreen for Paul last year. I never dealt with him myself."

"Me and Mahesh are mates. We go way back. He can do all that shit—and hacking too, just never talk about it. D'you want to brief me and I'll take your phone to him?"

"Yes. And I would like to accept your offer to come along to the Spiritualist Church."

"Good decision, Rache. It's a guest medium this Sunday. Ralph Elliott. He's supposed to be hot. We start at ten. You know where we are?"

"Yes, Oak Street. Do I have to bring anything?"

"Just an open mind and a heart full of love. If Eve is waiting on the other side and has a message for you, the medium will channel it. If not, he won't shit you pretending. He'll say sorry and move on to the next person. Be prepared for anything."

"I will. Kiz, did Paul tell you our other news?"

The secretary hesitated. "He did, but asked me to keep it under me hat, so I didn't know whether to congratulate you or not. I guess I can now! Let me give you a hug."

Kizzy rose from her seat and approached Rachel, her face split into a huge smile. "I am so thrilled. You clever thing! And Paul too. He is so chuffed and so concerned. He wouldn't have took off this morning unless it was real important."

"Life or death, you mean." They hugged, Kizzy's dimpled arms enveloping Rachel.

Raffles let out two short, sharp barks. He'd heard something before they had.

The PA broke free. "Are you expecting a delivery? I'm not."

A small, white, unmarked van came into view and parked next to the Renault. A young man with short, tidy hair, dressed in a suit and tie, stepped out. Seeing the office lit up and its two occupants standing looking at him, he scurried towards them in the drizzle.

Kizzy opened the glass-panelled door. "Yeah, man? What you got?"

"Delivery for Mrs. Rachel Phelps."

"That's me. You can leave it here." Perhaps it was a bunch of flowers or some chocolates, a guilty peace offering from Paul. If so, it wouldn't impress Rachel much.

The lad returned to his van. He came back bearing a package the size of a shoebox, with cardboard carry handles.

"Leave it in the corner," Rachel instructed him. Maybe it was a cake with "Sorry, Babe" piped on in pink icing.

The driver produced a carbonless delivery note, which Rachel signed. He bowed his head and turned to go.

The box was surprisingly heavy. Not flowers, chocs, or a cake. Rachel put it down with a thump on the round conference table.

She bent over to read the label pasted on top.

"Oh God, no . . ."

She let out a low moan and was just aware of Kizzy rushing to prevent her falling as a greasy darkness encroached on her vision and all the lights dimmed and went out.

23

SHE CAME ROUND from the faint. Kizzy had kicked a chair into position and lowered Rachel into it. "Rache? Rache? Are you all right, love? Shall I call the ambulance?"

"It's Mum," Rachel moaned. "Mum's ashes. They've cremated her and I never knew. What did my husband think he was doing?"

Kizzy crossed to the kitchenette for a glass of water. She sat opposite Rachel, the box of ashes between them on the table, and scanned her employer's face. "Sure you don't need a doctor?"

Rachel sipped, ran her hand through her hair, and breathed in and out twice. "No, I only blacked out for a few seconds. The shock."

"So you wasn't expecting this?"

"Not at all. Pass me the phone please, Kiz."

Rachel dialled Brown Brothers Funeral Directors. She knew their number by heart, she'd called them so many times over the past ten days.

"Rachel Phelps here, who am I speaking to?"

"Ah, yes, Mrs. Phelps. Bernard Brown here. Is everything in order with the ashes? You may wish to choose a suitable box or urn for them, unless you plan to scatter them soon. I do trust you are feeling better now the formalities are concluded."

"Not at all. I had no idea the cremation went ahead. When did it happen? I assume my husband Paul arranged everything?"

"You didn't know? Mr. Phelps said the family wished the cremation to proceed forthwith. We completed the procedure the day after the service, finishing just in time. The police had visited first thing to give the go-ahead. I telephoned your husband and he agreed. You see, by law we are allowed only twenty-four hours after the committal. There was no option, frankly. I'm sorry if you didn't know, but you need to discuss that with Mr. Phelps."

"I was in hospital on Friday and over the weekend. I arrived home this morning. The first I knew was when your driver appeared with Mum's ashes in a cardboard box."

"Dear me. Tut tut. How distressing for you. I take it your husband is out at work?"

"Something like that. I wish people would consult me about these matters. It was *my* mother, after all."

"Only the police could have halted the cremation. It has to be performed in a timely manner, for obvious health and safety reasons and to comply with legislation."

"I thought they'd call the coroner back in."

"Once the authority for cremation is issued, it can't be revoked except by court order. There is no precedent for postponing a cremation after the service and committal. If the police required the body for forensic examination, they would have had to apply to a judge in chambers for an emergency order. I read all this up on the Thursday afternoon after your, er . . . intervention."

"Thank you, Mr. Brown. You only did your duty."

Rachel had spent the day thanking people for doing things she didn't want them to do and apologising for her own existence.

Everyone assumed a husband and wife would work together and support each other at a time of bereavement.

Why hadn't Paul phoned her on the Nokia to keep her informed, or told her when he visited? Maybe he'd believed her too ill to cope, or feared she would resist the police decision to shelve the case.

Which she would have.

And still she wouldn't give up, even though her mother's body had been reduced to a cardboard box of ashes weighing the same as two large bags of sugar.

Rachel left Kizzy dealing with Mr. Jackson, who was becoming more frustrated by the day over the lack of progress on his conservatory. She retreated to the bungalow, took notepad and biro, and sat at the kitchen table.

It was time to make sense of the extraordinary events of the past fortnight, which to her mind were all interlinked. Only, she couldn't see the connections. She needed to find the missing piece of jigsaw that would reveal the whole picture.

She wrote down *Mum—cause of death?* Two doctors had confirmed this to be bronchopneumonia. Why did she doubt it? She had Googled the disease and discovered that it could indeed progress with frightening rapidity in an old and frail person, the malevolent infection multiplying exponentially, filling the lungs with mucus. Victims drowned in their own bodily fluids. Also, Dr. Thorpe had mentioned that there were several types of pneumonia, which made diagnosis and treatment difficult. This too Rachel had confirmed.

Eve's medical notes had presumably rung no alarm bells with the coroner. Rachel was forced to admit that they were unlikely to reveal anything untoward.

Given all that, the main evidence suggesting foul play was the three-word message.

The incredible vanishing text.

She'd seen it for a fleeting moment, in the anteroom of the crematorium chapel. She wrote it on her notepad now, to make it feel real.

I was murdered.

She would give her smartphone to Kizzy to take to Mahesh the phone unlocker and hacker, who would dive in at chip level or whatever.

When Mahesh undeleted the text, she would return hotfoot to Ryan, force him to reopen his enquiry, and request the metadata and tower dump from the phone company.

Paul must have deleted it, as she'd suspected on the day. When her husband returned from his "business trip," she would confront him.

At the back of Rachel's mind, a tiny voice told her that Paul had indeed deleted the text, and not through any motive to protect Rachel either.

Had Paul sent the message as well?

Incredible to contemplate, her loving partner as a conspirator in ... what?

Why would anyone send such a message ... unless it was true?

Who else could have snatched Eve's mobile? She scribbled "Suspects" on her pad and listed them in order of probability: Alma, Leelo, Paul, Terry the Taxi, Howard Plumb.

She crossed the bank manager off the list.

No way.

Terry? No, not him either.

Besides Paul, that left the two care home staff.

Leelo must be a suspect, because she'd had ample opportunity to steal the phone, and she was present in the crematorium and able to time the sending of the text perfectly. She had been sitting next to Rachel at the exact instant the text arrived.

Did Leelo have a phone out at the crucial moment?

Possibly. The crematorium manager had just entered and reminded everyone to turn off their mobiles. Leelo was ideally placed to compose and send the text, while pretending to power down the phone. Rachel racked her brain to try and remember if Leelo had done that.

Rachel had her own phone out at the time to turn it off, and wasn't looking around at others doing the same.

Try as she might, she couldn't remember. People had their phones in their hands half the time.

Why would Leelo send the text?

To drive me mad?

It made no sense.

Did Leelo know about the bequest to her in Mum's will? If so, she would have no motive for halting the funeral and holding up probate.

If only Rachel could persuade the police to request the call records and the tower dump! That would confirm if someone in the crematorium had sent Rachel a text message at the precise time of 10:59 a.m.

The main suspect remained Alma, the mysterious vanishing care assistant. She too had every opportunity to steal the phone. More than Leelo, in truth, because Alma attended Eve throughout the day—to get her up, help her to the loo, serve her meals.

Where had Alma gone? She'd told Rachel she too would attend the funeral.

Rachel wrote, "Action Points:"

1) Retrieve deleted text
2) Quiz Leelo, find Alma
3) Follow the money

It had to be the money at the root of the mystery.

Unable to action her first point until Ryan arrived, she moved on to the second item.

The receptionist at the Willows put her straight through to Guy Lane.

"I need to contact Alma and Leelo. May I have their details, please?"

"Mrs. Phelps, I do hope you are feeling better? We were all—"

"Yes, yes, I'm fine. May I have the girls' details, please?"

"I'm afraid that information is confidential, Mrs. Phelps."

"It will be to their advantage if I can contact them."

"Ah, I understand. Perhaps your solicitor would write to them care of the Willows and I will forward the letters."

Rachel ground her teeth in frustration. "All I need is their phone numbers, or emails. Surely you can provide that? Failing which, may I visit Leelo again? To give her the good news in person?"

"I assume Eve has generously left a gift to those ladies. Mrs. Phelps, I don't want to tell you your business, but I suspect your solicitor would advise you to delay informing the legatees until probate is granted, given the unfortunate circumstances with the bank. Unless that has been cleared up?"

"No, that's ongoing. Why so secretive?"

"I must safeguard our employees' and volunteers' personal data. The police interviewed both Leelo and Alma. Did you check with your detective if he took their contact details?"

This wasn't going well, and Rachel sensed that Lane was giving her the run-around.

"At the very least, may I come and visit Leelo again? You can't have a problem with that, surely?"

"Neither Leelo nor Alma work here anymore."

Rachel raised her eyebrows in surprise. "They *both* resigned? At the same time?"

"Leelo offered us her services for six months. That period was up, and she left to pursue other interests."

"What happened to Alma? I thought she was one of your best and most loyal carers?"

Rachel heard him sigh. "Yes, but these girls come and go. They have no roots in the United Kingdom. Sometimes they stay a month, sometimes a year, sometimes they meet a man and settle down. Then they get pregnant. It's all very challenging."

"Did Alma have a boyfriend?"

"Mrs. Phelps, I have told you too much already. I am sorry to appear unhelpful; I have no wish to add to your woes. I will forward messages to Alma and Leelo. Email me, if that's easier for you. More than that I regret I cannot do. My apologies. Oh, I have another call waiting. Please excuse me."

"Of course, thank you for your time, Mr. Lane. I will do as you suggest." Rachel waited for an answer, but the line was already dead.

In fact, she had thought of a far better idea while on the phone.

There were emails from Leelo to Eve on the iPad, test messages sent to Mum. All Rachel needed to do was reply to one of these!

As for Alma ... if the carer had Eve's phone, Rachel could call it, or send a text.

Why didn't I think of this sooner?

She fetched her mother's iPad and scrolled to an email Leelo had sent. It read:

> *Hi Eve, now you can receive emails from people all over the world! To reply to me, press the little crooked arrow symbol at the top of your screen.*
> *Love Leelo xx*

Rachel pressed Reply.

> *Hi Leelo, thank you for attending Eve's funeral. I am sorry for the commotion I caused, resulting in the cancellation of the wake at the pub. All is well, and I am much better now. I have news to your advantage, so do reply. Please give me a phone number, as I prefer not to put details in writing. Best wishes, Rachel Phelps.*

She changed the reply-to address to her own email. Leelo would get a shock, as Rachel had done, seeing a message arrive apparently from beyond the grave. The reason would become obvious soon enough.

Next, on the landline, she selected her mother's mobile number, heart thumping.

She tensed, half expecting to hear, "Your call cannot be connected . . ."

She heard the ringing tone.

Two rings, three, four, five ... then her mother's voice sounded in her ear, as clear as if she were still alive.

"Eve Miller speaking. I'm told you can leave a message for me after the pips. You'll have to speak slowly and clearly." After a pause she heard, distantly, "How was that, Rachel?"

It didn't mean anything, didn't even suggest the phone was turned on. Just the voicemail Rachel had helped Mum record one drizzly morning at the Willows.

Rachel fought back tears for the second time in an hour. She redialled. "Hi, Alma. Rachel here. I desperately need to speak to you. You're not in trouble, and no one knows I am calling you. I received your text. Phone me back on this number, love, saying when I can reach you."

Next she called the bank. "Howard, I want to thank you for attending the service at the crematorium last week and to apologise for my outburst. I was taken ill. I'm much better now."

"Pleased to hear it, Rachel. We were all concerned for your well-being."

"Any more news about the wire fraud? The police are scaling back their investigation."

"I regret not. Grimshaw's are holding the line, refusing to divulge the identity of their account holder. I shouldn't say this, but your best course now would be to issue a formal complaint against us, in your capacity as your mother's executor."

"That's unfair on you. You were tricked as surely as my mother was."

"Yes. I am always alert to the possibility of fraud against my more senior customers. Unfortunately your mother issued clear instructions for the wire transfer, with a convincing explanation of what the money was for. Had I refused to give her access to her own funds, I would have been in equal trouble. I tried a delaying tactic by stating that for money-laundering prevention I would need Eve to return another time with her passport and proof of address. Blow me, she produced both! A valid passport with a year to run and a copy of her account with the Willows. Even now I'm not sure what more I could have done. If only she had granted you power of attorney, I could have telephoned you ... but it's too late for hindsight. Don't worry about me—my career is almost at an end anyway. File your complaint. Claim negligence on my part. Just don't say I recommended you to!"

"That is most generous of you."

"While you are on the line, Rachel ..."

"Yes?"

"I am a tad concerned about Phelps & Son. The current account has breached the overdraft limit today by a little over five thousand pounds. I tried to telephone your husband, but the young lady said he was away for a few days. As a director of the company, are you in a position to reassure me that funds are on their way to reduce the deficit?"

Rachel closed her eyes. "I don't have day-to-day dealings with the business since we appointed an excellent assistant-cum-bookkeeper earlier this year. Kizzy—the girl you spoke to. Paul should be back before the end of the week. Can you indulge us until then?"

"Certainly, Rachel. Only my discretion is much reduced from the good old days. The computer flags up delinquent accounts automatically and copies the information to my area manager. I can't let an unauthorised overdraft run unchecked. I fear automatic penalty interest will be applied daily in the meantime. Just so you know. How is business?"

"We have plenty of work on the books. Cash flow is the constant challenge."

"Quite so, quite so. Perhaps you could encourage Kizzy to collect in any payments due? And would Newsome's extend your credit for a few weeks? Just ideas. Don't let me tell you how to run an old-established family business."

"I will certainly ask Kizzy to do those things in Paul's absence. Goodbye, and thank you again, Howard."

"Remember me to Robbie. He read the T. S. Eliot most movingly."

"I'll be sure to tell him." Rachel rang off.

She dialled Paul's mobile yet again.

Still switched off, or out of range.

If this was his strategy to help her rest and avoid stress, it wasn't working. If she used the automatic blood pressure monitor the hospital had loaned her, the cuff would surely go on pumping until it exploded.

Her baby must come first. She heaved herself up, exhausted all of a sudden. She hadn't had a good night's sleep for days.

The phone rang yet again, this time with the warble that signified an internal call.

"Hi, Rache. Would you like me to come across and make your lunch?"

"No thanks, Kiz. I can heat the soup. Then I plan to lie down for an hour. Listen, love, you didn't mention that Howard Plumb had rung this morning about the overdraft."

"Didn't want to worry you. Did Plumby get hold of you?"

"Kizzy, Paul is away. God knows where or why. I am a director of the company. Keeping things from me won't help. Your loyalty must be to the business."

"Sorry. I should have told you, but what with you coming home from hospital an' all . . ."

"Level with me from now on, promise?"

"Will do. Any word from Paul?"

"No."

Rachel heated her soup and ate it with a handful of cream crackers and an apple. Weary beyond belief, she trudged to the bedroom.

Wardrobe doors and drawers stood open. Paul's sports holdall was gone, along with his bedside phone charger and reading glasses. She poked her head into the en suite shower room. His toothbrush and electric razor were missing too.

She closed the curtains, kicked off her shoes, and lay down fully clothed on the unmade bed.

24

RACHEL AWOKE to her doorbell sounding the chimes of Big Ben.

Groggy, she scrabbled for the bedside alarm clock.

Half past two! She'd been asleep for over an hour.

The doorbell chimed again. "Coming!" she yelled in the general direction of the sound.

In the hall, she glanced at her face, haggard in the mirror, before opening the door.

Detective Sergeant Jim Ryan said, "I hope I didn't disturb you. Here's your phone."

"Sorry, I was asleep. The ward was bedlam day and night. Come in, Jim."

"Are you sure, Rachel?"

"Yes. I'd like to continue our discussion."

Ryan stepped inside. He was wearing black skinny jeans and, under his trademark leather jacket, a white tailored shirt that emphasised a well-honed upper body. Rachel wondered if he worked out at the gym or used weights at home. He looked ridiculously young and bouncy today, while she felt as old as Methuselah.

"Tea? Coffee?"

"A glass of tap water would be fine."

In the sitting room they sat at right angles to each other, as at their first meeting. Rachel twisted her hair and snapped a band around it. She needed to wash it, and wished she'd done so before Ryan's visit.

He said, "How are you?"

"I've been better. I learned after I spoke to you that my mother was cremated last Friday. Paul didn't tell me."

Ryan shifted in his seat and made a lemon-sucking face. "I guessed that much, when you asked about your mum's body. I couldn't bring myself to break the news over the phone. Sorry, I chickened out of that one." He managed a rueful smile.

"But my dear husband did find time to divulge to you that I'm pregnant. At the age of forty-eight."

"Yes. Any word from him?" Ryan sipped from his glass.

"Nothing. His mobile is off, or out of range. He's packed for a short trip, two or three days. He snatched a couple of shirts and changes of underwear. It's completely out of character. He never, ever does this. I'm worried to death. How soon can you start a missing persons enquiry?"

"Any idea why he took off?"

"Yes. Our family business is in trouble. Paul has fallen out with Fletcher Groundworks, run by a guy named Phil Fletcher, who looks like an old-fashioned East End gangster. Paul bribed one of Fletcher's foremen to get work done on the cheap. It all went pear-shaped, and this morning a digger turned up at the cottages we are renovating and demolished the lot. Aren't you going to record this as a statement?"

"Rachel, I'm not supposed to be here." Ryan got up from his seat, as if to emphasise the point. He stood at the window, staring out at the grey afternoon. "My boss thinks you're a hysterical attention-seeker." Rachel gasped in surprise. He turned to face her. "Sorry, but you need to know. Your breakdown at the crematorium confirmed that for him. If you want to go down the station and make a complaint about Fletcher Groundworks, or file a missing person report, that's up to you."

"So why are we even talking about it?"

Ryan sat again and leaned forward. "I believe you. There's something going on and we can see only part of the picture."

Rachel took a deep breath. "I fear Paul is involved with the theft of Mother's money. I think he has taken off to start a new life."

"Is it possible he's having an affair? That's often the reason husbands do a runner."

"If so, he has covered his tracks very well."

"He would, wouldn't he? Another possibility: the news of your pregnancy scared him witless, and he can't cope with the prospect of fatherhood. He needed to get away, come to terms with it. How did he react when he heard?"

"As he learned it from a junior doctor in A&E, his first reaction was amazement. Kizzy our secretary says he was overjoyed when he told her."

Ryan didn't reply, and the two of them sat for a moment.

Rachel broke the silence. "Paul has gone with his pickup. It's a distinctive vehicle, a Ford Ranger double-cab with Phelps & Son wraparound livery and lots of chrome bars, lights, and accessories. Will you put out an alert for it? Please? I can find a photo."

"Rachel, we don't put out alerts these days. We use Automatic Number Plate Recognition, ANPR for short. The police computer at Hendon tracks a hundred million hits a day and we can find just about any vehicle on the roads, even track it in real time like on the movies."

"Great. Find Paul's pickup. Please, Jim."

"I can't simply log into my computer and do it. Access to the system requires authority at superintendent level and is only approved for the detection of serious or organised crime. A husband who left a note saying he was going on a business trip doesn't qualify."

"So I have to wait for news?"

"Yes. If you learn anything that makes you suspect a crime has been committed by Paul, against Paul, or involving Paul in any way, I'll reopen the file. Until then, I'm officially off your case. That doesn't prevent me supporting you, or seeing you when I'm off duty, or acting as a sounding board for your concerns. I'd like to offer you that. You're pregnant, you're not well, and you have all the cares of the world on your shoulders."

He smiled. His teeth were white and even. Rachel fought to stay businesslike.

He stood again. "Whose dog is it—the lovely rough collie? I saw Kizzy letting him out for a pee."

"Raffles? He's ours. He dotes on Paul, thinks he's God."

"We had border collies when I was a boy. Wonderful dogs, as long as you can keep up with them. You won't find a more loyal companion." Ryan gave Rachel what she interpreted as a meaningful look.

Is the detective coming on to me? What do I think about that, if he is?

Definitely time to end the meeting.

She rose to her feet and held out her hand. "Thanks for everything, Jim. I'm disappointed you can do no more for now, but I understand why."

They shook hands, and Rachel showed Ryan out.

Time for that shower.

In the bathroom, she changed her mind and drew a deep bath. Not too hot—that might be bad for baby—but warm enough to soak away some of her tensions, aided by a generous glug of lotion.

Afterwards, wrapped in her fluffy bathrobe, she dried her hair in front of the full-length bedroom mirror. Her underwear from this morning was clean, but she tossed it into the laundry basket anyway. There was a faint whiff of antiseptic about everything that had come back from the ward.

She dressed in her comfiest old boyfriend jeans, a T-shirt, and cardie, then padded into the en suite bathroom to apply her makeup.

She dabbed her lips and dropped the red-stained tissue in the pedal bin.

Hold on—what was that? Half hidden by older tissues, dental floss, and an empty shampoo bottle?

She bent down and caught the faintest scent.

She extracted the item with forensic caution, holding it between her fingernails. It was a small, lavender-coloured and scented envelope such as Eve had used for thank-you notes. It had been sealed and—earlier that day?—torn open. On the address side was written the one word *Rachel* in her mother's hand.

Without a doubt Paul had ripped opened this envelope, removed whatever was inside, and gone with it, leaving the envelope poorly concealed in the bin.

Presumably Eve had handed it to him, for onward delivery to Rachel.

Why had he not done this?

Perhaps Paul had forgotten the note, found it in the pocket of whatever trousers he had worn for his trip, read the note guiltily, and kept it with him, intending to seal it in a fresh envelope and give it to Rachel on his return.

Or maybe the contents had been the impetus for his hasty departure—not the state of the business's finances.

Feeling more and more like Inspector Morse, Rachel went to the kitchen and found a zip-up sandwich bag, into which she sealed the envelope.

She finished her makeup, then took the bathroom waste out of the kitchen door to the wheelie bins.

Her tummy lurched when, at the bottom of the big green recycling bin, she discovered two empty own-brand vodka bottles hidden in a shoebox.

Perhaps they aren't Paul's?

But she knew they were.

Vodka was a devious choice: less detectable on his breath.

She tidied the bedroom, which resembled the scene of a burglary. She put away Paul's thick builder's socks and poked around in his knicker drawer for other evidence. She found a little stash of betting slips. Losing bets, obviously. She flipped through them. Mostly from the Tote, issued at local race meetings that year. Towcester, Huntingdon, Leicester . . . with the average bet one hundred pounds.

She sat on the sofa in the sitting room and checked her returned mobile phone.

Perhaps there would be a text or voicemail from Alma. Or a message from Paul.

Plenty of unread emails; but no little red numbers adorned the phone or message icons.

Her emails were the usual collection of sale announcements, Facebook alerts, and stuff about dancing, plus a few concerned messages from friends.

The hospital consultant had advised her to avoid stress and to take a week off work, but enforced idleness was more stressful than working, to Rachel's mind.

Am I fit to work?

From her handbag, she took the battery-powered blood pressure monitor and tightened it on her upper arm. She was supposed to do this four times a day. She was on blood-pressure tablets too ... and daily low-dose aspirin ... with twice-weekly check-ups.

She leaned back and pressed the button. The device buzzed and whirred and the pressure grew until it hurt. Then beeping began in sync with her heartbeat and the pressure eased as the air hissed out.

A long bleep announced the end of the reading.

She glanced at the LED display: 148 over 98.

Yikes.

The consultant had told her to go straight to the surgery or A&E if the numbers ever exceeded 150 over 100.

But Rachel refused to play the role of invalid.

She decided she would attend the beginners' class on the next day, show her face, announce her pregnancy, and then keep off her feet for most of the evening. Barry, Monica, and the students would be happy with that. So would Robbie.

Robbie.

If Paul didn't reappear or get in contact soon, she'd have to tell her kid brother something.

She hadn't tried Paul from her own phone and did so now. The call went straight to voicemail. "Paulie, love, I'm so worried that you haven't been in touch. Whatever the problem is, we can sort it out. I went up to the cottages with Kizzy. I made her take me. They're all rubble, but hey, we can rebuild them. I'll stand by you, but I need to know you're all right. If you don't want to tell me where you are, that's fine. I spoke to the bank today and I know about the money situation. You don't have to carry this by yourself. I'm feeling much better and my blood pressure is under control." *Liar, liar!* "Call or text me. Love you."

She checked the Nokia. Nothing new.

She looked at her notes and to-do list.

Retrieve text from own phone.

About the only thing she could progress.

She turned her smartphone over and over in her hands. She realised she had been daft to make a call to Paul from it, because now she needed to hand it to Kizzy to pass to Mahesh.

If Paul did respond to her voicemail while the phone was in bits on Mahesh's workbench, he wouldn't reach her and might panic.

She conjured up a vision of him standing on the clifftop at Beachy Head, phone in hand, or sitting in his pickup in a dark layby, a hose leading from the exhaust through the cab's window.

She resolved to keep her phone for now, plus the old Nokia.

She opened her laptop to focus on her dance business. She needed to update her Facebook page with the Christmas arrangements.

She managed five minutes, her heart not in it.

The low winter sun broke through the clouds and a shaft of sunlight lit up the table in front of her.

She'd take Raffles for a run before his tea.

25

PAUL DIDN'T get in contact that evening.

Rachel, prey to powerful misgivings, kept calling his mobile and sending text after text, in case he was in a poor service area and they were not getting through. In her heart she knew his phone was off.

The next day, she sat down with Kizzy and confirmed what she'd feared, that Phelps & Son's finances were in a critical condition. There wouldn't be enough coming in to meet the salaries at the end of the month, six days away.

After lunch of sausage rolls and apples, which she shared with Kizzy in the office, Rachel ordered a new flip key for her Fiat. The dealership said it would arrive the next day and they would bring it to her, which was good of them. The cost, however, nearly made her faint all over again.

Back in the bungalow, she couldn't settle. Her feelings for Paul veered between panicky concern and anger.

One moment, anxiety came to the fore and she could almost feel her blood pressure increasing as she thought of the anguish he must be suffering, away on a desperate mission to raise money, or retrieve the bribe cash from the chap at Fletcher's. What had he said? "I'll sort young Mervyn out and be home for tea."

Perhaps he'd had his fight with Mervyn, lost, and ended up in a truckload of Readymix, poured into the foundations of a filling station?

Rachel had considered telephoning or even visiting this Mervyn character, to demand answers. Common sense prevailed. The man was corrupt. He would tell a pack of lies, deny everything.

When would the police treat Paul as a missing person? Not until the "few days" mentioned in his note had elapsed, that was for sure. She checked her watch. He'd been gone twenty-eight hours.

Her thoughts spun around in circles of increasing apprehension.

Then, after tying her stomach in knots with worry, she would feel anger growing to take its place.

He'd abandoned and betrayed her just when she was at her most vulnerable, ill and expectant.

No business worries justified his actions.

And what of the note from the lavender envelope? How was Paul connected to all that?

Had he stolen the £200,000 from Eve and made off with it to start a new life, perhaps with a new woman, as Jim had suggested?

Rachel had always seen her husband as strong, silent, steady. *Had he led a double life for years?* One read of such things—men who kept two women, neither of whom knew of the other.

She couldn't believe it of him. He'd shown no signs of straying. Their years together had been contented enough, albeit without the family she'd craved. Their sex life had been fine. Not so great or frequent recently, but wasn't that common enough with couples who'd been an item for so long?

Just before four o'clock, Kizzy's finishing time, she crossed the tarmac to the office and handed over her smartphone.

Still, there came no word from Paul.

At the kitchen table, shaky, tearful, and wishing she hadn't committed to attending the beginners' class, Rachel found herself reevaluating her relationship with the man she had married.

He'd always doted on her. Of that she was certain.

He'd always been honest with her—and, in his business dealings, seemed as straight as anyone in the trade.

Sure, he would sometimes overcharge older clients a little, or substitute cheap colour-mixed paint for the designer brands specified by wealthier customers. He'd overclaim expenses, put personal purchases through the company, take cash for smaller jobs and "forget" the VAT.

Minor stuff, so common and petty as hardly to count as dishonesty—although even the smallest misdemeanour made Rachel uneasy.

The fact that Paul had bribed this Mervyn character proved he was capable of more serious wrongdoing, and covering it up, and keeping it from her.

What of Kizzy's role? How much had she known? Had she even suggested the bribe?

Could she—and this made Rachel's heart skip a beat—could *she* be the other woman?

Rachel flopped on the sofa and watched *Pointless*. A couple from South Wales made it through to the final but failed to come up with an obscure Bruce Springsteen track, so didn't take the jackpot.

"Pointless" was certainly the word for Paul's behaviour.

Why had he packed an overnight bag? Did he have a journey to undertake—to Birmingham, London even? Or did he simply need somewhere to stay that wasn't home?

"Business trip" implied travel. She'd imagined him meeting someone at a Premier Inn, having too much to drink, staying overnight.

Could he have gone instead to a friend or relative?

His parents were dead. He had a sister, Sandra, who lived in Redcar, but Rachel had met her only twice. Sandra and her husband hadn't attended the funeral.

There were various cousins, but none lived locally and he never saw them.

Mates? The guys from the bowls club? They all drank together at the Dog and Duck, but couldn't count as friends.

What about the reps from Newsome's, the builders' merchants? They weren't friends either, just business acquaintances keen to hold on to his account in return for tickets to the races and regular boozy lunches.

Like many men, Paul had few close friends.

Come to that, neither did Rachel. Work and home life had left her little time to keep up with her circle—who were all busy with hordes of children—and in recent years Facebook had become a virtual substitute for actual social contact with most of them.

Also, to be honest, many of them didn't think much of Paul.

She paced the bungalow. She fed Raffles and took him for a token walk to do his business.

Back indoors, she hung up his lead and opened the fridge. She chose a fish pie, jabbed at the film, and set it in the microwave.

The turntable rotated busily, and Rachel's thoughts went around in time with it; but when the pinger sounded, there were no answers to the questions that circled in her head.

26

BARRY PICKED her up as agreed, tooting cheerily from his big old Chevrolet. They set off to Hare House to collect Robbie, then retraced their route until they reached the road into town.

Rachel's spirits lifted when she entered the hall and saw a healthy turnout of beginners putting on their dancing shoes. She signed them into her register and took their money. By start time, she had more pupils than the previous week and a full cashbox.

Some good news at last.

She announced her pregnancy, and the class broke into cheers and spontaneous applause. A second later, Robbie cued up "Yes, Sir, That's My Baby," sung by Frank Sinatra, to further cheers.

Smiling broadly for what seemed like the first time in weeks, Rachel held up her hands to calm the excitement. Robbie faded Frank down.

"Thank you, all. I've come very late to the baby party, and I'm finding it exciting and terrifying in equal measure. I promise to come every week for as long as my doctor allows. I'll be arranging extra helpers for the classes, and lovely Monica will act as my deputy. The baby is due in April and I hope to bring him or her here to meet you all as soon as possible."

The smiles on everyone's faces raised her spirits still further. Robbie faded Frank back up to full volume, and as they'd planned in the car, Rachel danced the rest of the chorus to the line-dance steps, Barry and Monica joining in towards the end.

"Phew!" Exhilarated but a touch dizzy, Rachel retired to a stacking chair at the side of the hall.

Monica took over. "Let's start with a quickstep to get our circulations going! Music, maestro, please!" Robbie, whose gappy grin was the widest of all, fired up "Easter Parade."

Another clever nod to my condition and due date? He has hidden depths, that boy.

After class, Barry dropped her back at the bungalow.

Raffles knew the sound of every car that commonly arrived at the house, so he hadn't bothered to bark or even get out of his basket when Rachel fetched him from the office. The sad look in the collie's eyes suggested he had been hoping for Paul.

Rachel scratched the dog's ears in the way he loved. "You'll just have to make do with me for now, boy," she whispered. "Master has pissed off, God knows where."

Her home lay in darkness. The porch light clicked on as she unlocked the front door. She dumped her dancing shoes, register, and cash box on the hall chair. She tossed Raffles a dental stick, then fished the Nokia loan phone from her bag to check there were no calls or messages.

There weren't.

She lifted the cordless phone from its base, praying for the broken tone that would signify a voicemail.

A relentless, steady dial tone sounded in her ear.

With a sigh of frustration, she headed for the bedroom.

Without Paul's things lying around, it looked like a singleton's room.

She hoped it wouldn't become just that.

27

THE FINANCIER and the geneticist sat facing each other over a stainless-steel laboratory bench. Expensive equipment hummed and bleeped around them.

The money man, incongruous in his three-piece suit amid the high-tech surroundings, spoke. "Our client appreciates the long-term nature of this project, but human nature dictates that he is anxious for early results."

The young scientist looked up from his spreadsheet. His smooth face showed no emotion, and his voice was measured. "The first delivery will be soon. The challenge is getting the specimens. He must be patient. This is a marathon, not a sprint."

"An apt observation. Nevertheless, we feel you can do more. Trawl the city. Offer the service free."

"The target subjects are scarce."

The financier passed a photograph across the bench. "Without even trying, I have found one for you, arriving soon. So it can't be that hard."

28

A FIAT DEALERSHIP van arrived with her new keys the next day, as promised, and Rachel was mobile once more.

She called at the solicitor's, where she swore an oath on an old Bible produced by Gerald Smithers from the dusty depths of his filing cabinet. The solicitor congratulated her on her pregnancy and tut-tutted at the lack of progress in tracking down Eve's money. Rachel didn't dare suggest she feared her own husband was responsible—or even mention he was missing.

She and Kizzy worked together in the office, Rachel more wary than before. She shied away from physical contact with the PA, determined to put a little distance between herself and the girl, to reassert her position as director and employer.

She agonised over whether to attend the Spiritualist service coming up on the Sunday. Her head told her to cancel, but she missed her mother so much that she yearned to go along and maybe, just maybe, get a message that would give a clue as to what had happened and grant her some comfort.

On Friday evening she assembled Raffles's grooming equipment and gave him his regular brush and primp, talking to him the whole time. "So, boy, should I go to the police yet? Your master has been gone over four days."

Raffles seemed to roll his eyes.

"Is Master a wrong 'un? Has he been cheating on us?"

Raffles nuzzled her.

"Can I trust Kizzy? She seems so friendly. But she and Paul have been cooking the books, haven't they, old chap?"

Raffles grumbled as Rachel teased a tangle from his tail feathers with her stainless-steel comb.

"What are you going to say about having a little baby boy or girl around the house after all these years?"

Raffles gave no clue as to his opinion.

"You're no use, dog," she chided him. She gave him a big hug all the same when she'd finished grooming him.

29

RACHEL HAD the house and office all to herself.

Often, Paul would be out on a Saturday morning, visiting prospective customers to prepare estimates—or existing customers, to placate them after lack of progress during the previous week. But the bungalow always displayed evidence of his presence and imminent return. Boots stood in the porch, his hard hat hung on the hook, his large toolbox lay around waiting for her to trip over it, next to the extra-long spirit level propped up against a doorframe.

The complete absence of these familiar tokens of his existence troubled her.

This was beginning to feel like another bereavement.

She stood, sipping her meagre daily allowance of caffeine, looking out of the kitchen window. Raffles mooched about in the garden, sniffing the damp autumn turf. Then the collie looked up sharply, and his ears rotated forward.

Only the postman, his red van winding up the drive through the trees.

Rachel stepped outside to meet him, as much for the human contact as anything.

"Morning, Rachel. Chilly again. I'll have to start wearing me long trousers at this rate."

"Morning, Gary. At least it's stopped raining for now." She took the small bundle of mail.

In the office, the collie at her heels, she started the two PCs.

The password for both computers was the same hopeless choice: "Raffles."

Kizzy's computer finished loading Windows and announced itself ready for work. Rachel drew up the operator's chair, raising the seat with the lever by a good six inches.

She scrolled through the emails, on the hunt for clues.

A trend emerged: Phelps & Son Ltd. lived hand-to-mouth, robbing Peter to pay Paul, juggling jobs according to which could be billed rather than which needed progressing.

Kizzy's role was firefighter, keeping the money flowing, placating tetchy customers, making excuses.

Rachel leaned back. Raffles put his nose on her thigh.

She opened the post. A statement from Newsome's, totalling £6,000. A cheque from Mr. Jackson. That was quick! She hoped the poor man would get his conservatory and not join the end of a queue of creditors.

The last envelope was addressed to Kizzy.

In Paul's handwriting.

Feverishly, Rachel tore it open.

Out fell a car park ticket.

It was from the Gatwick Short Stay, South Terminal, with the date of entry the previous Wednesday, timed at 6:50 a.m. Printed along the top was the personalised registration of the Ford Ranger.

So. Paul spent two days in the country, drove to Gatwick, checked in early on the Wednesday morning, and flew somewhere.

It wasn't much to go on, but it was her first inkling of his movements, and it suggested he was on the run—from his wife, at least.

Did Kizzy know of his plans?

Normally, the PA received the post, both business and personal, and handed over the private mail to Rachel when she popped in for her—now-abandoned—midmorning cappuccino and chat.

Why the short-term car park? That cost hundreds, if you left a vehicle there for over twenty-four hours.

The only reason Rachel could think of was a panicky dash to the airport to catch a plane booked at the last moment.

Paul had posted the ticket back here, so did not intend to collect the pickup himself. That was ominous. Perhaps, aware of the exorbitant cost of a long stay in this car park, he had mailed the ticket back so Billy could retrieve the truck.

Rachel scooted the chair with her feet to the second PC. This was the one Paul used, if he needed to look up something like building regulations.

She unlocked the home screen. "You're a security risk, dog," she informed Raffles.

The desktop appeared, cluttered with icons, the PC equivalent of an untidy building site.

She clicked Google Chrome, Menu, and History.

His most recent searches were the previous Monday morning, timed at 5:30 a.m.

> Cheap flights to Tallinn—Google Search
> Gatwick (LGW)—Tallinn (TLL)—EasyJet
> What is the currency in Estonia?—Google Search
> Car hire Tallinn—Google Search

Why hadn't she thought of this earlier? She could have saved herself nearly a week of anxiety and indecision.

Why hadn't she checked whether Paul's passport was missing?

The fuzzy picture in her head came into sharp focus.

Leelo!

Paul was having an affair with Eve's PC instructor, and had done a runner to live with her, leaving Rachel behind, unwell and pregnant, and the family firm failing, and only Rachel to look after her adult brother with Down's syndrome.

Leelo! The same plausible wretch who had wormed her way into her mother's affections, so poor Eve had thought her worthy of a handsome legacy. And who'd lied about having a boyfriend for whom she cooked cabbage.

Leelo had stayed until after the funeral to avoid arousing suspicions. Paul had planned to go with her, but had been delayed by Rachel's hospitalisation.

The incriminating search terms burned themselves into her brain.

Surely he'd realised she would eventually log on to his PC and do this?

Perhaps, consumed with guilt, he'd wanted to be found out, but was too much of a coward to admit the situation to his wife in person.

It was a despicable way to confess: leave incriminating evidence and scarper.

She guessed that, unable to get a flight until the Wednesday, he had left on the Monday morning and holed up in a cheap hotel or B&B, his phone turned off—or more likely with a new SIM slotted into it, to go with his new life, his new identity, and his new love.

It was equally obvious to Rachel that Paul and Leelo had stolen Mum's money.

The betrayal was so complete, so shocking, and so brazen that Rachel's brain struggled to take it in.

She turned away from the screen. Their faithful hound sat by her side, unaware of the sudden and total change in the family's fortunes, or that he would likely never see his adored master again.

The PCs hummed. The room was warm thanks to the night-storage heating. Everything looked as it had done for years—but all had changed in an instant.

One slim consolation: Kizzy was not the other woman. That meant Rachel could keep her as an ally.

Rachel drummed her fingernails on the desk.

Saturday was her regular day to pick up Robbie from his karate class, have lunch with him in town—always at Nando's—and then go shopping with him. The second-hand music store, with its racks of vinyl LPs, was always a favourite.

She'd chickened out of telling Robbie about Paul's absence.

Now she had to face that challenge too.

"Just you and me from now on, boy," she told Raffles. "And a little friend, if by a miracle I carry this baby to full term."

To discover more about her errant husband's movements and plans, she scrolled back through his search history. But the earliest entries were only a day before the Monday morning shockers. Either Paul or Google had deleted everything earlier.

Rachel raised an eyebrow at the number of online betting sites her husband had visited in those two days, including on the Monday morning, before he checked on Estonia.

How much of the family's—or even the firm's—earnings had disappeared into the coffers of Ladbrokes and Bet365?

She resisted the urge to brew up a cappuccino with the fancy machine endorsed by George Clooney.

Right now she could so do with an Irish coffee complete with whipped cream and three heaped spoonfuls of sugar.

She shut down Paul's PC and sat staring at the blank screen.

The warning signs had been there.

Paul's frequent visits to the Willows, ostensibly to visit Mum. Actual purpose: to see Leelo, plot, and doubtless canoodle with her in that little lounge on Primrose.

Paul's slip-up over Grimshaw's Bank.

The note from Mum, who'd smelled a rat, and, too weak to telephone, had scribbled a last desperate note to get word to her daughter, sealed it, and left it in the drawer by her deathbed.

Paul would have stumbled across the lavender envelope when he collected Eve's personal effects.

In the office filing cabinet, under "Motors," she found the spare set of keys to the Ford Ranger.

She'd take the train to Gatwick tomorrow, after the church service.

With a heavy heart, she shut down Kizzy's machine, pulled up the lever, and sank down as the seat lowered. How apt: she felt several inches shorter than a few minutes ago. She told

Raffles to go to his basket and was about to leave when her loan phone chimed out the Nokia ringtone.

She pounced on it.

"Number Withheld" showed on the display.

"Paul? Is that you, you bastard?"

30

"NO. MAHESH Choudra. Mr. Mobile."

"Whoops. Hi Mahesh. Sorry about that."

"I have the information you wanted."

"Tell me."

"Not on the phone. Come to me. Above the kebab shop in town, Flat 6A. The bill is fifty, cash only."

With £150 from her dancing cash box in her purse, Rachel headed for the Fiat, glancing at her watch. Plenty of time to visit Mahesh before Robbie's karate class finished at midday.

The drive into town was the usual Saturday morning stop-start affair. She found a parking space conveniently near the kebab shop.

On the first floor, the door to 6A stood ajar.

Bollywood-style music floated out, plus a curry odour.

A voice called, "Come."

She had a moment to glance around a flat devoted entirely to mobile phones and computers. They covered every surface in various states of disassembly.

Phones lay piled three deep on the hall table. Power supplies, boxes, and chargers encircled with leads lined the walls. To get into Mahesh's workroom, she had to turn sideways and edge through a doorway obstructed by an unstable-looking pile of PCs on their sides.

The technician sat hunched over his workbench, his back to her. Rachel recognised her phone, in pieces on a worktop scarred with soldering-iron scorch marks.

Mahesh twisted in his seat and beckoned. He was olive-skinned, tall, and lanky, in his twenties, with black curly hair swept up from a high forehead.

"Sorry. I had a tidy up, but no space." He smiled, revealing sparkling white teeth, which contrasted with the short beard under his chin. One of the upper teeth was solid gold.

He turned down the Bollywood. "You got the money?"

She took fifty out of her bag. He counted it and put it in his back jeans pocket, then handed her a sheet of printout.

It listed the texts and calls to and from her mobile.

The final entry was on the date of the cremation, and once more Rachel saw the text from her mother's phone:

I was murdered.

She looked over the sheet of paper at Mahesh. "This last text, it was deleted?"

"Yeah, fifteen minutes after it arrived."

She hadn't imagined it. And Paul had done it.

"May I show this to the police?"

"Sure. I done nothing illegal. It's your phone, yeah?"

"Yes. Thanks for doing this so quickly."

"Kiz said to get on the case. I don't understand. How can someone send a text if they've been murdered? A joke?"

"I hope so."

"Here is your phone." He slid on the back, deftly inserted two tiny screws, and tightened them with an equally tiny screwdriver. "I fitted a new battery. Yours had done nine hundred and forty cycles. A freebie for a friend of Kiz's."

"Thanks again, Mahesh."

"Will there be anything else?"

"Yes. Can you track a mobile—tell me where it is right now?"

"If it's switched on. Otherwise I can find out where it last registered on the network. Gimme the number, and I'll show you." He pulled his PC keyboard towards him.

"How about if someone has changed the SIM?"

"Even if you don't have the new number, I can still trace a phone most places with the IMEI. That stands for International Mobile Equipment Identity. The unique serial number, built in by the manufacturer."

"Suppose the phone is abroad—In Estonia, for example? Can you still find it?"

"Yeah, man. I can trace in UK, India, Pakistan, Bangladesh, almost all European countries. The databases for this work are not publicly available, though. You can't go telling the cops I did it, right? I won't give you anything in writing, like the tower encryption algorithms and stuff I shouldn't know."

"I understand. You can trust me. Where would I find the IMEI?"

"You got two options. First, look at the small print on the user's contract. They usually put the IMEI there somewhere. The best bet is if you have the original box. It's on the barcode label. Text me the number, I'll trace it." He reached for a business card and scribbled on the back. "Use this number. It's off the radar."

"I have another I'd like you to track—the one from which that weird text was sent. It's my mother's old phone. Someone stole it just before she died."

Mahesh stroked the wispy beard under his chin. "Didn't you cancel the phone? If so, I won't see it."

"No. It got overlooked. It was only pay-as-you-go."

"Wouldn't it have a new SIM too by now?"

"Maybe, maybe not."

"Let's check it out."

He keyed a website into his browser. It began with "darksidetracker" and contained a blizzard of hyphens, forward slashes, and full stops.

A login page appeared. Mahesh filled in the boxes, fingers flying over the keyboard.

After several more security steps, a plain white screen with a single outlined box came up, into which Mahesh typed Eve's number from the printout.

An egg timer faded up, rotating above the message: *Searching for phone . . . you gotta wait, dude!*

The timer disappeared and the word *Gotcha!* flashed up in red, above a Google map.

He tapped the minus key to zoom out. "Yeah, you were right. Estonia. You got family there?"

"Is it Tallinn?"

Mahesh zoomed out more. "Yeah. A suburb called ... Lasnamäe."

A "quick facts" box slid in from the left of the screen. Rachel read out loud, "'Lasnamäe is the most populous administrative district of Tallinn, the capital of Estonia. The population is about 119,000, the majority Russian-speaking. Local housing is mostly 5- to 16-storey panel blocks of flats, built in the 1970s to the 1990s.'" She looked up. "Is the phone in someone's home? Can you get the exact address?"

"Nah, this works by triangulation on towers nearby. It's accurate to within fifty metres or so. Let's have a look around." Satellite imagery appeared, together with a strip of photographs along the bottom. "Looks a nice place. Plenty of shopping. Uh-oh, this is more dodgy. Check out those crumby high-rises."

He centred the screen on the mobile phone icon, selected Map View, zoomed in, and pressed Print. A sheet of paper whirred out from under his bench. "There you go. The handset is within that area, right now. Mind, the user might not live there. Could be on their way to the shops, or to see a friend."

Rachel opened her handbag and took out the remaining hundred pounds. "Will this be enough to track the other number from the IMEI? And give me updates on this phone too?"

"Yeah, man. Why don't I try it now, see where it last logged in to the network?"

Rachel gave him the number. Mahesh's fingers danced on the keys.

They had to wait more than two minutes. "Don't reckon the phone has been switched on for a long time," Mahesh ventured. "Ah, here we are."

The egg timer faded away and the map appeared. Rachel leaned over. "Where is he?"

"Paul the Bastard?"

"Yes. Paul, my bastard of a husband."

31

THEY SAT IN a window booth at Nando's. Robbie, still in his karate whites, two napkins tucked into his collar, gnawed at a drumstick. "So Paul and Leelo got it on and left the country?"

"Yep."

"And they took a load of money from Mum—the money that was for me?"

"Yep."

Her brother wiped his lips. His face creased with sudden anxiety. "Did they take Raffles?"

"No, he's at home."

"That's all right then, Sis. I'll look after you. I can move in tonight. I don't need the money for now."

Rachel wanted to cry. "Thanks, you big softie. Yes, perhaps you can stay with me for a while. It's lonely without Paulie and Mum. Both gone."

Robbie raised his right hand, fingers together. His voice took on a sing-song quality. "Me no softie. Me blue belt. When Paul comes back, he'd better watch out for my *shutō-uchi*."

She reached over the table and took hold of his karate-chop hand, gently lowering it. "Shh, love, don't make people stare. We can look after each other. How about that? But let's not rush things. We have to square it up with Hare House. Also, I'll be away myself for a few days, so it won't be until next week."

Now alarm registered on Robbie's broad face, as when Rachel had broken the news to him, in the car before they entered the restaurant. "Away? You too? Where you going, Sis?"

"I'm flying to Estonia to find Paul and Leelo, tell them what I think of them, and get Mother's money back for you."

"You're pregnant, Sis. You just got out of hospital. You can't go travelling abroad by yourself. I'll worry about you. And what if you don't come back? Then I'm all alone too."

"Of course I'll be back, love. It's no distance and Estonia is a modern, safe country."

"Why don't the police go? Paul and Leelo stole Mum's money. That's a crime. Police are there to catch criminals."

She couldn't fault his logic. "I'm in touch with a detective. The fact Paul has fled is a complication." She picked up a chicken leg using a napkin. She'd chosen their mildest sauce, herb and lemon.

Robbie drained his Coke. "Can I get another?"

"Half a cup. You know what your doctor says about too much sugar."

Robbie waddled over to the drinks dispenser, white trouser bottoms flapping, while Rachel toyed with her food and glanced around the busy restaurant. This branch of Nando's featured mobiles hanging from the ceiling, made of large plastic chillies. On the far wall hung a poster of Marilyn Monroe in *Some Like It Hot*.

Her kid brother, as so often, was the voice of reason. Her impulsive plan to fly to Tallinn was plainly barmy. She was setting herself up for failure on the one hand, or humiliation on the other. They'd never admit to stealing the money, and she had no proof they had.

Would I even find them?

Robbie returned with his Coke. She changed the subject to cats and dogs, and he soon had her smiling with the latest antics of the Scottie and the Doberman.

Back home, she let a grateful Raffles out. He scampered off around the garden. In the office, she found the box for Paul's phone and texted the IMEI to Mahesh.

Sitting at the conference table, mobile in hand, she phoned Ryan. "Jim? Is this convenient? Are you on duty?"

"Yes and yes. Is this official or personal?"

"Official. I took my phone to a technician and have confirmation of the murder text. Paul's pickup is at Gatwick and he was Googling travel to Estonia." She knew from Mahesh, but didn't mention, that his phone had last registered on the network the previous Tuesday night, also at Gatwick.

"Sounds like you've been doing my job. Any evidence of criminal acts, or that Paul is in any danger?"

"I think he's run off with Leelo."

"That did occur to me too. I'm very sorry. You've been treated miserably."

"I now also suspect Paul and Leelo of the scam to rob Mum. To answer your question, I have no evidence. But our business is in trouble, cash has gone missing, and Paul's gambling is out of control."

"I'm sorry again. I'll report all this straight away to my DCI." After a pause, he continued, in a quieter voice, "How are you coping?"

She sighed. "Surviving. It's a relief to know where Paul is, at least. I was beginning to fear the worst."

He replied, "Tomorrow will be difficult for you. Shall I come over in the afternoon?"

It was her turn to say, "Official or personal?"

"Official first. I'll report back if I can get reassigned to your case. Then personal. We'll take Raffles for a walk along the riverbank. The forecast is warm and sunny, the best day for weeks."

"That would be nice. I value your support. I'm out at church in the morning and I believe there will be refreshments after. How about one o'clock, while there's still sun? The days are getting so short."

"I'll be there, Rachel."

32

RACHEL SAT between Kizzy and Kizzy's mum in the fourth row. Both of the black women had gone to great lengths with their dress and appearance. Kizzy had braided her long, dark locks and applied copious glittery lipstick. Her mum wore a voluminous floral skirt and jacket, accessorised by a wide-brimmed floppy hat adorned with a crimson ribbon and a diamante brooch.

Rachel, smart enough in her jersey trousers, wraparound top, and sparkly scarf, nevertheless felt dowdy sandwiched between the two exuberant women.

Her eyes darted around the church. A good attendance: maybe eighty people, with about one in three of African-Caribbean extraction.

She hoped the service wouldn't be too happy-clappy.

She was already regretting coming, but it would have upset Kizzy to pull out, and she needed Kizzy. She'd phoned Kiz the previous afternoon and filled her in about the car park ticket and Paul's movements. She hadn't mentioned her own travel plans, undecided about what to do.

"Here they come," Kizzy whispered.

The preachers, or whatever you called them in this church, filed out from the side door and took their places on the dais. They wore smart-but-everyday clothes. Two were older black men, the rest middle-aged white men and women.

A stout, comfortable-looking woman about Rachel's age, wearing a rather masculine suit with a pinstripe, stood up to the microphone. She spread her arms wide.

"A warm welcome, ladies and gentlemen, to our service of communion with the spirit world. I am delighted to see new faces amongst us this morning. You are particularly welcome, and I hope we will bring at least some of you a measure of comfort, even joy during our time together in this special place.

"We know that life is eternal. Here at the Spiritualist Church, we believe that there is no death, that life continues. We are in this world now and we will go home to the spirit world. Our duty here on the platform is to provide clear evidence that life does indeed go on. Also, knowing that life continues helps us put our present existence into clearer perspective.

"We have no dogma and no liturgy in our church; however we do have a few important guiding principles. We believe in the fatherhood of God, the brotherhood of man, the communion of spirits and the ministry of angels, the continued existence of the human soul, personal responsibility, compensation and retribution hereafter for all the good and evil deeds we do on earth. So let us start with a prayer.

"Almighty Spirit, you who rule the oceans and the land, come amongst us today we pray, and guide our loved ones as they reach out to us from the other side. Help us to understand our place in the great order of creation as we strive to bridge the gulf between this world and the next, in the sure and certain knowledge that death has no dominion, no power over us. We are never alone. Amen."

A hearty answering "Amen" sounded out from the congregation.

"Before I introduce you to our medium this morning, I would like to begin with a poem by Henry Scott Holland."

Rachel let out an involuntary gasp. Kizzy squeezed her hand.

> "Death is nothing at all.
> It does not count.
> I have only slipped away into the next room . . ."

Although the poem was well known and often read at such occasions, Rachel felt a nervous fluttering in her tummy as the words she'd heard so recently rolled around the church.

> "What is this death but a negligible accident?
> Why should I be out of mind because I am
>   out of sight?
> I am but waiting for you, for an interval,
> Somewhere, very near,
> Just around the corner.
> All is well."

The speaker looked from face to face, lingering on Rachel, who blushed. "I sense that the words of my poem may be of particular resonance to some in our midst today. So let me straightaway introduce you to Ralph Elliott. I first saw Ralph in action six years ago, at a healing committee in the beautiful town of Rye. I was very impressed by his gift and his sensitive interpretations. We kept in touch, and I have been privileged to witness his mediumship many times since. I am pleased that my persistence—nay, badgering—in asking Ralph to visit us has finally paid off, and he is here this morning as our guest. Please welcome him with open minds and open hearts."

Rachel joined in the applause. At that instant, she experienced the same little flutter in her tummy again. A thought struck her.

Could it be the baby?

She'd read about the sensation, which mothers-to-be likened to popcorn crunching inside them.

Surely it was much too early for this? Nerves, more likely, she told herself.

The stout lady took her seat, and Ralph Elliott mounted the dais. Smart in a plain grey suit and striped blue tie, smooth-faced and bushy-eyebrowed, with a bulbous nose, he could have been an estate agent or accountant during the week.

"Thank you, Daphne, for that generous and warm introduction, and for inviting me to visit your beautiful church today. Spiritualism as we know it started, ladies and gentlemen, with physical phenomena experienced by the Fox sisters—Leah, Maggie, and Kate—in New York. The movement went from strength to strength and now encompasses many different kinds of mediumship, clairvoyance, and healing. My own journey began—"

He froze.

Then, as if an unseen puppeteer had jerked his strings, he reanimated. "I am being reached out to with unprecedented urgency from the spirit dimension. A mother. A mother's mother, is linking to me here. She's coming across very strongly, and standing at the side of the church, looking, searching . . . and now she sees her daughter, and is moving down the fourth row.

"She is passing behind the lady with the wonderful hat and ribbon. I'm not seeing a person of colour, so can it be . . . Yes, it is your friend on your right. Yes, yes, my dear. You."

"Me?" Rachel's pulse pounded in her ears. The heat in her cheeks was spreading down her neck.

Has Kizzy set this up?

"Your mother is right behind you. She is much less tall than you. Her head, standing, is the same level as yours sitting. She is reaching out, putting her hands gently on your head."

Rachel experienced a light touch on her hair. *The power of suggestion?* She flinched and twisted in her seat.

"You sense her presence. Your mother is with you. Do not fear. You are safe in this place. You have children?"

"No," Rachel said. "At least, not yet. I am expecting."

"Ah, that clarifies things. Your mum is saying she didn't know of a grandchild when she was on the worldly plane, is that correct?"

"Yes. I only discovered I was pregnant after she passed away."

"Passed on, we say. Passed on. No one passes *away*, we believe. Life is eternal. Your mother is with you in spirit always. Today we have bridged the narrow chasm between our world and hers. Your mother has a message for you."

Total silence reigned. The medium bowed his head for a good thirty seconds. Then he raised his eyes, fixed Rachel in a steady-but-friendly gaze, and spoke again. "Mum says she was sorry to leave you as she did. The time of her passing on was right, but not the manner of it. I sense sorrow and guilt. Mum kept a secret from you and fears you will never know it. I am seeing something like a letter, or note, and I am sensing an odour . . . sweet, floral."

"Lavender," Rachel whispered. "Mum had lavender-coloured notepaper, and she would spray a few drops of essence on each sheet as she wrote."

"Lavender, yes that is it. I'm afraid I am not much of a horticulturalist and I have a poor sense of smell myself. My wife says that is strange, given the size of my schnozzle."

Everyone chuckled, grateful for a chance to break the suspense.

The medium continued, "Mum will not tell me what was in her last note to you. She was a private woman, I sense?"

"Yes."

"Mum is asking for your forgiveness and vows to be with you always. She says she will try to make her presence felt, but only in a gentle and subtle way, and will never frighten or startle you. So I think you could look out for little tokens of her continued existence, particularly in places she frequented and loved in happier days."

"Thank you." Rachel's eyes brimmed with tears, but she smiled and looked from face to face, seeing answering expressions of sympathy from the people near her.

On the stage, the speaker said, "Mum is leaving."

Rachel couldn't concentrate on the rest of the service, or "meeting," as they called it. The medium communicated with spirits of wives, fathers, brothers, and aunts. Around fifteen people received messages or sentiments. She didn't pay much attention to these, or to Daphne when she thanked Ralph Elliott and embarked on a lengthy reminiscence of a family who had endowed the church, whose matriarch would have had her 150th birthday that day.

She could think of nothing except her mother's message, and remained distracted as hymns were sung, and conclusions reached, and parting prayers intoned.

The congregation broke up and headed for tables laden with tempting refreshments.

Still shaken, she thanked Kizzy and her mother. Everyone hugged.

On her way home, she glanced at the dashboard clock. Half past twelve. Just time to change before Jim Ryan arrived, and to adapt her makeup to something more casual and outdoorsy.

33

SHE HADN'T EXPECTED him to turn up in full cycling gear, on an expensive bike.

He looked ridiculously young, fit, and un-detectivelike, the cycling top accentuating his muscular torso.

Rachel let Raffles squeeze around her legs to inspect the new arrival. Jim Ryan bent down to tickle his ear. "Hi Raffles!"

"Would you like to come in?"

"Why don't we set straight off, if you're ready?"

"Yes, I need the fresh air." She shrugged on her fleece, grabbed Raffles's lead, and shouldered the backpack containing her phone, purse, and bottle of water. "We can walk from here to the river."

"May I leave my bike somewhere secure? There's been a rash of thefts. I've got two constables looking for the perps."

She unlocked the office, and they stowed the bike inside. Rachel dropped the blinds for good measure.

The low midday sun shone across the field as they set off towards the gate, Raffles bounding ahead.

"He's a handsome boy. An original, old-fashioned Lassie dog. It must take a lot of grooming to keep him so smart."

"He's beautiful and he knows it. He can spot a camera at a hundred yards and strike a pose. If you groom him little and often, with a full comb once a week, it's not as hard as you'd imagine."

"Does he need loads of exercise? We had border collies, and you couldn't keep them still for a moment. Always looking for something to round up."

"Not the rough collie so much. Raffles is happy with one or two walks a day plus a scamper in the garden. During the working week he sits up front in the pickup with Paul. From behind, it looks like Paul has a scruffy hippie hitchhiker." She paused, the thought that Paul and Raffles might never see each other again provoking a pang of distress. "Now, enough small talk. You said business first. Did you speak to your boss?"

"Yes."

"And?"

"The news about the text being authentic shook him. He'd convinced himself, without ever meeting you, that you were a neurotic."

"Had he taken the trouble to meet me, he might have realised otherwise. Jim, you've been great, but you're the least senior detective at the station, aren't you? Is it fair to say I haven't received a high priority?"

Ahead, Raffles, nose to the ground, followed an alluring scent. Ryan said, "You're right. Apart from Detective Constable Timmins, I'm the most junior. I've tried to make the boss take an interest, and I thought that verifying the text would do the job. Do you have something on paper from your man?"

"Yes, I'll give it to you when we get home. The text says that murder has been committed. Surely that's a top priority?"

Ryan sighed. "You'd hope so. Detective Chief Inspector Geddes—he's my superior—brushed it aside, saying that because the words were 'I was murdered,' it must be a prank. Unless the message came from beyond the grave, of course."

Rachel stiffened in her step.

He continued, "Rachel, Geddes ordered me to shelve your case. There's no evidence of foul play on your mum, and the police aren't interested in bank or credit card fraud. I'm ashamed to admit it, and you didn't hear me say it, but it's true. Besides, we're overstretched."

"Trying to catch bike thieves."

"You're right. It makes no sense. I even worry, and I shouldn't be sharing this with you . . . but you deserve to know . . . I worry that someone is leaning on Geddes."

"Really? Why?"

"Only two reasons. One, this is all linked to something much more serious and organised, which is being run by some other force, and they don't want us queering their pitch. Two, there's a rotten copper somewhere up the chain."

"You think the bank scam is part of a pattern? Have there been similar cases?"

"Not in this county recently, and never on this scale."

"So where does that leave me?"

"Waiting for Paul to get in touch."

They walked on in silence. Rachel couldn't decide how much to trust Ryan. She wondered whether he had been tasked to strike up a relationship with her so he could gain her confidence and find out what she was hiding. In that case, his talk of organised crime and officers higher up being involved would be a smart-but-manipulative double bluff.

Well, two could play at that game. So choosing her words with care, she said, "I'm desperate to trace Mum's stolen phone—the one I believe Alma used to send the murder warning text. Can you not at least access your system to find out where the phone is now?"

"Sorry, Rachel. I'd love to, but I have been expressly forbidden to follow that line of enquiry. 'A prank message on a cheap pay-as-you-go phone,' as Geddes put it."

"Can't you get one of your colleagues to do it on the hush-hush?"

"Nope. Anyway, they're too busy hunting down stolen racing bikes."

"Jim, that's not funny."

"Sorry. I apologise. I'm spoiling this lovely day for you instead of providing the promised support."

They reached the lane. Raffles ducked under the stile, and Ryan went over, then waited for Rachel as she climbed up. She took his outstretched hand. It would have been rude not to. They turned left, and the tower of St. Mary's Church came into sight above the ash and oak trees lining the road. Raffles trotted at Rachel's heel, now on a short lead, Ryan following behind in single file.

They encountered no cars and soon arrived at the church. Here the road widened, and there was a pavement leading to the village and the river. Ryan moved to her side.

The sun warmed Rachel's back. The fleece was too snug for the rising temperature. Her flushes and sweats had become less troublesome since she knew she was pregnant, but she still tended to overheat. She unzipped the front.

She didn't want to believe ill of Ryan's intentions. She liked him, and in another life, if she wasn't spoken for—and if she were twenty years younger—she could imagine falling for his puppy-dog charm and good looks.

Right now, she was a married woman with a missing husband and no interest in the opposite sex.

"How long before you count Paul as a missing person?" she asked, to stop that train of thought.

"It depends on a risk assessment. Someone who takes their passport, clothes, wallet, and car and leaves a note would not be considered a risk—they'd be a low priority. That can change with the passage of time. The two considerations for us are the risk of self-harm, and of a crime being committed against, or by, the person in question. I suggest tomorrow is the day for you to come to the station and file a report. Geddes can't stop the process. Our manual on missing persons is one hundred and fifty pages long, and we must follow it."

"Paul is presumably still abroad in Estonia."

"That will complicate matters. We have no authority to visit another country or carry out investigations overseas. We could put Paul on the Schengen system through the national police computer. That's a sophisticated tool for tracing people. Estonia is signed up, and so are we—for now. But unless Geddes agrees that Paul is at risk, all we can issue is something called an Article 32 Alert. When he shows up—say at passport control, if he flies out—he'll be invited to get in touch with us.

"The missing person does not have to agree to share their contact details, and officers must not pressure them into doing so. Many people do not wish their location disclosed and want no contact with their family. Everyone must take great care not to disclose the missing person's location without their consent."

"So he can choose to disappear, and I have no right to know where he is?"

"It works both ways. Often an abused wife or an unhappy girlfriend will sever all ties, go to live somewhere else and make a fresh start. That's what Geddes thinks Paul has done."

"Without duly carrying out the risk assessment first."

"Yep. Although you haven't filed a missing-person report, on my advice, so officially nothing has happened yet."

"I'll do that tomorrow."

They walked on through the village. Everything was closed except the Dog and Duck, which always did a brisk trade on Sundays with their carvery roast. At least a dozen people sat in the sunshine, waiting with drinks until their tables inside became ready. Children ran in all directions.

"Fancy a quick half?" Ryan asked. "That's the business part over, I hope."

"Sure, why not? Raffles will think it odd if we pass by without stopping."

A couple vacated a table for two. Ryan fetched a beer for himself, a lime cordial for Rachel, and a packet of potato crisps for Raffles.

Rachel's phone pinged. "Excuse me." She flipped open the cover.

"Not Paul, by any happy chance?"

"No, just one of those texts saying I could claim thousands for missold payment protection insurance."

She surreptitiously switched the phone to silent and slipped it back in her rucksack.

34

HOME ALONE, Raffles at her feet gnawing a treat, Ryan's bike disappearing down the drive, Rachel took out her phone.

The sender was "Mum," and the message read:

> *Hope UR well. At home Estonia. Sorry miss funeral & u getting silly msg, my brother (10) playing tricks. Eve giving me her mobile the day B4 she dying. Alma xxx.*

Her phone pinged again.

This text *was* from Paul, and on his original number.

Suddenly faint, she pulled out a kitchen chair and slumped into it. She put her head between her knees and took several deep breaths, pushed the hair out of her eyes, and swiped to read the message.

> *Hi darling! Sorry outta contact so long—phone playing up big time. All sorted back soon luv u missing u xxx.*

With shaking fingers, she called him.

After six rings, the voicemail cut in. "Hi, this is Paul Phelps of Phelps & Son—"

She pressed Cancel, returned to texts, and replied to Paul's:

> *Hi Paulie where RU? Call me now! xxx*

She sent this and swiped to Alma's text, replying:

> *Hi Alma gr8 2 hear from u all fine here stay in touch Rachel xx.*

Finally, she called Jim Ryan's number. He at least answered.

She blurted out, "I heard from Alma and Paul!"

"Oh, that's a relief. Hold on, let me get off the carriageway." She heard cars whizzing by in the background. He came back. "Are they both all right?"

"Yes! Alma is in Estonia. Mum gave her her phone, and the text was a joke by her little brother. Boy, am I relieved. Next thing, Paul texts. He didn't let on where he was, but said he'd be home soon."

"I guess he needed breathing space. As for Alma, I'm pleased she's fine too. So everything is back to normal. I'm guessing that Paul may get an earful when he shows up."

"Indeed."

"So no need for you to attend at the station tomorrow after all?"

"No. Jim, thank you for the walk and the drink today. I think we should leave matters there. I appreciate all you've done for me and the family. I won't relax until Paul walks in the front door, but at least I should get a better night's sleep tonight."

"Pleased to be of help. Sorry things got tense. I won't give up on the fraud, trust me."

"Thank you, Jim. Bye for now."

Raffles, in the corner, finished his chew and emitted a satisfied belch.

"Raffles! Manners! I have great news for you. You're off to the Korner Kennels."

The collie cocked his head on one side. Maybe he understood the phrase "Korner Kennels." More likely, he had picked up the false jollity in Rachel's tone of voice. He let out a little whimper, lay full length on the floor, and put a paw over each eye.

He hadn't been fooled.

And they hadn't fooled Rachel—whoever "they" were.

The text was from Paul's number, but it had not come from Paul.

Alma's text had come from Mum's phone, but not from Alma.

Had Rachel fooled them in return?

She picked up her phone and read the messages again.

Paul never called her "darling." It was always "babe," unless she was out of favour, in which case he would call her "Rachel." Or if extremely provoked, or teasing her, "Rachel Kimberly Phelps"—her middle name was of her Canadian father's choosing.

Alma didn't have a brother aged ten or any other age. She was an only child.

Whoever had these phones wanted to throw Rachel off the scent.

In turn, she'd deliberately misled Jim Ryan, pretending everything was all right. It would have been hopeless to tell him about the texts, and then get him to believe they were from imposters. Even if he had believed, the wretched Geddes character would have vetoed further action for days.

She texted Mahesh.

Her phone rang at once.

"Hi Mahesh. I just got a text from Paul's phone, on the original number."

"Gimme a second." She waited, visualising Mahesh at his workbench in his chaotic flat, staring at his monitor on which the egg timer rotated. "Yeah man, I see it. I ran a trace on the IMEI this morning and got the same registration as when you visited. Gatwick. Now the phone is in Tallinn. Switched on thirty minutes ago. Before you ask, yeah, I also checked the other one—your mum's. Its last location was also Tallinn, an hour ago. Another suburb, three miles away. The two phones are in different places, or someone has both and turned them on one at a time."

"Thanks, Mahesh. Give me the location of Paul's phone, please."

When he rang off, Rachel paced around her kitchen. She had a lot of information to process.

Paul's phone was in Tallinn: logically, so was Paul. But he hadn't sent that text. The same thing went for Alma.

What to do?

Stay at home, marking time, plodding through the motions of work and daily life, waiting for news, getting bigger and more bloated by the day — or jump on the next plane and fly out?

Raffles growled and barked twice.

A visitor, and not a regular one.

Big Ben chimed.

Robbie stood on the doorstep, backpack at his feet. The Hare House minibus waited outside, its headlights bright in the gathering gloom. She waved to the driver, who, seeing Robbie safely admitted, reversed his vehicle and departed.

She hugged Robbie. "I wasn't expecting you tonight, but welcome anyway, Bro. Come in."

"You said I could move in for a while. I said I could move in straightaway. Here I am."

"Yes, but I also . . ."

He picked up his rucksack. She stepped aside, and he entered. Raffles bounded up, tail wagging furiously. Her brother crouched down and fussed over the collie for a moment, then looked up. "I thought you might take off to Estonia without me. So I came to mind you. Everywhere you go, I go too, Sis. I got my passport from the office. I got my money, nearly forty pounds. I got my mini DVD player and my Nintendo and my phone so I won't be bored ever, even if you read a long book. What's for tea?"

In the kitchen, Rachel peered into her fridge while Robbie and Raffles began a game of tug-the-rubber-bone. "Lasagne it is."

"Great, I'm starving. Put the kettle on, Sis."

Ten minutes later, courtesy of her trusty microwave, they ate, Robbie with a paper napkin tucked into his collar. He said, "What time is our flight?"

"It's a crazy plan for us to go."

"Crazier for you to go on your own. I'm a good traveller. I enjoyed Malaga."

"A little too much."

Her brother snapped his fingers. "I get it. It could be dangerous. In which case you really *do* need me to watch your back, Sis."

"What about the kennels?"

"We have to drop Raffles off, right? We tell Julia there's a family emergency, say Paul is abroad, give her our hotel number. Julia will be cool. We're not busy, and she can get by without me for a few days."

Rachel couldn't fault Robbie's simple logic. She sighed. "I'll let Kizzy know our plans. She'll run us to the kennels tomorrow, then on to the station. The Ranger is already at Gatwick, and we don't want another vehicle parked up there."

"Plenty of room in the Ranger for the three of us and Raffles when we all come home together."

"Assuming we find Paulie and he wants to return with us."

Robbie looked grave. "We'll find him. He'll come back. He wouldn't want to live abroad long without Raffles."

Rachel put her head on one side and pursed her lips. Robbie was joking. His broad face broke into a gap-toothed grin. He roared with laughter and slapped his thigh.

Rachel made a face and poked her tongue out at him. It would be nice to have his company. He could stay in the hotel playing games and watching videos. Also, if he was there, she wouldn't have to worry about him on his own with no family support. Hopefully there wouldn't be a repeat of Malaga. Rachel and Paul had taken Robbie with them for a week's all-inclusive break. Robbie had met a Down's girl there, half his age, and fallen madly in love. Luckily the girl, who was with her parents, was at the end of her holiday, and had flown home before things could get out of hand.

"Finished?" she asked.

"Yes. I'll wash up and tidy your mucky kitchen while you book the flights."

She punched him playfully on the arm. "Hey kiddo, since when did you give the orders around here? You're the little nipper, remember?"

"Sis, I'm head of the household now. I'm the man." He stood and adopted his karate pose. "They better watch out for my *shutō-uchi*. Here, you'll need this." He pulled his passport from his baggy jeans.

In the office, Rachel fought with her conscience.

So much could go wrong.

If Paul and Alma were in trouble, things could indeed get dangerous.

For all his bravado, Robbie was a child in a podgy adult's body. He'd be a liability in any difficult situation.

Still, she couldn't pull out now and go on sleepwalking through the chaotic remnants of her life until the news came through that a body had been found ... Or worse, to have no news at all, while her baby was born, then started to grow up with no daddy ...

She fetched her own passport from the safe, went online, and bought two tickets for the next day's noon flight to Tallinn.

She booked a family room with two double beds in a three-star hotel in Lasnamäe.

The only train to Gatwick that suited them was the 6:30 a.m. She reserved two seats.

She phoned Julia at the Korner Kennels. Julia confirmed they were quiet and Robbie could have the whole week off.

She booked Terry the Taxi.

She phoned Monica, who assured her that the beginners, Latin improvers, and medal class would be well cared for.

She phoned Kizzy and thanked her for inviting her to the church.

"No worries, Rache. We'll do it again next week or whenever. Eve may come through with another message. The spirits can be shy first time. I guess it's pretty mind-blowing for them too."

"Kiz, Robbie and I are flying to Estonia tomorrow. We'll be gone by the time you arrive for work."

"Great idea. I'll take care of business, no worries."

"I'll leave our itinerary and hotel details on your desk. I'll check in at least twice a day with you. If you don't hear from me for over twenty-four hours, call Detective Sergeant Ryan at the station. I'm leaving his numbers too."

"Gotcha. Good luck, girl. I'll be rooting for you. Luv ya."

Weary to the bone, Rachel gathered her paperwork together, locked up, and trudged the few yards to her bungalow.

The kitchen worktops sparkled. The dishwasher gurgled. Raffles lay curled up in his basket, sound asleep.

She found Robbie in the sitting room, watching *Milo and Otis*, his audio-visual comfort blanket, on DVD.

She slumped down on the sofa and took his hand in hers.

"You missed the racoons and the seagulls, Sis. Watch, this bit is good. Milo is in that hole and Otis pulls him out with the rope. Way-hey! There they go! Next, they find mates of their own."

Rachel, who had endured many enforced viewings of the Disneyesque film narrated by Dudley Moore, smiled. She knew, because she'd looked it up on the movie database, that dozens of animals had allegedly been maimed, drowned, and killed during the filming. Robbie would be horrified if he ever discovered that Milo was not a single tabby kitten but many different lookalikes.

One thing she knew for certain. For all his fighting talk, with a mental age of ten, Robbie could never protect her.

For as long as they both lived, he would be her responsibility.

35

THE YOUNG ASSISTANT hesitated, then knocked on the laboratory door.

"Come!"

"Director, pardon me, but some of the results from last night's run appear anomalous. There seem too many—"

"Show me."

She passed him the printout. The geneticist speed-read it, his eyes darting from line to line.

"I see what you mean. I will rerun these myself tonight using the B samples. It's probably a calibration error. You were right to alert me."

She turned to leave.

"One more thing."

"Yes, Director?"

"Tell no one of this."

36

"IS THAT SNOW?" Robbie turned to Rachel, anxiety etched on his face.

"Yes, love." The plane's engines whined as the pilot struggled to maintain his glide path amid the buffeting of the storm. The flight attendants, making their final check of seat belts and tray tables, clung to seat backs as they passed down the aisle.

Outside, the snow rushed past in the darkness, illuminated by the flashing lights on the wingtips. Rachel gripped her armrests, regretting their madcap adventure more by the minute.

She'd known roughly where Estonia was, but hadn't realised it was on a similar latitude to the Outer Hebrides. They'd be there at the worst time of year, with early snows reducing the roads to slush, and little prospect of any sunshine. Temperatures would hover around freezing point by day and night. Besides near-continuous cloud cover, they could expect only seven hours of daylight. All this she'd learned from the in-flight magazine.

Despite his bravado, Robbie was an inexperienced flyer, and his journeys had consisted entirely of short hops to France and Spain. He looked ashen in the beam of his reading light.

Rachel reached for his hand. "We'll be down soon."

Hopefully on the runway and not in the lake, she added to herself.

She craned her neck to see past Robbie's broad head. No lights were visible on the ground through the gloom and cloud.

Sooner than she expected, they touched down. Robbie gasped in alarm when the pilot deployed the thrust reversers.

"Welcome to Tallinn, where the local time is five twenty-two p.m. and the temperature is one degree Celsius. Please remain seated with your seat belt fastened . . ."

The plane taxied to the gate, and they disembarked into the terminal, which was bright, modern, warm, and efficient.

Passport control was fully automated, with shiny gates and scanners and plenty of smartly uniformed officials to assist.

In arrivals, they passed the waiting group of taxi drivers holding up passengers' names. Rachel looked this way and that for directions. It helped that all the signage was in English as well as Estonian.

While they stood undecided, an elderly woman, hunched, and dressed in a ragged shawl, shuffled towards them. She held out a bunch of heather, its stems wrapped in tinfoil.

Rachel had encountered Romanians before, on the Underground in London, begging from tourists with their "cross my palm with silver for luck" line.

"No thank you, we're—"

Only it wasn't heather in the old woman's gnarled fist. The faintest odour confirmed it.

The crone spoke in heavily accented English. "For good fortune in our country. The hotel buses are through those doors."

"Thanks." Rachel handed over a five-euro note. She accepted the small bunch of lavender. The woman melted away into the throng hurrying to leave the airport.

"Mum's favourite," Robbie said. "I'll carry them, Sis. I got a hand free." He took the stems with exaggerated care.

Conditions outside were filthy, with thick, damp snowflakes reducing visibility and making it treacherous underfoot. A minibus with Hotel Raadiku livery appeared within minutes, for which Rachel was grateful.

One other couple boarded with them, Eastern Europeans in their early twenties.

The bus pulled away, its wheels swishing on the wet roadway.

"You have family in Tallinn?" the man asked in perfect English.

"My husband's here on business," Rachel replied. "We're meeting up and going home together."

"I guessed. No tourists visit Tallinn in November. This is just the start." He waved at the darkened windows. The bus's wipers, on top speed, were barely keeping up with the blizzard. "We're from Finland, stopping over a few days."

Robbie said, "I'm here to look after my sister. I'm a blue belt in karate."

The young woman, all blonde hair and wide eyes, said, "That's nice of you. You need not worry. We used to work in London, and we feel safer here."

Rachel smiled and looked out of the window. They must be in Lasnamäe already. Tower blocks loomed over them, with many of the windows illuminated. These were the Soviet-era estates thrown up to house the inflow of Russian workers.

The bus continued past a building site announcing itself as a supermall. Then they were in the heart of the residential area.

Washed to a dingy pallor in the headlights, the brutal concrete wasteland made Rachel shiver with apprehension. It felt like they had been transported to a Russian gulag.

The hotel came into view ahead, its bright neon sign a welcoming beacon in the swirling snow. It appeared to occupy the first three floors of the block, which was of more recent construction than its neighbours.

The young man held the door for them. Inside, he took command, speaking in Russian or Estonian, Rachel could not tell which. The check-in process was smooth, with the equally young female receptionist all smiles.

The girls seemed to be pretty and courteous in this country. Rachel's stomach lurched as she thought of Paul and Leelo. No wonder her husband had fallen.

Mind you, the blokes were easy on the eye too. She hadn't seen an overweight man since landing.

The room was fine. A little spartan, but clean with no smell of smoke. She'd read that Estonians were compulsive smokers and that even nonsmoking hotel rooms often reeked of stale tobacco.

Robbie put the bunch of lavender in a plastic beaker of water and picked up the guest folder. "Great, the Wi-Fi is free and unlimited. But no restaurant or bar, Sis. Just a coffee machine and pastries for breakfast. I'm starving now. That snack on the plane was pants."

"According to TripAdvisor, there's a big shopping centre in walking distance with plenty of dining."

"We'd better not walk at night in this weather. Can we get a cab?"

"OK, love." Rachel would have been happy to make a cup of tea and retire to bed.

Downstairs, the receptionist phoned for a taxi. "Five minutes, sir and madam."

Robbie stood at the rack of leaflets promoting the city.

"Hey, can we try the KGB Exit Room?" he said. "They lock you in and you have to find the clues to escape. It's an attraction. All about spies and stuff." He waved the leaflet at Rachel.

"If we have time, love." She scanned the flyers and took out a tourist map. Tallinn Old Town, Town Hall Square, Toompea Hill, Kadriorg Park—amazing in the snow, apparently. It all looked interesting, but she doubted they would have any chance to sightsee.

This was no holiday.

Then she found what she wanted: a leaflet for Lasnamäe Magnum. It claimed to be the biggest shopping centre in the area. It wasn't the local mall within walking distance, but that wouldn't matter in a taxi. Restaurants, shops, beauty salons, disabled access, all the usual, plus...

That confirmed it.

She held the leaflet up for Robbie. "Reckon we'll find Paul here."

37

SHE'D FEARED a dodgy minicab, but their taxi was smart and clean, with yellow-and-black chequered livery and "Takso" on the roof sign. En route, Rachel texted Kizzy their destination. She wanted to leave a trail of their movements, in case of trouble or danger.

The driver said, "Welcome to Tallinn. They call this district 'The Bronx of Estonia,' but it's a friendly place. Lots of young people."

Rachel wasn't convinced.

They passed a modern filling station, its fascia illuminated, but otherwise the area was poorly lit and scruffy, with cracked concrete roads, a bus graveyard, and the brutal Soviet tower blocks looming overhead like headstones in a giant's cemetery.

The snow had transformed into sleety rain.

Magnum was an oasis in a winter desert, brightly lit, multicoloured, and welcoming. The taxi driver handed Rachel his card. His name was Andrus. "Here you have everything you need. It's one of the biggest commerce centres in Tallinn. Call me fifteen minutes before you're ready to return to the hotel, I'll be here waiting."

"Thanks, Andrus."

Inside, light and sound assailed them. The place wasn't as big as Meadowhall, but it was new, clean, and warm.

"First things first! Feed me!" Robbie cried.

In the absence of a McDonald's, they chose Hesburger, the local equivalent. Perched on a round, padded stool, Robbie attacked his cheeseburger with gusto.

Rachel thought she felt her baby moving again. The sensation was strange, not unpleasant. She nibbled her chicken-salad burger.

"So, why do you reckon Paul is here? Do you think Leelo will be with him?" Robbie asked through a mouthful of fries.

Rachel had deflected the question in the taxi. She hadn't wanted the driver to overhear.

She took out the Magnum leaflet and pointed.

"Aha. The Casino Acropolis. Open twenty-four hours."

"Precisely. And while you were in the bathroom at the hotel, I texted my new friend Mahesh, who is tracking Paul's mobile from back home. Paul was in this centre half an hour ago. I'm guessing—hoping—he's settled in for the night."

"Paul doing the horses still?"

"Yep. And the dogs, and the football, and the Estonian Premier League for all I know. If you can back it to win, Paul is there." She couldn't keep the bitterness out of her voice.

They finished their food in silence. Robbie said, "That's better. Now what? Stake out the casino?"

"Yes."

"I can't wait to see Paulie's face when we walk in." He slithered off his stool.

On a large illuminated floor plan Rachel located the Casino Acropolis and set off with purposeful step, Robbie at her heel like a loyal puppy. "Whatever happens, love, keep calm. I'll do all the talking."

"Sure, Sis."

Before they saw the casino, they heard it: a chorus of bleeps, snatches of tinny music, and the clatter of coins cascading from slot machines.

At the entrance, Rachel gazed open-mouthed. They hadn't scrimped on the Ancient Greece theme. She took in ornate ceilings, statues of gods and goddesses, a fountain in the lobby. Artificial laurel wreaths wound themselves around Grecian columns.

The place thronged with people of all ages. Punters sat on high chairs upholstered in gold in front of towering slot machines that chattered, spun, and flashed.

The floors, carpeted in swirling patterns of blue and brown, made Rachel feel dizzy.

"Wow. Serious bling," Robbie commented.

They advanced with caution, passing an electronic roulette table resembling the control panel of the Tardis, with monitors at each player's seat. Rachel glanced around for croupiers, but the entire place seemed to be automated.

"Where do we start?" Robbie asked. It was like trying to find someone on the concourse of Birmingham New Street at rush hour.

"See the lounge bar over there? You case that out. I'll take the sports bar." She handed her brother a postcard-size photo of Paul, snapped that summer and printed the night before. "Be polite. If you spot a group of friendly people, just say 'Excuse me, I'm looking for my brother-in-law. Have you seen him?' If you find him, don't approach him. Text me, and I'll meet you at the entrance. Can you handle that?"

"Sure, Sis. Be polite, show the picture, ask if they've seen Paulie." Photo in hand, he ambled off in his trademark rolling gait.

Rachel set off through the crowds towards the Sports Bar.

Here, TV monitors hung on the walls, each tuned to a different sport: snooker, golf, soccer, cycling, even cricket. Punters stood at ranks of betting terminals. The bar, inlaid with purple and gold mosaic tiles, was a monument to bad taste. Gigantic golden coins in bas-relief adorned the back wall above rows of bottles on glass shelves. The migraine-inducing carpet gave the eye nowhere to rest.

She could see only the backs of the drinkers on the barstools, but none of them was Paul. The barman—young, slim and sporting the perfect amount of stubble—smiled and said, "Take a seat, madam. A member of our wait staff will serve you."

"I'm looking for my husband." She held up the photo.

The barman said, "He was here earlier. Maybe he plays the slots, or he left."

Rachel ground her teeth. So near, and she'd missed him! "May I have a sparkling water, please? I'll wait for him."

"Here you are. On the house."

She crossed to the lounge. Paul was not among the drinkers or the gamblers at the terminals. She decided it would be better to hunt elsewhere.

A pale-faced man around Paul's age caught her attention. Dressed in a designer suit of Italian cut, he sat by himself, phone to his ear, on one of a group of four armchairs. In front of him lay a document case in soft, expensive leather, next to a half-drunk cocktail in a highball tumbler.

Two more glasses on the table, both empty, suggested that the man was only temporarily alone.

Rachel perched on a chair by a betting terminal and sipped her water, keeping a surreptitious eye on the fellow.

He continued to talk into his phone, relaxed and confident.

Rachel was about to give up and search elsewhere when a waitress headed for the man's table. He didn't glance up as she removed the two empties and replaced them with fresh drinks, one a large beer and the other a colourful cocktail.

Then, so suddenly that it made her gasp, Paul appeared from around a screen.

He went to the table, sat, took up the beer, and drank.

The man in the suit didn't acknowledge his arrival but continued to murmur into his mobile phone.

She texted Robbie: *FOUND HIM, sports bar, come now.*

Head held high, she advanced towards the two men.

Mr. Suit spotted her approach and registered recognition but not surprise.

Her husband, facing away from her, gulped at his beer all unaware.

"May I join you?" She dropped into the seat where the cocktail awaited.

Paul looked up and almost choked. He put down his glass and spluttered, "Babe. You're not supposed to be here . . . yet. How did you find me?"

"Never mind that. You and your natty friend"—she nodded at Mr. Suit—"have the explaining to do."

Paul's eyes focused on someone approaching. Rachel twisted in her chair and said, "Oh dear. Have I taken your seat? I am most tremendously sorry. Would you like your cocktail . . . *bitch*?" Without waiting for an answer, she seized the glass of red-and-blue concoction and flung the contents at Leelo, who stood wide-eyed right behind her.

Throwing a drink at someone from a sitting position is not an easy feat, but Rachel's aim and technique were perfect, and she had the satisfaction of dowsing the Estonian woman's expensive-looking silky top without getting any liquid on herself.

Leelo let out a shriek of alarm. She turned and fled, presumably to the cloakrooms.

Paul said, "What's got into you, Rachel Kimberly Phelps? Was that necessary?"

She turned back to the table. "Completely necessary. As is this, you bastard."

She lunged, grabbed Paul's half-empty beer mug, and poured the remaining contents over his head. "You'd better go find your girlfriend and help dab her chest dry."

Meanwhile, the foppishly dressed man in the suit pocketed his phone, finished his own drink, leaned back in his chair, and roared with laughter.

"Who are you?" Rachel demanded. "And what's the big joke?"

Mr. Suit guffawed, his eyes moist with tears of mirth. Then he glanced up over Rachel's shoulder and spoke, the first time she had heard his voice. "To complete the merry party, here comes your chromosomally challenged sibling." His diction was posh and pompous, reminding Rachel of Stephen Fry, whom she detested.

She turned her head again. Robbie, at the entrance, spotted her and ambled over.

Paul said, "You brought Robbie with you? That was so irresponsible. This is nothing to do with him."

"He's the only member of my family I can trust. He's loyal. Not a word you'd understand."

Paul wiped his face with a paper tissue, which disintegrated into damp shreds. His soaked shirt clung to his chest.

Mr. Suit renewed his laughter, this time cackling to himself and saying, "Oh my. What a twist. 'Heaven has no rage like love to hatred turned, nor hell a fury like a woman scorned.'"

"What are you going on about?" Rachel snapped. "Who in '*hell*' are you?"

Robbie arrived. "Are you all right, Sis?"

"Yes, but your brother-in-law's spirits have been dampened."

Robbie's face creased with worry. "Paulie, what's going on?" His eyes darted from Paul to the suited man to Rachel. "Was that Leelo I passed outside with the wet top?"

Paul said, "Robbie, you shouldn't be here. This is business."

"Monkey business, I'll be bound," Robbie chanted, raising his voice.

Suited Man giggled. He seemed to possess a wide repertoire of laughing styles. Wiping his eyes, he said, "I feel I can contribute no more tonight and that my continued presence will be superfluous. Robbie, take my seat. Paul, we'll be in touch." He picked up his document case, bowed to Rachel while making a silly cap-doffing gesture, and strode off.

Robbie remained on his feet. The young barman approached with a bucket, sponge, and roll of washroom paper. "Is everything all right?"

"My husband had an accident with his drink. He's very careless. Even with things that are very important to him."

"Sir, shall I fetch you a fresh glass?"

Paul said, "Yes please" at exactly the same time as Rachel said, "No way."

The barman wiped at the beer dripping to the floor. "Could I suggest you move to the next table, so I may attend to the spillage?"

"I'm sorry my husband made such a mess on your carpet."

"Accidents can happen. People get carried away." He waved at the TV monitors. "Especially when Flora play Levadia in the Meistriliiga. That is like a Liverpool-Everton derby for you."

"I support Man. United," Robbie said. "I have a number ten shirt at home."

Paul glanced towards the entrance.

The barman straightened up, unable to clean further until they left.

Rachel said, "It's make-your-mind-up time, Paul. Either go and comfort your top-heavy totty in the loos and wait to hear from Gerald Smithers, or come home with me and Robbie."

"It's not how it seems," Paul replied, the hint of a whine in his voice. He addressed the waiter. "May I have some of that paper please?" He dabbed his trousers, then his hair, which hung in matted strands over his face. "Babe, I was about to call you to come here, but you jumped the gun."

"Not what you said in your text."

The barman said, "I do need to clean up under the table."

Rachel held her nerve. "What's it to be, Paul?"

Robbie chimed in, "You're in serious shit, Paul. I'm disappointed in you."

Paul rose from his seat. "Let's get out of here at least and let the guy clear up. Really, Rachel, that was childish."

Rachel picked up her handbag and unfolded her six-foot-one frame from the chair. She grasped Robbie's hand. Paul followed behind like a naughty dog that has rolled in silage and knows a serious hosing-down awaits it.

In the lobby, Rachel said, "I'll call the taxi."

"No need. I've got a car."

"What in God's name are you up to in this city?"

"I can explain everything. It's all about you, babe, though I forgive you for not appreciating that yet. I had to go, you see. Me and Leelo, it's not like you obviously think, there's nothing going on."

"Tell that to the Marines," Robbie said. "Be thankful you didn't get a *hiza geri* in the nuts back there."

"Robbie, you shouldn't be here. Be quiet. Rachel, what were you thinking?"

"What was *I* thinking? Paul Phelps, you abandoned your pregnant wife just out of hospital, you left your business in tatters, you stole my mother's life savings, and you eloped with an Estonian woman half your age. And you have the gall to ask me what am *I* thinking?"

Paul's eyes darted around.

"Well, what's it to be?" Rachel repeated. "Are you going to continue with the Lord Lucan act, or come home and face the music? I don't care which, I just want an answer so Robbie and I can get to our hotel and into our beds. We've been up since five this morning."

"I'll run you back. Where are you staying?"

"The Raadiku. What did you mean, saying this is all about me?"

"About you, and Robbie too. I've acted at all times in your interests. I've put you first. It's been hell without you. I needed a day or two more to get sorted, then I would have sent for you. Honest." He wouldn't meet her eye and kept glancing around.

"On the lookout for Leelo?"

"Of course not. Come on, let's take you back. I can't stand here in a wet shirt all night. I—"

"I, I, I, me, me, me. It's all about *you*, isn't it, Paul?"

"Give me a break. Hear me out."

"All right. A wet shirt won't kill you. We'll go back to the Hesburger. That was busy enough that we can talk without being overheard. Besides, you could do with a strong coffee."

Rachel had noticed that her husband's eyes were rimmed with black, and he was sweating despite the comfortable ambience of the shopping centre. He'd been on the booze, for hours, days . . . weeks, to judge by his dissolute appearance.

Her elder brother Simon had noticed Paul's decline. *Why hadn't I?*

"Fair enough. I need a pee first. That fizzy lager goes straight through a bloke."

"Robbie, accompany Paul, please. I don't want him running off again. I'll find us a table in the Hesburger."

"Sure thing, Sis. Paulie, come with me." Robbie took his brother-in-law's arm in a firm grip. Although he was much shorter than Paul, he made a convincing minder. Rachel couldn't help smiling.

After the adrenaline rush of the confrontation, Rachel drooped. This level of stress couldn't be good for her or the precious new life she carried.

Paul hadn't even asked about her baby. *Their* baby.

In the Hesburger, she found a table tucked away. The TV was playing a movie, the sound almost inaudible against the hiss of the espresso machine.

She took her hand mirror from her handbag and checked her face and hair. She didn't look as bad as Paul.

Her phone pinged.

Kizzy!

> *Mission HQ here. Have printed out Google map and am plotting your movements. Good luck xx*

She texted back:

> *R & me fine. FOUND PAUL! All 2gether in mall. More 2morrow! xx*

Out of curiosity, she tried dialling Alma on Mum's old number.

"Eve Miller speaking. I'm told you can leave a message for me after the pips. You'll have to speak slowly and clearly . . . How was that, Rachel?"

Her mother's voice comforted her. Then, with a pang of guilt, she thought of Eve's ashes in their cardboard box at the back of the wardrobe in the bungalow.

Her eyes flicked up to the TV monitor. A girl with a beautiful hourglass figure, in a flowing white dress, turned pirouettes alone in a dusty attic.

Not unlike me as a teenager. Nothing like as tall, though.

She recognised the actress as Lady Rose from *Downton Abbey*.

What was her real name? Lily Allen?

No, but something like that.

Whoever this is, she can dance.

On screen, a family of mice appeared on the attic floor. They didn't seem to faze the girl.

One mouse leapt up to a windowsill, then jumped again to cling on to the handle of a closed window.

Trying to open it? Perhaps the girl is locked in the attic.

The mouse wasn't heavy enough. A second mouse followed, clinging to the hindquarters of the first. Then a third leapt up. Teamwork in action.

The server behind the counter had finished steaming her cappuccinos.

The girl on screen sang, the soundtrack now clearly audible.

> "Lavender's blue, dilly dilly,
> Lavender's green,
> When I am king, dilly dilly,
> You shall be queen."

Rachel caught her breath.

Another coincidence?

Maybe, but so what?

She felt the comforting presence of her mother regardless, and let it flow around her like the waters of a warm bath, relaxing her tension, encouraging her, supporting, loving her unconditionally.

"Hi, Sis. He didn't dare try to leg it. Hey, *Cinderella* is on. Can I have a Coke?"

The song had ended. Rachel snapped out of her reverie.

"Paul, get Robbie a Coke and bring me a hot chocolate." Her husband had rinsed his hair and slicked it back off his forehead. He had recovered some of his composure. Rachel suspected he'd gone to the cloakroom for breathing space, to think what to say and do next.

He plodded obediently to the counter.

Robbie plopped onto the stool beside Rachel.

"Who's that playing Cinderella, love?"

"Lily James. We all watched it on Sky. The mice are the coolest bit. I can't wait to hear Paulie's excuse."

"Me too."

This was a complete role-reversal. For the past twenty-odd years, she and Paul had worked together for Robbie; helping Mum to cope with him, sorting out the sheltered accommodation and the job at the kennels, keeping him part of the family, feeding him, clothing him, taking him on holiday. Now Robbie was by Rachel's side, supporting her in her dealings with her wayward husband.

"I'm head of the household now. I'm the man," he'd announced, pride in his voice.

She'd better keep him grounded. For all his bravado, he was emotionally fragile.

God knows what damage this trip might do to him.

Paul returned with their drinks and a small espresso for himself. "Babe, this isn't the time or place. Me and you need to go somewhere private when you've calmed down. How's about we meet up tomorrow at your hotel? Robbie, you shouldn't have been involved and I'm sorry she brought you here, away from your home and your dogs."

Robbie sat up straight and puffed out his chest. "She needed someone to look after her. I asked to come, didn't I, Sis?"

Rachel said, "Paul, I'll decide whether we meet again after tonight. For now, have a go at convincing me it's worth the effort, because if you don't make a start, it will be too late. We're drooping with fatigue and we won't tolerate any more bullshit. The truth, please. Are you, or have you ever been, having an affair with Leelo?"

"No! Cross my heart. Leelo's with Richard. They're the item."

"Richard?"

"Richard Shackloth. The guy in the bar."

Rachel sipped her hot chocolate. "Go on. We're agog."

Paul ran his hand through his sticky hair. "It all started when I won a massive accumulator at Newbury in July. I got the winners of the first four races including Lathom with Tony Hamilton on board at thirty-five to one, and pocketed forty grand. I didn't tell you because I'd had some big losses before that over the year, and this brought me level plus a nice bit of bunce.

"I'd promised myself if I won that bet I'd give up. So I needed somewhere to stash the cash. The very next day, I overheard Leelo and Eve talking about investments. I was in the room installing those remote sockets on Mum's lights, so she could turn them on and off from her chair. They didn't think I was listening. Leelo told Mum that her boyfriend was a big knob in the City. A venture capitalist. She'd met him in the champagne bar at St. Andrews through colleagues at the Treasury, where she used to work."

Paul drew breath, gulped down his espresso, and looked from one to the other with his best George Clooney expression.

Robbie and Rachel sat stony-faced. Paul dropped his eyes to the table and continued. "I snuck out of Mum's room and hung around in reception. When Leelo came down, I asked her if this boyfriend would invest my winnings. Putting it in the bank was hopeless, you see. It would have earned nothing, and attracted the attention of Kizzy and you. I wanted to multiply it up quickly and without the taxman knowing."

Plausible?

Barely.

Rachel tossed her hair and glanced sideways at Robbie. "Go on," she repeated, her eyes narrowed.

"Leelo set up a meeting for me with Richard at the Dovedale Country Club. We had lunch, just the two of us. The place was dead posh. Richard spent the whole meal talking about his cars, and his properties—he owns over a hundred—and his motor yacht in the Med. I didn't say a word. Then right at the end, he pushes a piece of paper across the table and says, 'Leelo tells me you have forty to invest. Wire it to this account, don't ask questions, and I'll double it for you in a month.' And he did."

"How?"

"Derivatives or something. Who cares? He's a City boy. He manages the wealth of big names. Premier League footballers, film actresses: A-listers, the lot of 'em. I'd blagged my way into his inner circle!"

"So you got back eighty thousand. Then what?" Rachel noticed that Robbie's eyelids were drooping.

"Richard asked me that. He said it would be fine to pay me my winnings—sorry, dividends—in cash. Legal tender means just that. Only, I would need to declare the gain to the Inland Revenue, and I wasn't sure you would approve of that amount of holding-folding lying around."

"You're right there, at least."

"It all fell into place after I visited you at the hospital. I went home and looked up about amniocentesis and Down's—"

Robbie jerked awake. "Someone talking about me?" He wiped his big face with his pawlike hand.

Rachel said, "No, love." To Paul, she said, "Wherever you're headed with this saga, it must wait."

Paul glanced at Robbie. "Of course. Stupid of me. You two need your beauty sleep. You'll hear me out tomorrow?"

"It had better be good, Paul."

"I'll run you both back to the Raadiku. Come on Robbie, my man. You're about to fall off your perch, literally. My car is outside. We'll have you tucked up in ten minutes."

38

RACHEL LAY awake. The family room had been a bad idea: she'd forgotten that Robbie, like many with Down's, snored for Britain. Something to do with congenital misshaping of the nasal passages.

She turned and pulled the pillow over her uppermost ear. The bed was long enough—they often weren't—and the mattress wasn't uncomfortable, just rather firm, but she didn't sleep well at the best of times these days, and a strange bed was the final straw after the day they'd endured.

This is all about you, babe.

He'd calculated she would want to find out more.

He'd tried to give her a peck on the cheek when they parted at the doors of the Raadiku, but she'd kept her distance.

Rachel had meant what she said: if Paul had robbed Eve and been screwing Leelo, her solicitor would hunt down every penny he had, in dodgy cash or otherwise, and claim it for Rachel and her unborn child. Gerald Smithers would do it, too, with the help of "Young Mr. James."

A massive accumulator ... forty grand. Do I believe him? It sounded an awful lot of money to win in one bet. Could he have kept such a triumph secret?

There again, he'd admitted losing big bucks up until then.

That she *could* believe.

He'd certainly been very chipper in the summer, readily agreeing the purchase of the iPad for Eve out of the joint account. The high cost of the device had worried Rachel. That must also have been around the time she conceived ... which led her wandering, restless thoughts to her own condition.

Why had Paul mentioned Down's? It was the last thing on Rachel's mind. She'd parked the problem as she boarded the plane at Gatwick, planning to discuss it with Dr. Tomkins on her return home.

Listening to Robbie grunting and snorting brought it all to the forefront.

Should I risk an amniocentesis? What if it shows the baby to be normal and then I miscarry?

Conversely, supposing it confirms Down's?

She loved her brother and had done so since she first set eyes on him. She'd been less bothered about his condition than her parents. In the early months it wasn't even apparent to the untrained eye. He was a happy baby, gurgling and smiling like any other. His development was slow, of course, but Rachel, aged seven and with no experience of babies, didn't care. She was by his side to applaud as he sat up (six months), stood unsteadily holding on to his playpen (thirteen months), and uttered his first intelligible word ("doggie," at two years and four months).

Talk about mother's helper! Only too willing to share in the childcare: the dressing, the feeding, the bathing . . . she was big sister, and that was what big sisters did.

Brother Simon, being that much older, took less interest in Robbie. Aged twelve when Robbie was born, he was on the verge of adolescence, with his own issues. One of them the realisation he was gay, Rachel suspected.

Robbie grew up with Rachel as his standby mother, such as when Eve was ill with gallstones and went into hospital to have her gallbladder taken out.

The move to Hare House had proved a watershed. At first Robbie missed living with his mum, but he soon made friends and blossomed into an independent-minded, socially functional adult who almost passed for normal—whatever that was these days.

In recent years, as Eve's health declined, Rachel—and Paul, to be fair—had taken on a growing share of Robbie-care.

Could Rachel, approaching fifty, start again with a Down's son or daughter? Robbie would still be there, needing family support, both practical and financial, for as long as he lived.

And sad to contemplate, medical issues were likely to affect his quality of life and foreshorten it.

Caring for a Down's child was the easiest stage. Down's children invariably brought joy to their parents, and children need feeding and their bottoms wiped whether or not they have an extra copy of chromosome 21, that genetic stowaway in a single tiny twisted strand of DNA in each cell of their body that causes all the problems.

Society was more often the issue; other parents with "normal" children were reluctant to let their children mix with Down's kids. Segregation began at an early age, compounded by ignorance and prejudice. Rachel still heard the word "Mongol" used, particularly by the older generation. And what about that idiot Ricky Gervais, who'd posted jokes about "mongs" on Twitter alongside pictures of himself gurning, pulling his features into the shape of someone with Down's? At a stroke, he'd undone years of efforts to include Down's people in society, and given schoolchildren a hateful new term of abuse to fling around the playground.

Apart from the learning difficulties experienced by all Down's children, they faced a panoply of medical problems ranging from the mild, such as snoring, to the life-threatening, like congenital heart defects.

Adulthood brought new challenges and concerns. All relatives of those with Down's particularly dreaded dementia, ten times more common than among the general population. It was a cruel irony: thanks to better care and regular screening, people with Down's now often survived into their sixties, even seventies. Previous generations hadn't lived long enough for dementia to be a problem.

It was a rocky road for parents to travel at any age, never mind in their fifties. The fact that Rachel might be a single parent brought the choices into starker relief.

Robbie, having been quiet for some while, let out a sudden grunt.

Sleep apnoea. The sufferer stops breathing for up to a minute, then inhales with a snort that usually awakens them.

Rachel raised her head and listened, in case Robbie was awake and confused as to his whereabouts.

He started snoring gently again.

She turned on her back and pushed the ends of her pillow against each ear.

This is actually all about you, babe.

What had Paul meant by that curious pronouncement?

She so wanted to believe in him.

He'd been weak. Had he been unfaithful?

Weakness was forgivable. Provided he faced up to his gambling demons, she would support him.

He needed to cut down on the booze, though. Drink and gambling were a toxic brew of vices.

Rachel didn't think he was alcoholic, just a heavy drinker. A change of habits would set him on the right path.

No more nightly walkies to the Dog and Duck.

Turn left out of the front door instead of the other way.

Simple.

The birth of his baby would surely give him motivation to clean himself up.

For how long had Paul been on the wrong path, so to speak?

The death of his father, Peter: that was the turning point.

Paul had respected, even feared his dad. Up until the day he died from a massive heart attack, the old man kept an iron grip on the business, countersigning every cheque.

The firm passed to Paul, together with the bungalow in which they now lived.

The first thing Paul did was buy himself a brand-new 4x4. Rachel should have seen the warning signs then.

Poor decisions followed. A string of speculative projects brought more effort and worry than profit. Bread-and-butter work such as extensions, conservatories, and driveways dried up.

Rachel, with her own dance business booming, had relinquished hold of the admin to Kizzy. In hindsight, that was a mistake too. Giving Paul free rein with the money.

He'd capped it all by buying the row of derelict cottages at the local auction, not even telling Rachel he planned to bid.

He hadn't asked her about the cottages this evening, or mentioned the building business once. This Richard Shackloth fellow had seduced him with the promise of easy money.

Now Rachel started to overheat, smothered by the pillow wrapped around her head. She shoved it aside again.

How to handle Paul?

If he'd acted at all times in her interests, albeit misguidedly, he deserved her support.

Rachel was certain his story would be full of half-truths.

But deep down, can I still trust him?

He'd skipped without warning to Tallinn, in close company with an attractive, clever young woman from that city.

But people under mental duress did act crazy. Respectable professionals like doctors and lawyers did a "Reggie Perrin" and vanished. Some were found wandering and confused in shopping centres and railway stations.

Others — and this must be considered — killed themselves.

If Paul's problems came down to money, she'd cope with that. If the building business failed, she'd handle that. If he'd lost Mum's money on the horses ... that would be harder, but she knew she could cope with even that scenario, if only Paul loved her and wanted to be with her and the new baby.

She didn't want to return home without him, and it wouldn't be in his best interests.

Perhaps Leelo had turned his head by introducing him to the jet set. What had he termed them? *A-listers.*

Perhaps she had got him into her bed.

What man could have resisted?

If he'd weakened, maybe just once, was that forgivable? Possibly.

But he must confess.

He must tell the truth.

He must return to Earth from whatever mental planet he had jetted off to, then she'd decide.

Calmed by this rationalisation of her situation, she counted sheep up to four hundred, then danced her way through a rhumba and an Argentinian tango.

Stop snoring, Robbie love!

Wake him, or gently turn him on one side?

As if her thoughts had reached him by telepathy, her brother snorted once more, then heaved himself into a different position and lay quietly at last.

A few minutes later, Rachel drifted into the realm of sleep, where she dreamed of herself, in a white gown and ballet shoes, dancing alone around a deserted ballroom, while her baby slept in a cot in one corner.

The baby awoke and began to cry, or grunt, rather.

In the strange logic of her dream, Rachel had forgotten what her baby looked like, or even if it was a boy or a girl.

She crossed the ballroom to the cot on her points and looked down at her squealing infant.

It wasn't a baby at all.

Dressed in a Victorian nightdress, like that illustration from *Alice in Wonderland*, staring up at her, was a piglet.

It snorted.

She awoke in a sweat, her sheets tangled and damp, her pulse hammering.

Could I cope with a Down's child?

39

BREAKFAST WAS better than advertised. Rachel and Robbie helped themselves to fruit and cereal with yoghurt, followed by croissants and peach jam. Rachel sipped her caffeine ration.

She'd got back to sleep in the end, fatigue overcoming worry.

She didn't feel too bad, and Robbie seemed positively chipper.

"I'm meeting Paul alone this morning, love. Can you play on your Nintendo, or watch a movie for an hour or two?"

"Sure can, Sis. I think I'll watch"—he pretended to consider—"*Milo and Otis!* Where you seeing him?"

"Right here, in the breakfast room. We'll sit in the window."

"Give him hell, girl."

"I want him to tell the truth. Then we can move on."

"I hope Raffles is happy and not pining."

"He's at the best kennels in the country. Message Julia if you want."

"Is it cheap to use my mobile? I don't want a bill for three thousand pounds like Betty got in Orlando."

"You can text and check emails. Just don't watch any movies online."

"No need. I have them all with me. I love you, Rachel."

He rarely called her "Rachel."

"I love you too, little bro. Now, if you've had enough to eat, off you go. Paul will be here in twenty minutes."

"If you need me, text me under the table."

The hotel was lightly occupied, and with Robbie gone, Rachel was the only guest in the pleasant breakfast room.

She moved to the window and sat on a sofa. The arrangement of seating was the same as in the Willows, reminding her again of her first meeting with Detective Ryan.

How did he—and the police force—fit into all this? His suggestion of corruption at high levels was unsettling.

She fidgeted, worried that Paul had been sucked into an international crime syndicate.

She hadn't liked the look of Richard Shackloth one bit.

The breakfast waitress wiped the table they had vacated and pushed through the swing doors to the kitchen, leaving Rachel alone.

Paul showed up five minutes late. He looked better than the night before, with his salt-and-pepper hair washed and swept back from his high forehead, and wearing a clean shirt under his leather jacket.

"Good morning, Rachel."

"Hello, Paul. Would you like a coffee? Help yourself from the machine. I'm fine for now."

She watched as he fixed his drink. Even in his short time away, he'd put on weight. That would be the booze and restaurant food.

It felt at once completely normal and completely weird. Here was a man who looked like her husband of old, the husband she had lived with, slept with, conceived a baby with.

But he wasn't the same man.

He had changed, a caterpillar morphing into a butterfly, except in reverse. It was as if an alien had taken him over, like in another of Robbie's favourite movies, *Invasion of the Body Snatchers*.

Rachel's resolve faltered.

Do I really want him home? Can I ever trust him again?

He returned with an espresso and sat where she pointed, where she could see his face in a good light and he couldn't touch her.

"Robbie all right?" he asked.

"Yep."

"And you?"

"What do you think?"

"I guess not."

"Correct."

"I mean your health . . . the baby . . . ?"

"I didn't bring my blood-pressure monitor. I know the baby's alive, at least. I can feel movement. I'm taking my medication."

"Wow. That's great."

"No, it's not great. Now stop flannelling and trying to soft-soap me. Explain yourself, from the start."

Paul drained his coffee and set the cup down softly on the saucer. "I made bad calls. Now I've come good. I'm sorry about the business. Dad so wanted me to make a success of it."

"You're a skilled builder, Paul."

"Yeah. I can lay a level patio. I can tile a roof. I can plaster and paint and I'm not too shabby at the carpentry. I'm just shit with the money side of building. I realise that now. When Dad was alive, I resented him holding the purse strings. But I needed him."

"I understand. You miss him too, don't you?"

"Yes. After losing my mum so young an' all . . . which is when I started on the horses, looking back. Dad paid me a wage, I had no outgoings, I could have a flutter on the gee-gees and I got good: kept my nose in front. But I kicked it, babe. I haven't had a bet since the big win."

Rachel met his eyes. "You were on the computer the morning you scarpered. You logged into all the online bookies. I'm not stupid, Paul. Don't lie to me."

"I was closing the accounts. I got bigger fish to fry now."

"With your new A-list friends?"

He sat forward. "I believe I can be a successful investor. I'm learning fast from Richard."

"Why is that guy here? Why are *you* here, with Leelo, hanging around him like a lap dog?"

"He's shown me the way to a secure and prosperous future. He's kind of taken me under his wing."

"Why here?" Rachel repeated. "And what did you mean, this is all about me?"

"Richard gave me a list of the companies he invests in. He's a business angel, like that smooth bastard on *Dragons' Den*. Richard picks businesses and puts money into them in return for a stake. It's similar to backing a racehorse, but you get a share of the animal and all its future winnings, not just the winnings on one race like a punter does."

Rachel resisted the urge to roll her eyeballs. "I understand the concept. So what's this Richard character got you into?"

"I put my eighty grand into a company right here in Tallinn. It's a biomedical outfit, run by an Estonian scientist and a Russian engineer. Richard insisted I see the facilities, meet the founders. Babe, they specialise in genetic research for human reproduction. Get this: they are world leaders in Down's syndrome screening."

Rachel said, "You've known I am pregnant for under two weeks. This is all bullshit, Paul. You've had no time to set up anything to help with my condition. If you did have contacts in that area of medicine, why didn't you tell me back home?"

"It all happened so fast. You would never have let me do this. I had to take a flyer, come out here, and check it for myself. I've done that. It's all kosher. The beauty of it is, because I'm an important shareholder, they'll treat you free." With a flourish, he produced a business card and laid it on the table.

"Tamm Bok Genomics Services," announced the card, which was stiff and glossy. "Advancing the Human Race." The visuals comprised chemical symbols and diagrams of molecules.

"My doctor has it all under control," Rachel said, turning the card over in her fingers. "What can they do here that they can't in the King Edward?"

Paul laughed. "The National Health Service is twenty years behind the curve. They're still in the Jurassic era compared to these dudes. Apart from what you already had, the only test available if you go home is an amniocentesis. We both know that's risky. At least a five percent chance of a miscarriage at your age. Maybe ten."

"So what does this outfit offer?" All Rachel's instincts put her on guard.

Paul sat back, more at ease now. "The fastest, most reliable, comprehensive screening service for all major foetal genetic abnormalities. Completely noninvasive. You give a small blood sample. They extract the baby's DNA, grow it in a test tube, and see if it's got the right number of bits. They don't just screen for Down's, they pick up other bad stuff too."

"Why couldn't I get this back home?" Rachel repeated.

"The NHS doesn't provide it and won't any time soon. You have to go private. They send your blood sample to America or Switzerland. It takes much longer. And it costs up to a thousand pounds. Time isn't on our side, babe. We need to know *now* that our baby is healthy and normal."

Rachel bridled at the word. "Are you saying Robbie isn't normal?"

"You know what I mean. Genetically normal. Don't pretend. I love him too, but do we want another Down's child in the family?"

Rachel, who had asked herself the same question in the small hours of the night, could not argue. "You say the test costs a thousand pounds. That's not much to a high roller like you, Paulie." She caught herself using his pet name.

Stay detached.

He spoke with quiet urgency now, warming to his theme. "The money's nothing. I'd lay out the whole eighty grand to look after you and baby. It's about technology, and speed, and thoroughness. These guys can follow up straightaway if the test is positive, to confirm for sure, with the world's safest amniocentesis. They use a graphene-coated asymmetric needle only ten gauges thick. I got the leaflets. I studied it good."

Rachel pushed her hair behind her ears and leaned forward. "If your wonderful new friend and mentor Richard Shackloth has my interests so much at heart, he showed it in a strange way last night."

"The rich can be like that. They don't have to be polite to anyone. Your sudden appearance amused him, and he enjoyed the show."

"So if you're a businessman now, what were you doing in the sports bar of the casino?"

"Just keeping Richard company. You gotta stay close to these people."

"You say Leelo and he are an item?"

"Yes."

"She's half his age."

"So what? He's a big entrepreneur. He's got a yacht and stuff. He can pull younger birds."

"Leelo seems to be more than totty. She worked for the Estonian government, they seconded her to the British Treasury. She's a high flyer. Why would she take up with a jerk like Richard Sackcloth?"

"Shackloth. He may be a jerk, but he's a serious player."

"Why would she tolerate being laughed at? He didn't even get out of his seat when I soaked her."

"I told you, the rich are different. I'm getting another espresso. Anything for you, babe?"

"They have a ginger infusion in the box on top."

"Right-oh."

Rachel was grateful for a moment to think.

His story was so preposterous that it could just be true.

Paul had first learned of her pregnancy in the hospital. That was Thursday afternoon, after the cremation service.

The next Monday, the day she was discharged, he was on his computer Googling flights to Tallinn.

Does he expect me to believe he set up an investment in an Estonian biomedical company over that weekend, with the sole aim of getting me better tests and diagnoses than in the United Kingdom?

He returned with a second espresso for himself and a tall mug with a string and label hanging over the side for her.

"Why didn't you just *tell* me all this? Instead of leaving me sitting by my bed in the hospital, waiting for you to pick me up?"

"I handled it badly. I see that now. I did leave a note."

Rachel opened her bag and took out the piece of paper in question. She unfolded it and held it in front of his nose. "This was the last I heard from you until I got the text. I waited all week for you to call me, Paul. I tried to text and phone you. You put me through a hell of worry, on top of my pregnancy complications. Not to mention saddling me with four demolished cottages. What were you thinking?"

He drained his espresso in one gulp. "It all got too much. I wanted to help you, but you would never have approved this trip. As for the cottages, yeah, that was a cock-up. I owe Kizzy an apology too. But you gotta trust me, babe. I was about to call you, saying come over to meet me. You jumped the gun."

"What would you have done in my position? Sat at home feeling sick? I had the detective all ready to put out a missing-person alert. Finally you deigned to send that text . . ."

"I didn't send no text."

Rachel unzipped her bag and withdrew her phone. She swiped to Messages and held the screen out to Paul. She read aloud in a sarcastic tone. "Hi darling! Sorry outta contact so long—phone playing up big time. All sorted back home soon luv u missing u xxx."

"I didn't write that."

"It came from your phone. Where is your phone? Who's had access to it? This message was your attempt to keep me in England."

"I lost my phone. I left it in the toilet at arrivals, I think. Somebody stole it. I put it down on a shelf above the basin while I dried my hands. I'm sure I did. I walked straight out, through passport control, got outside the terminal, patted my pockets, and realised. I went back but they wouldn't let me airside. I filled in a form. I haven't heard since."

Rachel looked in her husband's eyes. "Why didn't you cancel the phone?"

"I hoped it would be found. If so, I wanted it working. To call you, babe."

Rachel could take no more. "Other people have phones you could have borrowed. You could have bought a phone and a SIM. Hotels have phones, and PCs connected to the internet. They even still have payphones. There's one in reception over there. It is not difficult to get a message to your wife."

"Just confused ... not thinking straight. Yeah, you're right."

"When I mislay my mobile at home, I call it from another phone. Simple! Shall we try that with yours? We might even hear it ringing."

"No, babe. Don't ... ." But Rachel had her own phone out again.

She pressed Call, and a second later the familiar ringtone sounded from Paul's leather jacket. He took out his phone and cancelled the call.

Rachel said, "You are a lying bastard, and there is no reason I should believe a word you say."

"Fair enough, but I didn't personally send the text. It was just easier—"

"Easier to make up any old story rather than tell the truth? How many other lies have you told me today ... last night ... for the last twenty-five years?"

"None, babe. Honest. I swear on our baby's life—"

"Don't you dare bring my baby into this. And for God's sake stop calling me 'babe.' You've patronised me ever since we got married, kept me in the dark, gambled and drank behind my back. I've been the major breadwinner for the last two years, and you never gave me credit for my hard work."

"Yeah. Sorry."

She could feel her blood pressure rocketing.

As if in protest at having his or her name taken in vain, her baby shifted position.

She carried on in a level, calm tone, but inside, fury at her betrayal burned bright and hot. "You abandoned your business and vanished, for reasons I still don't understand. Instead of contacting me, you flew here, leaving your precious bloody customised vanity-plated pickup in the short-term car park racking up fifty pounds a day in charges, you hired a car here, since when you've bummed around in the casino all day and night, drinking, gambling, having a high old time. And you have the gall to spin me a story about medical testing. I can never trust you again, Paul. I don't believe what you've told me. I don't know what's going on between you and Leelo, but it stinks. For all I know, you, Sackcloth, and Leelo are having a threesome. You're not the man I married, the man I loved."

She stood up.

"I'm leaving you here, returning to London and then home, which will be *my* home from now on. You'll be hearing from my solicitor. Don't expect to have anything to do with my baby except paying the bills for its upbringing and education for the rest of your deadbeat life."

Paul stood too. He reached out both hands. Rachel backed away.

He said, "I know I've blown it, Rache. I know I've been flaky. But the stuff about the clinic is true. One day the full story will come out. I hoped it would be today, but you've made it clear you don't want to listen."

"I listened. What I heard was a mixture of lies, half-truths, and pure fantasy. You as a big-time investor! It would be funny if it wasn't so pathetic. Your idea of an investment is a hundred pounds on a dog at Nottingham."

"Fair do's. I haven't been a good husband these last weeks. For our baby's sake, I beg you, take the card and check out the clinic. Have a look around. Speak to the staff. Ask to see the equipment. What's to lose? They're expecting you, your bills are taken care of, and the test just means a tiny prick on the arm and a small sample of blood. Can you go home without doing that, Rachel?"

"It can't be that simple."

"It is. I don't expect you to believe me again, but Leelo could explain. She's more technical than I am."

"Leelo? I trust her even less than I trust you. I'm more certain than ever that you and she robbed Mum of her life savings."

"No, no, we didn't. That's completely wrong. All we did was help Eve."

"What do you mean, help her?"

Paul stammered, "I—I—we—"

"You stole her money, didn't you?"

"No. Not a penny. No way. Your mum explained what happened. Some conman, then the bank screwed up, then the police—"

"I'm going home to start divorce proceedings. Goodbye, Paul." Rachel snatched her handbag, drew herself up to her full height, and marched towards the exit, leaving her husband, with a look of pure desperation on his sweaty face, rooted to the spot, his arms held wide apart like the sculpture the *Angel of the North*.

40

RACHEL AND ROBBIE lunched in another Hesburger, this one within walking distance of the hotel. The snow had relented, leaving slushy puddles on the roads and pavements. The temperature hovered just above freezing.

Robbie hadn't brought footwear suitable for the cold and wet. His training shoes were soaked through, Rachel noticed guiltily. And he was prone to athlete's foot. She had been mad to bring him, as Paul had said.

"So we leave without Paulie?"

"Yes. Oh, that's our order." The server at the counter beckoned. Robbie lumbered up to collect the paper bags and polystyrene mugs. It was an unsuitable diet for a mum-to-be, but Rachel had higher priorities. She needed to get Robbie home, take stock, and start divorce proceedings.

She must see her doctor. This crazy trip had done nothing for her health.

Robbie sorted out the burgers and fries between them. Rachel uncapped her paper mug of water.

"Have we got time to do the KGB Exit Room? They lock you in and you have to find the clues to get out."

"You told me, love. I don't know. This afternoon I'll check flight times and book our return tickets."

"It looks really cool, and has a hundred and fifty-nine 'Excellent' reviews on TripAdvisor."

"The Old Town is worth visiting too, but I'm not in the mood for sightseeing. So we'll do the KGB Room if there's time, I promise."

"Yay!" Robbie thrust the flyer back into his pocket. "I texted Julia. Raffles is fine. He sends his love with a woof and a wag!"

"Paul didn't even ask about him," Rachel murmured.

"Why won't he come home? He loves Raffles."

"I don't want him home. He's got involved with Leelo and that man, and despite his blustering assurances, I still suspect them of stealing Mum's money. Though Paul protests his innocence and insists that Leelo and the ghastly Shackloth are the item."

"In that case, what's keeping Paul here?"

"Business."

"Monkey business?"

"For sure."

Rachel's phone pinged. She dived for her bag. *Why? Do I hope it's Paul, texting his remorse?*

"It's Kizzy, wanting an update."

"What you going to tell her?"

"Just the essentials. I'm booking our return flights and Paul won't be with us."

Robbie wiped his hands on a paper napkin. "I could get used to the food here. Not sure about the weather." While they had been in the restaurant, the sky outside had darkened with the prospect of renewed snow. It hadn't got properly light at all so far that day. He continued, "Won't you let me speak to Paulie, man to man? I'll get the truth out of him."

"Thanks, love, but no. He's past caring about us."

"What about the baby? Doesn't he care about my new nephew or niece? I'd like a niece, by the way."

Rachel smiled. "I'll do my best." She considered a moment. She hadn't told Robbie about the clinic and Paul's plea for her to investigate it.

Can you go home without checking it out? he'd said.

Could she?

She sniffed the air and looked around for anything lavender scented or coloured, but to no avail.

Make up your own mind, Rachel Phelps!

After a moment's hesitation, she reached into her bag and handed the business card across the shiny red table.

He studied it. "What's genom . . . genomics, Sis?"

"The study of the human gene, the code that each of us carries in every cell of our body. DNA."

"The code that's a bit different in me? T21?"

"Yes."

"Paul gave you this?"

"Yes again. He said he was an investor in the business."

"I don't want a niece with T21. They're not all as clever or athletic as me back at Hare House. Thelma is thick and Freddie can't breathe very well. I'm lucky. I'm perfect." He breathed on his fingernails and mimed polishing them. "Can these people tell if your baby is all right?"

"Paul says so."

"That's more important than escaping from the KGB, isn't it?"

"Yes, but—"

"They won't upload your mind like in *Avatar*?"

"I guess not."

Robbie slurped his Coke. Outside, heavy snow began to fall, the sky as dark as Rachel's mood.

A tiny prick on the arm and a small sample of blood.

She didn't want Robbie out and about in this weather, and she had no wish to be locked into any room, let alone a KGB Exit Room.

So, rationalising that it was for Robbie's benefit, and because he'd already suggested it, she said, "I'll check out the clinic on the internet. We won't have time for attractions as well."

"No worries, Sis. I have to finish watching *Milo and Otis* anyway."

Robbie tipped the waste into the bin and they trudged back to the hotel in swirling, puffy snow that clung to their coats in messy blobs. In their room, Rachel made sure that Robbie washed and dried his feet and put on clean socks. He'd brought his bedroom slippers, so that was fine. She placed his wet trainers upside down on the radiator, where they began to steam odorously, and hung up his hoodie in the bathroom.

"I'll be downstairs, on the computer."

Her brother, busy with his portable DVD player, half turned his head. "Sure, Sis."

She rode down to the first floor where a small lounge, unoccupied at this hour of the afternoon, provided a desk and PC.

She typed "Tamm Bok Genomics Services" into Google.

Many of the results linked to research papers published by the two founders. Rachel scanned the abstracts. They meant nothing to her, but they showed that the founders were serious scientists.

She clicked on the firm's website and selected the Union Jack logo for the English version.

Tamm Bok had two arms: the research company and the clinic. Each complemented the other. Research in the lab carried over into clinical trials. Some of these used volunteers. Once approved to European Union standards, the clinic offered the treatments and tests commercially, ploughing the profits from these activities back into research.

Tamm Bok claimed to be at the forefront of *in vitro* fertilisation, or IVF. Photos showed proud parents holding shiny infants conceived with the help of their advanced fertility techniques.

She found the section on foetal screening. The story was the same as Paul had told; he had memorised whole chunks of copy from the website. She clicked through to a technical drawing of the amniocentesis needle developed by the lab. Graphene-tipped, 10 gauge, ensuring a clean penetration of the abdominal wall and amniotic membrane with a 75 percent reduction in cell trauma.

Even reading about it made her feel faint.

Where was the company based? The science park.

This was the largest such park in the Baltic, with over two hundred tech companies. There was a business incubator programme for start-ups, with funding from the EU. They emphasised information technology, green technology, and healthcare.

She watched a short video. Everything looked glossy and futuristic.

Rachel had to admit that the facilities rather eclipsed those in her local hospital.

She wavered. *What's to be lost? A blood test can't harm me.*

She could take the results back to Dr. Tomkins.

She turned the business card over and over, tapping its edges on the computer desk.

She got up, walked around the tiny lounge, and sat down again.

Heart pounding, she took out her phone and dialled the number for private individuals seeking prenatal and fertility services.

A pleasant female voice answered, in Estonian and then, before Rachel could speak, in English. "Tamm Bok Health Clinic, how may I help you?"

"Oh . . . my name is Rachel Phelps. My husband, Paul, gave me your card. I'm pregnant and I am interested in your foetal screening."

"Certainly, Mrs. Phelps. Everything is prebooked for you. How soon can you come in?"

"Right now? I'm sorry it's short notice, but I need to return to London. I'm here with my brother who has Down's syndrome, and he's outside his comfort zone."

"I understand. Can you be ready in half an hour?"

"I guess . . . I'm not sure how long it will take in the taxi. I'm in Lasnamäe."

"We'll send a car for you. Please confirm you are staying at the Raadiku Hotel, Mrs. Phelps?"

"Yes. How did you—"

"The car will be with you within thirty minutes. A black Mercedes saloon."

"Was Paul right—I won't have to pay?"

"Yes, he's taken care of all that with the directors."

"Do I need to bring anything? How long will I be there? I can't leave Robbie for hours and hours."

"We just need you and your bump. There will be paperwork, an exam, and ultrasound. You'll see the haematologist to give your samples, then we'll drive you back to the hotel. Tell your brother to expect you by five this evening."

"What about the results?"

"One day."

"Can you send them through to my doctor in the UK?"

"Of course. So we'll pick you up in half an hour? Any more questions?"

"No. I'll be ready."

So slick. So professional. They had been expecting my call. They'd even known where I was staying.

She logged off and returned to their room.

Robbie was sound asleep, snoring. Dudley Moore's unctuous narration issued from the flat-screen television on the wall.

Rachel touched her brother on the shoulder.

"Oh, Sis. I nodded off." He raised his head. "I'll rewind fifteen minutes." He rubbed his eyes and felt around for the DVD remote.

"I'm off to the clinic, love. I'll be back by five. You stay here in the room with your movies." She paused, then added, "Don't leave the hotel. I'll hang the Do Not Disturb sign on the knob. Don't answer the door if anyone knocks. Keep your phone handy, and text me at once if anything strange happens."

Robbie's eyes opened wide. "What are you worried about, Sis?"

"I'm not worried. I want to be certain you are safe here and haven't gone out in the wet and snow."

"Right-oh. Stay in the room, don't answer the door. I copy we're in lockdown."

41

THE CAR ARRIVED, a big black beast with tinted windows such as a reclusive film star might choose. The driver, uniformed and capped, stepped out to open a rear door for Rachel.

She did a double take. "Andrus! We meet again! What a coincidence!"

If he was surprised, his face didn't betray it. "I work for Tamm Bok some days and taxi the others. The clinic helped me and my wife to have our baby. They would take no payment. I said, 'May I do driving at least, to show my appreciation?'" He looked Rachel in the eye. "Did you take another cab to return here last night? I waited for your call the longest while. A little concerned."

"Sorry, I should have let you know. We met my husband and he drove us back."

"He is minding your brother, I guess?"

"Something like that."

"Please get in, you will feel the cold."

Andrus gave a commentary as they sped through the urban landscape. "We're running alongside the lake, but you can't see it behind the pine trees. Notice the cycle lane? That's the old railroad line. Cycling is big here. It's all flat with plenty of dedicated tracks . . ."

Meanwhile, Rachel worried about whether his reappearance was a coincidence or not. She leaned back and tried to relax.

The reception area at the clinic was light and cheerful, with playthings for young children at one end. All was new, clean, and bright. Unusually for such a place, it didn't smell of surgical spirit or disinfectant.

No other clients waited, but a few technicians and lab assistant types scurried through as Rachel glanced about her.

The receptionist took her coat, sat her down, and handed her a long form to fill in. Name, address, date of birth, email, whether she had undergone fertility treatment, whether she'd had previous abnormal pregnancies or miscarriages, whether she'd experienced early bleeding, which could have been a "vanishing twin" pregnancy—she had—what medication she was on, consent to the tests, and data release.

She completed everything and handed it in, feeling like a schoolgirl submitting an exam paper. A few minutes later, a white-coated man appeared. Young, like all the staff that Rachel had seen so far: early thirties, she guessed. He approached Rachel with a friendly smile and they shook hands. He introduced himself as Dr. Yevstigneyev. She glanced down to his name badge. He said, "Don't worry, many of my colleagues can't pronounce it either. You can call me Stig. How would you prefer me to address you?" His eyes were startling: a piercing blue, even bluer than Paul's. His complexion was fair, his skin smooth as a child's. Somehow, he already had a copy of her form.

"Rachel is fine."

He led her to a windowless room equipped with couch, washbasin, and scales.

"Slip off your shoes and jumper, and I'll measure your height and weight."

This accomplished, he produced the device she had grown to dread, tightened the Velcro cuff around her upper arm, pumped, and listened through his stethoscope.

"It's 154 over 99. Too high for comfort. I will measure again later and administer a supplementary injection if needed." He unwound the cuff. "The Noninvasive Pregnancy Test, NIPT for short, will give a probability that your pregnancy is affected by one of three syndromes: Down, or Down's as you call it, Edwards, and Patau. Do you wish me to explain these?"

"Down's is my main concern. My brother has it."

"So you are already informed about the condition and you know it is not normally inherited. First, we will perform an ultrasound scan. We will date your pregnancy again and compare our findings with what you were told in the United Kingdom. We need to be sure you are not carrying twins. We should also be able to determine the gender, but I see you ticked the box to say you don't wish to know?"

"That's right."

"The sonographer will note any structural abnormalities apparent from the scan. Hopefully none. Then we take two small blood specimens. One is for testing, the second is for reserve in the unusual event that the first test fails."

"How might it fail?"

"If we don't gather enough markers for your baby's DNA. It doesn't mean you are positive, it means the test hasn't given a result. We then retry with the backup specimen. We will have a result from the first sample well within twenty-four hours, the fastest turnaround for this procedure anywhere in the world." Rachel could hear the pride in his voice. "Using the spare sample will add another day. To date, we've never failed to produce a result once we include the backup."

"Does the test say for certain that my baby is normal?"

"It's not quite that simple. We are screening, not diagnosing. The results will be in the form of probabilities. We give a different number for each trisomy. A normal result will show a very low risk of your pregnancy being affected; maybe one in ten thousand. As negligible as the chance of snow in London in July." He smiled, and his bright-blue eyes held hers in an unwavering gaze. The combination of his fixed stare and his baby-faced complexion was unnerving. He reminded Rachel of the androids in one of Robbie's movies. "A high-risk result might give a probability as great as one in two of being affected. In that event, we will need to discuss the options. We would recommend you follow up with an invasive test called an amniocentesis, which I am sure you have heard of?"

"Yes."

"Just to let you know, Rachel, should that be necessary, we can conduct it here. Although the procedure carries a small risk of miscarriage, we have never had a client suffer that in over two hundred tests carried out in the past three years. We use an advanced technique and equipment patented by Dr. Tamm."

"I'll bear that in mind. How will you let me know the results?"

"Many mothers-to-be opt to have a phone call, with a written copy of the findings emailed to their doctor. For you, it would be better to return to the clinic and get the results in person, with your husband."

"I'll think about that too. I was hoping to fly home tomorrow."

"You might want to delay your return home, just in case. Discuss it with your husband. No need to decide now. Do you have questions?"

"No."

"Then let's take you down to Agnetha, who is waiting to perform your ultrasound."

Agnetha was a petite, almost birdlike woman with thin, straight, mousy hair and round spectacles, as friendly as everyone else in the clinic. She turned on music, which Rachel recognised at Tchaikovsky's *Nutcracker*. Rachel lay back on the couch and shrieked as the operator applied the cold gel to her tummy. They both laughed.

Rachel looked down.

Can I see a bump? Hard to be sure.

There was definite thickening of her midriff, but that could be her recent junk diet.

She watched the big monitor on the wall as Agnetha moved the probe and pressed keys on her machine.

Dotted lines appeared as she measured Rachel's baby. There wasn't much to see in this mode. Then her baby's heartbeat sounded out in the room, accompanied by a trace along the bottom of the screen.

"We're too late for the nuchal transparency or nasal bone tests, but I note you had those back home. Why couldn't the sonographer get a clear view? Did she say?"

"She said the baby was on the borderline of being too big."

"That makes sense. I calculate you're at seventeen weeks now. He or she is a lively little thing. Are you feeling some bumps?"

"Yes. Perhaps baby will be a dancer, like me."

Appropriately, "The Waltz of the Flowers" was playing.

"Every possibility. Shall we have a look at those moves?" The sonographer switched to a full-colour, 3D view. Rachel gasped at the detail and clarity. Her baby was squirming around, clasping and unclasping tiny hands.

Agnetha said, "Baby is waving at us!"

"Oh my." Tears of joy filled Rachel's eyes as she watched, transfixed by the moving pictures of the precious life growing within her.

The images were so clear and colourful she felt she could reach out to the screen and touch the baby, even take gentle hold of one of its perfect little fingers. Despite herself, she looked for signs of the gender of her unborn child. Her untrained eye couldn't make out any distinguishing features, and Agnetha was giving nothing away.

The waltz played on. Baby seemed to move in time to the music for a few seconds.

The sonographer made notes on her clipboard, pressed keys on her instrument, and said, "Finished! I see nothing to raise concerns. Baby looks in great shape. I cannot see chromosomal abnormalities with this equipment, only signs that may indicate them, and those are not present, although the foetus is too big for the main checks. That's where the blood test steps in, to give a probability, as I'm sure the director explained. Now let's wipe up my messy gel. I'll call the haematologist to take your bloods in here, to save you getting dressed and undressed again. Would you like me to email you a movie of the scan to show your family and friends?"

"Yes please." Rachel lay back and smiled, more relaxed than she had been for weeks. Agnetha wiped her tummy with wads of paper towelling and left the room. Moments later, another technician appeared.

She was younger, in her twenties, with the blonde hair, wide mouth, and full lips that seemed to characterise the Estonian female. She had a Slavic look around the eyes. Unlike the other staff Rachel had encountered, this girl wore a stony expression.

She was Helena, according to her name tag, and the first thing she did was turn off the music. "I will take two samples," she intoned, avoiding eye contact as she swabbed Rachel's inner elbow with an antiseptic wipe.

"This is a nice facility you have here. It's far posher than in my country," Rachel ventured, but the girl merely said, "Please hold still for me. A small pinprick coming."

Rachel looked away.

"All done. I suggest you sit for a few moments in case of faintness, then make your way back to reception. Turn left out of the door."

The technician applied a plaster to Rachel's arm, then she was gone in a flurry of white coat, clipboard, and test tubes.

That was brusque to the point of rudeness, Rachel thought. *Perhaps not a good time of the month for her. Or boyfriend trouble.*

She did as instructed, listening to the hum of the air-conditioning and reliving the images of her baby doing that funny hand-jive.

She needed the loo. They hadn't wanted her to go before the ultrasound, as it made it easier to see the baby if her bladder was full. The prodding and pushing of the probe had combined with the large glass of mineral water she'd accepted on arrival to make her distinctly uncomfortable now.

She shrugged on her jumper, retrieved her handbag, and opened the door.

Which way?

Reception was to the left, but she had an idea the toilets were farther down the corridor, to the right.

A little strange she'd been abandoned in the ultrasound suite. Didn't Stig want to recheck her BP?

She turned right. The brightly lit passageway stretched ahead, then there was a T-junction.

Now which way?

No signs gave any clue.

The doors bore cryptic labels in Estonian, or numbers.

Where is everybody?

She proceeded down the side corridor and came to the next junction.

This place is like a rabbit warren!

She turned again, lost and a touch panicky. She was well out of the patient area now and into the research department. She passed a door displaying a yellow-and-black radiation warning sign. Another silently screamed "BIOHAZARD."

She needed directions. Here was a door ajar, with lights on inside. She knocked gingerly.

No reply.

She opened the door wider.

It was an office and laboratory. Complicated equipment with computer terminals occupied the length of the wall. One machine looked like a photocopier but wasn't. She took in arrays of tiny glass dishes, two machines that resembled drinks dispensers but had test tubes under them instead of mugs, a Perspex-sided box that could be an incubator, a shiny sink, and three microscopes.

In a corner stood a desk with a laptop open and running. Above it was a stainless-steel notice board filled with pictures and papers attached by coloured mini-magnets. There were dozens of photographs of athletes, male and female, of all nationalities. Many of the photos were of the London Olympics.

Runners, hurdlers, jumpers, javelin throwers: the whole range of track and field athletics was represented. Plus swimmers and ice skaters.

Underneath these were several photos of Asian-looking tribes in colourful national costume.

Perhaps they also deal with sports medicine here, or conduct antidoping tests?

Anyway, there was no one to direct her and she was bursting for a wee by now.

Rachel backed out and retraced her steps. The obvious solution was to follow the illuminated exit signs to reception and start again.

She had a nasty moment trying to remember which way she'd turned. The fire exit signs didn't help: they seemed to point in all directions. You could escape many ways. She took a deep breath and set off again. Then she reached familiar territory and soon came back to the treatment rooms. She'd only needed to turn left out of the ultrasound suite and she would have arrived at the toilets within a few paces.

She entered the Ladies. Inside were three stalls, the leftmost one occupied, a red circle by its latch. She took the rightmost stall, closed the door silently, undid her jeans, sat down, and relieved herself.

A noise came from whoever was in the far cubicle.

She froze.

And heard it again.

Only somebody blowing their nose.

Then the nose-blowing was followed by the faint but unmistakable sound of sobbing: small, jerky breaths in and out, with little whimpers in between.

Instantly back on edge, Rachel held her breath.

The occupant of the end cubicle was in distress.

A patient who'd received bad news, most probably. A mother-to-be like herself, only an unlucky one.

Nothing to do with Rachel; but curiosity and concern united to root her to the seat, quiet and immobile.

The sobbing continued, now accompanied by little phrases in Estonian or Russian. It sounded as if the woman was scolding herself.

Rachel waited until the whimpering and self-reproach ceased. After more rustling, the toilet flushed and the door latch clicked open.

Rachel pulled up her jeans, waved her hand to flush her own toilet, opened the door, and stepped out.

Facing her was Helena the haematologist.

She looked very different to the stony-faced professional who'd attended Rachel ten minutes earlier. Her bottom lip quivered, and her eyes were moist.

Rachel's mouth fell open. "Are you all right?" she asked, as you do even when you can see that someone is definitely *not* all right.

"Yes, madam. Of course. I thought you would have left by now."

"What's the problem? Is it to do with me?" Rachel stepped over to rinse her hands.

The clinician stole a glance at Rachel in the washbasin mirror, then looked away. "Everything is just fine and perfect."

"Have you tested my samples? Is anything wrong? Did Agnetha see something on my scan?"

"No, no, madam. Your samples have gone for analysis. And I know nothing of your ultrasound. Please, leave at once."

"You don't look well," Rachel persisted. "You should go home."

"No! I am perfectly well. I have a touch of allergy. To the powder on the gloves. Do not concern yourself."

Rachel saw in the mirror that the girl clutched papers in her right hand, which she was attempting to conceal behind her back.

Not very hygienic to take those into the toilet.

But Helena probably hadn't used the toilet, had just come in here for the privacy.

Are those my records?

Helena advanced towards Rachel. "I will show you the way back to reception, madam."

Rachel stood her ground. "Aren't you going to wash your hands?" she enquired.

"You made me forget," the woman countered, directing a sulky look at Rachel.

"Why were you crying in there?"

"I was sniffing, not crying. Why are you being so unpleasant? Please let me pass."

"I thought you wanted to wash your hands?"

With an exasperated exhalation, Helena turned, placed her sheaf of paperwork on the shelf above the basins, and ran the tap.

Rachel, acting out of character, which she could only justify through a vague suspicion of the other woman's behaviour, lunged forward.

Helena, her hands in the basin, washing them in the clinically approved manner, had no opportunity to resist as Rachel snatched the papers, turned, and stepped into the stall she had just vacated. Inside, she flipped the lock.

A shriek from Helena was followed by hammering on the toilet door. "Those are confidential client records! Give them back this moment or I shall call security!"

Rachel, sitting on the toilet lid, flicked through the sheets. "I don't think so, Helena," she called. "You should never have taken these out of the laboratory."

"They are my notes! What are you doing?"

The three pages were handwritten. Helena had ruled in six columns in ballpoint pen, headed:

Фамилия	вес	высоты	+	-	?

The first column contained women's names, some in regular English letters, others in Cyrillic. Amelia Richter, Liisa Koppel, Kristine Balodis, Jane Doe...

The second column contained numbers between 1.3 and 1.9. The third column contained numbers between 41 and 90, the majority in the 50s and 60s. For each woman except the final one on the list there was a handwritten pencil tick in one of the three rightmost columns.

The names meant nothing to Rachel—except the last, which was her own.

42

THE ASSAULT on the toilet door continued. As Rachel had anticipated, the woman hadn't gone for help.

Rachel opened her door. Helena grabbed the papers. "You must not tell!"

"I will not tell if *you* tell me what this is all about."

Helena stuffed the papers into the pocket of her white coat. "They are my working notes. Confidential client data. You should not have taken them."

"Perhaps not, but now I've seen my name on the list I demand to know what they're about."

The other woman turned her head, listening. "You will tell no one?"

"What is the list?"

"I meet you later. Not here. In town. You go now."

"How do I know you will show up?"

"They are coming!"

Rachel too heard approaching footsteps.

Helena thrust the notes back at Rachel. "Here. Hide them. Tell no one! Then you can be sure I will come. Quick. Into your handbag. Hurry, hurry!"

Rachel unclasped her bag and slipped the papers inside as the door of the cloakroom opened.

Yevstigneyev's piercing gaze took in the situation. His eyes were extraordinary: it was as if he'd had blue LEDs implanted in his eyeballs. "Is everything all right? Helena? Rachel?"

"Yes, Director, all is in order," Helena replied.

"I got stuck in the toilet," Rachel said. "The latch jammed. It was all very comical. Helena set me free with a little brute force."

"I will tell maintenance," Helena added.

"Which door?"

"The right-hand one," Rachel said.

Yevstigneyev entered the stall, closed the door, slid the latch, and the red circle appeared. He reopened the door. "Seems fine. Are you sure nothing else is amiss? I heard shouts and quite a commotion."

"The noise was me," Rachel said. "I got a little panicky when I was trapped. I couldn't work out which way to turn the catch. I think I jammed it myself. All's well."

Yevstigneyev stood for a moment, looking from woman to woman. "Your driver awaits," he said to Rachel. "Come."

In the black Mercedes, Rachel flopped back against the squashy leather and tried to calm her racing heartbeat.

What had that all been about? Why had Helena been by turns brusque, then tearful, then aggressive, and finally panic-stricken?

She realised Yevstigneyev had forgotten to recheck her blood pressure. Perhaps she should telephone Dr. Tomkins tomorrow for advice.

Andrus was silent on the return journey, and Rachel didn't speak either. Outside, darkness encroached. Cars turned on their headlights, illuminating snowflakes that fell softly, quietening the noise of the tyres so that the inside of the luxury car felt as cosy and quiet as the womb.

Perhaps the haematologist is neurotic.

Anyway, it makes no difference, Rachel realised.

She'd reached her decision.

She texted Robbie:

On my way back. All fine.

She stared out of the window. The grey tower blocks flashed by. She closed her eyes and relived the ultrasound pictures of her baby waving.

Her phone pinged.

CU soon Sis.

They'd spend a final night in the Raadiku, then fly home.

43

SHE FOUND ROBBIE in the same position as she'd left him, on his bed, *Milo and Otis* playing softly on the TV. He'd had time to watch the whole thing through twice. Perhaps he had.

But Robbie announced, "Paulie was here."

"He came here? Into our room?"

"Yes. He said it was important, about you."

"He tricked his way in and talked to you?"

"I know you told me to let no one in, but Paul isn't no one. I thought you might have had an accident."

"What did he want?"

"He said he's done nothing wrong. He and Leelo did meet up back home but only to plan this trip. He doesn't understand why you don't believe him."

This was not what Rachel needed. Robbie was eminently suggestible. Paul had no right to use his brother-in-law as a go-between.

"Will you give him one more chance, Sis?"

"Paul has behaved badly, love. Disappearing from home, hanging out in casinos . . . claiming it's all for my benefit."

"He did line up the clinic for you, though."

Yes, and that's not all it seems, Rachel wanted to say. But she bit her tongue.

"How did you get on? Have you had the tests?"

"Yes. They gave me an ultrasound, which showed the baby moving around."

"Does it look like a proper baby, or all globby like an alien?"

"It looks like a little baby. Every feature is formed and perfect and lovely. Just tiny. They're sending me the files to play on the computer. We'll watch together."

"Paul wants to see you again. He was real upset, Sis."

"Maybe later, back home. Not here. Not after the way he behaved. I'm angry he came here and worked on you, love."

"Right-oh." Robbie turned to the TV.

"Did you tell Paul where I was?"

"He knew. I thought perhaps you told him."

"No. He must have found out from Leelo or Shackloth."

"Whatever. Does it matter?"

She let it pass. "I'm going down to the PC room to book our return flights."

"What about our tea? Can we eat at the Hesburger again? I haven't tried their chicken nuggets yet."

"I'll order something in by phone. It's cold and snowing hard out there. Look, your trainers are still steaming."

Down in the lounge, she was again the only occupant. She logged on and navigated to her webmail.

She keyed in her email address and password.

Password incorrect.

Careless! She tried again, pressing the keys with more care.

Password incorrect.

Weird. She took out her phone and selected the mail app, clicking the envelope icon. A dialogue popped up.

Enter password.

She entered her password for the third time.

Password incorrect.

Someone had accessed her email and locked her out!
Paul!
He had to be the culprit. She'd meant to change her passwords from "Raffles" days ago, but hadn't.

With a sigh, she gave up and returned to the browser. She wouldn't need email to book her flights. She could do it all on Chrome, then print out the boarding cards using the printer under the desk.

She brought up the airline's site and clicked to log in to her account.

> *Account email or password not recognised.*
> *Retry?*

She did, with the same result.

Damn him!

To get a new password, she needed to log in to her email, which she couldn't. She let out a howl of frustration and beat the desk with clenched fists.

Count to ten. Mind your blood pressure. Think of your happy, dancing baby.

She counted to ten and felt the same hard, cold anger. Whatever Paul was up to, her interests were at the bottom of the heap.

She drummed her fingernails on the desktop, got out her phone, and called him.

He answered at once. "How'd you get on?"

"Never mind that. Why have you hacked into my email and my travel accounts and changed the passwords? I want to go home, Paul, and take Robbie with me."

After a moment, he replied, "Hacked your email? Not me, babe. Honest."

"Honest isn't the first word I'd associate with you over the last few weeks."

"I know. That's why you must hear me out. I popped over earlier to see you. I found you were out, and hoped it was at the clinic. Robbie was evasive, but he's not too hard to read. So how did it go?"

She glanced at her handbag, in which the crumpled sheets of paper from Helena were visible.

"The ultrasound was normal, the NIPT blood test will be available tomorrow."

"So you'll stay? Get the result?"

"No, Paul. Whatever the result, I don't want to be here. I told you, I am going home with Robbie. Unblock my emails, please."

"I never touched them."

"Who, then?"

"A Chinaman or a Russian or that bloke from WikiLeaks. Not me. Let me come over. I'll book your tickets."

"So that was your plan? To make yourself indispensable to me?"

"How many times must I—"

She pressed the red Cancel icon and sat back.

How else to book flights? A travel agent.

Back on the PC, she searched near her location. Travellinn, a short cab ride from the hotel, opened at nine o'clock.

Further research on the Ryanair site produced a flight to London Stansted for only €54 per person. It wasn't ideal, because she'd moved Paul's Ford pickup to the long-term parking at Gatwick. She'd send the lads down to collect it, then take it straight to a local car auction to raise money.

Right now, all Rachel cared about was going home.

She logged off and descended to reception.

The rack contained leaflets for takeaways that would deliver. Provided Robbie got a pizza in front of him soon, he'd be fine for another night.

As she waited for the lift to take her back to the room, her phone rang.

It would be Paul again.

With a sigh, she looked at the screen but saw a number she didn't recognise, prefixed by +372.

"Helena from the clinic, Mrs. Phelps. Can you talk?"

The lift pinged to announce its arrival.

"Hold on." She ignored the opening doors, headed for the breakfast room, and peered in. Empty. "Yes, I'm alone." She sat at the nearest table.

"They searched me. It was lucky you took the list."

"Look, I'm going home tomorrow. I'm not staying for the results of the test. They'll phone them through and email the details."

"I need my notes back. Very important, very urgent."

"What do they mean?"

"I can't explain on the phone. I come to you now. Are you sure you are alone? Where are you?"

"Yes, I'm in the Raadiku Hotel, but I don't have long. I must order supper for my brother and get an early night."

"Tell no one. I am on my way. Fifteen minutes on my feet."

Rachel took the handwritten list from her handbag and examined it again.

The heading of the first column, in Russian script, was clearly Name.

The final three columns were also obvious enough: Positive, Negative, and Not Known. The ticks in these columns must refer to the results of medical tests, and as Rachel was last on the list, it suggested that the NIPT was the test at issue.

Around a third of the ticks were in the Positive column. The rest were Negative, except for seven names where "?" was ticked.

There was no mark in any column next to her own name at the bottom of the third page.

She counted fifty-four women altogether.

There seemed to be a high proportion of positives. That could be explained by the clinic attracting women at greater risk, prepared to pay their fees. Although the clinic also did *pro bono* work, so perhaps poorer women at high risk were also represented.

What did the numbers in the second and third columns mean? Blood sugar levels? Cholesterol? She couldn't Google the headings without being able to type them in Cyrillic. She could ask the receptionist, who might read Russian.

Rachel scanned the takeaway menus. There was no Domino's, but she found a lookalike. She phoned, spoke to a helpful girl with perfect English, and ordered two Four Seasons and a salad for delivery in half an hour.

She'd give Helena fifteen minutes, assuming she arrived when she said.

She texted Robbie and told him to answer the door only to Peetri Pizza.

Exhausted by the events of the day, she yawned and glanced at her watch. Helena should be here any minute.

She crossed to the drinks dispenser, took a sachet of ginger infusion, added hot water from the boiler tap, and sat again.

Time passed.

Where is the woman? The pizzas will arrive soon.

Ten minutes later, her mug empty and cold on the table, her phone pinged.

"Food here."

Helena wasn't coming after all.

44

THE CARD MACHINE buzzed and ejected a slip of paper. The young woman in the travel agency looked up with an apologetic smile.

"I am sorry, madam. The transaction has been declined."

"There's plenty of credit. Perhaps I got the PIN wrong. Let me try again."

Rachel had left Robbie—yet again—in their room. Her brother was showing signs of cabin fever. Small wonder, holed up in a family suite in a strange hotel in a foreign country as the Baltic winter tightened its icy grip.

It never seems to get properly light in this city.

When she'd come down to reception, she'd found the Finnish couple and the receptionist glued to the wall-mounted TV. The news report showed police cars and crime-scene tape.

"Just near here!" the receptionist had said, white-faced.

The travel agent said, "The PIN was correct, some problem with the bank. It happens all the time. Do you have another means of payment?"

Rachel fumbled for her purse. Besides her Visa card, she had the joint account debit card. Something told her this would be no more successful.

After a long wait the machine ejected a second declined slip.

Rachel felt herself colouring. "Oh dear. I must phone the bank and find out what the problem is. I'll come straight back."

"No worries, Mrs. Phelps. I expect their automated fraud system gave an alert because you are in a foreign country. I reserved the tickets for you. I'll need payment by midday, and you must be at the airport by 1600 hours."

Anger and anxiety fought for dominance in Rachel's mind. She exited into light rain. She put up the hood of her parka. The snow of the previous day had melted, leaving puddles on the pavement and in the road. Staying clear of the kerb to avoid being soaked by passing cars, she hurried along, wondering about the crime scene on the TV. The Finnish guy had said something about a serious mugging nearby, and all three of them had appeared very shocked.

Hadn't the Finn woman said that Tallinn was safer than London?

Rachel hugged the buildings and came to the coffee shop she'd noticed from the cab.

Inside, she ordered a decaf cappuccino, sat in an alcove, and counted the money in her purse.

Enough for the coffee and the taxi back to the hotel, no more.

She took out her phone and called the international helpline.

"My card has been declined. I'm in Estonia." She gave her account number and personal details.

"Thank you for clearing security, Mrs. Phelps. Please hold while I look into this for you."

She sipped her cappuccino, unwrapped and ate the little biscuit supplied.

"Sorry to keep you waiting, Mrs. Phelps. Our records show you reported your card stolen last night. Have you found it again?"

"I didn't report it stolen."

"My screen says you phoned, cleared security, and reported the theft of your purse by a pickpocket at four forty-five p.m. yesterday."

"Not me. Someone impersonating me. Can you reactivate the card, please?"

"I'm afraid not. We can issue a replacement in the post to your home address within the next three days."

"Were there any transactions attempted before the card was cancelled?"

"No."

"Why would someone else report my card stolen?" But Rachel already knew the answer to that. They wanted to keep her here in Estonia, to block off her escape route.

This was serious. Rachel contemplated phoning Detective Ryan; but if the culprit was Paul, Ryan couldn't help her. Besides, Ryan was in the United Kingdom.

She swiped to her Favourites and jabbed "Paul."

"Good morning, darling! I'm pleased you've called."

"My cards have been blocked. What's going on, Paul? Don't play the innocent abroad. You know my date of birth, mother's maiden name, all that stuff. You cancelled my cards, didn't you? Or had Leelo do it, more likely."

"Slow down, Rachel. I swear I did nothing. I want to help you, love. You have to calm down, see me. I've got cash, plenty."

"Well, bring it now. I'm in a coffee shop called ..." she glanced at the menu on the table and gave the address.

"I'll be there. Ten minutes."

"Don't keep me waiting." Rachel seethed. All this was a ploy to stay in contact with her, to work on her. It was the dirtiest of tricks to play on your pregnant wife.

She picked up her phone again and scrolled to Helena's number in the list.

A guttural man's voice answered in a foreign language. Either Estonian or Russian: Rachel couldn't tell them apart.

"Is Helena there?"

"Who is this?" Heavily accented English.

"Never mind who I am. Where is Helena, please?"

"Ah, you are the English patient. Helena has a message for you. She is sorry, she could not make the appointment with you last night. She received an urgent call from the clinic. An emergency. She spent the night on duty. She is leaving there just now and will come to you. Please, tell me where you are? I will pass it on to her."

"Who are you?"

"I am Fredo, her husband."

"It is a confidential matter. Why do you have her phone?"

"She is leaving it behind in her great hurry. Please, be telling me your location."

"Ask Helena to call me back. I have to go." Hands shaking, Rachel selected Tamm Bok Genomics Services from her called list. "Hello, this is Rachel Phelps. I was with you having tests yesterday. May I speak to Helena, your haematologist?"

"Helena is not here. May I help you?"

"Have I missed her? Her husband said she was leaving after the emergency last night."

A moment's silence followed. "Mrs. Phelps, I believe you are misinformed. Helena does not have a husband, and there was no emergency here last night."

"In that case, where is she?"

"I cannot say."

"Someone has her cell phone and is pretending to be her husband. Please tell me where she is. She may be in danger."

"In danger? How so?"

"I don't know exactly. I arranged to meet her last night, and she never showed."

"You arranged to meet Helena? Why?"

"We got talking about dancing. I am a dance teacher. Helena was a champion dancer in her teenage years and spent time in London studying with Billie Gieves, the legendary tap dancer. We agreed to have a drink together and reminisce."

Well, everyone else is telling a pack of lies!

"Please hold."

A different voice came on. "Mrs. Phelps? Dr. Yevstigneyev here. I regret that Helena no longer works for the company. There was an issue with patient confidentiality. Do not try to contact her again. Can you confirm you will return to the clinic later today to get your results? With your husband?"

"I'm flying back to London with my brother on the afternoon Ryanair flight." She realised her mistake as soon as the words left her mouth. Now they would know where to find her! "Why am I of such interest to you, Doctor?"

"I have all my patients' best interests at heart. I advise you not to go home today."

"Why not? It's my business what I do. You said most people opt to phone in for their results."

"Your blood pressure is too high for you to fly. When you return, I will give you a supplementary injection and more tablets. Even then, no flying for forty-eight hours."

She looked up. Paul stood outside in the rain. "I'll discuss it with my husband. He's here now. Goodbye, Doctor."

Paul pushed open the glass door and slipped into the booth next to her.

Despite her misgivings, something like relief flooded through her.

"Sorry to hear of your woes with the cards. It wasn't me. I'm horrified you would think so ill of me. Now, how much cash do you want?"

"Five hundred euros, Paul. For the hotel, the return air tickets, cabs. I need sterling too, for our arrival back home. A hundred minimum."

"No problem." With something of a flourish, he produced a thick wallet bulging with cash and peeled off the euros she'd asked for, then counted out ten fifty-pound notes. "There's a monkey to see you right until the new cards come."

She seized the banknotes and stuffed them into her purse. "Pay for my coffee. I'll be in touch." She wriggled and slid off the bench seat.

"Rachel, don't go. Wait for the results of the NIPT test. One more day."

"Not you too! Did Yevstigneyev call you this morning?"

"No. It seems crazy to leave when all these facilities are at your disposal."

"Tough. Robbie and I are out of here."

Paul rose, unable to stand upright unless Rachel moved out of his way. He remained, bent into an *S* shape, while she looked him up and down. He lowered his voice to an entreating whisper. "At least let me come with you to buy your tickets, then I'll run you back to the hotel. You two fly home, I'll follow in a day or two, max. We'll take it from there. I know you're angry and upset, but the top priority must be our baby boy—"

She interrupted, "And how do you know it's a boy?"

"Or girl. You didn't let me finish. Of course I don't know. Do you?"

"No."

"But he or she is doing well?"

"Amazingly, yes."

Paul took the bill for Rachel's coffee to the counter. He held the door for her and they walked back to the travel agency.

Minutes later, two boarding passes stowed in a zipped compartment of Rachel's handbag, they were in Paul's hired Skoda.

During the short journey to the Raadiku, Paul kept silent and made no further attempt to persuade Rachel to stay. She sat tight-lipped on his right, her bag clasped on her lap.

They drew up outside the hotel. Paul said, "I love you, Rachel. Take care of yourself."

"I'd better, because no one else will take care of me." Her voice choked. This could be the final parting. Paul would drive off, back to Leelo and whatever strange new life he'd constructed for himself. Only their unborn baby united them now. He'd surely want to see him or her, be involved. He'd have rights of access, presumably.

She got out, closed the door, and marched into the hotel foyer.

The reception desk was unmanned.

She pressed the lift call button and took her room key from her handbag. She wouldn't knock and alarm Robbie.

On the third floor, she padded down the corridor, slid the key into their door, and opened it.

The TV was on, hooked up to Robbie's portable DVD player. The sound was muted. On screen, the wretched puppy and kitten were up to their antics again. The kitten was in the box floating down the river.

No Robbie on the bed. She peered around the room divider. Not in her alcove either.

In the bathroom?

"Robbie, love, it's me," she called out.

No answer.

Anxiety tightened her chest. She opened the bathroom door and clicked on the light.

No Robbie.

He'd wandered out, bored and lonely, or gone in search of her, concerned that she'd taken far longer than she said to pick up the tickets.

I should have texted him from the coffee shop!

She checked her phone to see if she'd missed a call or message from him.

Nothing.

Don't panic. Your brother is sensible, and he's been trained how to behave in the world.

She called his mobile.

At once, from Robbie's bedside table, she heard his ringtone. A chorus of dogs barking "How Much Is That Doggie in the Window?" in tune.

Wherever he was, he hadn't taken his phone. That meant he couldn't be far away.

She left the room but didn't lock it, in case he was nearby and returned without his own key.

The lift was in the basement. Instead of summoning it, she bounded down the metal-banistered stairwell.

On the first floor, she dived into the little lounge with the internet access.

Empty.

At ground level, out of breath, she hurried up to the receptionist, back at her desk. "Have you seen my brother? You know, the stocky fellow with the moonlike face and the gappy teeth."

"Yes, madam. He went out a short while ago."

"Did he say where he was going?"

"For something to eat."

Robbie! Always thinking of your stomach! It's nowhere near lunchtime!

"When was this?"

"Just now. A few minutes."

"What exactly did Robbie say, please? He has Down's syndrome. He has a mental age of ten and he can get lost in strange surroundings and panic."

"I realised that. I would have asked where he was going, only as he was with your husband—"

"Sorry, did you say he was with my husband?"

"Yes, so I thought that would be fine, that he had collected your brother to meet up with you for an early lunch."

"My husband just dropped me off when I came in a minute ago. I don't understand."

The girl looked bewildered. "Have I done the wrong thing?"

"No, no. It's . . . oh, it's complicated. Any idea where they might have gone? The Hesburger perhaps?"

"Your brother simply said they were going to eat."

"Leaving no message for me if I returned?"

"No, I assumed they were meeting with you. I didn't realise you were in the hotel."

"I came in a few minutes ago."

"I was in the toilet. I stepped out only for a minute—"

"I'm not blaming you, but I do need to find Robbie."

"Perhaps you could call your husband and see where they are? Plainly a small misunderstanding has occurred."

"Yes, good idea. Silly me, wasting time." Rachel's phone was already in her hand. She called Paul as she stepped away from the reception desk towards the entrance doors and the rack of leaflets.

"Hello, Rachel. Changed your mind?"

She hissed, "Where are you, Paul? How did you pull that trick?"

"Eh? What trick?"

"Sneaking out with Robbie while I was in the lift. Did you have him waiting in the breakfast room so he could nip out and avoid me?"

"What are you talking about, Rachel?"

"You haven't got Robbie with you?"

"No. I dropped you off and I'm still in the car. I shouldn't be on the phone. Let me stop somewhere."

Rachel heard the background noise of traffic and the metallic squeal of a tram's wheels taking a tight corner.

If Robbie isn't with Paul, where is he? And who is he with?

"I pulled in."

"Robbie left the hotel moments ago. The receptionist said he was with you."

"No. Didn't you see me drive away? How could Robbie be with me?"

Rachel turned to the receptionist. "Did you recognise my husband from when he came here before? Are you sure it was him?"

"I don't recall seeing him before, madam."

"Can you describe him?"

"Tall, smartly dressed."

"Wearing a leather jacket?"

"No, a suit and tie. But surely your brother knows your husband? Why would he—"

Rachel closed her eyes.

This can't be happening.

Into her phone, she said, trying not to yell, "Your so-called friend Shackloth has abducted Robbie. Get your sorry arse back to the hotel. We must find them."

45

RACHEL PACED the lobby. She hadn't liked the look of the Shackloth fellow from the moment she'd set eyes on him. An unpleasant piece of work, he had sat smugly in the casino bar while she dowsed Paul and Leelo with their drinks. What had he said, in that know-it-all Stephen Fry voice of his? Something about "your chromosome-challenged brother?"

Paul had said he'd be less than five minutes. He'd asked where Robbie and Shackloth had gone, and Rachel had answered "to eat," voicing her opinion that a burger would have been enough temptation to prise Robbie from his room and forget his solemn vow to open the door to no one.

"Did they leave in a car?" she asked the receptionist.

"Your husband didn't have an umbrella or overcoat, so I guess, in this weather. But I can't see the parking from my desk."

"He's not my husband—he's a friend of my husband."

The girl looked relieved. "Oh, that's all right then?"

"Let's hope so."

"Your brother seemed to know this friend of your husband's."

Rachel smiled reassuringly. "Yes, he knows him. I'm sure they are fine." In truth she was not sure, not sure at all that her beloved brother was fine, or even safe.

She glanced at her watch. Time had slowed to a crawl. Only two minutes since she spoke to Paul. She turned around on the spot and knew her teeth were grinding.

My blood pressure must be through the roof.

She sat on the bench seat near the door, breathing in slowly through her nose and out through her mouth.

"May I fetch you a glass of water?" the receptionist asked.

"No, Paul will he here any min—" At that instant, her phone rang.

She leapt up, mobile clamped to her ear. "Where are you, man? For God's sake, hurry."

"Relax, I've found them. They're at the Hesburger joint around the corner from you. Robbie has a family bucket of chicken nuggets and a gallon of Coke. He's happy as Larry."

"Shackloth there?"

"Yes, he came looking for me after I called him and couldn't get through. He thought I might be at the hotel with you and came by on the off chance. Robbie answered the door and said he was bored and hungry, so Richard offered him a bite. They're getting on fine. I think Richard wanted to apologise to Robbie for the way he spoke about him too."

"Paul, bring Robbie back here this instant. Shackloth abducted him."

"Chill out, babe. You're overreacting. Let Robbie finish his meal."

"No, leave the wretched junk food and bring him back."

"Speak to him yourself."

Robbie's voice came on. "Hi, Sis. Am I in trouble? Only you were out such a long time, I was worried. I was about to call you when there was a knock at the door. I thought it was you. It was Richard, looking for Paulie. These nuggets are fab, Sis. They got a Peri-Peri sauce like Nando's but even more spicy. Boy, they're hot!"

"Stay right there, Robbie." Rachel rushed for the door. She didn't trust Paul to bring him back.

What are these men up to?

With a backward glance at the receptionist, a forced smile, and a thumbs-up sign, she hurried out into the cold.

The burger joint was only minutes away. It would be quicker to run there than spend more time arguing with her husband.

Fresh snow was falling, or rather sleet. She stood under the glass canopy of the hotel and wavered. Visibility was dreadful. It was dark as night. The vehicles that swished past all showed headlights.

She took out her pocket umbrella and unfurled it. A tremendous gust of wind blew it inside out, and it threated to take off with her underneath, clinging on like Mary Poppins.

She fought to furl it again.

Her parka would keep out the wind and was showerproof, but not blizzard-proof. Even with the hood up, her hair would be soaked in seconds. She stood, undecided, while the sleet, driving in under the canopy, started to spot her jeans with cold, wet patches.

Her hair blew in her eyes.

She wanted to cry.

Then a taxi approached.

She waved frantically before realising he didn't have his light on, so wouldn't stop.

But he did.

Rachel's jeans were soaked by now. Sleety rain dripped from her hood and ran down her face like icy tears.

The driver leapt out of his cab, leaving his engine running and the windscreen wipers on high speed.

"Mrs. Phelps? Please ride up front with me for the heater. Also more room for your long legs. Let me take your umbrella." Andrus opened the passenger door.

Rachel climbed in gratefully. "Hello again! Andrus, how come you're always here when I need you?"

"Let's go."

A small car, headlights on full beam, travelling at high speed, crossed the road and swerved towards them. Andrus let out an exclamation, spun his steering wheel, pulled away from the kerb, and accelerated on the snowy road, his rear wheels fishtailing.

The other car narrowly missed them before skidding to a halt right outside the double doors of the hotel.

Rachel, not properly seated or buckled in, yelled, "Hey! What is that lunatic doing?" She twisted to look out of the rear window.

Before they turned the corner, she glimpsed a female figure leap from the sports car and tug at the hotel door. Rachel couldn't see her face, and she wore a woolly hat.

Helena?

Rachel faced forwards again and secured her seat belt.

"Sorry, Mrs. Phelps. I thought that car was coming to collide with us. Tallinn drivers are mad, they take no heed of the weather, speeding all over."

"I don't need that kind of shock," Rachel puffed out her cheeks and leant back. "That was lucky, Andrus, you passing precisely when I needed you!"

"Not luck. Your husband sent me to collect you."

"Oh, that was good of him." Whatever his motive, Rachel was grateful not to be out in the open, buffeted by the swirling, sleety rain and wind.

"Let me turn up the heat and dry you out. What weather! And the winter only beginning."

"It's hardly worth it. We'll be there in a minute."

"Not quite a minute! More like fifteen. Twenty, if we hit traffic through town."

"What are you talking about? The Hesburger is just around the corner from the hotel."

"Hesburger? No Hesburger. Mr. Phelps said to take you to Tamm Bok Clinic."

"He did what? I don't want to go there! Stop the taxi! I must phone him. He's playing some game! Pull up, please. Anywhere. My brother is at the burger bar."

"I must take you straight to the clinic. Those are my instructions, Mrs. Phelps."

"I refuse to go there! Why are you driving on? I won't be hijacked by my own husband!" She felt the colour rising in her cheeks. The hot air from the heater was overpowering. Her wet jeans clung to her legs. They'd be steaming any second. Her chest tightened, a wave of dizziness washed over her, and she knew her blood pressure was heading off the scale.

"Mrs. Phelps, it is all in your interests. Your husband and brother will be waiting for you at the clinic. Please sit back and relax. I will drive you smoothly. Would you like classical music on?" He reached out and turned on the radio.

All in your interests. That old lie from Paul again!

Raising her voice, she said, "No, take me back to the Hesburger. I order you, driver."

He shot her a sympathetic glance. "Mr. Paul said you were likely to be upset. I'm sure everything will be all right. I cannot take you to the Hesburger. They are not there. That would waste time."

There must be something dreadfully wrong. Perhaps my baby is dying. Perhaps I am dying.

Rachel's head pounded.

What could the clinic have discovered—and why wasn't I the first to know?

She took out her phone and dialled Paul.

"Hi, this is Paul Phelps of Phelps & Son Builders. I'm not available right now. You can leave a message—"

She called Robbie's phone, which rang once, twice . . . before she remembered he'd left it behind in the hotel room.

Who else to call? Kizzy!

She scrolled to her Favourites.

Andrus reached out, slid his right hand behind her head, and snatched the phone from her ear. The driver pocketed her phone in his left jacket pocket, out of her reach.

"Hey! Andrus! What are you doing? I thought you were looking after me!"

"The way to look after you is to take you with all haste to the clinic."

Rachel was near to tears. "I . . . I don't want to go there. There's something horribly wrong."

"I'm sure they can treat you. It is one of the most leading clinics in the country."

"I mean there's something wrong with the clinic. I don't know what—"

"Sit back, Rachel."

She stiffened at the use of her Christian name and the hint of menace in his tone.

Is Andrus part of a plot to abduct me? Why doesn't Paul answer his phone? Where is poor Robbie?

The taxi raced along the dual carriageway alongside the old railway line at ninety kilometres an hour. A crosswind howled over the scrubby plain and buffeted the car.

She raised her voice over the wind and engine noise. "Stop and let me out. You have no right to take me against my will."

Nothing happened. Andrus fixed his eyes on the road ahead and, if anything, accelerated.

She'd make him stop. She counted to three, leaned over, and grabbed the wheel.

The taxi swerved leftwards towards the central reservation. With an oath in his own language, Andrus wrenched the wheel back. The taxi bounced on its suspension. A car overtaking them on their left had to brake and swerve to avoid a collision. The blare of its horn sounded and receded behind them as Andrus regained control and sped on.

"Are you trying to kill us all?" he yelled. "You, me, and your baby? Paul told me you were a little crazy. I see it is so. Do not try anything like that again."

He'd clearly invited her into the front passenger seat so he could see her and keep her within reach, and prevent her leaping out of the cab at a traffic light.

This was a setup.

She'd been kidnapped.

She also now knew what the numbers in Helena's notes meant.

46

"YOU WILL LOSE your licence, treating a passenger like this."

No answer.

"When did Paul book you to pick me up?"

No answer.

"Why won't you obey me? Are you abducting me?"

No answer.

"You knew we were in Tallinn right from the start, didn't you? The Romany woman at the airport with the lavender. She was looking out for us, wasn't she? Then you fixed it somehow so you were standing by to collect us on the first evening. Did you intercept the cab the receptionist ordered and pay him to go away? Or were you just waiting, the nearest cab on call, knowing we'd need a taxi?"

No answer.

"What do you want with us?"

No answer.

"Give me my phone, please."

As if knowing it was being talked about, her phone rang from inside the driver's pocket.

Andrus removed it and held it against the steering wheel, his eyes darting down to the phone and back to the road.

"Who is Jim Ryan?"

"A friend from home."

"Talk to him and say all is fine, you are having the lovely time and wish he was here."

"No."

"You love your brother, do you not? Speak." The driver thumbed the screen to answer the call and turned on the loudspeaker.

"Hello, Jim," Rachel called out towards the handset. "I'm driving at the moment, but I'm on hands-free, so go ahead."

"Are you alone, Rachel? Can you talk?"

Andrus nodded his head and mouthed, "Yes."

"Sure, Jim. Just sightseeing. I'm taking the hire car to the hotel to pick up Robbie and Paul."

"So you're all coming home together?"

"Yes, of course. Paul's little adventure is over. He's been a silly boy, but everything's fine now."

"You mustn't travel back with him, Rachel. There are things going on you don't understand."

"How do you mean, Jim?" Rachel felt perspiration beading on her brow.

Andrus smiled and raised his eyebrows.

"Listen, Rachel. I need you to stay clear of Paul for twenty-four hours. Make any excuse. Get out of the country with Robbie."

"Jim, this is crazy talk. Please ring off. I can't concentrate while I'm driving and you keep breaking up."

Andrus, steering with one hand, thumbed Rachel's touchscreen with his other hand to mute the microphone. "He's police, isn't he? Ask him where he is now."

"He's not police," hissed Rachel. "He's in England."

"You lie. Ask your friendly policeman where he is, if you wish to see your brother again soon." He unmuted the microphone.

Rachel blurted out, "Jim, I'm in a taxi and I'm being taken against my w—"

With a curse, Andrus cancelled the call. He powered down his window. Cold air and sleet blasted in. He flung Rachel's phone out into the swirling wintry snow.

She shrieked in horror.

The window slid shut, and the car sped along.

"Are you going to rape me and kill me?"

No answer again. The driver had his orders and was intent on following them. She'd wait until the cab stopped for a red light, or drew up at its destination—then move like lightning.

Are we heading for the clinic? Or a deserted back street, far from any help?

None of this made sense, and once again her husband seemed behind everything.

She closed her eyes.

"That is good. You try to rest and relax. Believe me, you are safe as long as you behave in a sensible manner. All will become clear."

This time it was her turn to stay mute.

When the cab turned off the dual carriageway, Rachel opened one eye and peeped.

She recognised a junction. This *was* the way to the clinic. Andrus would have to stop at the next intersection.

Little by little, she inched her right hand towards the armrest in the door.

Here was her chance. A red light at the entrance to the science park. Many offices lined the boulevard beyond; she'd find sanctuary there.

As the cab approached the light, it changed to green and Andrus accelerated over the junction.

Damn . . . and now we're almost there.

The clinic's illuminated sign appeared ahead. Before she could form a new plan, the taxi pulled up outside the main doors on a yellow-hatched area with the word "KIIRABI" stencilled on the ground.

Rachel lunged for the door handle anyway. Andrus, anticipating her move, pressed his lock button.

The snow fluttered down, now in larger, fluffier flakes that fell silently, unlike the earlier sleet that had lashed the car.

Andrus was murmuring into his own phone.

Then the doors of the clinic slid open and two figures appeared, wheeling a gurney. Porters, in the clinic's distinctive green uniform.

The taxi doors clicked open. The porters lifted Rachel bodily from the passenger seat and onto the trolley. They buckled her on with click straps.

"Put your head back, Mrs. Phelps," the porter by her head said. "You will be fine if you don't exert or stress yourself. The team are ready for you."

Tickly snowflakes fell on her face. She couldn't wipe them away. "Is my husband here? And my brother?"

"A little bump as we go over the door sill. Nice and warm and dry inside."

She stared upwards at the ceiling lights of the lobby. The inner set of doors hissed open and the trolley rolled into the reception area.

A face appeared above her. Silhouetted against the bright overhead fluorescents, she didn't recognise him until he spoke.

"I am so pleased you returned."

Dr. Yevstigneyev. *Call me Stig.*

"Why am I here?"

"For your sake, and the baby's. Lie still."

"I have little choice. You've strapped me down."

"Just a precaution against you falling or having a seizure, Rachel. Relax."

The trolley trundled along a corridor and pushed through a set of double doors with big rubbery flaps.

The ceiling lights in here were blindingly bright, and a sharp scent of antiseptic assailed her nostrils.

Yevstigneyev gave an order in his own language.

Another face she recognised loomed over her.

Round specs, straight and mousy brown hair.

"Agnetha! What are you all doing to me?"

The sonographer who had shown Rachel her baby dancing on the large screen smiled. "We are so sorry for all the cloaks and daggers. We want the best for you, and it was an emergency. May I please take your blood pressure?"

"If it's high, it's because I've been kidnapped and brought here against my will. The driver said that Paul, my husband, had hired him."

"Quite right. Mr. Phelps insisted that you must return to us. You are safer here than back in your homeland, Rachel. They have obsolete methods in the United Kingdom. Last-generation screening, old-fashioned, unreliable diagnostic techniques. Paul didn't want that for you. Nor do we. I need to wrap the cuff around your upper arm. Please stop wriggling."

"What is this room?" Rachel turned her head from left to right, as far as she could with her arms restrained. She glimpsed ranks of shiny clinical equipment with keypads and monitor screens and wires and tubes. The two porters hadn't gone. They stood a few paces off, as if guarding her. Now Yevstigneyev's face loomed over her again, with those alien blue eyes.

Rachel focused instead on Agnetha, who was busying herself with the monitor. With a whirr, the cuff inflated, compressing Rachel's arm until she could feel her heart thumping away like a drum hit by a hammer.

"Well, what is it?"

Agnetha said, "It's 195 over 115. But don't worry."

Yevstigneyev said, "Monitor the electrocardiograph and put in an intravenous line. Rachel, everything will be fine. You are lucky you are in Estonia. This is the most advanced prenatal facility in Europe."

"The driver locked me in his cab and destroyed my phone. Is that in your patient care guidelines?"

"I am displeased to hear Andrus took that action. He was overzealous. He knew it was urgent you returned for treatment. You need to speak to your husband. He instructed Andrus to hurry you back here."

"Treatment for what?"

"Your blood pressure yesterday was also high, though nothing like this. To have embarked on an airline flight to London could have been catastrophic both for you and your baby."

During this exchange, a second female nurse clipped a small device resembling a hi-tech clothes peg to Rachel's right forefinger. It emitted a red light. Meanwhile, Agnetha had rolled back Rachel's other sleeve and said, "Just a little prick. I am putting a line into a vein so we can administer medication to bring down your pressure. Ready?"

"What choice do I have?" Rachel whispered, half to herself. Being told she was ill had made her feel ill, whereas an hour ago she'd felt not too bad, considering the stress she was under.

My baby must come first.

Maybe all this *was* in baby's best interests.

But what a way to treat a pregnant woman!

Like an experimental animal in a vivisection laboratory.

"Where is my husband? What happened to Helena?" She needed information: facts she could act upon.

Yevstigneyev's head came into view overhead once more. "I explained about Helena. Paul is on his way. He'll be here soon." The doctor's head disappeared from her field of vision, and she heard him murmur to Agnetha, "Administer twenty milligrams of Labetalol. Push slowly. Monitor her, and after five minutes inject double doses if necessary. Let me know when she is stable, and we'll move on to the procedure."

Rachel closed her eyes against the glare of the examination light. More murmured conversation followed, not in English. Then she heard the swish of the doors to the suite. She opened her eyes and tried to turn her head to see who was leaving and who remained in the room, without success. Agnetha smiled down. "They are all gone except me. It will take five minutes for the Labetalol to work. The drug is the safest choice for your baby and you, and we'll use the absolute minimum."

"I think that's what they gave me back home after the funeral."

"Very likely. So you know, if we'd allowed your BP to stay as high as it was, we'd be compromising blood circulation to the foetus and there would be a risk of you having a stroke. Once again, I am sorry for the way you were brought here."

"I need to speak to someone."

"You can borrow my phone. I am sure your husband will bring you a temporary one."

"Where is he? I'm worried sick about my brother. Where's my handbag? Did it come in with me, or did that wretched driver steal it too?"

"Shh, try to stay calm while the medication takes effect. Then, if Paul hasn't arrived, you can call him. I don't see your handbag, but I expect the porters brought it in. I'll go look when I'm relieved. I must remain close by to keep you under observation."

Rachel, who didn't actually wish to speak to Paul, but to Jim Ryan, said, "Do you know why Helena was dismissed, Agnetha?"

A brief silence followed. Rachel could hear machinery humming and a gentle bleeping from the heart monitor in time with her own pulse. Agnetha spoke quietly, so quietly Rachel could barely make out her words against the background noises. "Do not repeat this, or tell anyone we had this conversation. You agree?"

"Yes. I trust you."

"Helena is excitable and a little—what's the word in English—neurotic? She got into her head that the results she was obtaining from the sequencers were inconsistent. Director Yevstigneyev double-checked all her findings and ran tests on the equipment. He also reran tests on other machines using the reserve samples. Everything was fine, but Helena would not accept it. She talked to me—and anyone who would listen to her—alarming us with her fantastical notions. Dr. Yevstigneyev counselled her, and for a while all was right. Then Helena began to frighten the clients, telling them nonsense."

"What do you mean, nonsense?"

"That their results, particularly from the NIPT tests, were not to be trusted, and they should get a second test elsewhere. Well! That was outrageous. Disloyal and unprofessional. She received a final warning about her conduct. Then there was an incident yesterday. Maybe you were involved? Yes, that seems most likely. All that the rest of us know for sure is Helena was terminated."

"I found her in the toilets, crying. She had papers with handwritten notes about recent results. Why are so many of the positive results from tall and slim women like me, Agnetha?"

"Tall and slim?"

"Yes. Height over 1.75 metres, weight under 75 kilograms. Surely the opposite should be the case, that shorter, fatter women are more at risk? You must find my handbag. The notes are in it."

"I know nothing of these things. I am sorry Helena alarmed you. We never had troubles of this kind. Oh, good, your blood pressure is down already. I do not think we will need another dose for now. How do you feel?"

"Woozy. My scalp is tingling. It's the weirdest sensation."

"Just mild side effects, common with the medication at this level of dosage. They shouldn't last long, and soon we'll move you somewhere more comfortable and begin foetal monitoring."

"What did Stig mean about a procedure?"

"Let's wait for Paul, shall we? Then we can all have a discussion together."

"No—tell me now. What have you found? Why was it so urgent to rush me back here?"

"You heard the director explain."

"Please take these straps off me, Agnetha. I feel like a condemned prisoner. I'm going nowhere connected to all your tubes and wires. I'm not about to have a convulsion or seizure."

"The restraints are a safety precaution during patient movement. Fits and convulsions are always possible in your condition. I will take them off now, but no sudden movements, Rachel. Keep your head back, yes? If you sit up or make a rapid move, you could faint and fall, injuring yourself or your lovely baby."

Agnetha moved around the trolley, unfastening the webbing straps.

As soon as her right hand was free, Rachel reached out, taking care not to dislodge the sensor attached to her finger. She grasped Agnetha's wrist. "Please, we haven't got long. The others will return, and I want to know what's in store for me."

Agnetha's face wore a troubled frown. "This is a family matter. You need support. I must follow the protocol."

"For God's sake, I was kidnapped, brought here against my will. Tell me what's going on, at least as far as you know!"

Agnetha sighed. "I have spoken too much already, I fear. But very well. Later, you pretend you are hearing this for the first time, right? Or I will be in serious trouble. And I can't watch out for you if I am terminated also, like Helena."

"Yes. I agree. Quick, now. Is it to do with my scan?"

"No, I am telling you about the scan myself. All is as I said. It is the blood test. The NIPT."

"And?"

"The sequencers ran all night. The result came through this morning. They—"

Agnetha turned her head.

The rubber-lined doors to the suite swished open.

"How is the patient?"

"Director, Mrs. Phelps has responded well to the Labetalol and her BP is down to 155 over 100."

Yevstigneyev's face loomed over her, smooth as a boy doll's. "Good. Rachel, do you have any swelling of your feet or ankles?"

"No more than usual."

"Any headaches, nausea, or vomiting?"

"A thumping headache and dizziness."

"Pains in your stomach or shoulder?"

"No. I was fine until I was bundled into that taxi and brought here."

"Have you experienced any unusual or sudden weight gain in recent weeks?"

"No."

"Disturbances to your vision—flashing lights, blind spots?"

"No. Why are you asking me all these questions?"

"I am sure you are aware of the risks of preeclampsia. You are under my care now, and I must assess your condition. Any shortness of breath?"

"No."

"Rachel, I need you to give me a urine sample. I will check it here and now to be certain your kidney function is good. Agnetha, help the patient."

Rachel said, "I'm not ill, I'm angry. Before I agree to anything else at all, will someone please give me a mobile phone so I can call my husband? He must be worried sick about me."

"Paul is on his way."

Rachel raised her voice, though it came out more of a croak. "You told me that twenty minutes ago. He should be here by now."

"Very well." Yevstigneyev passed his own mobile to Rachel. "You will see his number in the recent callers list." Rachel selected Paul's number.

"Hi, this is Paul Phelps—"

She let the voicemail message play, then at the beep, said, "Paul, I'm back in the clinic, as you well know. Get here now, with Robbie." She sighed and ended the call. "All right, he's gone missing. Probably popped into the casino for a turn at the roulette table. Come on Agnetha, let's produce this urine sample."

"I will return shortly," Yevstigneyev said. The doors flapped to and fro once more.

Rachel said, "How are we going to get my jeans off? Let me sit up."

"No, you must not. The director does not wish you to be making sudden moves. I can manage."

"What were you about to tell me before he came back in?"

"There is no time. He will return. Let's undo your belt and zipper. We must have the urine sample ready for him, not be discovered talking. Now roll on your side."

"Tell me, tell me."

"You will know all in a few minutes. Make the water, Rachel. Please, hurry. Yes, that's good."

Scarcely had they finished when the doors opened. "Ready?"

"Here, Director."

Yevstigneyev seized the sample bottle and strode to a bench. Rachel couldn't see what he was doing as his back was to them. No more than two minutes passed before he returned to her side.

"Mrs. Phelps, I regret this is a medical emergency. Your urine shows a dangerously high level of proteins. This indicates serious stress on your kidneys and is a life-threatening risk to both you and your baby. But do not worry. We are fully equipped here to deal with your condition. I had hoped that Paul would arrive, but as you see, he has not. I tried his number myself while I was outside just now. I think we must assume he has been waylaid."

"What's the matter with me?" Rachel asked in a small voice.

Ignoring her question, Yevstigneyev said in a quiet aside, "Agnetha, leave the room, please. I need to consult with Mrs. Phelps in confidence."

"But Director, I know that—"

Yevstigneyev turned his laserlike eyes on the nurse. "Leave the treatment room at once."

"Yes, Director." The doors opened and closed. Rachel's only ally in this place had been despatched.

Yevstigneyev spoke in a low, urgent voice. "Your life is at risk, if we do not act."

"Act?"

"Before we discuss that, I must tell you the result of the tests you underwent yesterday. I am very sorry to inform you, but your baby is ninety-nine percent certain to be carrying the Down trisomy. I know that will come as a shock, but it may make things easier to bear in the longer term."

Rachel closed her eyes. She was living a nightmare. "My tests and scans back home showed nothing like that probability. Fifteen percent, they told me."

"They based those predictions on a crude test involving only maternal blood. The system we use here extracts fragments of the baby's actual DNA from your own blood, then amplifies them by polymerase chain reaction. The test is highly accurate. There is only a one in a hundred chance we are wrong. You must face it, Mrs. Phelps. You are carrying a Down baby."

"I don't believe it. There's been a mistake. Helena—"

"As I explained yesterday, in normal circumstances we would confirm with an amniocentesis."

"An invasive procedure where you stick a foot-long needle into my tummy. That isn't going to happen."

"No, it isn't. We are out of time. Even with our accelerated chromosome microarray test, it would take too long."

"What are you talking about, out of time?"

"I sensed something was wrong yesterday, but because you are under twenty weeks, I let it pass. It is unusual to contract preeclampsia at your stage, but your age may be a factor that has worked against you. Now do you see how urgent it was for you to return here, even against your immediate wishes, rather than board an aircraft?"

"You are telling me I have preeclampsia?"

"Yes. Early onset. Did your doctors not warn you of it?"

Panic rose in Rachel's chest. "Yes, of course, but not so soon . . . although I have already been in hospital with my blood pressure, so I guess . . . though I put that down to the stress of Mum's funeral . . ." Her voice tailed off.

"Now do you understand that we care about you?"

"So I have to remain here? In Estonia? I can't go home?"

"That would be out of the question."

"What is the treatment?"

"There is no treatment. If you wish to live, you must have an immediate termination."

47

HIS BLUE EYES bored into her soul. "We have the suite ready, and will perform it immediately. I have studied the ultrasounds. There is no doubt. Your baby has Down Syndrome. It is very small for the term, and that is good news in one way, namely I can conduct a vacuum aspiration. It will all be over in half an hour, Rachel."

"I don't agree. I want a second opinion. I won't go through with anything at all until Paul arrives."

"You may not live that long."

"Agnetha said my pressure was falling. Surely the immediate risk is past?"

"Not at all. Time is against us. Do you wish Paul to arrive and find you dead?"

Rachel looked up at the doctor's head hovering over her, bobbing in and out of her field of vision.

"Something is wrong here," she managed to whisper. "My lovely baby can't die. If baby dies, I want to die too. There will be nothing for me to go home to."

"Your brother needs you. Paul needs you. He is a good man, your husband."

"How do you know anything about him?"

"Why, he is a shareholder in this clinic. He did not tell you? He has been here, taken the tour, met our founders."

"So that much is true," Rachel sighed.

The doctor consulted the monitors attached to his patient. She heard him tut-tutting. "I need to administer more Labetalol. Stay quite still . . . another few seconds . . . a double dose . . . there we go. You should feel better in a few minutes.

But I fear we are fighting a losing battle. You must have the termination now."

The doors burst open with a rattle. Yevstigneyev said, "At long last! Here is your husband. Good day, Mr. Phelps."

Paul's face appeared next to Yevstigneyev's above her trolley. "Babe, darling. Rachel. Are you all right? Doctor, how is she?"

"Paulie, where have you been? That taxi driver kidnapped me and brought me here. Did you order him to do that?"

"It's complicated. There is no time to explain. The reason I took so long is that we lost Robbie."

"You lost him? How could you lose him in a burger bar? And why did you tell Andrus to hijack me against my wishes? He threatened me, said if I wanted to see Robbie again I had to do what he said. He knows where my brother is. He's kidnapped him too."

Yevstigneyev said, "We have no time to be sidetracked by all this foolishness. Mr. Phelps, here are the simple facts. One, your baby has Down Syndrome. Two, your wife has preeclampsia. I have tried to explain to her the urgent need for an immediate termination."

Paul's face registered bewilderment and shock. "Termination? As in abortion? I don't understand—"

"Yes. It will be quick and painless. Then you may all return home tomorrow. I am sure you will find Robbie safe and well. This talk of kidnapping is hysterical. He has wandered off. I believe Andrus was a trifle overenthusiastic in following his instructions to bring your wife here without delay. But he did the right thing. She is dangerously sick, sinking fast, and her condition is impairing her judgement."

Rachel's voice grew weaker and she struggled to make herself understood. "Paul, something is wrong. Get me out of here. I'll go to the city hospital. I don't believe I am as ill as this man is making out."

Paul's face contorted into a new expression of puzzlement and anxiety. "What have you done to Rachel, Doctor? Explain yourself, man."

Yevstigneyev replied, "We received the result of the NIPT test. I phoned you earlier with that information. In due course, Rachel arrived here, and I suspected an acute hypertensive episode. We took her blood pressure and I conducted a urine test. There is clear and present danger to her life. We must go ahead with the termination. I have the consent form here; Mr. Phelps, I will allow you and your wife to discuss this, and I need the signed consent from you. Do not delay. I will scrub up in the meantime. Mrs. Phelps, do you have any questions before I leave you two alone?"

"No. Just go."

"Very well. Give the signed consent to Agnetha, who waits outside at the nursing station." He handed a clipboard with a form to Paul.

The doors flapped, swung a couple of times, and settled. Silence descended, punctuated only by the bleeps of Rachel's monitors.

Paul brought a chair across from the side of the suite and sat.

"No way am I consenting to an abortion," Rachel said. "I repeat: get me out of here and let's find Robbie. I can't believe you abandoned both of us yet again."

"Richard Shackloth said he would run Robbie back to the hotel."

"While you ordered the taxi to abduct me from the street."

"Yes. Except I didn't tell him to mistreat you."

"Andrus strong-armed me, he threatened me and Robbie, he threw my mobile phone out of the window. No wonder I'm in this state."

"He has a reputation for being hotheaded, but why would he treat you that way? Are you sure you're not being oversensitive . . . paranoid?"

"Paul, he destroyed my phone."

"Any idea why?"

"Yes. I took a call from Jim Ryan."

"The boy detective? What in hell did he want?"

"I don't know. News on the scam to steal Mum's savings? Andrus didn't give me the opportunity to find out. So you're saying Yevstigneyev telephoned you with the test results?"

"Yes. He knew you were planning to fly out today, and was concerned for you."

"He seems to know everything about me and my movements."

"I'm guessing Richard updates him."

"That slimy jerk? What hold does he have over you all?" Rachel felt worse, if anything, than before Yevstigneyev had administered the medication: hot, shivery, and tearful.

"Money talks, babe. Even in healthcare. Think what this place takes to run. The sequencing machines cost six million dollars a pop, and they've got five of them. You need serious financial backing to keep up in the scientific arms race. Let's stick to the point. You and our baby. You're clearly unwell and must stay here."

"I don't accept the baby has Down's. The haematologist who treated me yesterday, Helena, suspected that results are being falsified. She was dismissed and now she's disappeared. Paul, she had a handwritten list of patients, and my name was on it. The taller, slimmer women had the most positive tests."

"Babe, this *is* paranoid. Why would a reputable clinic like this falsify results? What possible benefit would it bring them?"

"I don't know, but I suspect your so-called A-list investor friend Shackloth does. Now, for about the fifth time of asking, get me out of this place! I don't trust Yevstigneyev. He seems hand in glove with that thug Andrus. Nor do I buy his explanation of Helena's disappearance. I think she was on to them, and they silenced her."

"Babe, you're slurring your words."

"I feel as if I'm floating. On a boat, perhaps."

"I'll never forgive myself if you come to harm. I love you, Rachel. I want to go home with you and live with you."

With an effort, she forced herself to listen and reply to him. "It won't be just me. Remember baby. Maybe I am being paranoid. Maybe I am positive. Will you love a Down's child and bring it up?"

"I don't know. It's a big ask, love. Robbie is enough of a handful and we're responsible for him now Eve has gone."

"And her money has gone too."

Money makes the world go around. Who sang that? Liza Minnelli.

Rachel's blood rushed in her ears. It reminded her of standing behind the waterfall at Niagara. They'd holidayed there when Robbie was ... what, eight years old? He'd been entranced by the cascades. They'd been visiting her dad's Canadian relatives.

She struggled back to reality and tried to focus on her husband's words.

Talk, talk. That's all people do. Talk at me.

"Never mind the money. All that matters is your well-being. I don't know what to do for the best. You're in the most advanced prenatal clinic in the Baltic. If you have preeclampsia, it makes no difference whether the baby has Down's or not. You'll both die. Oh God, what should I do?" He ran his hands through his hair, stood and paced around, out of Rachel's view, muttering to himself.

Rachel was beginning not to care. A tidal wave of dizziness swept through her and rolled her back and forth like a log on a beach in the surf. The gurney on which she lay seemed to lift at one end and spin. Just like that time she'd got drunk on champagne cocktails at Perry and Julie's wedding.

The whole room was going around, actually. Quite a pleasant feeling, once you got used to the spinning. As a girl, she'd loved the travelling funfair that set up in the park every Whitsun bank holiday. She closed her eyes and seemed to see the horses of the carousel rising and falling in time with the organ.

She heard Paul's voice through a roaring mist of music. "Babe, can you hear me? Answer me, love. Dear God, we're losing her! Wait there, babe. I'm going for help!"

She smiled.

What could she do but wait?

Perhaps I can get up, now I'm alone in the room. Yes!

She stood, still connected to the drip thing and the electric clothes peg thing. She put her arms up as if going into hold.

Who is my partner? Oh—Barry!

Robbie started up the music. "Moon River." She danced with Barry in front of her beginners' group. Barry guided her around the ballroom. Except it wasn't a ballroom, or even the school hall. More like a dusty attic.

She glanced down and saw a white mouse standing on its hind feet, looking up at her. Surely they shouldn't allow mice in a clinic? But it was a pretty little mouse.

Barry led her into a reverse turn, then he disappeared.

Perhaps she should go to bed and have a little sleep.

So tired.

Somehow she was on her back again, drifting in the bottom of the boat in a calm bay.

Am I asleep? Dead, even?

It isn't too bad, if the latter. Like being in the womb. Cosy, and dreamy, with nothing to do, no responsibilities, no need to breathe, even.

Mum provides everything: my food, my oxygen.

All I have to myself is my blood supply, going around and around and around and . . .

48

IT WAS NOT a gentle awakening, such as she might enjoy at home, with the early morning rays of sunshine stealing through the gap in the curtains and caressing her into the new day. Rather, Rachel rose from the abyss of unconsciousness at breakneck speed, like a diver surfacing too quickly from the depths.

One moment she was living a weird, freaky dream in which a snarling, disembodied head made of sand floated around her, its mouth wide, trying to eat her. Then she opened her eyes and every shape loomed vivid, bright and oversaturated with colour, like a children's cartoon. And the sounds: they too were overamplified. Tweets and warbles. Birdsong? She struggled to bring her hearing into focus. No, just the bleeps and buzzes of medical monitors.

She was still in the clinic.

She'd been anaesthetised and was coming round.

Panic rose in her chest and she cried out weakly, "My baby! My lovely dancing baby!"

She was all alone.

No one came.

She tried to feel her tummy.

"They've taken my baby!"

She attempted to raise her head.

No way. Had they buckled her down again?

Bleep, bleep, bleep . . .

Her pulse accelerated like a microwave oven gone mad, the monitors seemed to jeer at her, the colours ran together like a child's painting under the tap, and her head began to spin like a gyroscope, faster and faster, spinning and wobbling, threatening to explode.

"Help me! I'm dying too . . ."

A door clicked open and someone entered, hurried to her side, held her hand, stroked it, and said, "You're fine, love. It's me. Paul. You're safe. I'm here with you. Sorry, I had to pop out for a pee."

She wanted to sit up but couldn't. "Where have they taken my baby? I want to see the baby! Don't let him burn it."

"Hush, love. Everything is fine."

"Is it a boy or a girl? It must be so tiny . . . let me see it."

"The baby is safe inside you. You haven't had an abortion, or a miscarriage. Baby is doing well."

"Quick, then! We have to escape from the clinic. He'll come back as soon as you leave and suck my baby out of me with his vacuum tube."

"You *are* out of the clinic. We're in the city hospital. Look around—it's all different. You're in a private room in the mother-and-baby unit."

"He can get to us here! We must slip out and go home!"

"Shh. No one can get you. That's just the medication talking."

"What about the preeclampsia? Where are the nurses?"

"I'll call for the doctor, now you're awake."

"No! No doctors!"

"We are not in the Tamm Bok clinic and Yevstigneyev cannot get to you."

"How can I be sure of that . . . of anything? What happened, Paulie? I had such dreadful nightmares. I don't know what is real any more. If this isn't Tamm Bok, how did you spirit me away?" The words tumbled from Rachel's mouth.

"Me and Agnetha took you out the back door."

"How? I don't remember a thing."

"You wouldn't. You were well out of it, love. I thought you'd had a stroke. I ran for help. Agnetha rushed in and said your blood pressure was going up again. 'I must fetch the director! She will die! Sign the form!' she kept on saying. I said, 'No, she wants a second opinion from the city hospital, and that's where I'm taking her.' Agnetha said, 'You stupid man! She has preeclampsia! I will show you the result!' She wrestled the top off the clinical waste bin and rooted around in it, then came back, white as a ghost, holding the test strip. In a tiny voice she said, 'The result is normal. There is no protein! He lied.' She said that meant you didn't have preeclampsia and there was no reason you should have an abortion. Then she whispered to me, 'That is why Helena is gone! Rachel was right. We must get her and you away!'

"Agnetha took the tubes and things out of you, I scouted outside, and we pushed you down the corridor, desperate not to attract Yevstigneyev. He was in the abortion suite. I knew if we went out through an emergency exit it would trigger an alarm. So once round the corner, I had a bright idea for once. As we passed, I smashed the glass with my elbow and set off the fire alarm!

"That caused a big panic. We heard Yevstigneyev shouting. Luckily he ran the other way, back to the examination suite. We hared down the corridor, getting drenched by the sprinklers, doing racing turns at the corners, and skidded out the rear emergency exit straight into the car park. The alarms were all going off anyway, so no one was alerted to our departure. We bundled you in the back of my car, and Agnetha sat in the front and gave me directions here. We left Agnetha at the hospital doors. I told her to flee the city, turn off her mobile and throw it away, visit no one, draw out loads of cash then not use any cards again so as to leave no tracks."

Rachel said, "Yevstigneyev or Andrus will find us here. It's the obvious place to look. They want me dead, Paulie. I can't stay. I'll be terrified of every nurse that comes in to check me. I *knew* Yevstigneyev was evil. Why do they want to hurt me—*kill* me and our baby? It's all connected with Shackloth somehow. He's the common thread. I always thought it was incredible that he should have made you an investor in that clinic. It was a con, Paul. You've been set up as a fall guy, a patsy. You've landed us in the deepest trouble."

Paul said, "Babe, you're hyped up. You're gabbling. Try to stay calm. I've been here all night, by your side. Your blood pressure is down, your temperature is normal. Don't worry about me. Now let me call for the duty doctor and get you checked."

"No! I don't want any doctors, Paulie."

Paul reached for the button on its cord and pressed it anyway. She blinked and focused on his face. His eyes were sunken and black-rimmed with tiredness.

What has he got us all into?

In turn she'd involved Robbie . . .

"Oh my God!" She clasped Paul's hand. "Where is Robbie?"

A white-coated female doctor about half Rachel's age entered the room, stethoscope over her shoulder. She stepped over to the bedside, took the clipboard from the end of the bed, and studied it before addressing Rachel.

"I am pleased to see you are awake, Mrs. Phelps. I'm Dr. Lill. How are you this morning?"

Rachel squirmed, trying to hide under the hospital sheets. "Stay away from me! I refuse all treatment."

The doctor seemed unsurprised by her patient's reaction. "That is the MDMA talking," she said to Paul. "Paranoia is a common effect during the come-down."

"MDMA? What's that?" Paul asked.

"Methylenedioxymethamphetamine. A bit of a mouthful of a word. You know it as Ecstasy, or plain old *E*. We see plenty of it. Our young people are susceptible."

"I've never taken an illegal drug in my life," Rachel whispered. "Yevstigneyev must have injected it into the line. To make me worse, so he could carry out the abortion without suspicion."

Dr. Lill addressed both Rachel and Paul, turning her head from one to the other. "The good news is, the blood and urine tests we ran last night show no other abnormalities. Your pressure has stabilised overnight, and we can take out the intravenous line. I recommend we keep you for another twenty-four hours, Mrs. Phelps, to monitor you and your baby. You need to seek support with the drugs issue. It is rare to see Ecstasy used by expectant mothers of your age, and you should know, and Mr. Phelps too, that the drug is potentially harmful to your baby. Were you being treated for this problem at the other clinic? Is that why you discharged yourself in a hurry, and will not even tell us which clinic it was?"

Rachel said, "Get me out of here. My brother has been kidnapped. He's been missing since lunchtime yesterday. He has Down's syndrome and is very vulnerable."

The doctor said, "You are showing signs of psychosis, a result of the high dosage of *E* you took. I will not authorise discharge until the effects have dissipated."

"I didn't take any drug, it was given to me, forcibly! Paulie, tell her."

"It's complicated, Doctor, but my wife is right. She would never take anything that would harm her baby."

"I'd never take anything, full stop!" Rachel shrieked.

Dr. Lill pursed her lips. "You are visitors to Estonia so perhaps you do not know. Our country has decriminalised the possession of small amounts of drugs for personal use, so you should not fear charges. There is no need to protest your innocence. Be assured, we will not disclose your use to anyone outside this hospital. However, as in your country and throughout Europe, the police do not tolerate trafficking. They are keen to stop foreigners using Estonia as a transit route to and from Russia and the Netherlands."

"We're not drug users or pushers," Paul said.

The young doctor replaced the clipboard on the hook at the end of the bed and said, "A nurse will remove the drip, and I believe refreshments are on their way." She smiled. "Don't be too hard on yourselves. You're going to have a lovely baby. Do get help."

She left and almost at once, a nurse entered. She snapped on gloves and set about removing the transparent tape from the catheter in Rachel's arm. Rachel turned her head and said, "Paulie, we have to find Robbie. We must call the pol—"

Paul put his finger to his mouth to hush her. She realised the nurse would understand English.

The nurse applied a plaster, bagged up the used tubes and dressings, and left with a sympathetic smile.

"No need for the police. I've got Leelo on the case. She was out until midnight."

"Leelo? Can't you see that Shackloth is behind all this? He's the one who tempted Robbie out of the hotel. He's holding him. And, at least according to you, Leelo is his girlfriend."

"Not anymore. She realised yesterday that something big was going down, something stank. She drove to the hotel to prevent you taking the taxi. She's with us. On our side."

"Does she have a small sports car and wear a woolly hat?"

"Yes. You saw her?"

"She almost ran us down. Where has she been looking?"

"She's been searching for Shackloth. Like you said, find him and we find Robbie."

"That could be risky for her. Why not involve the police?"

Paul's phone rang. He glanced at the screen. "This is her now." He answered the call. "Yeah? Phew. Great. Where are you, Leelo? Really? Yes, stay there. Rachel is all right. And the baby. Yeah. I'm on my way." He cancelled the call and punched the air with his clenched left hand. "She's found Robbie!"

"Where? Is he unharmed?"

"Yep. She found him half an hour ago in an all-night Hesburger. Not the one by the hotel, another branch out of town, on the lake road. God knows how he ended up there. I assume Richard dropped him off, but why there and not at the hotel? Anyway, Robbie is fine and says 'hi' to both of us. He wasn't too keen on going with Leelo, apparently, but he was so tired and had consumed so much Coke and junk food that he couldn't refuse. She took him straight to my apartment. The two of them are there now, and she won't leave his side until I arrive." Paul reached for his leather jacket, draped over a chair.

"I'm coming with you. I'm not letting *you* out of my sight either. Then we go together to the travel agent, buy new tickets for this afternoon's flight. Once we're on British soil we'll talk about what happens next."

"Babe—"

"Paul. This is nonnegotiable. Help me get up and dressed."

"You heard the call. I can be at my place in fifteen minutes. You must stay here. The doctor said."

Rachel struggled to pull herself up in the bed. "I've had enough of clinics and hospitals. If I'm paranoid for a while, that's no bad thing. I trust no one. Find my clothes, Paul. We're wasting time."

Paul opened the wardrobe next to the bedside table. "I can handle this on my own," he said, but he handed out her jeans and top anyway.

Rachel pushed aside the bedsheets and swung down her legs. He helped her to dress, clipping her bra and steadying her as she climbed into the jeans. She felt dizzy and faint, but hoped that was just a side effect of the cocktail of drugs she'd been administered.

"Handbag?"

"Here. Agnetha found it. And I have your parka."

She opened her bag. The three sheets of paper from Helena were gone. She hoped that Agnetha had them, and not someone else. She took her comb and stepped to the mirror by the door, unsteady and shaky, Paul at her elbow.

"Where is this apartment of yours and how do you come to be staying there?"

"It's one of Richard's. In the heart of Lasnamäe. He owns the block and lets the flats out to students, nurses, Russian immigrant workers. The gaff is a bit basic and the gas heater doesn't work, but it's been good enough for me to crash."

She combed her hair but couldn't remove all the tangles. "That's another place they'll look for us. Tell them here I'm discharging myself."

"Right-oh." Paul left. Rachel glanced around. The room was en suite, with its own toilet and shower. She opened the extra-wide door, sat, and peed.

She washed her face and applied a little lipstick, put on her jacket, opened the door of the suite, looked to left and right, and hurried out.

Paul stood at the ward's reception desk. He said, "There's paperwork to do, and we have to pay."

"Later. This is an emergency."

The orderly said, "You must settle your account on discharge, madam, as you have no European Health Insurance Card."

"Paul, leave your credit card as security, plus that Rolex you've somehow acquired. Let's go! Now! Go, go, go!" She gave him a shove for emphasis.

He did as he was told. She took him by the arm and propelled him towards the exit, leaving the orderly and the two nurses open-mouthed.

They rode down in the lift and hurried through the bustling main reception to the car park, Paul supporting her.

Light drizzle fell, and the sudden cold made Rachel shiver. She wrapped her jacket more tightly around her.

"The car's over there." Paul, holding her arm, unlocked the Skoda with the remote.

The engine started at the third attempt and they pulled out into the traffic.

"How long?" she asked.

"Fifteen minutes. Longer if this jam doesn't clear."

They crept along, wipers going, in slow-moving traffic such as encircles every city-centre hospital.

"Leelo was with Robbie when she called?"

"Yes."

"The poor boy, abandoned in a burger joint."

"His idea of a perfect night out."

"Don't joke, Paul. Robbie might appear to cope, but this will shake him to the core. What was Shackloth playing at?"

Paul didn't answer.

They inched forward. Lights ahead at the junction with the main road allowed only a few vehicles through before changing back to red. Rachel beat her clenched fist on the armrest in the passenger door. "Bloody traffic! Bloody weather! Whatever possessed you to come here?"

"Cool it, Rachel. Think of your blood pressure." The small car ahead braked unnecessarily. The traffic lights changed to red, and they all halted again. "Idiot!" Paul leaned on his horn.

"Now who needs to stay calm? Give me your phone. I want to speak to Robbie myself. And Leelo. She must get out of your flat—it's the obvious place to find them both."

Rachel redialled the last number.

The ringing tone sounded, on and on.

"Leelo doesn't answer!" Rachel shrieked. "She's not there."

"Hush. Here we go. Just a few minutes more." The lights changed, the car ahead pulled out, and they were on the main road, Paul tailgating the slowcoach. "Probably poor reception."

"You have five bars, and everywhere I've gone the signal has been perfect."

"The apartments are solid concrete. It blocks the phones. Don't panic, we're almost there." Paul gunned the engine, turned the wheel, overtook the laggard in front, and accelerated down a clear stretch of road. The towers of Lasnamäe lay ahead, dingy grey fingers scattered across a featureless suburban plain, pointing upwards at a rain-laden sky.

She pressed Call again, with the same result. "Are you certain you can trust Leelo?"

"Sure. She's a bright girl. She lost her father when she was fourteen. He was a top civil servant. Her family is very academic. She's Mensa material. A class act."

"Leelo wasn't very bright to take up with Shackloth."

"He's a charmer and a chancer, a lone wolf. He has a sense of humour, which Estonian men famously lack. He's a self-made man, a multimillionaire. The Estonians aren't great funsters. They're almost as dour as the Finns. Richard took me in too, babe."

"That I *can* believe. How much farther?"

"Next turning off this drag."

No more was said as they approached a residential tower, its concrete stained black where water had run down the walls from faulty guttering. Paul indicated and lurched onto a side road so cracked and potholed that he had to slow to walking pace.

Elderly cars and vans lined both kerbs, including one that was burnt-out.

"You've been staying *here*? Leelo brought Robbie *here*? Why? This makes Moss Side look gentrified."

"It's fine inside. Ah, good. There's Leelo's car." Paul pointed at a sleek sports Mercedes, conspicuous among the old bangers. He found a parking space, leapt out, rushed around to Rachel's door, and opened it like a chauffeur.

A little late for gallantry.

The rain fell in relentless sheets, filling up the potholes and puddling the cracked walkway to the tower block's entrance. Rachel picked her way down the path as fast as she dared.

Stay positive. Pick up Robbie, back to the hotel for luggage and passports, and we'll be home tonight.

She pictured the happy reunion of Raffles with Paul and Robbie.

Beside the entrance door was a panel of buttons for the entry phones. Paul pushed one labelled "Müller."

"Let me in. I'm freezing and soaking," Rachel said. "Haven't you got a key?"

"Leelo has it. Why doesn't she answer?" He pressed the button again, letting the buzzer squawk for a good ten seconds.

Still no response.

"Shit," Paul said.

"Now what? Where have they gone?"

"I don't know. Give me my phone. I'll try calling her again."

He took back his mobile, jabbed the touchscreen, and held it to his ear. "No joy. Concrete too thick in this place."

"I'll sit in the car while you work out how to get in."

At that moment, a figure appeared behind the frosted glass of the entrance. A man emerged wearing a raincoat and beret. He put up an umbrella and hurried away. Paul caught the door before it swung back on its latch, and they entered.

The lobby was lit by a single, dusty light bulb. A side table stood strewn with takeaway menus, newspapers, and post for residents.

A sign hung by the lifts.

"Out of order still. We'll have to walk up. Can you make it? It's thirteen flights."

"Do I have a choice?"

They set off up the stairwell, which was littered with empty cigarette packets, sweet wrappers, and dead leaves. Rachel climbed steadily but slowly. Her level of fitness was high—or had been before this trip—but she didn't want to raise her pulse too much.

They reached the fifth floor and paused, more for Paul's benefit than Rachel's.

He panted, "Richard says he keeps trying to get the lift fixed but the parts are impossible to buy. Russian again."

"He sounds a model landlord."

They set off again, passing grimy windows at each turn in the stairs.

They were both panting hard by the time they reached the thirteenth floor.

"This way. Oh, good. The door's open." Paul stepped ahead of Rachel to the apartment labelled "Müller" and went in.

49

THEY STOOD IN a tiny hall with three doors leading off it, floored with what looked like thirty-year-old linoleum curling up at the edges.

The sitting room inside was icy cold—so cold that Rachel could see her breath—and displayed evidence of occupation by a slovenly male. Pizza boxes lay scattered on the threadbare carpet. Various articles of clothing adorned the furniture: underwear, socks, a crumpled shirt. On a rickety-looking gateleg table stood an empty bottle of vodka.

How could my husband have come to this?

Paul strode down the room and threw open another door. "Leelo! Robbie! Where are you?"

He turned to Rachel, his face pale, still panting for breath. "They're not here," he said unnecessarily. He retraced his steps and opened the bathroom door, poking his head in. "Not here. What's going on?" He flung open the final door, to the bedroom. Rachel glimpsed an unmade single bed and more signs of chaotic bachelor living.

She pursed her lips. "Have you called Shackloth?"

"No. He can't be trusted. Leelo gave me alarming information about him."

"Why am I not surprised? Where could Leelo and Robbie have gone, Paul? Is there a communal area, a games room, a laundry, somewhere warmer? Think!"

Her husband stood mute.

She grabbed him by both arms. "They couldn't have stayed here for long. It's freezing. You know how Robbie feels the cold. They've gone to get warm."

"The gas fire is dodgy. Richard advised against using it. I'm glad they didn't try to light it. Or perhaps they did, and the gas ran out. It's just a place to crash. I've hardly been here, babe." He spread his arms wide in a gesture of hopelessness.

"So this is the lifestyle of an international A-list investor?" Rachel shivered and pulled her coat around her.

"Leelo's Merc. is down below, so they can't have gone far. They must be on foot." His face lit up. "I know! There's a new centre in the next block. The students opened it the other day, a big room for art classes, yoga, all kinds of community crap. They do coffee. Robbie and Leelo will be there. Let's go!"

Rachel said, "Not so fast. I'll stay here in case they reappear. I don't want to climb those stairs again. Go down and check this community place. Give me your phone and call me on it with Leelo's phone if you find them. If they're not there, or you don't get a signal, sprint back up here pronto."

With a nod of agreement, Paul handed over his mobile and left.

Rachel reentered the living room. She looked around, shaking her head in disbelief.

Shackloth was a latter-day Rachman, renting flats to impoverished or desperate tenants, with no concern for their comfort or safety.

She didn't fancy sitting on any of the furniture. She stepped over to a greasy coffee table strewn with magazines. They all dealt with sports and betting. Paul had managed to acquire recent copies of *Racing Ahead* and the Irish publication *Racing Post*. His betting days were far from over. She prodded the pile of magazines gingerly, as if they could be laden with germs, which was possible if germs could survive in a fridge.

The Cricketer, Athletics Weekly, World Soccer, Rugby World . . . all kinds of sports that Paul did not follow.

A jotter pad protruded from underneath the pile. She pulled it out using her fingernails.

The pages were covered with scrawled notes—names, phone numbers, and dates.

Lots of dates.

He had written down the dates of the next soccer World Cup, the next two Olympics and Winter Olympics, and the upcoming Commonwealth Games.

Paul was keen on sport, but his main interests were horse racing, the dogs, and Premiership football. Whatever he was up to here in Tallinn involved international competition.

The cold was starting to seep into her feet, and she figured her nose must be blue.

How long has Paul been?

She wasn't wearing her watch. She'd lost it somewhere, taken off her wrist at one of the clinics. It was only a cheap Swatch. She realised she had Paul's phone in her hand and checked the time. 10:03 a.m. Only three minutes.

I should have stayed with him. Once we found Robbie, I would have had no reason to come back up here. I could have waited in the car with my brother, the heater going, while Paul packed his sorry collection of clothing.

She shivered again. She did need to sit down, and did so on the dusty, stained sofa. It was of ancient construction, with springs that groaned as she took the weight off her feet.

Yuck.

There was every chance the unsavoury upholstery harboured fleas. She leapt up again.

There must be a kettle in this dump, or a way to make a hot cup of tea at least.

The kitchen cupboards and worktops were the original Soviet fittings, made of thin Melamine that had swollen at the seams, exposing damp particleboard. She opened wall cupboards, found a packet of teabags. Kettle? Yes, a yellowed plastic-jug type. She filled it and switched it on.

She turned around. The kitchen door was open and pushed back against the wall. Only there was something behind the door. Also, a black and gooey substance had oozed over the floor.

This place is disgusting.

The kettle began to hiss and burble. She inched towards the door, eyes on the floor.

The gunky stuff was dark red, not black.

She seized the handle, pulled it towards her, and tried to make sense of what she saw.

A big, heavy-looking, old-fashioned ironing board, all rusty steel, stood propped up against the wall, wound around with masking tape like decorators use.

Some clothing or sheets or something was bound to the other side of the ironing board by this tape, sandwiched between the board and the wall. And there was hair, or possibly the stuffing from the old sofa, stuck to the tape.

She stepped forward and trod in a little puddle of the gooey liquid. Her foot shot out as if on a skating rink. She grabbed the ironing board to prevent herself falling. The board was indeed heavy. It fell away from the wall, together with whatever was secured to its other side. She let go and leapt backwards, skidding on the thin lino and leaving a red trail, but she kept her balance as the board clattered to the floor.

Lashed to the ironing board, staring up at her through sightless eyes, was a body.

Clumps of its hair had been ripped out, revealing bare patches on the skull. The mouth was covered with layers of the light-coloured tape. But despite the disfigurement, the taping up of the features, and the grey pallor of what remained of the face, Rachel saw that this was—or had been—Leelo.

Any doubt as to her fate was dispelled by the kitchen knife handle that protruded from her stomach. What had been a white T-shirt was now a red T-shirt with a few white patches. Multiple stab wounds pierced her upper body.

She had been trussed and tied to this ironing board like a battlefield casualty strapped to a field stretcher. Except the intention here was not to save life, but to end it.

The murderer had inflicted the knife wounds and stood the ironing board up, leaving the girl to bleed to death in agony, leaning upright against the wall.

Rachel gagged, and an acidic taste filled her mouth. She rushed to the sink, where the kettle was boiling away, billowing steam into the freezing air.

She leaned over and retched. There was no food in her stomach to bring up. She wiped her watering eyes, clung to the sink with one hand, and reached out to turn off the kettle with the other.

If Leelo is dead, then surely so is Robbie, probably in a similar manner.

Whoever had done this would return for her and Paul.

She ran her fingers through her hair, cupped her hands, and splashed freezing water on her face. She took a chipped mug from a hook, filled it, and rinsed out her mouth.

She could hardly bear to turn around and see the disfigured body on the floor. But she must find Robbie—alive or dead.

The tiny kitchen offered no concealment for a second corpse. Averting her gaze, Rachel stepped over Leelo back into the sitting room.

Nothing behind the sofa, and no other place to hide a victim.

Her shoes left bloody footprints as she searched.

Heart hammering, straining to hear any approaching footsteps, she entered the bedroom. The door was opened right against the wall, as in the kitchen. She yanked at the handle and peered around it.

Nothing.

With her anxiety at fever pitch, holding her breath, she stepped over to the wardrobe and snatched it open.

She exhaled.

Nothing inside except half a dozen wire coat hangers and a carrier bag of dirty washing.

That left only the bathroom. On tiptoe, she crossed the tiny lobby, pushed the flimsy door, and felt resistance from something bulky and soft behind it.

Oh God, no! Not my lovely brother!

She tugged at the light cord and entered.

Behind the door hung a fluffy white towelling robe from a Marriott hotel, presumably lifted by Paul at Gatwick. Never had she been so pleased to see such a mundane article of clothing.

The bath was empty, and the room showed no signs of a struggle. No blood anywhere, nothing smashed or on the floor.

So no dead Robbie. While there was hope, there was life. What was the saying? Her brain still refused to work. Like a car engine filled up with dirty fuel, it kept misfiring. She realised she was coming down from her drugged, hyped-up state.

So cold. Her teeth began to chatter, not only from the near-freezing temperature but also from visceral, bone-chilling fear.

She and Paul had been duped.

This is a trap.

We won't get out alive.

She had minutes to plan a course of action.

Hide in the apartment? Only the wardrobe offered concealment. It could work. A casual searcher in a hurry might not check, assume I fled.

Would that be a better idea—run for it?

Or just stand and await my fate?

No. Anything but that.

Call the police! Yes, that was the obvious thing. First, warn Paul.

Back in the lobby, she woke up Paul's phone. With cold, trembling fingers, and unfamiliar with the phone's operating system, it took precious seconds to find the list of recent callers.

Come on, come on.

Here we are.

She highlighted "Leelo" and pressed Call.

No answer.

Duh! She realised her mistake. Leelo lay dead in this very apartment. She wasn't with Paul, and she wouldn't be answering her phone—or anyone else's.

Rachel stepped into the sitting room. Now she heard the ringtone from the kitchen: the old-fashioned bell telephone that most iPhone owners choose. Leelo's phone was on her body.

She lowered Paul's phone to cancel the call. To cap it all, his was almost out of charge. Only one percent showed.

Maybe just enough to call the police. What was the emergency number? Not 999. She had a feeling it was 911.

She pecked out 9-1-1.

Nothing! Not even a message. Only silence.

Try 101.

No again!

As she stood looking at the touchscreen, hoping for inspiration, it turned black and a big red battery symbol appeared. Then that too faded.

She'd have to retrieve Leelo's phone from her bloodied body.

Right, let's do it—

What was that sound?

Footsteps, echoing up the stairwell. From maybe two floors below.

It could be Paul and Robbie. More likely not . . . Better get out of here.

She'd take the stairs upwards. She kicked off her shoes without unlacing them. Stained with Leelo's blood, they would leave tracks.

She flew to the front door, pulled it open, and let out a cry of anguish.

50

PAUL STOOD OUTSIDE, standing between Andrus, dressed all in black, and Shackloth, who wore a tweed suit and carried a small toolbox. Andrus held Paul's arm, while in Andrus's other hand was a glinting blade, long and wickedly thin, like a fish-filleting knife, pressed against Paul's neck, where an artery throbbed.

"You two have led me a merry dance, and I am seriously displeased with the pair of you," Shackloth said, out of breath, for all the world like a country gent who has suffered a lapse in standards from a couple in his domestic employ. "Hand me the phone, then back off into the apartment. Don't make a sound, Mrs. Phelps. Andrus won't make a sound killing your useless husband, and your useless husband won't make a sound because he will be dead before he hits the floor."

Paul's eyes bulged with terror. "Do as he says—he's not bluffing," he panted.

Rachel held out the phone, which Shackloth pocketed. She stepped backwards.

All four of them now stood in the tiny lobby. She could smell Paul's fear.

"Into the living room. Not a sound, Mrs. Phelps."

She complied, then everything happened at once.

Andrus twisted Paul's arm behind his back and kept his knife at Paul's neck. Not that Paul looked as if he would offer any resistance even if released.

Shackloth fetched one of the upright wooden chairs that stood around the gateleg dining table. "Sit," he commanded Rachel.

He produced a roll of two-inch masking tape from his toolbox. He positioned Rachel's arms on the arms of the chair and taped her wrists around and around the wood.

"Good stuff, this. Comes off cleanly without a trace, and just as effective as duct tape, provided you use enough turns."

He bent down to do the same with her legs. Rachel lunged and kicked out. Her stockinged feet caused little hindrance to her captor, who bound first one ankle and then the other to the front legs of the chair.

The man stood up and surveyed his handiwork. "Feisty to the end," he chuckled.

Rachel glared at Shackloth, buttoned up in his three-piece country suit. "Why are you persecuting us? We've done nothing to you. What is happening at that clinic?"

"I could tell you, but then I'd have to kill you. Oh, I just remembered! I *am* going to kill you. So I will tell you what you have achieved, you and your dope-on-a-rope husband."

Paul piped up, "Richard . . . stop all this. I invested in you. I trusted you. We're partners . . . I thought we was friends."

"We are neither of those things, and never were." Shackloth nodded to Andrus, who sheathed his knife, let go of Paul's arm, spun him around like a puppet, and unleashed a huge punch into his stomach. Paul collapsed, winded and gasping in agony, cracking his head on the corner of the coffee table in the process.

Bound hand and foot, watching Shackloth unwind more masking tape ready to truss Paul, all Rachel could think of doing was to keep the man talking.

"I'd like to know what cause is worth killing us for."

Shackloth pulled another dining chair from beside the table and positioned it in the middle of the room. He favoured Paul with a prod from his brogued right foot. Paul, moaning and writhing on the floor, looked up through watering eyes.

"Stop whimpering. Get up and take the other seat."

Paul hauled himself off the floor and collapsed onto the waiting chair. Shackloth set about binding him to the seat while turning his head to address Rachel on the other side of the room.

"You're a bright woman, Mrs. Phelps. Why did you marry this drongo? Did he come round to build a wall or lay tarmac or install kitchen units? And you were the prissy middle-class nose-in-the-air dance teacher who fancied a bit of rough? Did he say, 'I'll just wash me bucket out and then give you a good seeing-to, darling?'"

"No," Rachel said.

"Or were you opposites that attracted? Beauty and the Beast? The burly builder and the statuesque dancer? And then it all went wrong when he got stuck into the booze and the bets?"

"No," she whispered.

"Where's Leelo?" Paul's voice trembled.

"She went into the kitchen. She may be some time. Your wife has already paid her a courtesy visit, I see, by the mess on my nice clean carpet."

Paul's head jerked sideways. "Leelo dead? You killed her? You bastard."

"Where's my brother?" Rachel demanded. "Have you killed him too?"

Shackloth bent down to speak in Paul's ear, almost as if confiding in him. "Yes, Andrus killed Leelo—after persuading her to make the call to lure you here. He had to give her a good few jabs with his knife before she cracked. However, the police may see things differently. Leelo adorns your kitchen, with your knife in her vitals, rather like a Cluedo victim. Did you ever play that game? I loved it as a kid. 'Professor Plum, in the ballroom, with the candlestick.' Great stuff."

Shackloth finished securing Paul to the chair, straightened up, stepped back, put his thumbs into his suit waistcoat pockets, and continued. "Your wife asked what cause could justify the extreme measures you have obliged me to take. Paul, *you* tell her."

"So you knew all the time?" Rachel hissed across at Paul.

Paul wheezed, "I'm as in the dark as you are. It's as I told you. Richard invested my money and made me a partner in the Tamm Bok Clinic. I can't imagine why, because he didn't need the funds."

"No, but I needed you to hand over all your mother-in-law's money so I had you hooked, like a fish on a line. Give a man a sum of money, and he may be grateful to you for a day, or not. Appeal to his greed and vanity, persuade him to invest in you, and you have yourself an accomplice for life."

"I thought it was all about screening and sports medicine. Why did you use me?" Paul asked.

"You were useful for the holding company. Since the global crackdown on money laundering, it has become harder to guarantee one's anonymity in the British Virgin Islands and the Cayman Islands. Now they insist on a named individual. Paul Phelps, you are that individual. The Person of Significant Control. Any investigation of the company leads to you, and no one else."

"I'm the scapegoat—the fall guy if it all goes wrong?"

"Give the man a cigar! Yes. And your perceptive wife threatens everything we are working so hard to achieve. Which is why my good temper and bonhomie have evaporated. Andrus, time to move on."

"Wait!" Sensing that death was near for both her and Paul, and that Robbie was surely dead too, Rachel called out in desperation. "You said you would explain what this is all about. You owe us that, at least."

Keep him talking! Where there's life . . .

Shackloth said, "The clinic is everything it claims to be, and a lot more besides. Comrade Yevstigneyev's speciality is mitochondrial and genetic manipulation. He and I control Tamm Bok, and we have a lucrative contract with the Russian government to supply certain organic material advantageous to their plans.

"The techniques required are outlawed throughout the world except, interestingly, in the United Kingdom, but that would hardly be a productive territory for our efforts. Also, the samples we require must be at a later stage of development than is permitted under any nation's medical ethics code."

Rachel gasped, "You're harvesting live foetuses!"

"Well, dead ones would be of little use. We have a quota to achieve from tall and athletic women such as you. The technical details are beyond your comprehension, and I have neither the time nor the inclination to explain the process. But in brief, we take mitochondria and nuclei from pluripotent stem cells in the living foetus and use gene editing and DNA transfer to create new embryos with the attributes specified by our client. These embryos, with their tailored chromosomal characteristics, are implanted into sturdy young examples of orphaned Russian womanhood, peasant girls who have no special characteristics themselves beyond good health; they are mere surrogates.

"For many years Russia, and before it the Soviet Union, relied on doping. That all ended in tears. You remember the fiasco at the Winter Olympics; the tampered urine samples, the Federal Security Service agents passing clean samples back through a trapdoor. Childishly incompetent! It was all too easy for a single whistle-blower to undo years of work and make Russia a laughing stock! Not because they cheated — every single nation does that — but because they were found out. And then the debacle of the following Summer Olympics: the ultimate injustice, with the whole Russian track and field squad banned, and many other Russian competitors in a variety of sports disqualified too, and the entire Russian Paralympic team, while other countries continued with their own rampant doping programmes and competed with impunity.

"The Russian people needed a new way to assert their superiority. At the personal command of the president, a handpicked working group was assembled to devise a long-term plan to regain dominance of the medal tables.

"My name came up. My reputation had preceded me. With my international business and financial connections, and as a free operator with existing interests in Estonia, I was ideally placed to facilitate.

"Meeting Leelo—shy, serious, brainbox Leelo, so naïve in the ways of the world—unlocked more doors. She introduced me to Tamm and Bok. I provided thirty-five million dollars to upgrade their equipment, having recruited young Yevstigneyev as the cuckoo in the nest. He has the know-how, the ambition, the drive, and a ruthless hunger for personal gain and recognition.

"Single-handed, Yevstigneyev has achieved what four thousand Chinese equipped with one hundred and seventy-eight sequencers in their ludicrous factory in Shenzhen have failed to do.

"Tamm and Bok have no clue what is going on. Their heads are in the research clouds. All they know is that their own labs are groaning with brand-new kit."

"What are you and Yevstigneyev doing?"

"We have brought together the science and the technology, the perfect cover of a world-renowned clinic with easy road access to the Russian border. It is beyond the wildest dreams of a Third Reich Nazi! Yevstigneyev has already identified and isolated seventeen genes promoting athletic superiority, including the haemoglobin gene that enables certain tribes high in Tibet to thrive in a low-oxygen environment. Other genes target muscle cross-section, hand-eye coordination, and skeletal characteristics. With our designer embryos, we are breeding new generations of genetically modified children, destined from birth to become Olympians, with champions' genes hardwired into their DNA. And the beauty of it is that they will need no drugs to achieve that greatness!"

Shackloth paused for effect, then continued, "The first batch will be ready to compete at the third Olympics after next. At the following Games, four years later, which I think we will find are held in Moscow, the Russians have set themselves the target of winning one hundred gold medals—virtually every event. The current president plans to remain in office so he can attend and witness the triumph.

"But you, Mrs. Phelps, dancing teacher from the English Midlands, who threatens the whole programme, will see none of this, I fear. Because within approximately thirty minutes, you will be dead."

51

"SO MY BABY doesn't have Down's? That was all tricks and lies to get me to agree to an abortion?"

"Maybe it does, maybe it doesn't. Who cares? We just need foetuses from tall, fit mothers. Anyway, you have cleverly kept me on my hobbyhorse, talking longer than I planned. Enough. Mr. and Mrs. Phelps, I am sure you are freezing. Let's put the colour back in your cheeks. Andrus, light the fire. You'll need this."

Shackloth tossed over the roll of masking tape. At the fireplace, the black-clad henchman kneeled and applied the sticky tape to a grille in the floor. Using a screwdriver from the toolbox, he opened an inspection cover on the flue of the gas fire and stuffed a rag inside the pipe.

"No!" Paul cried out.

Andrus turned the tap and lit the fire with a Bic cigarette lighter.

"Should soon be nice and warm. What a thoughtful landlord I am. So merciful! No marks on your lily-white skin! No blood, no pain . . . just a comfy, cosy room in which to say goodbye to each other, and then to the world!"

"Will I gag them?" Andrus uttered the first words he had spoken since he appeared on the doorstep.

"Unnecessary. The more they gasp, the quicker they die. The other apartments on this floor are unoccupied and the good old cast-concrete floors will muffle any cries for help. Also, we must let them say their romantic goodbyes to each other and to their unborn child, which has been lucky to survive this long, frankly."

"What are you doing to us?" Rachel managed to speak in a level and clear voice.

"I told Paul the gas fire in this room was awaiting maintenance. Oh, if only he'd listened! Andrus, come. We have more cleansing to do elsewhere before we return here."

Andrus gathered up the tools. Shackloth took out Paul's mobile and prodded the buttons. "No charge. Perfect." He placed the phone on the windowsill. "We're off, Mr. and Mrs. Phelps. See you soon! Sorry, that was tactless. We'll see *you* soon, but you won't see us. So I am afraid this is goodbye."

The outer door closed, and the lock turned.

For a few seconds, the only sound was the hissing and spluttering of the gas fire in its grate.

"Shit," Paul said. "All the windows are shut, he's taped up the vents, and blocked the flue. The fire was well dodgy anyway. We'll die of carbon monoxide poisoning. Then they'll come back, untape us, replace everything as it was, and leave again. When someone eventually smells our decomposing bodies and the cops find us, they'll think I murdered Leelo and then we accidentally killed ourselves with the fire or had a suicide pact."

Rachel, who had already worked all this out for herself, replied, "How much did you know about the clinic?"

"I had no idea they were targeting innocent women for abortion. He told me the clinic hired Yevstigneyev to develop genetic enhancement of athletes. I saw how this could work for online betting syndicates. We'd know in advance who were the superathletes. Like Boris Becker, they'd appear from nowhere in their teens and win huge sporting events. Richard encouraged me. I saw how to make a killing."

"Paul, that's an unfortunate turn of phrase, and the time for talking is past. Can you get free?"

Paul strained at his bindings. "It's only paper, but it's so tight it might as well be handcuffs. I can only move my fingertips. I've got another idea." He rocked from side to side, building up momentum. The chair protested with squeaks and groans. After a minute he stopped and panted, "I was trying to tip it over, but I can't get any purchase with my feet. It's getting warm already. How long do we have?"

"He said thirty minutes. Topple the chair somehow—anyhow!" She jiggled her own chair, but it was difficult to achieve any movement at all, bound as she was at both wrists and ankles. "Those bastards knew what they were doing."

"I'll try rocking backwards and forwards instead." Paul brought his upper body forward, then crashed it onto the back of the chair, which didn't topple, but slid backwards a fraction on the worn carpet. Not much help, and he had no means of controlling its direction.

To Rachel it appeared futile. The exertion would only cause him to breathe more deeply, poisoning his blood with the deadly gas, driving out the oxygen of life. Paul renewed his frenzied efforts. He made progress backwards, but to what advantage?

Rachel had an idea. She bent forward. Could she get her teeth on the masking tape? She strained to lower her head to wrist level.

Impossible! Her back was too long. Her height was working against her. Perhaps Paul could succeed, with his stocky build. "Paul! Stop that and bite the tape!"

At once he tried as she suggested. His problem was the reverse: he was too thickset to bend down that far from the waist.

Rachel felt the first waves of dizziness and nausea lap over her. Her head pounded with a migraine-like pain, and her mouth filled with saliva.

Paul abandoned his bending efforts and resumed his frantic jerky rearward progress, an inch at a time, as he threw himself backwards and forwards. He was almost alongside the table now.

Then she saw it.

"The bottle!" she screamed. "Behind you, on your right-hand side!"

Paul gyrated like a convict in the electric chair. "I get the idea!" he gasped. The empty vodka bottle stood on the table.

Paul jerked backwards, until he could see the bottle himself. He couldn't reach it, but he got his fingertips on the leaf of the gateleg table and pushed down.

The bottle slid along the greasy surface towards him. Paul scrabbled to catch it.

"Don't let it fall!"

He didn't. Paul gripped the bottle and turned it sideways, keeping it from falling by holding his bound arm tight against the edge of the table. He worked his fingers until he held the bottle by its neck.

"Flip it at the window! As hard as you can! You have only one chance."

"I need more leverage." Paul wriggled his hand from side to side, still holding the neck of the bottle, loosening the bindings around his wrist.

Rachel felt herself drifting into unconsciousness. It was like falling asleep.

Not so bad. Better than drowning, anyway. Is my baby dead already?

No! She felt the slightest movement, almost a kick. Or was it a convulsion or seizure, as the oxygen-depleted blood reached its delicate, part-formed brain?

She closed her eyes.

Was that a voice calling her? Her father, she realised, beckoning her, helping her rise through the clouds to the warmth of his embrace.

Dreamy, comfortable . . . a lovely way to die.

Two sounds in quick succession jerked her awake.

The first was the noise of thin glass shattering.

The second was a loud metallic report from the kitchen.

Her head pounded with new pain as a gust of pure, cold winter air blew into the room through the broken window. She sucked it into her tortured lungs, which burned as if she'd inhaled napalm.

Paul gasped and sobbed as he also drew in the life-giving air.

"We did it, we did it," he repeated between breaths.

What was that sound? Is a rescue party breaking in through the kitchen window?

Rachel kept her eyes glued on the kitchen doorway, desperate to see rescuers emerge.

As she puzzled over the noise, still befuddled by the poisonous fumes, she saw it.

"The fire's out!"

"The gods are with us. I thought I'd lost you there when you stopped answering me."

More fresh air wafted her way, and she breathed in more deeply, replenishing the oxygen in her blood and, she hoped, her baby's. The tightness in her chest abated.

Shackloth had forgotten that the fire worked on a coin meter.

The gas had run out and turned itself off with a clunk.

After a few minutes, both she and Paul were breathing normally. Rachel's head began to clear. The headache remained, but at least she could think with a degree of clarity again.

They were alive—for now.

Paul, over by the table, echoed her own thoughts. "We're not out of danger. They will return, discover we're not dead, and finish us off."

"Can you work the bindings off one of your wrists?"

Paul strained with both arms, grunting with the exertion, but at least he had the oxygen now to fuel his muscles.

For minute after minute, he laboured away.

"It's not working!" he called over his shoulder. "I'm just turning the flat tapes into strings that cut into me more. Can we manoeuvre our chairs together and help each other?"

"Let's try," Rachel said. She started to jiggle, squirm, and bounce her own chair. It didn't budge. The carpet nearer the fire retained some pile, preventing any sliding at all. "No go!" she called. "We need another plan. Shout for help. Somebody outside may hear through the broken window."

So, in unison, they shrieked, "Help! Help! Help!" then paused to listen for response.

"Again."

Paul shouted and Rachel screamed. "Help! Floor thirteen!"

They paused again.

"Anyone coming?" Rachel panted.

"No. It's like they said. We're going to die, babe. Only not through fumes. I expect Andrus will suffocate us, one after the other. He won't want to leave a mark. Oh God, I've been such a fool. I love you, Rachel. How could it have come to this? All I wanted was a better life for you, me, and our baby . . . Now all three of us are dead . . ." He began to sob and whimper.

"We're not dead yet, but we soon will be if you wallow in self-pity! Stop feeling sorry for yourself and let's work this problem out!"

"It's hopeless, babe . . ."

"You saved our lives with the bottle. We can survive this. One more shout for help, then we sit quietly listening, and use the time to think."

They shouted, and they listened, and they thought, or at least Rachel did—she didn't know if her husband was in any state to think clearly, or at all.

Ten long minutes passed before Paul said, "We play dead."

"Yes, yes! That is genius. We sit here, heads lolling. It should be easy not to move, trussed up like this. With a little luck, they won't check on us, just leave to come back later. Then we have much longer to work on the tapes and shout for help."

"Only one problem. The fire is out and it's getting colder again. They'll notice."

"It's our only chance, Paulie. *Oh no!*"

"What?"

"Can't you hear?"

"You're nearer the door. What is it?"

"Footsteps. We've got less than a minute."

"It could be rescuers, the police, or Special Services or whatever. Or neighbours who heard us hollering."

"In which case we can stop playing dead when we're sure it's not Shackloth and Co. Slow your breathing right down."

"I hear them now too. Babe, if they get us, know that I love you, and always have done."

"I love you too, you big dope."

Rescuers would be hurrying, and shouting or talking.

These footsteps were steady, measured, unhurried.

Two sets.

Both male.

Rachel spoke in a low, urgent tone. "Heads down and face away from the door as much as you can."

"Eyes open or closed?"

"I've no idea, I never got poisoned by carbon monoxide before. Open seems more likely. Be sure you don't move your eyeballs."

"Shouldn't our lips be blue?"

"Shh. Here they come. If they enter with a key, they're baddies. If they knock and try the door, they're good guys."

Rachel lolled her head and let her tongue protrude a little. Rather than holding her breath, she took the tiniest breaths possible, keeping her shoulders down.

This could just work.

Lucky, lucky . . . be a lucky baby, she whispered to her unborn child.

In the door of the apartment, a key turned.

52

RACHEL COULDN'T SEE who entered, but all hopes of rescue vanished when Shackloth, very out of breath from his second long climb up the stairs, gasped, "Check they're both dead."

Andrus's feet made no sound on the carpet.

Where is he?

Then hot breath raised the hairs on the back of her neck and fingers probed for the carotid arteries on either side of her throat.

No way to fake it.

"Boss, this one's unconscious but alive!"

"Damn. And the fire is out. The meter! Go to the kitchen and relight the gas."

"The window is broken. He let the air in."

Shackloth said, "I see it. Looking more closely, our two guests appear to be in the pink, literally. I do believe a little playacting is going on here. Andrus, put your gloves back on, extract the knife from Leelo, come back, and stick it in Mrs. Phelps's stomach. Kill two birds with one stone, so to speak."

"Yeah, good. They will think he slit her too. What about him?"

Rachel listened to what were surely the final words she would hear in this world. Her lifespan now could be measured in seconds.

Andrus stepped around the chair. She could see his feet. She didn't dare raise her head, although what difference that would make she could not quite fathom. Playing dead just felt more natural. At least she wouldn't have to engage Shackloth or his sidekick in more conversation.

"Block up that windowpane and bring him over by the fire. Nice and close. Leave him again, and this time no mistakes. Get the knife and start the gas first."

She watched the black-trousered, booted legs of the taxi driver until they disappeared from view.

Tense moments of silence followed. Perhaps Andrus was surveying the carnage he had inflicted in the kitchen, or searching for a euro coin. Eventually he called out, "I'm ready to start the gas."

"I'll relight it," Shackloth shouted back.

Rachel saw Shackloth's legs passing her chair. Then, when the man kneeled down at the grate, his whole body entered her field of vision.

A clunk from the kitchen signified that Andrus had restarted the supply.

Paul spoke from across the room. "Richard, leave now. There's been too much killing already. The police are on to you. Your scheme is finished, and so are you. Escape while you can."

Shackloth produced an old-fashioned silver cigarette lighter from his waistcoat pocket and clicked it. The gas fire came back to life with a *whoomph*.

He didn't bother to answer Paul.

Andrus now reappeared in Rachel's line of sight.

No point in maintaining the pretence. Rachel too raised her head and said, "You won't get away with this."

"Famous last words," Shackloth replied. "How laughable they can be. I have a book of them. Did you know that Marie Antoinette stepped on her executioner's foot on her way to the guillotine? Her last words were, 'Pardonnez-moi, monsieur.'" He snorted with laughter. "A surgeon called Green was checking his own pulse as he lay dying. His last word: 'Stopped.' What a classic! And tall, graceful Mrs. Rachel Phelps, instead of asking the good Lord to pardon her wicked soul, tells her executioners they won't get away with it. I regret you will be proved wrong. Come on, Andrus. Make it fast. Cut her throat. He wouldn't torture her. Then tape up the window.

We have much else to do. We must eliminate Agnetha. I'm told she has arrived at her sister's."

"I'm here, Boss." Bloodied kitchen knife clasped in gloved hand, he advanced on Rachel and disappeared from view once more behind her chair.

He would grab her hair; yank her head back. She hoped he would make a clean, quick job of it.

Will it hurt? Or will the pain messages have no time to reach my brain before my blood pressure drops to zero and I black out? What about the baby? Will that go on living for a few seconds, its tiny heart circulating blood that is suddenly unoxygenated?

She thought of her mum, and wondered if she would see her again soon.

Shackloth got up on one knee in preparation for standing. "Hold it," he commanded.

A reprieve? A change of mind?

"Move the happy husband so he can watch the performance."

No—a vicious final act of cruelty.

Andrus crossed to Paul.

"*Aaaaiiieeeowww-ya-ya-ya!*"

A crash from the front door and a bellowing war cry made all turn their heads in startled unison, although Rachel couldn't yet see the source of the commotion.

Then everything happened so fast that her mind couldn't keep up with the sounds and images her brain was receiving.

The thump-thump on the carpet of someone running . . . and as that someone passed her chair, a rear view of a stout figure in a hoodie charging towards Andrus, who stood transfixed by the sudden entrance.

The newcomer seemed to elevate his body and fly. A leg shot out in front of him and connected with Andrus's midriff. The thug dropped his knife.

Andrus rose bodily into the air for an instant. Propelled by a perfect flying sidekick, he staggered backwards, arms outstretched.

Out of the corner of her eye, Rachel noticed that Shackloth, still on one knee, was reaching for the bloody knife.

"Robbie! Shackloth has the knife."

Andrus tumbled over the back of the sofa, disappearing from view in a bundle of limbs. Robbie rushed to the sofa and shoved it hard against the wall, pinning the man behind it. Not that he would be offering more violence any time soon; the winding from the enormous karate blow would surely immobilise him for minutes.

"Right-oh, Sis. I'm on it." Robbie twisted around and faced up to Shackloth, who abandoned his knife and reached into his jacket breast pocket.

"Oh no you don't, sunshine!" Robbie shouted at the top of his sing-song voice. He adopted a crouching posture.

Both Robbie and Shackloth froze. Then, with a smooth motion, the suited man produced a small handgun and levelled it.

Robbie scuttled forwards, bandy-legged.

He isn't going to make it.

A bullet outruns a charging bull.

"No!" Rachel shrieked. "Don't shoot!" She closed her eyes.

The gun fired, a single sharp report that echoed around the shabby living room.

A bellowing scream assailed her ears.

It took her a second to realise that the animal howl of agony came not from Robbie—but Paul.

She opened her eyes again.

In front of the fireplace, Robbie, apparently uninjured, let out a cry of *"Shutō-uchi!"* and chopped at Shackloth's outstretched gun hand. The weapon clattered onto the tiling surrounding the grate.

Shackloth yelped. Robbie, now down at Shackloth's level, held the man by the lapels of his expensive suit jacket and performed a vicious head butt.

Shackloth fell backwards. His head crashed against the red-hot ceramic radiants of the ancient gas fire.

The smell of burning hair and skin mixed with the acrid odour of gunpowder.

"The fire! I'm stuck to it! My head's alight!" Shackloth screamed in a falsetto wail.

"Good," Robbie replied, panting. But after a moment, he reached forward and pulled the man away from the fire, tearing out chunks of hair and scalp, which sizzled on the bars in a gruesome parody of a barbecue.

Paul, meanwhile, let out cry after cry of pain, and between cries gasped, "I'm bleeding bad, babe! Robbie, quick!"

Hell could be no worse than this.

"Quick, Bro! Cut off these tapes so I can help Paulie!"

"Right-oh, Sis. I'll get a clean knife from the kitchen!"

"No! Don't go in there! Use the one on the floor."

Robbie picked up the bloody knife and the pistol. "Hey! It's hot!" he said, looking down at the weapon. He approached Rachel and, with four careful movements, slit the bindings around her limbs.

"Cover the two of them. Any attempt to move, shoot them in the head," she told her brother.

"Right-oh, Sis," Robbie chanted for the third time.

Rachel rose too quickly for her own good from the chair that had been her prison. A wave of faintness threatened to overcome her and she had to bend down for a moment, wasting precious seconds. She straightened up with more care and hurried to the bedroom. She snatched the bag of dirty laundry from the wardrobe and dashed back to Paul's side.

"My thigh," he whispered. The left leg of his jeans was no longer blue, but bright red with arterial blood.

Robbie had already sliced off Paul's bonds. Paul now pointed at the site of the injury.

Rachel said, "Phone the emergency services, Bro, while I make some sort of tourniquet."

Robbie said, "No, not a tourniquet, you want to apply pressure, not wind it round, Sis. We did it in First Aid. And we should get him on the floor, with his legs higher than his heart."

"Right, let's tip him backwards." Rachel and Robbie lowered the back of the chair until it lay on the carpet. Paul's legs were now in the air, like an upended beetle.

Rachel emptied the laundry onto the floor. She seized a white T-shirt, folded it, crouched down, and applied it to Paul's leg near the groin.

She pushed hard.

Paul howled with pain.

"Sorry, Paulie, but we must staunch the bleeding. Shackloth, what's the emergency number?" She pushed harder still.

"It's 112, Sis," Robbie said, his phone in hand. "Ringing now."

Shackloth called out, "Quick! I need urgent medical attention."

"Don't move a muscle, or you won't need any attention except from the undertaker," Robbie said.

The bleeding from Paul's thigh seemed to be slowing under the pressure Rachel was applying. But he had already lost much blood: the carpet was pooled with it. He wasn't yelling any more, or even moaning, and the reason soon became obvious: he was losing consciousness.

"Stay with me," Rachel urged. She pushed with both hands.

No sound.

Robbie was through to the emergency services. Shackloth told him the address of the apartment and Robbie sang it out while Rachel leaned on Paul's leg. She couldn't keep this up; her arm muscles were already burning.

She glanced over at the sofa. No movement from behind it. No sudden counterattack likely from that direction. Now she must be patient again, waiting for the paramedics and police.

"How did you get here, love?" she asked Robbie. "I'm guessing Leelo never brought you here."

"Leelo? No, she never did. After lunch that bugger"— Robbie indicated Shackloth—"said he would take me back to the hotel, but he drove me instead to an old house. He frisked me, but luckily I had left my phone in the hotel. He locked me up in the cellar. There was a guy living there who he called Fredo, who was my jailer. I spent the night down in the cellar with only a bucket for company and it was cold and boring with no phone or TV. I wasn't too worried though, because it was like *Firewall* with Harrison Ford and that all ended well, except for the baddies.

"In the morning Fredo checked on me and brought me a Coke and a bun. I acted all frightened and wimpy. Next time he came down, about an hour ago, I gave him a good *hiza geri* in the nuts. I locked him in, ran up the cellar stairs and out of the house, stopped a taxi like I do when we go to London, went back to the hotel, got my phone, and tried calling you both but no answer. So I used my locator app.

"The reception lady said I should not go out again alone, but I told her to chill as I was high functioning. My taxi was waiting, and he took me to where you were showing on my phone, Sis, but you weren't there, it was just road. So I knew your phone was lost and I told the taxi to come here where Paulie's phone said he was, and I showed a man down below in a funny hat the photo of Paulie and had he seen him and he said yes. He let me in, so I climbed up and up until I heard voices on this floor and I tiptoed in and saw what was going down."

He drew breath while Rachel examined Paul again; his eyes rolled and he couldn't focus.

"He seems out of it. Where's that ambulance? You were so brave to do all that, love." She flashed a smile at her wonderful little brother.

"Yeah, well, whatever. No point being a blue belt, then not using it in an emergency. That's allowed."

"Didn't . . . didn't . . ."

Paul was trying to speak.

"Yes, love?"

Her husband's voice was a faint whisper.

She bent down. "The ambulance is on its way. Hold on."

"Didn't steal . . . did it for us . . ."

"We'll have all the time in the world to straighten everything out." Rachel spoke near his ear.

"Letter ... take it ... " He tried to move his hand towards the breast pocket of his leather jacket, but winced with pain.

Rachel's arms were on fire from the effort of maintaining the compress. "Robbie, swap places with me. I can't keep up the pressure."

Only then could she reach, ever so gently, inside Paul's jacket. She withdrew two sheets of notepaper folded together, releasing the faintest odour of lavender, as if an unseen hand had sprayed room freshener to mask the hellish smells in the sordid room.

"Read ... read it ... out loud ... for Robbie too. I want you both to know. I don't think I am going to make it, babe."

"Shh, love. Of course you will make it. The bleeding seems much better." In truth, the bleeding, though reduced, had not stopped by any means. Paul, on his back in the upturned chair, lay in a widening pool of his own blood.

"Read it for me," he pleaded, his voice weaker still.

"Keep those clowns covered," Robbie commanded. So she took up the gun, and keeping one eye on Shackloth, read the lavender letter out loud, because she too feared that Paul would be dead before the paramedics arrived.

> *My darling Rachel,*
>
> *By the time you read this I will be gone. I have done a stupid thing.*
>
> *The fees here at the Willows are three thousand a month, and I am running through my capital at a rate of knots.*
>
> *Should I survive five more years, and with my heart strong that is all too possible, I would get through the lot with not a farthing left for Robbie!*
>
> *So I cooked up a plot to make it appear my savings had been stolen. Leelo agreed to help me and spoke to her financier boyfriend, called Richard but I never met him, and he got together with Paul.*

We decided to trick poor Howard Plumb into wiring my money to Richard. Richard would put it into an offshore account in Paul's name. Paul would keep the money and the secret until my death.

The beauty of it was, once I was bankrupt, the local authority would have to pay for my care! And Robbie's inheritance would be safe, with no tax to pay!

The instant I arrived back from the bank I regretted the madcap venture. It was criminal, and I had drawn your dear husband and lovely Leelo into my net of wickedness. I phoned Paul and said I must confess at once. He came over and told me it was a victimless crime, wholly justifiable in my circumstances, and if I confessed we would all go to prison.

Now I was in a pretty pickle! With no idea what to do!

Later you appeared, and to my eternal shame I did not confess to you. You must have thought I had taken leave of my senses, the rubbish I talked!

Rachel, I have decided to end my life tonight. I know that is wicked too in the eyes of the Lord, but He will just have to get over it!

I considered doing this earlier in the year, and prepared carefully. Instead of taking my sleeping pills, I fooled the night nurse for a whole month by swallowing regular paracetamol, which Audrey smuggled in, and palming the real pills.

Then I heard on the radio about bank scams targeting the elderly. I thought Aha! I could have my cake, and eat it! Put my money safely aside, and continue to enjoy what life is left to me with my beloved family around me.

And so the crazy plan. I felt so guilty involving dear Leelo that I changed my will to leave her some money as compensation. I expect she'll give it to charity.

> *But I can't live with myself. So I will end it all, and tonight is the night. Luckily (!) as you know I have a nasty chest cold, which that lazy arrogant fool Thorpe will happily state as the cause of death.*
>
> *I love you, Rachel. Forgive me my sins. Don't blame Paul or Leelo. They simply did my bidding.*
>
> *Now you have read my letter, destroy it.*
>
> *Paul will tell Richard to send the money straight back. No crime will have been committed, so don't tell the police or anyone about the conspiracy.*
>
> *Mum xx*

Rachel reached the end of the letter, reading her mother's closing words through tear-filled eyes. She refolded the lavender paper.

The metallic wail of sirens floated up from thirteen floors below through the broken windowpane. She crouched down close beside Robbie, held Paul's hand, and bowed her head to speak into his ear.

"Everything is fine. There is nothing to forgive. I love you."

"Me too, I guess," Robbie added. "Even though you've been a twat, Paulie."

No answer.

Rachel leaned in closer still. "Can you hear the ambulance? The paramedics will arrive soon. Stay with us, love."

Paul stared up unseeingly.

"Paulie! Paulie!"

Nothing.

"Blink if you hear me. Hold on, hold on."

No response.

Just as Andrus had done with her, but searching for confirmation of life rather than death, Rachel felt her husband's neck for a pulse.

53

RACHEL GLANCED around.

She counted eighteen friends and family.

Not a bad turnout.

The two lady sidesmen, Barbara and Alison, notoriously competitive, had vied with each other to produce the most elaborate arrangements of seasonal flowers.

Everyone waited for the entry of the vicar, while Mark the organist improvised on gentle stops.

Her family wasn't that religious—and neither was Paul's—but the village church had been the focus for many of the turning points in their lives. She'd been baptised here, and twenty-four years later, she and Paul had stood side by side to be married, a few steps ahead of where she now sat.

Dad's funeral had packed out the little church, with many standing.

A long time ago now . . . sixteen years.

She reached down to tickle the left ear of Raffles. "Good boy," she whispered.

After the debacle of Mum's funeral, Rachel had happily agreed that Raffles could attend this service. She couldn't deny Robbie that, after all he'd been through. And her little brother was right—the collie would sit still for as long as required.

Robbie sat on the other side of Raffles. He'd bought a shirt for the day from the market, which he wore outside his chinos, both lovingly pressed by Rachel.

Where was the vicar? Rachel twisted around. She'd greeted everyone at the door on their way in, but now she was nowhere to be seen. Robing up, Rachel guessed.

Despite her best efforts, she found her thoughts returning to the tumultuous recent events in her life.

Certain scenes kept repeating like an old newsreel on an endless loop in her mind.

She relived the short, dark days in midwinter Tallinn ... she and Robbie daily visiting Paul, who had been rushed to the same hospital where Rachel had been treated ... the nervous waits in the hospital café for news, following the three separate operations Paul had endured ... then the setback, the superbug infection, the long faces from Paul's medical team as drug after drug failed to halt the downward spiral.

Before the infection took hold, Rachel and Paul had spent hours together, she by his bedside, holding his hand while they chatted, or watching in silence as he dozed, each rise and fall of his chest marking another few seconds of his survival against all the odds.

He was physically tough, at least.

Shackloth's bullet had nicked Paul's left femoral artery. Robbie's timely advice about applying pressure to the wound had saved his life. Even so, by the time he arrived in the emergency room, he had lost over two litres of blood. Besides the arterial damage, the bullet had chipped his femur, causing further internal bleeding and nerve damage.

After the operations began the slow process of recovery.

Despite the circumstances, this period of forced confinement provided an opportunity for Rachel and Paul to start rebuilding their relationship.

Once he was well enough, sitting up, alert and getting bored, she broached the subject of his disappearance and subsequent activities.

"Tell me about the cottages, and Fletcher, and the business. If you're happy to talk."

"I'll tell you everything," he replied. Over several sessions, that day and the following week, he led Rachel through what he'd done and why.

The money he'd claimed to have won on the horses had been a fiction. The only money had come from Eve's bank transfer.

Paul had planned to spend some of it on the cottage renovation, and in particular on bribing Mervyn at Fletcher's to underprice the structural work on the buildings. "I'd have paid it back at the end of the project," he insisted. "But Richard held on to the lot. So I didn't have the five grand when I needed it."

On learning of Rachel's pregnancy, Paul went to Shackloth, who persuaded him instead to invest all £200,000 of Eve's money in the Tamm Bok Clinic. "He offered me a directorship of the company," Paul said. "Now we know why, but back then I was taken in hook, line, and chequebook. Once on record as a named director in the British Virgin Islands, I would be the fall guy for any investigation into the business. Shackloth and Yevstigneyev could melt away if it all went belly-up ... flee to Russia. Your pregnancy was an added bonus. They could exploit both of us."

With no cash to fulfil the bribe, Paul couldn't pay for the underpinning work in progress on the cottages and Mervyn had betrayed him. At a showdown that fateful Monday morning, Paul told Fletcher, "Knock the bloody cottages down as far as I am concerned." He had bigger plans. He'd previously coached Eve to say the fictitious conman was called Fletcher. "I hoped that might get the bastard into trouble. He was always ripping me off."

"At that point, I reached rock bottom," Paul continued. "I was boozing and betting like a whore, Phelps & Son was on the ropes, I'd conspired to steal your mum's life savings and handed them to Richard Shackloth to invest in a medical business in a country which I couldn't even place on the map.

"Richard flew over here with Leelo, and he invited me to join them and check it all out. He installed me in that fleapit of a flat, hired me a car, and paid me an allowance which I spent on yet more drink and bets. He gave me a tour of the clinic, made me feel big, convinced me the place was kosher, and said it was nearly time to bring you over. I thought he was doing us a favour, babe! A high-tech Down's test for you ... and I'd already seen a chance to make a killing through online betting in the future. Win-win!

"I kept my phone off because I couldn't bear to see or hear the messages I knew you'd send. In the end I snapped and sent you that half-arsed text ... to let you know I was alive, and to play for time. I know it didn't sound like me, but it was. I turned the phone off before you could reply. Then you and Robbie appeared in Tallinn. Shackloth was expecting you, but I wasn't."

Rachel stroked his hand as the confessions tumbled out of him, wondering if she could trust him even now. "So you did delete the murder text in the crematorium?"

"Yes. The last thing I needed was for you to halt the service, get an autopsy, and discover your mum killed herself. I could hardly come to terms with it myself. I hid the letter because I needed the money in the short term for the cottages."

"And you did cancel my email accounts and cards?"

"Yep. Guilty again. I couldn't bear you leaving Estonia without me, so mad at me. I was concerned about your NIPT test. I didn't know they would fake it. And you weren't fit to fly. That was true enough."

"How about Leelo? What was her role in all this?"

"Shackloth used her—for her connections, her knowledge of the Estonian financial and medical system, and as attractive arm-candy. She introduced him to Tamm and Bok. When Leelo realised the clinic was working for the Russians, doctoring test results and harvesting healthy foetuses for research into athlete breeding, she tried to warn you. Shackloth sent Andrus to lure her to my flat, where he murdered her and framed me."

"How did Leelo find out the truth in the first place?"

"Shackloth and Yevstigneyev needed to prevent Helena visiting you that night. They had Andrus follow her on foot. He stabbed Helena, made it look like a mugging. It was on the TV news with Helena's picture, wearing her Tamm Bok uniform. Leelo saw it, challenged Shackloth, and phoned me with her concerns. That sealed Leelo's death warrant. And ours too, almost."

"That's enough for today," Rachel had told Paul, rising from her bedside chair, grim-faced. Two innocent women had died horrific deaths and dozens of mothers-to-be had lost healthy babies.

The next day, Paul developed a fever. Soon the downward spiral of infection took hold. Four days later, Paul lay in a coma on a respirator in intensive care, and his consultant told Rachel they had reached the drug of last resort. "We must now give Paul colistin," he said quietly. "It's our final hope. It's an old, crude drug from the 1950s, the pharmaceutical equivalent of a blunderbuss. There's a risk it will damage his kidneys, but there's nothing to be lost, as without it he will die anyway."

Mark the organist struck up the opening bars of the first hymn, jerking Rachel out of her reverie and back to the present day.

She rose along with everyone else. Amusingly, Raffles also stood.

To her left, Paul took a while to struggle to his feet. It wasn't so easy for him to get up, not because he was still suffering any serious ill effects from his injuries—he'd been declared fit to return to work without physical exertion—but because he was holding a tiny, two-month-old, squirming baby.

Rachel glanced sidelong at him. He grinned at her, restraining a pink finger that threatened to poke him in the eye.

He had responded to the last-ditch antibiotic. He'd been out of danger within forty-eight hours, his kidneys undamaged.

"Probably so pickled in alcohol no germ could survive," Rachel had ventured.

The congregation launched into the first hymn, singing lustily and more than making up for their limited numbers.

> "All things bright and beautiful,
> All creatures great and small . . ."

Rachel turned her head and caught Kizzy's eye. She sat next to her mum, who was wearing another extraordinary hat, this one replete with so many feathers that it resembled a bird's nest.

Kizzy gave a thumbs-up and flashed her widest smile. Rachel had attended the Spiritualist Church twice more since returning to the United Kingdom. There had been no more messages for her from the spirit world, for which she was grateful. She'd stick to the good old C. of E. in future. She would never know whether the medium was genuine, or had been given clues, maybe inadvertently, by Kizzy or her mum. Either way, Kizzy had Rachel's best interests at heart.

Just before the christening, Rachel, Paul, and Robbie had laid flowers on the stone in the churchyard marking where Eve's ashes were buried, next to her dad.

"Rest in peace, Mum," Rachel had whispered. "I'm only sorry you never got to meet your grandchild."

> "He made their glowing colours,
> He made their tiny wings..."

Right on cue, a ray of June sunshine shone through the stained-glass window high in the nave. It painted the stone columns in rainbow hues, as if a child had scribbled with crayons of coloured light.

I am a mum! Rachel could still scarcely believe it. She tried to focus on the words of the hymn, to savour every moment, to fix the occasion in her memory.

> "All things wise and wonderful,
> The Lord God made them all."

The vicar spread her arms in welcome. "The grace of our Lord Jesus Christ, the love of God, and the fellowship of the Holy Spirit be with you all."

"And also with you," the congregation responded.

Rachel spotted Detective Sergeant Jim Ryan sliding into a pew on the other side of the aisle. She was pleased he'd made it; he'd promised to try, but was still involved in the aftermath of the Tamm Bok affair, helping the Estonian police through Europol. Shackloth awaited trial in Tallinn on charges of conspiracy to murder, attempted murder, money laundering, racketeering, and a slew of other counts. Andrus likewise was in custody, charged with two counts of murder and two of attempted murder. Yevstigneyev had fled across the border to Russia, his homeland. He would never face justice, at least not from the West. His fate lay in the hands of the Russian president, a man who viewed failure as a capital crime in itself.

While Rachel was in Estonia, Ryan had been freelancing on her behalf. He'd put out a watch for Paul's name on an international financial tracking system, which had thrown up his directorship in the British Virgin Islands. When Rachel missed two check-ins by text, Kizzy informed Ryan, who tried to warn Rachel. He'd realised Rachel was under duress in the taxi when he called her and contacted Europol, but events had moved too swiftly for his intervention to influence the immediate outcome.

Ryan had told Rachel why his boss, DCI Geddes, ordered him off the case. "The relationship between Geddes and Shackloth is the subject of a Corruption Unit enquiry. It turns out the two of them attend the same Masonic Lodge in Peterborough. Bank records show transfers from Shackloth to Geddes: hush money, we're certain, though Geddes protests otherwise. We'll apply to extradite Shackloth back to the United Kingdom as soon as the Estonians have finished with him. Meanwhile, Geddes is on indefinite gardening leave."

Jim Ryan, now in his place with service sheet in hand, caught her eye and smiled.

Rachel allowed the vicar's words to wash over and around her, cocooning her in contentment and joy. She kept glancing at her baby, squirming in Paul's arms.

Her perfect baby! At least, perfect as far as she was concerned.

She turned. Only the top of Alma's head was visible above the high front of the little carer's pew.

Rachel had responded to the doorbell in early March to find Alma on the doorstep, holding out Eve's phone, a worried look on her face. Rachel, so big that she feared the baby would arrive any minute, ushered Alma in and sat her down with a cup of coffee.

Alma explained she was back at the Willows. "On the evening before Eve died, Mr. Paul and Leelo were talking together before you arrived. I stood outside the lounge and listened. Mr. Paul was saying, 'Keep cool, Leelo. The money is safe, and provided no one talks, we're in the clear.' Leelo is replying with words like, 'This is evil thing we do.'

"That night I say to Eve, 'Be careful, Mr. Paul and Leelo did the trick with your money and now they plan to kill you!' Your mum says, 'Rubbish, Alma, you are a silly little girl. Don't dare say such wicked things to anyone. Get my iPad out, I want to send an email.' Next morning I go in to Eve with her tea. It is very hard to wake her. She sends me away, still very cross cross. When I go back, Leelo is coming out of her room saying Eve dead!

"I fear Leelo has put the pillow over her head! I say Leelo, what have you done, she says nothing, nothing at all. I am frightened. I take Eve's phone so I can contact you. I say nothing to the detective, as you instruct me, I pretend all fine, but I fly from England quick quick and go home."

"You sent me that text just before the funeral to warn me?"

"Yes. For the longest while I am too scared, I turn phone on to text you, I turn it straight off with my hands shaking. Then on the day of funeral I get up my courage to send you just a short message. I look up time difference, Tallinn is three hours ahead of London, so I send the text one hour before the funeral. I am hoping you will stop the funeral and make them do autopsy. I did not say my name, to keep me out of trouble because Leelo was back in Tallinn and she knew where I live."

Rachel smiled. "You got the time difference wrong, love. We were still on British Summer Time, an hour ahead of Greenwich Mean Time. Your text arrived not one hour, but one *minute* before the service began. Even so, I'm glad you

314

sent it, because otherwise the truth would never have come out. Tell me, why did you text me again later, saying it was all a silly trick by your brother?"

"Mr. Paul called me, said my first text driving you crazy crazy, and tells me to send another to set your mind at rest. I did it because I was scared of him and Leelo."

"I see..."

"But I put in little clues so you would be uncertain and go on searching for the truth."

Rachel assured Alma that Eve hadn't been murdered by Leelo or by anyone. She showed Alma the lavender note and went on to explain that she had obtained her mother's medical records, revealing that Dr. Thorpe had prescribed Eve with Ramitax, a sleeping tablet, in August. "Ramitax, which you might know as Ramelteon, is a safe medication, and it is virtually impossible to kill yourself with an overdose. The amount Mum took that night would not have been fatal, though it would have made her very groggy the next day."

It appeared Eve had indeed succumbed to pneumonia.

Relief was palpable on Alma's face.

Rachel had also learned from Google that long-term use of Ramitax, a powerful hypnotic, could explain her mother's change of personality in her final months and her extraordinary decision, completely out of character, to embark on the bank scam.

So much trouble had flowed from that fateful lapse in poor Mum's common sense.

The vicar announced the final hymn.

Rachel stole another glance at her husband. He smiled back, looking nervous, as well he might. He'd been off the drink since the shooting and now attended the local Alcoholics Anonymous group every week. He'd quit gambling, too, telling Rachel he had deleted all his online gaming accounts. She checked his phone and PC several times a week to make sure they didn't creep back.

Money was no longer the problem. The family finances, at one point so dire, had recovered. Four weeks ago Grimshaw's

Bank, satisfied that Shackloth had no right to Eve's money, had relented and returned the whole £200,000—plus interest, much to Howard Plumb's joy. He too was in church today. Robbie's inheritance was safe, and Rachel had authorised the purchase of a new stereo system and record deck for him.

Even the cottages fiasco had proved a blessing in disguise. The owner of the neighbouring land, a farmer, had approached Paul to buy the plots on which the cottages had stood, as they provided the only viable road access to his top field, which he wished to sell to an energy consortium for a wind farm.

The farmer had offered Phelps & Son (Builders) Ltd. five times the market value of the land.

When the money arrived, Rachel, who now countersigned every cheque and contract, would ensure it was put to good use.

They were approaching the business end of the service. Rachel concentrated on savouring every second.

During the last hymn, Rachel, Paul—with baby—and the godparents—Robbie, Simon and Kizzy—left their pews, followed the vicar, and gathered around the stone font at the west end of the church.

The vicar led them through the liturgy. They all duly rejected the devil, denounced the deceit and corruption of evil, and repented of their sins.

Rachel was happy to recite words that a year earlier would have seemed like abstract concepts. This world *was* full of evil and corruption.

Unfortunately, the weak and the gullible—like Paul—would always be drawn in.

But Rachel wouldn't be taken for a fool any longer.

God knows she'd given him enough chances. Too many, in truth.

If he couldn't clean himself up now, he never would.

She'd told him on the plane home from Tallinn that if he so much as sniffed a wine cork, bought a single National Lottery ticket, or fiddled a brass farthing from the business ever again he would be out of the bungalow, never to return—with a divorce petition hard on his heels.

She would not tolerate her child growing up with a loser for a father.

The vicar took the baby, dressed in a traditional long white christening robe, from Paul's arms.

She dipped her silver dish in the water she'd blessed, chuckling as the little candidate attempted to poke out her eye too.

"Lavender Eve, I baptise you in the name of the Father, and of the Son, and of the Holy Spirit."

"Amen," the congregation chorused, and in the pause that followed Robbie sang out, "Nice one, Vicar!" at which point happy laughter and hearty applause rang out from all sides, echoing around the walls and rafters of the little church.

T. J. FROST

T. J. Frost lives near the sea in Norfolk, England with his wife Liz. He began writing as a student, but a career as an advertising copywriter intervened, and it was many years before he accomplished his lifelong ambition of writing a full-length novel.

His books have sold over 100,000 copies, the majority as eBooks on Amazon Kindle.

Author's website: www.timothyfrost.com

Printed in Great Britain
by Amazon